IN THE GRAVE
WHERE THE BONES
ARE STILL WET

.-. .-. .-.

KALVIN ELLIS

In the Grave Where the Bones Are Still Wet by Kalvin Ellis
Published by Infinite Key Media PO BOX 351501
Westminster, CO. 80035
KALVINELLIS.COM

Cover by: Dusty "Duck" LaPerriere - https://dvcx.design/
Hardback ISBN: 978-1-7342526-5-1
Paperback ISBN: 978-1-7342526-3-7
Ebook ISBN: 978-1-7342526-4-4
Library of Congress Control Number: 2024911717

,⁻, ,⁻, ,⁻,

Also by the Author

Novels
In the Hills Above the Gristmill

Short Story Collections
Bury My Body Somewhere Nice (COMING SOON)

Middle Grade Fiction
Don't Turn Around - A FrightVision Tale

Note from the Author and Content Warning

In the Grave Where the Bones Are Still Wet is a true sequel to my first book In the Hills Above the Gristmill. If you haven't read that book you should hold off on this one until you've read that one. This story will be much more enjoyable if you've been properly introduced to the characters, I promise.

Unlike a lot of series we are not going to ignore the trauma experienced by the characters in the first book. This story is about how people process trauma and how we let others help us do that. This book is also about loss. The loss of a sibling is sadly something I know all too well, and I share a bit of that with you in this story. I hope I've done them justice. Enjoy.

Kalvin

Content Warnings

This book is much darker than the first so I wanted to offer content warnings for it. To avoid unintentional spoilers I have placed a full list of content warnings on the very, very last page of this book. Updated lists are also available if you scan the QR code below.

Content warning QR Code:

Dedication

For the ones I've lost.
Donny, Katie, and Kody.
I'd do anything to find you.

1

On average the human body contains more than one skeleton. That was the statement that stuck with Alisha Lipari as she kicked at the empty soda cans that rolled around in the passenger side footwell as endless miles of night rolled past outside.

"What did you mean by that, sweetie?" She asked, turning to look at the child stretched haphazardly across the backseat.

Millicent lay with her eyes closed, and one little arm pulled up under her cheek, squeezing a crochet turtle that served as a makeshift pillow. She responded without ever opening her eyes. She carried the burden of sleep and could trudge on no longer.

"Matt told me that if you had all the people in the world, and you counted the skeletons in their body, they would average more than one," Millicent said, her soft voice fading but confident.

"Oh did he now?" Alisha asked but got no response save for the soft, rhythmic breath of a sleeping child. She turned to her husband who smirked as he drove. "You told her that?"

"I did. She's likely the smartest seven year old on the planet. Might as well teach her some things that they won't teach in school."

"But what does that even mean?" Alisha sat back in her seat and crossed her arms. "Like because people swallow like chicken bones or something?"

"Think about this; people, on average, have less than two hands," Matt responded.

She thought for a moment then raised her own hands to look at them.

"I don't get it."

"Ponder it for a while." He yawned and stretched in his seat.

Alisha thought about it while she allowed herself to be hypnotized by the trees nearest the road. They would appear and then vanish in the darkness just behind them as the old Buick rolled through the black blanket of a cloudless night.

Rumble strips ripped at the bald tires as the car drifted over the white line and grew dangerously close to the edge of the highway.

"Matt!"

"I'm fine," he snapped, pulling the vehicle back into the center of the lane.

"Do you need me to take over for a while?" she asked.

"No, I'm fine."

"Do you want to stop somewhere and get some sleep?"

"I said I'm fine."

"It isn't like we have anywhere to be," Alisha said. They had packed up and left their trailer earlier that day. The money they got from the state for fostering Millicent and the measly money she pulled in from working at a laundromat wasn't enough to keep them from wanting to escape the nightmare their life had become. They were headed nowhere in particular, so they were in no rush. They just needed to be somewhere people didn't know them and wouldn't ask too many questions. People were looking for them, and they owed a lot of money. So it was best to disappear.

"I said I was fine. I was just lost in thought for a minute, that's all. Did you figure out the..." A heavy beam of light exploded over the small crest in the road behind them and hit the rearview mirror like a flash grenade. "Fuck! What is this guy's fucking problem?"

Alisha turned to look out the back window holding up a hand to block out the lights.

"Looks like a truck," she said.

"No shit. Why's he up my ass?"

The truck sped up and started to cross the dotted yellow line to pass the slower moving Buick.

2

"Oh hell no," Matt said drifting into the other lane to block the truck.

"Just let him go around."

"No, he can suck my dick if he thinks he's going to come up on me like that and then just go around. The asshole must have had his lights off so he could creep up on me," Matt growled, moving the car into the path of the truck once again.

"Just let it go. Maybe you just didn't see the lights. Not everything has to be about you proving how big your dick is. Just let him go around."

"Shut the fuck up and let me drive, please!"

The truck roared again, moving closer to the Buick's side. The smaller vehicle dipped over, pressing the truck toward the ditch. Matt stuck his hand out the window, stretching his middle finger skyward.

"Matt, stop!" Alisha yelled, but it was too late. The truck's engine bellowed like an angry giant and flung itself forward. Matt swung the wheel to block the truck's maneuver. The back tires broke loose of their hold on the asphalt and skipped like stones on a glassy lake. Light filled the car as it turned sideways, and the truck came barreling down on them.

"Momma?" Millicent's voice broke through the noise as she sat up in the back seat. Alisha had the time to register that this was the first time in the years they'd had Millicent that she had called her mom. The last thing she saw before hell and all of eternity came crashing down on them was the light from the truck shining through the fine golden-blonde hair of the girl she chose to be her daughter. Her life hung in that moment. Frozen in place like a picture hung in a gallery. She tried to hold that thought, knowing that whatever happened next, nothing would be the same.

Glass exploded inward as the front of the truck smashed the side of the Buick. Millicent, who had not been buckled, was thrown directly into the rusted grill of the truck. The driver side door bent inward around the brush guard of the truck and Matt's body folded around it. Something snapped deep inside of Alisha as the seatbelt caught and stopped her from flying into her husband's twisted lap. The world spun as the car flipped, spitting broken glass and debris into the night air like blood from a pierced artery. The passenger side door crumpled and came off on the second roll. The force of the spin partially pulled Alisha out of the vehicle. Her futile attempt to pull herself back in ended abruptly when her head swung wide and connected with the ground on the last few flips, nearly splitting her in half. The car bounced off an embankment and came to a stop upside down on the side of the road.

Alisha's right eye had been pulled away from her face and hung, flattened and useless, like snot on the side of her tattered cheek. She tried to scream but couldn't. One of her lungs was filling with fluid and the other nearly ripped from her body. She could see the truck driver's boots as he approached the car. Matt was gone. Presumably thrown from the wreck since he never wore his seatbelt, no matter how many times she had told him to. The only sign that he had been there at all was a dark streak of blood and his lone left hand. The ring she had put on his finger the day they got married still shined. The truck driver stopped and turned.

"Well shoot," he said.

Alisha tried to look up at him but the torn tendons holding her remaining eye would not respond to the command. The man knelt down and gently lifted something from the thick grass. One of the last things Alisha would see before death took her was the man's giant, dirty hand lifting the bloody and disfigured body of what remained of the girl she had promised to care for. As the dark enveloped her, she focused on her husband's severed hand lying inches from her face, and she wished she could hold it. The last thought that went through her head before she died was about hands. And how not everyone had two.

2

Night gripped the edges of the world and folded them in on itself like nightmare origami. Paisley looked up from where she sat on a stone at the edge of a fire pit. Smoldering ashes provided dim light, just bright enough for her to distinguish the shape of a book sitting on the side of the stone pit. She reached for it and only then realized that there was already something in her hand. It was a hot dog fork. The shiny metal reflected the amber embers. She stared at it, not remembering having picked it up. A branch broke somewhere in the woods behind her, and she turned. An unnaturally large shadow loomed at the farthest edge of the light.

"Get back," she yelled, raising the fork. It had changed. The tines were covered in rust and dripped with blood. She examined the fork as she turned it in her hand.

The shadow moved, closing the distance between them, and standing directly before her. It was a raven. Eyes as black as its feathers stared down at her, its beak gnashing as if grinding bone.

Paisley jumped off the rock, but the monster in front of her grabbed her leg with a human hand that shot out from beneath its Stygian wing. She screamed in pain and kicked at the giant bird, but as her foot connected with what she expected to be feathers, it met a white button-up shirt instead. She knew who it was. It was the same person it always was. She looked up into his face. She had to.

"Hey, pickle," Hollis said. That southern accent was thick and alluring, as always. Paisley kicked hard again, but his grip on her ankle was like an iron vice. He twisted, and she felt it snap off in his hand.

Paisley opened her eyes. Not in the jolt of someone waking

from a nightmare, but the slow, delayed, experienced opening of exhaustion. Breath filled her lungs to capacity. She held it for a beat and released it. She had to prepare herself; she knew that. She owed it to him not to roll over and scream. Another deep breath.

Paisley turned and found the man she had been sharing a bed with off and on for the last ten days was gone. Some nights, he stayed the whole night. If the nightmares were bad, and she tossed and turned a lot, he would.

A sound from the hallway through the open door let her know that he had stayed with her at least until morning. She locked that door every night, and he knew to lock it behind him if he left before the sun was up. If it was open, he stayed and had gotten up recently. She leaned back onto her pillow and inhaled.

"Well, good morning, beautiful," his voice entered the room before he did. Paisley kept her gaze on the duvet, she wasn't ready, and hearing Rowan's soft southern accent, didn't help. She had to separate it from the dream, from Hollis, the man who tried to kill her. She sat up and met his eyes. Her cheeks fought to pull the corners of her mouth into a smile.

Rowan Bloom was a tall, well-built, white man. He stood in the doorway holding a small plate with a donut with chocolate icing in one hand and a cup of coffee in the other. His dark red hair hung in loops on his forehead and bounced as he came closer.

"Breakfast?" he asked.

Paisley contorted her face and stretched out her hands. She opened and closed them in a "gimmie" gesture. The corner of the bed sank under Rowan's weight as he sat and handed her the treats.

"How did you sleep?" he asked.

The sound of large paws on hardwood drew their attention and signaled the interest of Pilot, a large gray and black Irish Wolfhound. She ambled toward the bed and placed her giant head next to Paisley.

Paisley set the coffee on the nightstand and ran her hand through the tufts of fur on Pilot's head. Rowan ran his hands along the side of the dog. It was quiet for a moment. Both using the petting of the dog to mask the silence.

Paisley broke off a small piece of the bread from the donut, careful not to get any of the chocolate icing, and fed it to Pilot. As if the animal was a troll waiting for payment for passage across her bridge, once she had what she came for, she disappeared through the bedroom door.

"What's wrong?" Rowan asked.

Paisley kept focus on the pastry in front of her. She pulled off bits and popped them into her mouth.

"Nothing, just feeling a little sick," she said.

"How's your leg feeling?" he asked after a beat of silence. His hand glided gently over her bare leg where the skin was still a few shades lighter than usual, thanks to the recently removed cast.

"It is a little sore, but it should be fine, thank you." She still wasn't sure how she felt about talking about it. It reminded her of him, of Hollis, but then everything reminded her of him.

Another beat of silence.

"Am I bothering you?" Rowan finally asked.

Paisley swung her feet off the bed and away from his hand, making a show of needing to place the plate on the nightstand.

"No, you're no bother. Why do you ask?"

"You just seem really annoyed with me sometimes, and I don't get it."

Of course, he didn't get it. He couldn't know what it is like to have feelings for someone who looks like the man who tried to murder you. Rowan wasn't Hollis, though. Rowan was smart and kind. He was more Hyacinth than he was Hollis, but she couldn't get past the fact that he sounded like him, and other than the red hair and larger frame, he looked a lot like him, too. If you had taken Hyacinth's beautiful green eyes, Cleopatra smile, and dark red hair, slapped them on Hollis Grimm, and pumped him with some human growth hormone, you'd have

Rowan Bloom. Paisley couldn't help sometimes thinking of him as Frankenstein's monster. Just an amalgamation of other people's parts.

"I'm just tired, that's all. It isn't you," she lied.

"I know you've got a ton going on, and you've been through a lot, and I know you've been thinking about what you'll do next..." he let that hang there for a moment.

Paisley fixed her attention to the floor.

"If you are worried we are moving too fast, I can give you some space," he said.

Rowan put his hand back on her leg, and this time, she left it. His hands were rough but always warm. She forced herself to look at it resting there. Forced herself to know that it was Rowan's hand and not Hollis's.

"That's not it," she said.

"So what is it?"

Paisley put her hand on his and squeezed.

"It's nothing. I don't know what I want to do yet. I'm just trying to get myself back to normal."

"Or para...normal," he joked.

Paisley bunched up her face as if smelling something foul and gave him the stink eye.

"Or not, Paisley Mott," he followed.

Paisley said nothing. She reached for a pillow and swung it at him, connecting solidly with his face. Rowan let out an oof and added a comical look of surprise that made her laugh. He stood, towering over her.

"You dare strike me?" his voice in a mock boom. He reached down to scoop her into his arms, intending to then toss her playfully back onto the bed, but as soon as his hands touched her, she stopped him.

"Wait!"

"What? I'm sorry, what is it?"

"My leg is still really sore, I can't..." she started.

Rowan looked instantly apologetic, which made it even more surprising when Paisley smashed him in the face with the pillow again.

"Oh, I see how it is going to be," the large man said as he descended upon her.

Her laughter filled the room. A welcome sound. For the time being, she allowed herself to be convinced that the terror was over.

3

The truck barreled down the highway, ripping through the night toward the town of Howling Ivy. The demolished car sat on the back of the flatbed but, without close inspection, you couldn't see the damage the truck took for its part in the incident. There were a few scratches. And if you leaned in, you'd see blood, hair, and maybe even some brain matter stuck in the grill. Nothing that wouldn't wash off with a quick spray from the power washer back at the shop. The truck swung up to the gate of Peck Salvage and Recycling on the edge of town. The driver jumped down and unlocked the gate. It groaned and screeched under its own weight as the man shoved it open.

"Hey, man, what are you doing working this late?" a voice called from the door of the trailer, the yard's office, on the other side of the gate. The driver masked his surprise.

"Oh, hey, not much. Just had to pick this one up and bring it in," the driver said, signaling to the destroyed Buick on the flatbed. "What about you? I didn't expect anyone to still be here."

"Just logging a few pulls we had today," the man said, stepping down from the trailer and walking toward the truck. "Jesus, man. That thing looks like it got hit by a train. And then hit by another train. And then pushed off a cliff."

"Yeah, it was one of them rally race things they do out in Westerville. This one finally gave up the ghost," the driver said as he climbed back into the cab of the truck and pulled the door closed.

"I don't remember seeing that on the manifest for today. Want me to put the papers together?"

"Nah, this one was just a little moonlighting side job," the driver said, winking. "Do me a favor and don't tell the boss, would ya'?" He nodded toward the small house pushed back on a hill overlooking the salvage yard.

The man looked over at the house and laughed.

"No problem. Your secret is safe with me," he said.

"You mind swinging that gate closed?" The driver rolled the truck in and headed toward the rear of the yard past rows of dilapidated cars left to rust unless saved by the pickers who came like carrion birds to strip whatever could be salvaged from them. The earth was eroding in the rear of the yard, and parts of the ground had already dropped. They didn't allow anyone back in that area, and eventually anything parked back there would fall as well. Out of sight, out of mind.

The driver pulled the truck into the restricted area, backed in near a line of old cars, disconnected the Buick, and lowered it. Since no one ever went back there, the bodies would do what bodies do when left in the trunk of a car over a long enough timeline. And they'd be disposed of when their faces had all but gone, and their flesh gave way to nothing but bone. The thought made his stomach churn. He walked around the vehicle wiping away any last spots of blood on the outside. Unless someone leaned in the broken windows, risking cutting themselves on the mangled frame, they couldn't see the carnage on the inside.

He planned to take the plates off the car with the intent to toss them in a dumpster next time he was in town. A muffled cry punctuated the air.

"What the hell?" He looked around to make sure nobody was nearby. His hand went to his mouth when the cry sliced through the quiet of the night once more. He didn't mean to hurt anyone. He wanted to call the sheriff and report the accident but she already hated him and he couldn't risk being charged with three counts of vehicular manslaughter. The asshole driving the Buick did appear to be falling asleep and then cut him off when he tried to pass. He had rammed the car and caused it to flip, so it was his fault. Had he known there was a kid in the car he wouldn't have been up on them like that. He just saw the out of state plates and lost it. He was tired of out-of-towners getting on the highway in the middle of the night and coasting.

"Help?" a cry came from the trunk of the car. "Help, please?" the voice croaked.

"Oh God," the driver said. He was certain that they were dead when he put them in the trunk. He didn't take a pulse, but they all looked like they were gone. There was so much blood. He circled the back of the car and pulled the keys he had taken from the ignition from his pocket.

"Hello?" he said.

"Help me! It's dark," the small voice came from the trunk.

The driver bent and picked up a piece of rebar from the weeds.

"I'm so sorry." He popped the trunk and prepared to swing.

4

The kitchen at Raven Bloom, expertly designed and everything in it purposefully placed, had been the staging ground for years worth of the photos that helped make the owner of the property an internet celebrity. When Paisley entered, Hyacinth Bloom sat at a refinished farm table sipping coffee from a stark white mug. She gathered herself a cup of coffee and slipped into the chair across from Hyacinth.

"Mornin'," Hyacinth said. She passed the platter with sugar cubes and milk toward Paisley.

"Good morning," Paisley replied, preparing her coffee.

"Sleep well?"

"I'm pretty sure that bed is literally made out of clouds. Thank you again for letting me stay," Paisley said.

"Of course. I really appreciate you offering to stay and help. With everything that happened, I'm just not ready to have to do all of this alone. Take care of Grover, help the town grieve and then rebuild, and figure out all the legal stuff with the properties since he dumped this crap on me too." Hyacinth hadn't called Hollis by his name since the event.

The search for Hollis started immediately but was reduced from a manhunt to a search for remains quickly. They'd discovered the site of the attack. A blood spatter analyst said that it appeared something had cracked his chest and ripped it open in two, like someone throwing open the doors on a refrigerator, spilling his insides on the ground. But the body was gone.

They said that whatever took him away must have been massive because there was no evidence that the body had been dragged. Paisley feared Hollis could still be alive, somehow. Law enforcement and forensic specialists assured her that the internal organs all belonged to Hollis. But with him gone, the property reverted to the Bloom Estate which Hyacinth had to deal with.

"I'll do whatever I can to help. I'm just glad not to be back home with my dad falling all over himself trying to take care of me," Paisley said.

"Oh, come on, he was adorable when he was here," Hyacinth said.

Paisley's dad came as soon as he heard what happened and stayed in a hotel until both Paisley and Hyacinth were out of the hospital. He wanted her to go back to Oregon with him, but Paisley wanted to stay and help with Grover.

"I'm so grateful, really," Paisley said. "But can I tell you something?"

"You can tell me whatever you want."

"I know you don't want to hear about this, but I have to talk to someone, and you are, for better or worse, currently my best friend," Paisley said.

Hyacinth sat back from the table with a comically stung look.

"I just mean that we met like two months ago but you are the only person I feel I can really talk to," Paisley said.

"That should worry me since you are also currently in some sort of weird relationship with my little brother and I would hope you could talk to him."

"I mean, I can talk to Rowan, I just can't talk to Rowan about Rowan. You know what I mean?"

Hyacinth giggled and nodded, sipping her coffee.

"Yeah, I'm just giving you shit. What is it? Does he snore? Does he hog the covers? Are you tired of pulling handfuls of his long red fur out of your shower drain?"

"No," Paisley started. "I don't know. I guess I just have a hard time because..."

"Because of *him*?"

Paisley was silent. Hollis was Hyacinth's half-brother and it was awkward to talk to her about being afraid of him, but if anyone would understand the type of monster he was it was her. After all, he wanted to kill both women. He tried with Paisley, but with Hyacinth, he came dangerously close to succeeding.

"I get it, Paisley. I do. You can't look at Rowan without thinking of him, right?"

"It isn't just that. It's the dreams... I've been having these nightmares about him. About Hollis, I mean."

"I have them too." Her gaze held in the middle distance as the courage to admit her weakness spilled out.

"Each morning, I roll over and can't tell if I am awake or asleep because his face is staring back at me," Paisley said. "In the dark Rowan's hair looks black. And if his eyes are closed and he isn't smiling, the similarity is just too much."

"I can't say that I have that same issue exactly," Hyacinth said, "but the day he returned from his little disappearing act, after it all happened, or whatever, I came in the front door and he was standing there. It was dark, and I thought it was *him*. I screamed and he turned the light on. When I saw it was Rowan I felt terrible. He looked so sad. I just couldn't help it."

"I can't tell him. He'll take it so hard. I'm sure it'll just take time." Paisley sighed.

"That isn't fair to either of you. You have to talk to him, hun." Hyacinth's southern drawl came out and it sounded more like Rowan than Hollis, which Paisley appreciated.

Hyacinth and Rowan, the youngest siblings, grew up in a lavish home with their mother and their father. Hollis and his brother Cecil were left to be raised by their father, a penniless, overly strict preacher. Everyone from that part of Appalachia had a specific harmony to their voice, but Hyacinth and Rowan spoke with poise, whereas Hollis was more rugged.

"I think you owe it to him to have that conversation."

"He is just so sensitive and I don't want to hurt him. None of this is his fault."

"He's a big boy. He can take it. Rowan doesn't like to get close to people, and there's a lot about him that you still don't know, but it will hurt a lot more if he finds out, in like six months, that you can't stand to be around him, it will kill him."

Paisley looked at Hyacinth as Hyacinth looked at the floor.

"You okay?" Paisley's voice finally broke the silence.

"Do me a favor, will you?" Hyacinth said ignoring the question. "Anything."

"Don't break his heart."

"He deserves better than that," Paisley said.

"I don't think I can handle trying to mend his figuratively broken heart while trying to fix Grover's literally broken one." Hyacinth tipped her coffee cup back and took what was left in a single gulp and then banged the cup onto the table like it was a bar.

"I'll do my very best. I promise," Paisley said.

"But what about you? You can't just stay here hiding in my guest room forever. You've got to get out and continue your story."

"Hey, that guest room is bigger than my apartment back home."

They laughed, the sound nearly foreign to them, given the circumstances.

"And you are welcome to it for as long as you'd like. But I have a feeling that you wouldn't be so worried about my brother if you got back out there and took another case," Hyacinth said.

Paisley searched for the words. "I don't know. After editing all that stuff for the last one and seeing all the shit that I missed, the signs I should have seen earlier, I have to ask myself if I'm actually good at this. If I'm doing more harm than good. Seeing faces of people who were alive before I got here, and aren't now, was hard."

"You should talk to someone," Hyacinth suggested.

"I'm just so twisted up right now. It's making me sick."

"Listen, Pais, shit got real down here. And you saved us. You saved both of us. But that doesn't mean you didn't earn some scars. And you'll carry that shit for the rest of your life. So maybe it would be a good idea to talk to someone about it. I was seeing a therapist before all of this, but I've had to up my visits to three times a week."

"Seriously?" Paisley asked.

"Yeah, seriously."

"I mean, there is a therapist here in Grey Water?" Paisley joked to deflect and lighten the mood, but Hyacinth didn't bite.

"No, we meet virtually. I can't sleep. I can't eat. I can't stop thinking about what I could have done. What I *should* have done. She prescribed me some things. But I'm feeling a lot of resentment toward Grover, so she is helping me work through that also." Hyacinth scratched unconsciously at the back of her hand.

"Grover? Why?"

"This is all just so fucked up. My brother tried to kill me. He killed others. I need time to heal. I've got scars, too. Emotional and physical, and they are deep. But instead of healing, I'm taking care of everything. *He* nearly cut Grover in two. And I am here putting him back together when all I want to do is fall apart. And the one person I thought would be here helping me disappeared, and when he came back, he fell for my best friend."

"So, I am still your best friend?"

"You've seen the people in this town, right? The competition isn't very stiff," Hyacinth said in a flat tone, trying to mask the smile that Paisley could see growing on her face.

"I'm so sorry, Hy. I should've thought about how hard this is for you."

"Don't worry about me. I'll be fine. I'm rich and gorgeous. Not to mention that I plan on writing a book about this whole thing, which will be a bestseller. Then I'll sell the rights to it and they'll make a movie based on it all."

"Can Jenna Ortega play me?" Paisley asked.

"We'll see."

The two sat quietly again, and again it was Paisley that broke the silence.

"Maybe I should go back to Oregon."

"And do what?"

"I don't know. I don't know what I am going to do with my life." Paisley took in the view of the trees that covered most of that part of the Appalachian mountains, trying to ground herself amidst the doubt.

"What are you talking about? You're an investigator. It's what you are built to do."

"I don't know." Paisley shrugged. "I don't know if I am good enough at it."

"Good enough? You literally stopped a serial killer and saved how many people on your first attempt?"

"Well, technically it wasn't my first one. Just the first with this high of stakes."

"Girl, I think you need another case."

"Case? Who am I? Hercule Poirot?"

"Paisley, this is America, and in America, we say Sherlock Holmes, not some British guy."

"First off, you realize that Sherlock Holmes is British, right? And Poriot is actually Belgian. And both Dame Agatha Christie and Sir Arthur Conan Doyle are British. So..."

Paisley waited for a reply but none immediately came. She was instead met with what sounded like a small rhythmic motor. "Are you sleeping?" Paisley turned back to Hyacinth.

"Huh, what?" Hyacinth jerked as if being startled awake.

"Funny," Paisley said. "I don't know about another investigation. The last one literally almost killed me."

"So what will you do instead? Your YouTube channel is blowing up right now. You're on the news every day. You've got people dying to see what you do next. You're hot, sis, and you need to cash in on this."

"Do I want to cash in on this? What about you? You were already a major influencer and you haven't posted since the incident," Paisley pointed out.

"And I don't know if I will. I've got the marketing company to run still. It isn't exactly like I need money or anything. Plus, there are a lot of terrified and confused people in town.

Besides, this house is only big enough for one social media influencer." Hyacinth threw in a wink and Paisley smiled.

"First off, this house is big enough for a hundred social media influencers and their families. Second, I haven't even logged into YouTube since I uploaded the completed documentary stuff. It's all just a bit much."

"What, really? You're literally a sensation right now. You went from a few hundred followers to full on internet celebrity status in no time. Everyone wants a piece of Paisley Mott."

"I'm sure that isn't true," Paisley said.

"Here, look at this." Hyacinth pulled out her phone, tapped some things, and then handed the phone to Paisley.

Paisley rearranged the apps for her email, social media, and YouTube off the main screen of her phone so she couldn't see the growing number of notifications. The text and call notifications weren't too bad, as she had changed her number after the incident, and only a handful of people received the new number. She had yet to see how well her videos were actually doing.

Hyacinth had pulled up Paisley's *Paranormal or Not* YouTube page. Each video in the "Grey Water Ridge" series had millions of views. The one with the footage of the attack at the fire pit had hundreds of millions.

"Brace yourself," Hyacinth said.

"This is insane."

"Click on the last video."

Paisley clicked on the final video in the series, which was the debrief she had done after publishing all the finished videos. She watched her own face but clicked the sound off. She knew what she had said. She talked about how much the anxiety would eat her up. How often she'd want to just crawl into a hole and hide. How many times she thought about running, going home, and forgetting Grey Water Ridge. Then she talked about how she knew she had to get past it. That if she didn't take control of her life and reclaim it from the crippling anxiety and depression, she didn't think she ever would.

"What am I looking for?" Paisley asked.

"Check the comments."

"You never look at the comments; that's day one stuff."

"Read them out loud," Hyacinth said.

"Joker60434 said that I look like the ass end of a baboon. Oh, and this other guy said that I should have just killed myself to save Hollis the trouble. This person thinks I faked the entire thing to get attention." Paisley tried to hand the phone back to Hyacinth, but she wouldn't take it. "Why did you want me to look at this?"

"Keep scrolling."

Paisley looked back at the phone and smiled.

"Hey, I know this one!" Seeing the screen name was like running into an old friend in a foreign city. The name on the comment was 'WhyItHurts,' someone who had supported her during the event but that she had not talked to since. She read the comment out loud. "Paisley Mott is one of the bravest individuals I've ever seen. Her persistence and drive in the face of terror are things to celebrate. Paisley, if you read this, know that we are with you. Reach out if you need anything. I'll be here."

"See, and there are thousands more like that. There are more positive than negative ones," Hyacinth said as she got up and stood behind Paisley so she could look over her shoulder.

"That can't be the case," Paisley said, going to the next comment. "Okay, here's a long one. *Djradmaddi* says, Paisley Mott is my hero. I'm fourteen years old, and I have bad anxiety. People at school made fun of me for it. They would do stuff to upset me, and it would set me off. I used to cry in class. I didn't like that. Once, I thought about killing myself, and I searched online for a good place to throw myself off a cliff and make it look like an accident, and that's how I found Paisley. She was doing a video about her mom dying. She was so sad. I just wished I could give her a hug. She said she was having anxiety and that it was hard for her. So, she made a video in a lighthouse, which made her feel strong. She made me feel like I could be strong, too. Then she went to that town and almost died. I was so scared. I felt like..." Paisley's voice cracked, and her eyes welled.

Hyacinth continued reading where she left off.

"I felt like my friend was in trouble, and because of that, the anxiety didn't matter. I knew what Paisley felt like when her friend was in trouble. I knew for the first time in my whole life what it was like to be part of something. Paisley saved my life. She showed me I could beat my anxiety and my depression. She is the best. Now, I make my own videos. They are just makeup tutorials, but they make me feel powerful," Hyacinth stopped. "There are thousands like this, Pais. You did something special. You mean something to people. That doesn't mean you owe them anything. It just means they are out there, and you got to them."

Paisley skimmed some other comments and saw that the majority were in fact positive.

"I didn't do anything," Paisley finally said.

"You saved my life," Hyacinth said. "You saved Grover's life. You gave closure to the families of a bunch of people who may never have gotten that by exposing their killer. You cleared Rowan's name. You found a body that may have never been found of a poor child who died ages ago. You saved the lives of countless women that *he* might have taken. You saved our town from being sold to the highest bidder. And you did it all while you were so scared that you couldn't even plug my Instagram account in your final wrap-up video." Hyacinth teased. She squeezed Paisley's shoulders and then sat back down.

Paisley coughed and then cawed with laughter.

"My bad," she said.

"I mean, I still got a bump. Because of the whole thing, I think I passed three more boy bands and two Kardashians in follower count," Hyacinth joked.

"Congratulations, I guess?"

"If I ever get back on again it will be nice to know I have a following."

"A following is nice, but maybe I should find a job and stop playing vlogger," Paisley said. "I can't justify paying for an apartment I am not living in, and my bank account is dwindling as we speak."

"Come now, woman. You know those videos are raking in the dough. I mean you did monetize your channel, right?" Hyacinth asked.

"Yeah, but really how much could I get off of that?"

"You're kidding, right?"

"No. I haven't looked at any of it since I uploaded the videos. I've avoided all connection with the outside world. The only people I've talked to are you, Rowan, Grover, and my dad."

"Girl, you need to check and see what kind of coin you have pulled in off that. I bring in a lot of money every month with my photos and videos, and none of them have even a tenth of your viewership. Do you ever check your bank account?"

"Of course I do. I just don't have YouTube set to deposit yet," Paisley tapped a few things on her phone. "Holy forking shirt balls. That's a lot of money!"

"Right?" Hyacinth said.

"Hy, I think I'm rich. Is this what you get every month?" She turned the phone to Hyacinth.

"Not from my influencer stuff, not even close. I get a lot from that, but that all goes to charity. It isn't near what you are sitting on there," Hyacinth said, nodding to the phone.

Paisley knew that Hyacinth's fortune was old money and that she probably could not fathom exactly how much she was worth.

"You donate all your internet money?" Paisley asked.

"Yeah, why wouldn't I?"

"So why even do it?"

"I enjoyed it. It was a great way to get beyond the four walls of Raven Bloom and outside the limits of this tiny ass little town."

"Huh, I guess that makes sense. I'm sorry," Paisley said. She had never really considered what it must be like to be Hyacinth, forced to stay somewhere because of family money.

"So you can afford to take off if you want. I would, if I could. But I'd pick up a camera on my way out of town."

"You would? But you just said you were trying to stay off social media."

"Being pretty isn't a talent. I want to display talent," Hyacinth said.

"You are very talented. I've seen how much work you put into your photos and videos. On top of that, you run a successful marketing company, and according to every source I've seen, the stuff you do with your dad's company is also incredible."

"There's no risk in any of that. If I fail at any of it, there is a pillow-shaped pile of money to catch me. I want to be like you. I want to be brave enough to do something that matters."

This statement hung in the air like smoke from a lit firecracker waiting to explode. Hyacinth Bloom, supermodel and billionaire heiress to the Bloom fortune, just said she wanted to be like Paisley Mott. Paisley, who always felt she was never good enough. Who felt like she was always at a disadvantage. Who always wondered what it would be like to be one of the popular girls or any other girl. Hyacinth Bloom said she wanted to be like her.

"Hyacinth," Paisley started but Hyacinth cut her off.

"I love you, lady. I've thanked you a million times for saving my life, but it will never be enough. I should have seen it. I should have stopped it. But he was my brother, and I was blind to it all."

Shame appeared on Hyacinth's otherwise perfect face.

"You don't have to thank me. I was just doing what I thought needed to be done. You would have done the same thing," Paisley said.

"I wouldn't have. I couldn't have. I thought it could have been Rowan. I'm so sorry."

"Hyacinth, stop. You have nothing to be sorry for."

"I just want to see what it feels like to be needed the way you are. I want to know what it's like to have people ask me what I think about interesting stuff, not just makeup, lighting, and clothes."

"Those things are important to a lot of people. Don't knock them. I mean that kid just said she has a makeup channel and that doing it saved her life!"

"I'm not knocking them. That's literally my life. I just want a purpose, you know?"

"Maybe we both need something to focus on?" Paisley said.

"As soon as Grover is healthy enough that he doesn't need me, I plan on completely falling apart until I figure out what's next. You don't have anything holding you back."

"Maybe I need to see what is out there again," Paisley said.

"I'm sure you will find something, and that something will be important."

5

Moisture dripped down Millicent's chin and soaked into the dirt floor. She could no longer tell if it was sweat or tears, but it didn't matter. She had lost track of the number of days she had been down there. She had been there long enough for her wounds to heal, and for that, she was grateful.

The chain wrapped around her waist wasn't so thick that it felt heavy but too thick for her to be able to break through, and even if she could, what would she do? It was easy to hear the door at the top of the stairs lock when the man would leave. She tried screaming for help the first day but, when she had, the man had taken a piece of rope and tied it around her head and put it in her mouth. The taste of the rope stuck with her. The way the little pieces would tickle the inside of her mouth, and when she breathed in a few would come off and stick in her throat. When the man took it out the next morning, she begged him not to put it back in. Millicent promised she wouldn't scream again. The man agreed but told her that if she did, he would have to hurt her very badly.

The following morning, he came down with a towel or cloth of some kind. He told Millicent that it wouldn't hurt as much, but it had to be in her mouth while he was gone, and he would take it out as soon as he got home. He had mostly kept that promise.

Millicent got food once a day, in the morning. He left three plastic water bottles for her, which he would fill daily. If she needed to go to the bathroom, there was a bucket, and early on the man would take it out every night to clean it and then return it when he brought food in the morning.

Millicent couldn't hold it one night, and she peed in the dirt. She had stretched the chain as far as she could and gone in the corner. She worried the man would be mad at her, but he wasn't. He just kicked some dirt over the spot and apologized to her for not having the bucket there. That night, he took the bucket, cleaned it, and brought it back right away. He also left a small stack of three chocolate chip cookies wrapped in a paper towel when he left. After that, the man would clean the bucket each evening and return it before he went away for the night.

Millicent could hear the man walking around upstairs when he was home, which wasn't often. She could hear another voice - a woman who sounded mean.

Another night, the man came home upset. He came down the stairs and looked panicked running his hands through his hair and looking around the basement as if an answer to whatever problem was following him was hiding there. He told Millicent she had to be quiet, and didn't remove the cloth from her mouth. He just stood there looking down at her, his eyes showing a darkness she wasn't familiar with. After a moment he grabbed the water bottles and left.

Counting days after that was nearly impossible. The light from a small window high up on the wall was the only indicator of time passing. Sometimes she felt like she slept for days and missed the light. The best Millicent could figure was that it was at least six days before she heard another voice upstairs again. She wished every day that someone would find her or that she could just stay asleep.

6

Paisley sat on one of the many balconies that adorned Raven Bloom, staring at her phone. She looked at the messages she had received but had been too anxious to read. There were tens of thousands of them. It was an insurmountable hill to try and poke through, so instead, she clicked on the search function and typed in a name. It showed only three messages. Paisley read them and saw they were checking in to see if she was okay. They said they would always be there if she needed anything. Paisley sent a message and waited for the reply. It only took a moment for a response to come.

ParanormalOrNot - *Hi there.*

WhyItHurts - *Well hello there!*

ParanormalOrNot - *I'm so sorry that I haven't responded. You deserve so much more after all the support you gave me.*

WhyItHurts - *Think nothing of it. I was glad to be of whatever service I could. How are you doing? Are you okay?*

ParanormalOrNot - *Yeah, I'm doing okay. It has been a bit of a whirlwind. I edited the videos and such from the hospital and when I got back to Hyacinth's I uploaded them and went into hiding.*

WhyItHurts - *How is your leg?*

ParanormalOrNot - *It's okay. Just got the cast off.*

WhyItHurts - *So what are you up to now that it appears you are coming out of hiding?*

ParanormalOrNot - *Well that's just it. I'm not sure what's next.*

WhyItHurts - *Are you thinking of picking up another investigation?*

ParanormalOrNot - *I don't know. Is it too soon?*

WhyItHurts - *Too soon for what?*

ParanormalOrNot - *People died here. A lot of people. If I start looking into something else, is that disrespecting the memory of those people?*

WhyItHurts - *As investigators, our job is to solve something. Once solved, we owe it to the victims of that case to move as quickly as we can on to the next. It was that quick movement that got us to their case. There will always be more puzzles, more mysteries to solve, and the longer you wait, the fewer you'll be able to save.*

ParanormalOrNot - *I never thought of it that way.*

WhyItHurts - *Few often do.*

ParanormalOrNot - *So how do I find an investigation? The last one just fell into my lap.*

WhyItHurts - *I've watched all of your videos and read thousands of the comments on them. And one thing is for certain. There is absolutely no shortage of people seeking your help.*

ParanormalOrNot - *I guess I can start looking. Thank you!*

WhyItHurts - *You're very welcome.*

ParanormalOrNot - *Can I ask one more question?*

WhyItHurts - *Sure thing...*

ParanormalOrNot - *Who are you?*

WhyItHurts - *That is a big question. But the short answer is that I am just a bored, retired detective who has an interest in all things strange and unusual.*

ParanormalOrNot - *Retired detective, huh? That explains a lot. How long were you active?*

WhyItHurts - *Not long enough. I was injured in the line of duty.*

ParanormalOrNot - *Oh no! I'm so sorry.*

WhyItHurts - *Me too. After it happened I was forced to retire, then my boyfriend left because he didn't want to take care of me. He said he was too young to be stuck tending to someone who needs to have their backside wiped for them. It is a lot of work to have to nurse someone back from the brink.*

ParanormalOrNot - *I'm hearing that a lot lately.*

WhyItHurts - *My advice to you is to pick an investigation that speaks to you. Something that motivates you to help because they need you and not just because it seems interesting.*

ParanormalOrNot - *That's good advice. Thank you.*

WhyItHurts - *You're welcome. Be sure to reach out if I can help with anything.*

ParanormalOrNot - *I will, thank you.*

WhyItHurts - *Be careful out there. Xoxo*

7

"You okay, darlin'?" Rowan said, his voice preceding him from the bathroom as he entered the bedroom.

"Huh?" Paisley asked from her perch on the corner of the bed.

"When you came in, you asked if we could talk. I said I had something, too, but you said you wanted to get it out first. Is everything okay?" Rowan asked.

"Oh, I'm not gonna lie, I sort of forgot you were in there for a moment, and I was just sort of zoned out," she admitted. She looked up at the bedroom door as if it could offer some sort of clarification.

"What's up, Paisley?"

She liked it when Rowan used her name. Hollis never called her by her name. He always called her "Pickle," or some other pet name. Rowan's use of her name helped her to differentiate between the two. That thought helped jog her memory of what she wanted to talk about.

"I'm struggling." It came out quicker than she intended, staggering him a bit. "It's not you," she added, hoping to soften the blow.

"Oookay. Did I do something wrong? What are you struggling with? How can I support you?"

"No, you did nothing wrong. This is just a really messed up situation, and I am having a hard time processing it all. It's not you." She could already feel the tears threatening to climb up into her eyes. She wanted to pretend that it wasn't happening. She didn't want to cry over a guy, especially since it was still new, and she wasn't exactly sure how she felt about him. No, that was just a lie she was telling herself. She knew.

"Oh, hey, is this the 'it's not you it's me,' talk?" he asked.

"No, no, it's not that."

"No?"

"No."

"No?"

"Well, maybe," she said. "Shit, I don't know, man. Should I be rushing into a relationship right now? I've been through a lot."

"I get that. It complicates things, I'm sure, that I am the brother of the man who tried to kill you." His voice was so calm. However, the light reflecting off the bottoms of his eyes betrayed his true feelings. Paisley wasn't the only one fighting back tears.

"I think I just need time, you know?"

"How much time?" he asked, stuffing his hands, rough from carpentry, into the pockets of his jeans and adding a shoulder shrug for good measure.

"I don't know that," she said.

"And when it's been enough time? What then?"

"I don't know."

"And what about me until then?"

Paisley pulled her feet up onto the bed and brought her knees to her chest.

"I don't know. I'm sorry."

"Do I get any say in this?"

His soft voice wrapped Paisley up like a hug, even in such a tense moment. She hated it. She wanted him to be mad to justify all of this.

"I just need time," she said, putting her face between her knees so that Rowan couldn't see the tears if they came.

"I'm here, Paisley. When you're ready. *If* you're ever ready, I'm here." The floor creaked as the big man moved closer to the bed.

Paisley said nothing. She just stuck out her hand and he took it as she knew he would.

"Thank you," she whispered. He answered with a squeeze.

After a moment, Paisley spoke. "You said you had something you wanted to talk about too?"

"It seems completely unimportant at this particular moment, but I went over to pick up some of Pilot's stuff from Boyd's mom's house yesterday," he started.

"Oh, God, Boyd," Paisley said, pulling her hand back and wiping a tear from her cheek to make room for another set of tears she knew would be coming. "Is his mom okay?"

"She's doing a little bit better every day. But something came up, and she didn't know what to do, so she asked me. And I think it may be something that is better left to you."

"What is it?" Paisley asked, finally looking up at him.

His gentle eyes and the mounting pain of everything happening sat there like dew drops hanging from the tip of a leaf on a fall morning.

Her shoulders slumped. She had processed the toll this all had on her. She'd talked to Hyacinth about what it had done to her. She even helped Hyacinth work through what Grover must be feeling. But neither she nor Hyacinth had stopped to consider Rowan. Rowan, whose brother tried to frame him for multiple murders. Rowan, whose sister was nearly killed because of his perceived inaction. Rowan, whose best friend was shot in cold blood for no other reason than he was in the wrong place at the wrong time and wanted to help stop a madman.

Everyone just assumed that when Rowan disappeared after the attack that he had worked through it all, but how could he? His family was broken, and his community, the one he got away from and chose to come back to, was in ruins. Now, he was showing Paisley grace simply because she needed it. All of that hung in those deep, sorrow-filled eyes. "What does she need?"

"She said Boyd was working on something weird when he died. She gave me a letter to give to you. She wanted your phone number but I said no. I told her I'd bring you the letter and she could explain all this stuff to you."

"What is it?"

Rowan pulled an envelope from his back pocket. There was a moment of wonder about men's pockets being like little magical black holes that could hold anything, including a full-size letter envelope, without bending it.

"Something about a ghost, or something," Rowan said. "I'm not sure why Boyd was wrapped up in any of it, but she said he was."

"A ghost?" Paisley said, flopping her feet onto the floor and pulling herself up by Rowan's hand. "Did you say a ghost?"

"Yeah, something like that, I think. None of it makes sense to me."

Paisley snatched the letter. The envelope was blank minus the letters "PM" written across the front. She tore it open and plucked out the single yellow sheet of legal paper inside. She read it aloud.

"Dear Missus Mott, I know we haven't officially met, but my name is Sylvia Gunnerson. I believe you spoke with my son, Boyd, before he passed. This seems forward, but someone reached out to me and said Boyd was trying to help solve a mystery. And that someone really needed his help. The person who called me said that he was a friend of Boyd's, but I didn't know him. He said Boyd had uncovered information that there may have been a murder..." Paisley stopped reading and looked at Rowan. "A murder? I thought it was a ghost? What sort of weird shit was Boyd into?"

Rowan's brow dropped a nearly imperceptible amount.

"Oh, jeez, I'm sorry. I didn't mean it that way. I meant it as a compliment," Paisley said.

Rowan raised an eyebrow.

"As in the way that I am also into some weird shit. I traveled across the country looking for Bigfoot," she said.

"A sasquatch," Rowan said.

At this point it was less a mistake when she said it and more like a Catholic call and repeat where she knew exactly what they would say.

"Right, sasquatch. Anyway, I thought this was ghost stuff,

not murder stuff," she said. "Though one usually leads to the other."

"Keep reading," Rowan said, nodding to the letter.

"... Boyd had uncovered information that there may have been a murder in some town in Indiana. They said my son had single-handedly come closer to cracking the case. He said that Boyd had tracked everything through a series of ghost sightings, leading to some sort of break. I don't know what any of it means, but he said they were too close to quit now and needed someone else who could pick up the case. The guy asked if I knew you since you caught Hollis. I said I didn't but that I knew someone who did. So I asked Rowan to bring you this letter. I don't know anything more than what I just said. My friend and I are going to Florida for a few weeks while the diner gets fixed up or torn down. Either way, we are leaving. You don't know me, but I am begging you for help. If this meant something to Boyd then it had to be important. Please help finish whatever it was that Boyd started. Yours truly, Sylvia Gunnerson."

Paisley read over a few key parts again.

"There's a screen name there at the bottom," Rowan said, pointing at the bottom of the letter. "He told her that if you agreed, you could message him there, and he'd fill you in on the little information he has so you can try and pick up the trail that Boyd was on."

"Well, I can genuinely tell you that when I woke up this morning, I did not think I'd break up with my boyfriend and be asked to track a murderer because someone is seeing ghosts in Indiana," she said.

"So, I was your boyfriend?"

"Yeah, at least I hope you were."

Her eyes met his.

"Then I hope to be again sometime," he said before leaving the room. Paisley watched him go, wanting him to come back but knowing it would prolong the inevitable. She thought it could possibly work once she had some time between her and what had happened with Hollis.

"I hope so, too," she whispered. "I hope so, too."

8

ParanormalOrNot - *Who is this?*
TheEndJustifies - *Is this Paisley Mott?*
ParanormalOrNot - *I asked first.*
TheEndJustifies - *Yes, but either you are Paisley Mott, and we can talk, or you aren't and I can disconnect now and ditch this account.*
ParanormalOrNot - *Why the secrecy?*
TheEndJustifies - *Is this Paisley Mott?*
ParanormalOrNot - *It is.*
TheEndJustifies - *Send a pic...*
ParanormalOrNot - *Ew, eat a bag of dicks, pervert.*
TheEndJustifies - *A picture of your face, and hold up three fingers, facing away from you, so we can verify it is you.*
ParanormalOrNot - *And you'll do the same thing?*
TheEndJustifies - *No, our identity must remain hidden. Please send the photo now.*

Paisley did as was requested, almost. She set the self facing camera up and set a timer. She held two fingers up on her right hand, facing toward the camera and away from herself, but with her left she was giving the middle finger. She uploaded the photo and hit send.

ParanormalOrNot - [Image sent]
TheEndJustifies - *Very funny, Miss Mott. I hope that your investigation techniques are less elementary than your skills of communication.*
ParanormalOrNot - *I'm not a fan of being in the dark.*
TheEndJustifies - *We understand. And if it were not completely necessary, we would be happy to share our identity, but knowing who we*

are will not help you.

ParanormalOrNot - *I don't like it, but I'm listening.*

TheEndJustifies - *In an attempt to not contaminate your investigation, we feel it better to give you no information other than to point you to the most recent lead in the case. Boyd had found a boy in Indiana who he believed had been seeing the spirit of his dead sister. We had been trying to determine if the hauntings were real. If they are, it could potentially lead to information that could solve the case. If you are interested in picking up the case, I will send you a link to a podcast that could have busted this whole thing wide open if Boyd had still been here. It contains solid evidence of the existence of a spirit. It doesn't hurt that the two teen boys who produce the show are fans of yours and may be willing to work with you more cooperatively than they would with us.*

ParanormalOrNot - *Send it.*

9

"So, was there a bigfoot or nah?" Steven "Patch" Simply, co-host of the Simply Knot Paranormal Podcast asked, pulling the worn-out boxing glove that served as a makeshift microphone stand closer to his mouth, careful not to knock over the table the two teen boys huddled around.

"No, buddy, because as Paisley said in the documentary, a number of times, Bigfoot is a name, not a genus," Darius "Derry" Knot, the podcast host, replied.

"I didn't say it was smart. I just asked if it was a bigfoot?"

"What does the thing being smart have to do with anything at all?"

"You said he wasn't a genius," Patch said.

Derry pulled the microphone close to his lips so he could whisper. He knew Patch would hear him, but even more importantly, the few hundred fans who listened to their podcast would hear it.

"So, I didn't say genius, genius. I said genus. Like the classification above species," Derry said.

"What do you mean?" Patch asked. Derry would say this about his best friend: he wasn't the smartest person in the world, but always tried to learn.

"A genus is a class of things with common characteristics that can be further divided into subordinate groups, or species. So it ranks just above species in an organism's taxonomic hierarchy," Derry explained. Patch just sat and stared for a moment.

"Explain," he finally said.

"So, let's take dogs."

"Love dogs."

"I know you do, buddy, that's why I am using them in the example."

"I'll allow it."

"What is your favorite kind of dog?" Derry asked.

"What kind of dog is Clifford?" Patch asked in return.

"You mean the Big Red Dog?"

"Yeah, that one."

"Well I believe he is just a giant Red Labrador retriever."

"Then that one."

"Seriously? Clifford?"

"Yeah, why?"

"You don't want to go with a real dog?"

"Nah, Clifford."

"Clifford the Big Red Dog is your favorite type of dog?"

"Yeah, I used to love that shit growing up."

"Okay," Derry processed for a moment and tried to decide where to take it. "Okay, so, let's say Clifford was real and that he is, in fact, a Red Labrador retriever. Now, Red Labrador Retriever would be his breed."

"And that is his genius?" Patch asked.

"No, not the *genus*," Derry said, leaving a little emphasis on the pronunciation.

"Oh, species I mean."

"Nope, but you are getting closer. So a Red Labrador Retriever would be the breed of dog that Clifford is."

"Oh, shit, I knew that."

"Right, a breed is an artificially selected designation given to different types of dogs that exist in the same subspecies. So his breed is Red Labrador, and his subspecies is Canis lupus familiaris, which contains other breeds of dogs," Derry said.

"Oh, like wolves and shit?"

"Not quite, but you're so dang close. So, a wolf and the common dog share the next level up from subspecies, which is species. In this case, Canis lupus. Then, and here is what we are talking about, you have the genus." Derry leveled his hands and made a row to demonstrate. "So this is wolf, common dog, and then canines that have a few more differences like a jackal."

"Cool, cool, cool. So then what comes after that?" Patch leaned forward, putting his arms on the rickety card table that held the microphones.

"Well then you have the family Canidae, which includes all of those plus things like a fox. Then above that you have order Carnivora, which are going to be animals that eat meat."

"My dawgs."

"Literally. But, that's going to include things like cats too. Then above that we include things that don't eat meat but are still mammals, like rabbits and squirrels and such. Then we step up again to the phylum, in this case Chordata, and that's when you start getting things like fish. Then it gets really big after that and we encompass the entire animal..." Derry paused to see if Patch would fill in the blank. He did not.

"Animal what?"

"Kingdom, the animal kingdom. That is the next level, Kingdom; in this case, it is Animalia. Then we kick up to basically most living things and get to the domain, which is Eukarya," Derry said. He sat back in his chair and smiled. It wasn't often in his daily life that he got to drop any of the knowledge he had picked up spending all his free time reading everything he could get his hands, or eyes, on.

"Dude, how in the fuck do you remember all that shit?" Patch asked, leaning back in his chair clapping.

"I wrote a paper on the sublevels of the taxonomic classification system of dogs in my honors science class. We had to pick a single animal and follow it all the way up."

"And what fancy-ass dog did you pick since Clifford wasn't good enough for you?" Patch asked.

"Blue," Derry replied.

"A blue dog?"

"No, Blue, from Blue's Clues," Derry said.

Patch broke. His laughter was loud and boisterous. Derry's face turned red and then he finally caved and started laughing as well.

"You're such a dick," Patch said.

"Anyway," Derry started, "Bigfoot is the name of a specific creature, just like Blue and Clifford are names of dogs, Bigfoot is the name of a Sasquatch."

"Oh, shit, that's why all those people kept getting pissed when she would call it Bigfoot?"

"Correct."

"So, was there really a sasquatch or nah?" Patch rephrased his original question.

"That's just it, we don't know. She leaves it very ambiguous on that point."

"Cause we know that preacher dude killed all them girls, right? If he did that then there was never a Bigfoot," Patch caught himself before Derry could correct him, "I mean sasquatch?"

"So there are a lot of reported sightings of what resembles a Sasquatch in that area over the last hundred or so years. It is possible that they see something, we just don't know what it is."

"I bet you could figure it out," Patch said.

"Thanks, buddy, but I don't know."

"You're a fucking genus cryptocurrency or whatever."

"Genius. And it is cryptozoologist. And no, I am not."

"Right, that. So you could figure that out. And about that fucking monster thing that everyone saw at the yard. And the ghosts. Oh, and the zombies!"

"That's all bullcrap and we both know it," Derry said.

"No way man. Which part?"

"All of it. There isn't any government conspiracy, and there wasn't any monster."

"Like three people at work said they heard a screeching noise, looked up, and some fucking weird long-legged mother fucker stepped out on all fours and ran off into a field or some shit," Patch refuted.

"And were you there?"

"Well, no. I wasn't working that night. But the guys told me all about it," Patch said.

"Right, and what were those guys doing that night when they saw it?"

"They was just sittin' out there at the trailer, having a beer."

"Right, they were drunk."

"C'mon, man. Just because they were drinking doesn't mean they were drunk, and it don't mean it didn't happen," Patch pleaded. "It was just like the thing that was behind the bar that one night."

"That carries just as much weight as your claim that the government has been hiding both aliens and zombies right here in town," Derry countered.

"Okay. Okay. I admit, some of it sounds crazy, but you can't deny that it is interesting."

"I will concede that the notions are interesting, but with that, our time is up."

"Already?" Patch looked at his cell phone.

"Yep. I've got homework and you've got video games to play."

"You're not wrong."

"So, until next time, I'm Darius Knot."

"And I'm Patch Simply."

"And you've been listening to The Simply Knot Paranormal Podcast. Please tune in next week when Patch and I discuss the rumor that zombies are walking among us. Have a great week, and keep it strange. See ya."

"Later," Patch added.

This was their signature sign-off at the end of every episode. Derry moved the mouse and clicked a few things, looking very official in what he was doing, and then hit the button to stop the recording. He took a deep breath and scanned back a few seconds to listen to the sign-off again.

Patch removed his headphones and wiped the sweat that always built up where they pushed against his massive head. Derry watched the green bars on the equalizer fade as the voices drifted from the machine.

"What the hell?" Derry said.

"Sup, my dude?" Patch asked.

Derry listened intently to the nothingness in the headphones. His face tightened.

"Dude?" Patch asked again.

"I thought I heard something," Derry said.

"What was it?"

"I don't know, maybe some interference or something. I hope it didn't jack the audio," he said.

"It good?" Patch asked, giving a thumbs up.

Derry returned the thumbs up.

"Seems okay."

"Cool, we had some gold there and I don't want to lose it," Patch said.

Derry leaned back in his chair. The episode was supposed to be about UFOs and crop circles, but before Derry could get into it, Patch started in on a documentary the two of them had watched on YouTube. Some random person on their social media kept commenting, saying that the lady who made it may be able to help them. The documentary was about a woman in the mountains in Kentucky who was nearly killed searching for a sasquatch. Derry had watched the documentary and all of the supplemental videos that went with it three times. He was impressed with Paisley Mott. Not just her developing skills as an investigator but her ability to overcome what appeared to be some pretty crippling anxiety.

"Gonna piss," Patch said, moving down the narrow, wood-paneled hallway of the trailer Derry shared with his dad.

Derry sat alone at his computer skipping back on the podcast. The banter of him and his friend bounced around in his ears. He wanted to hear it again.

"You've been listening to The Simply Knot Paranormal Podcast. Please tune in next week when Patch and I discuss the rumor that zombies are walking among us. Have a great week, and keep it strange. See ya'," Derry's own voice played back in the headphones. He had his mouse pointer hovering over the stop button and was prepared to click.

"Later," came Patch's usual response, but another voice came before the recording ended. A girl. A ball of ice formed in Derry's chest.

"Derry," the quiet voice came through the headphones. He looked around the room and saw nothing.

He stopped the playback and skimmed back again. His hands pressed the headphones closer to his ears.

"...tune in next week when Patch and I discuss the rumor that zombies are walking among us. Have a great week, and keep it strange. See ya."

"Later."

"Derry." The voice was soft, and the name came out like the last bit of air in a deflated balloon.

He skipped back again.

"...walking among us. Have a great week, and keep it strange. See ya."

"Later."

"Derry."

He skipped back again.

"See ya."

"Later."

"Derry."

Again.

"Later."

"Derry."

"Later."

"Derry."

"...ater."

"Derry."

"...ater."

"Derry."

"...ter."

"Derry."

"...ter."

"Derry."

"Derry."

"Derry."

He rubbed his eyes, stretched, and leaned back.

That voice hung in the air like a cobweb caught in a breeze. He closed his eyes and felt the air in the trailer change. It was as if someone was there, but he could not turn around. He was too afraid of what he would find in the dark.

"Dude?"

He jumped up dragging the headphone cord behind him and pulling his mixer off the table.

"Jesus Christ," Derry said, trying to pick everything up.

"Sorry man, didn't mean to scare you," Patch said.

"You didn't."

"Right, you were just so moved by my presence that you just had to jump out of your seat to greet me. I know you can feel me... coming..." Patch thrust his hips at Derry.

"Oh, God, do not say it like that. I was just focused on something else, so I didn't hear you," Derry said.

"Seriously though, you cool?" Patch helped Derry pick up the few other items that had come off the table.

Derry stopped collecting the scattered items and took a deep breath.

"There's something on the recording," he said. "A voice."

"Like an EVP?" Patch asked. Obsessed with the paranormal and conspiracy theories, he had always wanted real evidence. Electronic Voice Phenomenon or EVP was a good start. They were normally very easy to debunk, but you could get a lot of podcast mileage out of it first.

"Yeah," Derry replied.

"What did it say?"

"My name." His head and shoulders slumped, his eyes on the floor.

"No shit? Let me hear it!" Patch plopped down on the cheap, metal folding chair he had been sitting in to record and slipped the headphones back over his head.

Derry moved the cursor back and hit play. Patch listened intently and then mouthed the words of the sign-off as they went. Then his face twitched and froze. He sat holding his breath.

"Play it again," he finally said. His voice was low and flat.

Derry clicked the bar again and watched as Patch listened. Derry had not put the headphones on to listen again, he'd heard the sound enough times.

"Again," Patch said. The light reflected off of Patch's lower eyelids.

When Derry saw it he stopped resisting and allowed the tears in his own eyes to form.

"Again," Patch said, his voice hitching.

Derry clicked the bar. When it ended, he played it again, four more times, without Patch asking. Then Patch slipped the headphones off and looked at them. He inspected them as if there might be something wrong, then set them gingerly on the table. He looked up at Derry.

"What the fuck, man?" he said, his voice wavering.

Derry said nothing. He just shook his head.

"That was Lyds."

Derry nodded as the tears ran knowing that his friend believed him.

10

Paisley's breath caught in her throat as if a noose had been tightened around it. After the sign-off, she heard a terrified voice calling the host's name.

"Derry."

"Derry."

Paisley put her hand over her heart as the sound played over a few times before the host came back on to explain.

"At the end of tonight's recording, we captured what we believe to be an EVP, or electronic voice phenomenon," the host, Derry, explained. "I do not want to speculate as to what, or who, it is, or if it is indeed a true EVP. We have not yet investigated the sound, but we wanted to present it and let you decide. What was that sound? Was this a spirit from the other side? Did Patch just shart himself in a pleather chair? Let us know in the comments or on social media. Till next time. See ya." Paisley's anxiety crept in. The world sharpened and her eyes focused on things that she hadn't noticed before. The red squirrel, who sat in the tree about ten feet from her, watched for anything trying to challenge him while he enjoyed a snack of some ground nuts. A bird rested on the rail of the balcony just off the room to her right. The small, yellow stain on her pants from the filled doughnut she had before going out onto the balcony. No. That wasn't it. The doughnut wasn't custard, she remembered. The filling was white; therefore it was cream, not custard.

The stain would have had to be from the eggs that she made that morning. Over-easy, like she liked them. She didn't spill the eggs on herself, but she did drop her toast, which she had been using to mop up the yolk. Her anxiety-fueled hyper focus began organizing her normally scattered thoughts, and they fell into place in her mind.

A new side effect of this hyper focused state was that, when active, her memory was now near perfect. A gift for an investigator but a curse for a victim of violent trauma. The yellow stain on her pants left her mind and was replaced by his face. Hollis. She saw him that night, holding her by the leg, the madness in his eyes as she stabbed him with the hot dog fork.

Paisley jerked. Her hand shot down and grabbed her leg as her brain convinced her that the bone there, now healed, was broken again.

Memories flooded back, each clear and stuck in her brain like a harpoon. The clues she missed that could have led her to the truth about Hollis Grimm sooner. The anxiety caught everything, she saw it; she just wasn't adept at processing. That part was still coming. The connections between things were getting quicker. She saw the snapshot in her mind of Hollis digging at the scene of the first murder after she arrived in Grey Water Ridge. Then she remembered a subscriber asking if it was a watch Hollis had picked up and pocketed. The tan line around his wrist where his watch had been. She even recalled Hollis checking for the time and not having a watch to read. That seemed normal for most people but since Hollis rarely carried a cellphone, he relied on a watch. All of these things and more flashed like a zoetrope spinning in her head as she relived the horrific experience.

11

Millicent sat in the dark. The chains around her waist and hands pulled her down. Their weight increased with every passing day. It had been days since the man had last delivered food or water. He hadn't even been down to do laundry, as he usually would every few days. Moving her tongue in her mouth was like walking through a dry bramble on a hot July afternoon. She tried to cry out, but it was useless. The cloth between her teeth made it impossible to release more than a small whimper, and the desert that was her mouth wouldn't allow her to form words even without the cloth.

She clung to the sliver of light coming from the tiny, grimy window high on the wall, hoping to track the time as it passed. But countless times, it faded and she wasn't sure whether it was night overtaking day or if she had passed out. There were instances where she would sleep for what felt like days. She was so hungry, so thirsty, and so weak that she wished she could just stay asleep.

A sound, a rustle, crept across the basement floor. There was something there in the dark. Something small. Something as scared as Millicent herself. It scurried across the floor, little pink feet pattering. The mouse stopped to size Millicent up. It inched closer. She knew she should be scared of it, but instead, it brought her comfort. A living thing down there among the dust and cobwebs.

Dizziness flowed through her head like viscous jelly. She smiled beneath the gag in her mouth. She had a friend. The mouse watched her as she drifted off to sleep.

Millicent hoped it would be the last time. At least she wouldn't die alone.

12

Luggage dropped onto the conveyor belt and landed with a thud against the rim of the carousel. After collecting the checked bags, Paisley hauled them to the bathroom to take care of some quick, important business. She had to get ready before grabbing her rental car and heading to Howling Ivy to meet with Darius Knot.

Paisley entered the Ladies' Room, looking around she nodded at the empty room and then rolled her luggage into the far stall with the extra space and closed the door. Using her large suitcase as a table she opened her camera bag and spread out her new gear. She hoped this equipment, this potential case, was the "something new," she needed. Either way, she was armed with the tools to capture every moment. Hyacinth would be so proud. After deciding to make the trip to Indiana, Paisley ordered a few miniature clip cameras that could be attached via magnet to anything. They were small enough to go completely unnoticed unless you were looking for them but she had gone a step further and used Hyacinth's 3D printer to make housings for them that looked like pins she could wear on her clothes or bags.

Each camera sported a wide-angle lens, so just wearing one would capture almost everything she needed. The cameras recorded directly to a portable hard drive she planned to carry with her at all times.

Working in tandem with the camera was a small unidirectional microphone that could be slid into the pins and would allow audio to be recorded to the drive as well. Once on the drive, the files would be stored there and sent directly to a cloud service via a separate data line that served as a hotspot. After setting everything up, she gave Hyacinth and WhyItHurts the login credentials for the server. If anything happened to Paisley, either of them could log in and watch all the videos. They could even log in and watch Paisley live with a short delay if they felt the need.

The entire drive and wireless setup was almost completely unnoticeable and fit nicely into a hollowed paperback book. The book she chose was a mystery by Ellen Raskin called *The Westing Game*. She would keep the book in her bag most of the time but it would fit into her jacket pocket if needed. She slipped the hollowed-out book from the front pocket of her checked bag. She thought it better to check it and not stuff hard-to-identify electronics into a hollowed-out book and try to get that in her carry-on. Security made her take all her camera equipment out and show them each piece before she was allowed to board the plane with it, so this particular bit of kit was best left in the checked bag.

After getting the system set up she plucked a pin from the collection in her camera bag and put it on her jacket. This particular pin was shaped like a cat folded into a taco shell. The camera lens sat squarely in the cat's mouth. Paisley had planned on telling people there was a camera on them, but just in case, she had looked up the laws regarding recording people without consent. In Indiana, it was a "one-party consent" law. Meaning as long as one person in the conversation knew they were being recorded, it was legal, and Paisley knew, so she was golden.

Using her experience in Grey Water as a hard-learned lesson, this time, Paisley had done everything she could to control the outcome. She had redundant cameras, backup hard drives, a second drone, and even two camera bodies for quality footage. A stun gun and pepper spray had been obtained and were now out of her luggage and added to her bag. She had also reserved a car and rented an airbnb in town. Everything was all lined up and her confidence was at an all-time high.

"I'm very sorry, ma'am. We just don't have a reservation for you," the older man behind the check-out desk at the car rental company said. His beady brown eyes peered out through dirty, round lenses in his wire-framed glasses. He wore a little blue vest with a name tag that said "Carl."

"Carl, is it?" Paisley pointed to the tag.

Carl looked down at it, then back to Paisley, judging if the question demanded an answer, or at least the woman asking it did.

Carl nodded.

"Carl, I made a reservation. I have a confirmation email right here." Paisley held her phone up for Carl to see. He squinted and read the text on her screen.

"Well, sure, that's the confirmation for the reservation, but two days ago, that reservation was canceled," Carl said, turning his monitor to Paisley so she could see that, indeed, the reservation had been canceled.

"But I didn't cancel it. Why was it canceled?"

"Well, it looks like we canceled it. Doesn't give a reason, just that the reservation was canceled and that the vehicle wouldn't be needed." Carl looked from the screen to Paisley as he gave her the bad news.

"Why would they do that? Is that a thing that happens a lot?" Paisley settled back into her more casual demeanor in favor of the false bravado that she sometimes felt the need to portray in cases where she was worried that she was just going to get screwed over because she wasn't willing to make a fuss.

"No, it is pretty rare," Carl laughed.

"Okay. Uhm, no problem. Can I reserve a car now?" Paisley asked.

"That isn't possible, unfortunately. We've got a few conferences in town, and we share cars with some other services. So when the reservation was canceled we released the hold on the car."

"So, that's it? No car for me?"

"Afraid so."

"Well fuck me, Carl."

13

Derry walked into the diner and stood next to the host station. The smell was a mix of crayons and plastic with a hint of bacon and eggs. He stood with shoulders slumped, arms pulled in, and his face tilted downward. He stayed like that, waiting for the staff to notice him.

"Hey, sweetie. Sorry, I didn't see you standing over here," a woman said as she walked up to the stand. Derry tensed when he heard her. The duality of the situation forced a small bead of sweat to blister high on his forehead. He had both hoped that she would be his server and, at the same time, not. Derry was not new to having a boyhood crush, as he had one on a few girls on YouTube for years. But Khalida Walker was the first woman he had seen in real life that he was attracted to, and without Patch to break the tension, he was nervous.

He wasn't sure exactly how old she was, but she looked like she was in her mid-twenties. She had worked there for at least six years, so she must have had to have been pretty young when she started there.

Two things fueled the crush over time. He could not pinpoint which started it. She was an undeniably beautiful black woman, but that was just one aspect. She was also incredibly kind.

She often comped Derry's meals on the check when he came in with Patch for lunch. She would devise a silly bet that she would always lose, so she would have to give him the meal for free.

She was also the only adult in the neighborhood that would smile and wave at him if she saw him walking down the street. Khalida attempted to sing at the funerals of anyone in town, including his own sister's. When Patch's grandpa died, the only people at the service were him, Patch, Patch's grandma, and

Khalida Walker. Khalida sang the most beautiful song. Khalida, or Lida, as everyone in town came to know her, was a slight woman with a brilliant, wide smile. That day, her hair was pulled back tight, leading to a flourishing afro puff that bounced firmly on her head. The pale blue and white striped uniform she wore looked like it had seen years of wear and tear but was still clean. A small order book stuck out of the pocket of the apron around her waist, but Derry knew she didn't need it when she was taking orders and only used it to bring the checks back to the tables.

"No worries, Lida," he replied with a smile.

"Should have just given a holler, I'd have come-a-runnin'," she said, pulling a menu from below the podium that served as a host stand.

"I'm in no hurry," Derry said with a shrug.

"Is it just you today? Where's Patch?"

"He's working. I'm meeting someone else," then added, "a woman."

"Oh, well, well. Hot date. Would you like a booth then, or did you want to sit up at the counter?" She snatched another menu and signaled to the long white countertop that stretched the length of the place.

The counter was empty except for a man dressed in all black at the end. He appeared to be a preacher of some sort. Derry didn't recognize him, but there were more churches in town than there were bookstores, computer stores, or libraries all put together. One thing Derry knew was that when poor people ran out of money for everything else, they would invest what little they had left into one of two things: lotto tickets and God. Both in hopes of a miracle, and neither ever paying out.

"It's just a meeting, so a booth would be wonderful, if that is okay?" Derry said, raising his eyebrows.

"Of course, sweetie. Right this way."

"Thank you."

Lida led him down the aisle to a table about halfway. The choice of sitting him at that particular table felt so arbitrary that it caused Derry some anxiety. He always sat at the counter.

"Is this going to be okay for you?" she said, placing the menus on the table.

"This is great, thank you," he said, sliding into the booth on the right side. Once he was in, Lida placed a menu in front of him and left the other in the middle of the table.

"Can I get you anything while you wait for your date?" She winked at him.

"It isn't a date!" He held the menu up trying to hide the fact that his ears were turning red.

"My apologies, Mr. Bachelor. What can I get for you while you wait for your associate?"

"May I please just have a glass of water?"

She eyed him sideways.

"You sure you don't want a Pepsi? I still owe you one from when I bet you I could toss the tape and get it around the ketchup bottle on the counter in one try."

"I'm pretty sure you paid that bet off that day after we cleaned up all that ketchup when the bottle broke," Derry pointed out.

"I don't know my own strength," she joked.

They laughed, though his nerves prevented him from savoring the exchange.

"Just water today. Thank you."

"Of course, I'll be right back."

As far as patrons went, Derry saw that, it was just him and the preacher. It was too early for lunch and too late for breakfast. Lida returned with the water and set it in front of Derry with a straw.

"You need anything else before she gets here, you just holler, you hear?" Lida patted him on the shoulder.

"Thank you."

Then Lida was on the move again. She walked quickly in the heel toe manner that people who spend a lot of time on their feet tend to adopt. She turned past the counter and disappeared into the kitchen. Derry sat looking at the water bead on the outside of the glass and dragged a finger down the side tracing a line through the condensation. He was nearly twenty minutes early. He wasn't sure if Paisley would be on time but he knew he wanted to get there first.

He sat for ten minutes before he saw a black sedan turn onto the main street and pull to a stop in front of the diner.

"Thanks, darlin'," Lida said, somewhere off in the distance.

Derry heard the preacher get up and walk past the table where he sat staring at the woman in the car who could not yet see him.

14

The town came into view through the viewfinder of Paisley's camera from the back of a ride share car. She questioned her decision not to borrow Hyacinth's Hummer and drive up, which was not a mistake she planned to make twice.

Howling Ivy was dingy and dirty in the way only a town on the great American Rust Belt could be. Rows of abandoned houses stretched for miles as the grass broke through old concrete and asphalt, attempting to reclaim the land. Old factories sat boarded up; ghostly husks of the production giants they once were sat like slumbering behemoths among the fields. Paisley noted that certain colors stood out and gave a more stark contrast of the age of the buildings. Yellows and reds fade slower than blues and greens.

"Looks like if Warhol had painted dystopian landscapes," Paisley said.

"What's that?" the driver asked.

"Oh, no. I was just talking to the camera," she said.

The driver turned, and she tapped a finger on the camera as it recorded the scenery.

"Warhol? That's the soup guy, yeah?" the driver asked.

"Yep, that's the one. He did a lot of Pop Art."

"I never saw the stuff he did with soda pop, just the soup one," the driver said with a hint of pride in knowing the famous painter and his work.

"He used a lot of bright colors and heavy contrast."

"I'll Google it later."

"You may enjoy it," Paisley said.

"That why you're out here in bum fuck Indiana," the driver tripped over the phrase as if he didn't see it. "I'm sorry, I didn't mean to cuss."

"That's okay. I don't think my viewers will care."

"I mean, we just aren't supposed to when we are driving. Could cost us some stars."

She caught his eyes in the rear view mirror.

"Worry not, my friend. You get me there safely and your stars are safe with me." She smiled.

His eyes lingered for a moment longer in the rear view then flicked down to the road and back to her.

"Hey, I don't want to be rude, but do I know you from something?" he asked. "Are you famous?"

"Not really. Do you watch a lot of videos online?"

He laughed.

"That's about all I do when I'm not driving this car."

"Have you seen the one where the crazy preacher killed all those women in the mountains and then tried to kill a few more and one of them caught him on a drone?"

"Yeah, the one with the lady from the internet and the paranormal lady, right?"

"That's the one."

"Oh yeah, I've seen that one *so* many times. That dude was psycho. The way he just grabbed that lady by the leg and shook her like a rag doll and..." Then it hit him who she was. The car swerved as he hadn't been able to take his eyes off the mirror, and they crossed the rumble strip on the side of the highway. "Oh shit," he said, jerking the car back into the middle of the lane.

"That would be me. Raggedy Ann at your service," Paisley said.

"Whoa! Seriously? So what *are* you doing out here in the middle of nowhere? There isn't anything out this far, and Howling Ivy is like the armpit of the state. You'd be better off somewhere like Indianapolis, South Bend, or Fort Wayne. Maybe even Evansville. Unless you are looking for rock bottom prices on meth or real estate, you are in the wrong town."

"Maybe that's exactly what I am out here looking for, sir, and

I would thank you not to judge."

"Uh..."

"Kidding, obviously. I'm working on another story. Don't know if it will go anywhere, but as my dad likes to say, if you don't go you won't know."

"Smart guy, but I bet he never thought you'd be going to a place with more empty houses than full ones, and they still got people living on the streets."

"There are places like that all over the world, sadly." There was a moment of silence before the driver added some forced positivity.

"At least downtown isn't a *total* shit hole."

He was right. Most of the buildings downtown, even though they were old and run down, looked pristine in comparison to the rest of the town.

When the car turned onto the main street and rolled up in front of the diner, Paisley had a moment of panic. The small-town feel was almost too familiar. It was too much like the diner in Grey Water Ridge, where a gun-toting maniac who had already tried to kill her went in and killed a bunch of innocent people instead.

The blue sky and a singular cloud reflected on the diner's front window. That pale blue swath of sky wasn't possible in Grey Water Ridge. There were too many trees and mountains. You only got small slices of the sky there, not like this where even in the reflection of a window, the sky seemed to go on forever. That slight difference was what she used to ground herself.

The car door opened and the driver got out and went to the trunk to fetch her bags. She had even inventoried the sound his shoes made on the pavement. Her mind was sharp even if her emotions were still sitting in an Appalachian murder town.

"You okay?" the driver asked.

"Undecided." Paisley smiled and climbed out of the car. The driver set her luggage in front of her on the sidewalk.

"Okay then, are you going to be okay?" he asked.

"And if I'm not?"

"Um, I don't know. I can drive you someplace else, I guess?"

"As long as there isn't an insane preacher with a sexy accent in there waiting to kill me I think I will manage," she said and took her suitcase.

The driver laughed.

"Well, if so, I think you are uniquely equipped to handle that," he said.

Paisley pulled out her phone and opened the ride share app. A chime from inside the car rang as she clicked something on her phone.

"There you go, friend. Five stars. Thanks for getting me here alive."

"Hey, thanks. Be careful out here," he said.

"Honestly, how bad can my luck be?" Paisley said, turning back toward the diner just as the door opened.

The figure in the doorway stood in the harsh darkness set by the contrast of the midday sun. He was tall and stepped out into the sun as if it was a spotlight. Paisley inhaled as she realized the man was dressed in all black with a white collar just below his chin. A scream rose in her throat but she caught it as the man's face came into view. White tufts of hair speckled his head and the years hung loose off of his face like crepe paper days after a party. The man had to be in his eighties.

"You've got to be fucking kidding me," Paisley said as the man stepped down onto the sidewalk.

"I'm sorry?" The old preacher stopped and stared at Paisley. His eyes teetered between confused and angry.

A laugh like a window breaking split the tension as the driver stumbled around the front of his car.

"What are the odds?" he bellowed.

"I'm so sorry," Paisley said to the preacher. She raised a hand to assure him that it was a mistake, but he moved away from her as if she was infected with some hideous disease.

"Don't," the preacher said as he sidestepped away. Once he was safely out of her reach, he turned and walked up the street.

"I'm sorry!" Paisley called after him.

"I mean, what are the fucking odds?" the driver said through spits of laughter.

"I should just go home now."

"I can restart the meter?" the driver laughed.

Paisley looked up at the diner and saw a young face buried deep behind the reflection of the glass. She squinted and saw a hand wave at her from inside.

"Looks like he knows I'm here. I think I'm stuck," she said and then turned to look at the driver. "Thanks for the laugh. Take care."

With that, she grabbed her bag and headed into the diner.

15

Paisley hauled her bags into the diner and wheeled them down to where Derry stood before a table.

"Darius?" she said as she approached.

"That's me," the young man said.

He looked smaller than he had in the podcast cover art she had seen. If she had to guess, she would have said that the photo was two years old by now. His somewhat oily hair spilled off his head in every direction and could only be described as dirty dishwater blond. His shoulders tipped inward and seemed to have their own gravity as they pulled his chin down between them. The way he looked at her broke her heart. He wore a pleasant and practiced smile, but there was something about his eyes. They looked like the sky at noon, just as the sun had burned through the clouds, leaving only a milky memory that they had ever been there. They were the kind of eyes that if you looked into them long enough, you would find all of the hope that humankind could muster, but look too long, and you may see all of the pain that man has to bear. A stitch of guilt caught Paisley's side. She was looking at him as if he was a lost puppy. She worried that she was wearing her feelings on her face. She didn't mean to show pity. She hated it when people pitied her, and never wanted to do it to someone else. Sympathy was one thing, but pity was another altogether.

"It is very nice to meet you," she finally said as she took his hand. It was softer than she expected for a kid that looked so ragged. "I'm Paisley."

"Very nice to meet you, miss," Derry said. "I like your pin. Taco Cat. A palindrome, cool."

"Thank you." Paisley patted the little cat on its 3D-printed head. "It is actually a camera. I record everything. Is that going to be okay?"

"Yeah, that's fine. I figured it would be something like that."

"Yeah?"

"Yeah, that's what I would do."

"Perfect," Paisley said.

"Would you like to sit?" Derry stepped back and signaled to the booth.

After she was seated Derry dropped into the seat across from her.

"Thank you," she said.

"I have this." Derry pulled a paper from his pocket and handed it across the table.

"It's the release for the video you sent. My dad signed it."

"Oh, thank you so much," Paisley said, plucking the note from his hand and inspecting it. Satisfied that it looked legit, she tucked it in her bag.

"Thank you for coming all this way."

"Not a problem at all."

Something tickled at Paisley's brain and told her to be vigilant. Her eyes darted quickly around the diner as she took mental notes: the carpet that was pulled up at the corner where a vacuum likely pulled it free, the worn spots on the counter that didn't completely line up with the worn spots on the linoleum below the stools, meaning some past remodel likely caused a shift in the natural seating arrangement, and the fact that all that salt and pepper shakers were full, so the rush didn't just end because they had time to refill them all. After a moment of scanning she broke the awkward silence.

"What's bothering you?"

"Huh?" Derry said, looking up at her.

Paisley nodded at his hands.

"Oh, sorry," he said. He had been picking apart his straw wrapper. "I was just fidgeting."

"Maybe," she started. She had all the power in this interaction. She was here because Derry needed help. She could walk at any time. Yet the need to prove herself still loomed.

Her anxiety had kicked up the second she got on the plane in Kentucky, amplified when the rental car company said they lost her reservation and had no cars, and amped up to ten when she pulled up in front of the diner. Throw in the preacher, and it was cranked to a thousand. Everything was in such sharp focus to her. Her heart was racing. She was seeing everything.

Paisley took a deep breath and reminded herself again that she was there to help. She was going to show this kid what she could do. "Or maybe something is eating at you."

"I was just playing with the wrapper," Derry said.

"You specifically unwrapped the straw so you had something to pick at. You needed to occupy your hands."

Derry looked at the white bits piled beneath his fingers.

"How long have you been sitting here?" she asked.

"About twenty minutes or so," he answered.

"So, what's bothering you?"

Derry sized her up.

"The table placement," he finally said.

"What do you mean?"

"The table. Lida sat me here but there isn't anyone else in the restaurant. She didn't put us at the first table, or the last table, directly in the middle, or at a quarter point. We aren't at the table closest to the kitchen or the bathrooms. It's bothering me." He looked down and noticed he was picking apart the wrapper again.

"Ah. I think I get it," Paisley said.

"It isn't OCD. I don't have OCD."

"No, it would be fine if you did, but I think you just have to know how things work. You need to know why things are the way they are. You want to know the motives behind people's actions. Otherwise, it feels unsafe. Am I right?"

Derry stopped playing with the paper. His eyebrows lifted.

"Yeah, that's it. That's exactly it. How did you know that?"

Paisley smiled.

"Curiosity can be a real motherfucker," she said. "Oh, sorry. I shouldn't use that language."

"No, it's cool. I don't care. I say mother fucker too," he said, but the way it came out, Paisley doubted if that was true. "It's just how I am, you know?"

"It's a trauma thing, I think. You spend so much time trying to avoid conflict and pain when you can, to balance out the times you can't. You're always on high alert, and you have a desperate need to know everything."

Derry didn't respond. He just looked out the window and nodded his head, which was all the answer Paisley needed.

"Why did you sit on that side of the table?" she asked.

"What?"

"Lida, right?"

Derry nodded.

"Lida chose the table, but you chose the seat. Why did you choose to sit on that side of the booth as opposed to this side?"

"What makes you think I chose and she didn't just sit me here?"

"Do you know what you want to eat?" she asked.

"No, I'm not hungry."

"That's how I know you chose to sit there."

"How?"

"The menus," she said pointing to the two menus in the middle of the table. "They're in the middle of the table but facing this way."

"I could have had one and looked at it then decided that nothing looked good and put it with the other one."

"That is true, and it is a possibility, but doubtful. I think you picked a side, and Lida set your menu in front of you and then set mine facing this side of the booth, but in the middle, in case I sat on that side with you. I think you chose to sit there. Am I right?" Her head tilted back, and she gave him the *don't you lie to me* look.

"Yeah," he said reluctantly.

"Why? Both are equally catching the sun's reflection. No one was sitting next to you, so it wouldn't matter if you were a lefty or a righty. And, I would like to point out, this side faces the door and the kitchen, so technically it is the better seat. So why that side and not this side?"

"I wanted to be able to see when you were getting close," he said.

"And why would that side be better for that? It is a two-way road, after all."

"Yeah, but the highway is in that direction." He pointed in the direction from which Paisley was dropped off. "And it's the only way into Howling Ivy unless you take the county road. But that route is six miles out of the way."

"So..." Paisley nodded her head toward the counter side of the diner and then turned her head to look there herself.

Derry followed her gaze.

"Oh," Derry said as he realized he could see through the pickup window directly into the kitchen. He saw Lida from the chest up. She was sitting on a stool and focusing on her cell phone. "She put me here so she could see me through the window."

"Exactly," Paisley said only this time just a little louder.

Lida looked up and saw them looking at her, and she jumped from the stool.

"Cool," was all Derry had time to say before Lida was speed walking around the counter.

"So sorry about that, hun," Lida said as she came to an abrupt halt in front of the table.

"Not a problem," Paisley said.

"I just get so caught up in those new games on these phones. I got this one where you have to line up candies, and they disappear. Isn't that the funniest thing?" Lida said.

"Oh yeah, I get so lost in those," Paisley quipped.

"Can I get you something, hun?"

"I would love a Coke, if you don't mind?" Paisley asked.

"Pepsi okay?"

"That's great, thank you."

"Anything to eat for you?" Lida asked, raising her chin to point at the menus stacked on the table.

Paisley's eyes met Derry's.

"I haven't had a chance to look, I'm sorry," Paisley said, grabbing one of the menus.

"No need to be sorry, sweetie. As you can see, it is just the two of you at the moment. So it isn't like we need the space."

"Thank you," Paisley said.

"Ya'll just holler if you need something. I'll be right over there trying to get that darn moon-shaped candy to break. And I'll be right back with that pop."

"Thank you," Paisley repeated.

"Thank you," Derry parroted.

And with that Lida was off again and before Derry or Paisley could start the conversation again she was back placing Paisley's drink.

"Thank you," Paisley said.

"Thanks," Derry said.

"Welcome. Now you two just let me know if you need anything," Lida said and walked back to the kitchen. Paisley could see her sitting on her stool, brows furrowed and eyes fixed on the screen of her smartphone.

"So, Darius, what's your story?" Paisley asked, taking a sip of her soda.

"You can just call me Derry."

"Ah, Derry, got it. What's your story, Derry."

"There isn't much to tell, really."

"You are what, sixteen? And you already have a successful podcast about the paranormal. Clearly there is something to you."

"There's really not. I'm just a kid with some free time. I'd get a job, but there isn't anywhere I want to work here."

"Ah, work is overrated when you are a kid. You've got to have some fun."

"People's idea of fun around here is blowing things up, setting things on fire, shooting things, and riding dirt bikes or four-wheelers, neither of which I own," he said.

"That's it?"

"Well, and meth."

Paisley surprised both her and Derry with a sharp laugh.

"And I am assuming you don't have any of that either?" Paisley asked.

"Nope," he replied.

"That's good."

"Smoked it all," Derry said in a calm, even tone.

This time Paisley nearly spit soda. She took a moment to compose herself even though small spurts of laughter would come out every time she saw the innocent face across from her. The thought of this kid hitting a meth pipe seemed about as unlikely an image as she could come up with. He smiled at her from underneath his tattered bangs.

"Hey, there's a smile," Paisley said. "Does it hurt?"

"A little. Am I doing it right?" He stretched his mouth at the corners, looking less like a boy and more like a carp with human teeth.

Paisley laughed again.

"How come you aren't this funny on the podcast?" The question was meant to be rhetorical but Derry had an answer ready. His wit was quicker than Paisley was ready for.

"Because I can't be the smart one *and* the funny one."

Paisley laughed so hard at this that Lida stood up from her stool to look out the window at them. Paisley waved her off and she sat back down.

"Do you enjoy the podcast at least?" she asked.

"Yeah, I guess so."

"What do you mean, you guess so?"

"I like to learn things. Like you said, I like to study and figure out how things work."

"And you needed a podcast to do that?"

Derry started picking at his straw wrapper again.

"People out here don't like it when you learn things. They think you think you're better than them. Like learning what's outside this county means you think you deserve better than what they got."

"And how do you feel about that?"

"I don't deserve anything. I just want to learn," Derry said. When he talked about the town, his voice pitched, and it sounded like he was trying to blend in with his environment.

"That isn't true, you know?"

"Yeah, I know," he said. It sounded like a lie he had been telling his whole life, spoken with practiced ease.

"I heard the episode where you were telling your friend about the difference between saying Bigfoot and Sasquatch. I thought that was pretty cool."

"I guess. He just didn't get it."

"So did you watch all my videos from Grey Water Ridge?"

Derry nodded while still playing with the wrapper. He tore it to a pulp and he seemed to be trying to pry what was left of it apart. Paisley opened her straw and set it aside, then slid the wrapper into the cave that Derry had made with his head down and his slumped shoulders. He pulled the wrapper in like a log going into a mill.

"Yeah, I watched them all."

"What did you think? From a paranormal expert's point of view."

Derry sat up. His eyes peeked out from under his hair and Paisley thought he would flip his head and toss his hair to the side. Or at least bashfully brush it away from his eyes, but he never did. He stayed partially hidden behind that greasy curtain.

"What took him at the end?" he asked.

"If you've watched all of the videos, then you know I was knocked out, and when I came to, the first responders were there, and he was gone."

"Right," Derry said as if he expected the answer but didn't accept it.

"You don't believe me?"

"Do you believe there was a monster in the woods?"

It was Paisley's turn to lean back in the booth, assessing her inquisitive counter. "Hollis Grimm murdered those women," she said.

"That wasn't what I asked."

"Maybe you *are* too smart for your own good," Paisley said. "Or too smart for *my* own good."

"You said in your video that the Sasquatch had been seen in the town. Going back about a hundred or so years, right?" Derry asked.

"More than that, but basically," she replied.

"So if Hollis was basing his crimes off of actual sightings, then there is a possibility that there really is something in the hills above the pump house."

"Gristmill," Paisley said.

"Huh?"

"Gristmill. The bodies were found outside of town in the hills above the gristmill."

"Oh. That's right there was a stone grist wheel in the middle of the house, wasn't there?"

"Yeah. It was creepy."

"And you didn't see anything?" He leaned forward.

"Nope," Paisley said, popping the p at the end of the word.

"Interesting."

He knew something she didn't want him to know. He knew something that she didn't want anyone to know. That she did see something that night. The eyes that she saw looking back at her. She had slipped up somewhere, and she needed to move the conversation away from that point before this kid got her to do it again.

"What about you, though? There wasn't anything paranormal behind the murders in Grey Water, just some lunatic. But from what I understand, you may have something going on out here?" Paisley said, redirecting the conversation.

"I don't know. It's probably nothing," Derry said, returning to his paper shredding.

"I hope not. I came a long way to get here and I'd like to give my viewers some good ghostly stories."

"I worry that you are going to be disappointed."

"Why would I be disappointed?"

"It's just a voice."

"Was it your sister's voice?"

Derry sank further into the booth.

"I think so," he said.

"And it wasn't anything in the room? It wasn't a chair cushion, a cup sliding across a table, a fan in the other room?"

"I checked everything."

"Show me," Paisley said, setting a five dollar bill on the table and sliding out of the booth. Derry looked up at her.

"Now?"

"Yeah, you said you weren't hungry anyway, right?"

Derry glanced at the menu and then started to slide out of the booth. Paisley put a foot on the bench trapping him in.

"Wait," she said.

He looked up at her.

"You were just saying you weren't hungry because you don't have any money, weren't you?" she asked.

"What? No. I'm just not hungry," he said.

Paisley dropped her foot and slid back into the booth. Lida had seen her stand up and was now approaching the table.

"Did you decide what you wanted to eat?" she asked.

"Do you have a Reuben by chance?" Paisley asked.

"Best in the county," Lida responded.

"I'll have that with a side of fries, please," she said. "And since I don't like to eat alone, I am requesting that you force my friend here to eat with me. He will have..." Paisley looked across the table at Derry and Lida joined in on the staredown. He looked grateful and yet somewhat sad. "You look like a cheeseburger man. Am I right?"

"I do like a good cheeseburger," he said.

"Fries?" Paisley asked. Derry nodded. "And two strawberry milkshakes, as well. If he doesn't want one I will happily drink them both."

"I'll get that right out," Lida said and with a whoosh she was heading back toward the kitchen.

"Thank you," Paisley called after her.

"Thank you, Lida," Derry called out to the woman who was nearly in the kitchen already. Then to Paisley, "Thank you."

"No sweat," Paisley said.

"Clearly you've never eaten here before."

There was a beat while Paisley processed what he had said and then she laughed.

The two ate their meals as Paisley fielded tons of questions about the events of Grey Water Ridge, marketing a show on the internet, and what it was like to live near the ocean. It was a nice lunch with a very troubled kid.

16

The stairs thumped against the side of the trailer as Derry took them two at a time, carrying Paisley's bags. His youth grew more and more apparent the longer Paisley spent with him. He wore maturity like a suit of armor. He seemed to carry a weight on his shoulders and watching him lighten up a little was nice.

Paisley took the steps more casually, clamping down on the rail as she climbed. She didn't come from money, but this was her first experience climbing stairs that weren't actually attached to the structure they serviced.

Derry yanked open a broken screen door and plunged his hand into his pocket. When it emerged, a worn-out shoe string, with a key dangling on the end, was hooked around his index finger. It all felt so practiced. This kid used climbing the stairs and pulling out his key as some sort of ritual. The world applied undue pressure upon him, which was only shed when he entered this sacred hall. He pushed the door open with the familiar sound only the door of a trailer home can make, akin to an airlock being depressurized.

The pungent odor of stale cigarette smoke and cat urine flooded from the doorway like a backdraft. Paisley recoiled momentarily and expected Derry to do the same, but he was accustomed to it and plunged headlong into the trailer. Paisley glanced to see if the taxi that dropped them off was still there, but when she saw it wasn't, she inhaled another deep breath of fresh air and followed Derry through the door.

The room was small and crowded with mismatched furniture. Dark wood paneling covered the walls, making the room feel even smaller than it was. A shallow couch sat flat on the ground, the legs that held it up either removed or had given up and fallen off. The floral print faded into a mess of dark greens and browns indistinguishable from the grime rubbed into the fabric over what appeared to be a century of use. A newish-looking television sat atop an old printer cart. It didn't fit with the rest of the room. Everything else was old and broken, except the TV. Even the game console on the cart had duct tape holding it together.

"Most of this stuff my dad found," Derry said, catching her gaze.

"Found?"

"Yeah, he works for the sanitation district as his second job. People throw away a lot of usable stuff," he said.

"Oh," she started. "The TV is nice," she finally said, trying to paint a silver lining.

"Yeah, he brought that home a while back. It's mostly good." Derry reached over and pressed a button on the side of the unit. The screen came to life and it became clear why someone deemed it trash. When the screen blinked on, a chunk of missing pixels from the top made it look like a child missing their two front teeth. "Makes it hard to play games sometimes. But I manage." He clicked the button again and the screen went dark making the TV look new again.

"If this was the upgrade I hate to ask what you used before?" Paisley asked.

"You ever seen those sitcoms where the family is really poor and they've got those giant TV sets?"

"Yeah."

"Well I haven't," Derry said, not breaking eye contact with Paisley.

"So then how..." she started.

Derry blinked but held eye contact. His stoic face revealed nothing until a small smile percolated at the corner of his mouth.

"I haven't..." he repeated.

Laughter banged off the walls of the trailer like ball bearings in a spray can as Paisley let loose a cackle of laughter. A full-blown smile bloomed on Derry's face, revealing the child who lived under the weight of his unfair life.

"You're killing me, kid," Paisley finally said when she had calmed down.

"Sorry, I don't get many people around here that actually get my humor, so since you do I feel like I need to take every shot I can get," Derry said, pushing a hand through his dirty hair.

"I'm going to have to stay on my toes around you." Paisley returned to her visual tour of the trailer. "Is this where you record?" she asked, pointing to a folding card table against the opposite wall.

"Yep. As I always say, it isn't a lot, but it is what we've got," Derry said.

"Yeah? Is that what you always say?"

"Nope. That was the first time. And judging by your reaction, it shall be the last."

Paisley chuckled. Partially from the humor that Derry now projected that he was on his home turf but more from the relief. Her anxiety peaked because she was in a new place that was very uncomfortable for her. She wasn't too worried about her safety because she didn't think Derry was capable, either physically or emotionally, of hurting her. Plus, she had her stun gun and pepper spray at hand.

There were obvious visual similarities between Derry and the man who had tried to shoot her just six weeks earlier. The greasy hair, the different online persona, a possible obsession with her. She hadn't got the best look at Courtney Teere as she ran for her life, but she had seen plenty of pictures of him in news stories since, and the two weren't that dissimilar.

Paisley traced a finger across the pieced-together recording setup, wondering which parts came from the dump and which parts he bought.

"Where were you sitting when you heard the voice?" she asked.

"I was right here," Derry said, moving over and putting his hands on the back of a rusted, metal, folding chair with a worn-out cushion.

Paisley looked around, allowing her ability to pick up detail work to its fullest extent. What could have made a sound that would emulate a child perfectly?

The metal chair groaned as Paisley lowered herself into it. She stood and listened again as she sat. The sound the cushion made was too quiet to register, and the whine of the old metal was too high-pitched. She slid forward in the seat, allowing the friction from her jeans to pull against the worn cover of the cushion. A flatulent sound burped from under her. Derry suppressed a laugh.

"That was the chair," Paisley laughed.

"Right, sure it was," Derry responded, comically fanning in front of his face.

Paisley stood and pushed a small mixer across the torn cloth tabletop, producing a sound akin to stepping on someone's chest but not like a girl saying a name. She followed suit, moving everything she could around the table. She moved the makeshift microphone stands and the computer, and even took a book from a nearby shelf and ran it across the table.

"Did either of you have dishes on the table when you were recording?" she asked.

"Nope. Nothing on the table but what you see there," he answered, anticipating the question.

Paisley stopped moving things.

"I'm sure you've done all of this already, but I just have to know for myself, you know?"

Derry nodded.

"I totally get it. I appreciate your thoroughness," he said. "Do whatever you need to do. I'm going to go pee if you don't mind." Derry turned and started down the hall.

"Thanks for the briefing," Paisley said after him.

"Just thought you would want to listen to see if it sounded like a voice."

"I'm good, thanks," Paisley said as Derry closed the door at the end of the hall.

A sound rumbled down the hallway. Paisley jerked at the

suddenness of the roar before she could process what it was.

"It was the chair!" Derry yelled from the bathroom.

17

Squeaking woke Millicent from sleep. She wasn't sure how long she had been gone this time. The hunger pang in her stomach and the thirst in her throat suggested it had been a while. She couldn't remember if she had fallen asleep hungry. She didn't remember falling asleep at all. Which meant that something bad had happened.

She sat up, pulling the chain across the cement floor, and sitting cross-legged on the sleeping bag she had been given.

"Hi there," Millicent said. The mouse had returned a few times, and she was beginning to really like it. "You keep coming back here. Did you want to be my friend?"

The mouse crept back, threatening to run, as Millicent scooted toward it.

"My name is Millie."

The mouse took another step back, turning its body, ready to flee, but continued to look at the girl.

"It's okay, I won't hurt you. I just want to be friends. What's your name?"

The mouse's tiny nose bounced as it sniffed the air.

"Oh, Mr. Squeakers, that's a good name..." Millicent leaned in and looked closely at the mouse. "Oh, I don't know if you are a mister. Okay, just Squeakers."

The door at the top of the stairs unbolted with a crack, and the mouse vanished behind the washing machine, and the girl was left alone to face the person coming down the steps.

"Still here, huh," a woman's voice said. "I don't know what else to do to get rid of you."

Millicent looked where Squeakers had disappeared and wondered if the woman was talking to her or the mouse. She didn't see the woman usually. She normally just heard her voice. When she did hear it, it was never good.

The woman stopped and looked at Millicent. She always looked at her with her nose pulled up like Millicent smelled bad.

"You know, I don't want to keep you here, but he won't let me just leave you out there," the woman said as she loaded clothes into the washer.

"Can I have water?" Millicent asked.

The woman closed the lid on the washer, and it came to life, filling its chamber with the water she so desperately wanted. She said nothing. She just turned and went back up, slamming the bolt closed on the door at the top of the stairs.

"Squeakers?" Millicent called, but the mouse did not reply.

18

The awkwardly bright lights in the rental house that Paisley had found welcomed her as she came in. There weren't many options in Howling Ivy, but a converted bunkhouse at an old farm wasn't exactly on the bucket list of places to stay. It was a little farther outside town than she wanted, but the tourist market was weak, and her options were that or a motel with one and a half stars on Google. The small house, if it could be called that, had been fixed up and modernized in a way that crossed the Home and Garden Channel with the decor section of a craft store. Paisley set her bags down on a mass-produced bench that had been made to look distressed underneath a wood picket sign that read "Live, Laugh, Aloha" and had paintings of a pineapple and a coconut.

The exhaustion from the day was too much, so she fell onto a very trendy couch to make a phone call before worrying about getting settled.

"Hey, I was just talking about you," Hyacinth said on the other end of the line.

"To whom, and what was said? Am I an alibi? Yes, yes, in fact, I was with you at the aforementioned time at the aforementioned place. And yes, we did do the aforementioned activity which took exactly as long as Miss Bloom stated on the record," Paisley responded.

"Haha, no, silly, but I appreciate it. If I ever need an alibi, though, you will be my first call."

"Little harder when we aren't in the same state."

"Yeah, I guess that just means you have to come back to Grey Water when you're done with your case."

"Investigation."

"Right, investigation. How's it going so far? Is the kid super weird?" Hyacinth asked.

"He's a good kid, I think. There were a few weird things, but nothing outstanding. We are all weird at that age."

"Not me. I was fucking awesome."

"I actually believe you may have been the one and only non-awkward teen."

"Perhaps. Perhaps," Hyacinth replied.

"Who were you talking about me to?" Paisley asked, trying to turn the conversation.

"You really want to know?"

"Was it Rowan?"

"He isn't mad, Pais."

"He should be. I wish he was."

"So does he."

"Yeah," Paisley exhaled.

"I think he really likes you a lot."

"He is a great guy, I'm just not there yet."

"That is exactly what he said."

"That I wasn't there yet?"

"No, that he was a great guy." The two shared a chuckle.

"It's just too much, too fast. I really only just met him." Paisley said.

"I know, and so does he. Don't sweat it. Okay?"

"Thanks, Hy."

"So, tell me about the weirdo?"

"I think there is something out here."

"You mean you think the voice on the thing is real?"

"I don't know, but something is off. I haven't started digging yet, but I have a feeling that when I do, I'm going to find something."

"What makes you say that? Wasn't this supposed to be an easy one?"

"Yeah, but I think there's something here, and I think somehow this kid is at the center of it. It feels like there's something that he knows but isn't saying."

"Like that the kid is a murderer?" Hyacinth asked, rightfully alarmed.

"I don't know about that, but he is hiding something, that's for sure."

"Like bodies in the basement?"

"He doesn't have a basement."

"Someone else's basement then?"

"Maybe. I still haven't met this Patch kid yet."

"Maybe *he* has a basement?"

"Maybe," Paisley said. Another beat of silence.

"You okay out there alone?" Hyacinth asked.

"Yeah, I think so. I just have to focus and figure out what angle to take on this thing. On one hand, I've got this fairly convincing EVP and the story of a kidnapped and murdered sister."

"And on the other hand?"

"I don't know if I believe him."

"Does he seem like he faked it for clout?" Hyacinth asked.

"That's just it, no, he doesn't. He doesn't seem like the type to care about popularity at all."

"So why even do a podcast?"

"For three reasons, I think," Paisley said. "One is that he genuinely enjoys the research he has to put into it. The second is that he loves doing it with his best friend. He seems to adore the kid. The last thing is that it gives him a way to reach outside a town he will probably never leave."

"I mean, I guess that makes sense," Hyacinth said. The skepticism was thick in her voice.

"Why do you do the social media stuff you do?"

"What?"

"Why do you do it? You don't need the money. You just give away all the money you make from it anyway."

"For clout. I am a clout chaser of the finest order. I want those fans," Hyacinth said. She paused.

Paisley regretted asking the question when she followed the train of thought that Hyacinth must also be following.

"At least I used to," she finished.

"It's different," Paisley reassured her. "You wanted to build an audience that didn't judge you based on who your father was. You wanted those eyes on you. This kid has none of that."

"You don't think he wants to be judged for something other than the amount of money his parents have... or don't have?"

Paisley let the phone slip down in her hand.

"Damn, I hadn't even thought about that comparison. Shit, Hy, that's insightful as all hell."

"I'm not just another rich, beautiful, philanthropic, media mogul. I'm also brilliant."

"Truth," Paisley agreed.

There was a noise from somewhere in the background, and Paisley could hear Hyacinth take her earbuds out, say something to someone she couldn't understand, and then put them back in.

"Yo, Pais, I'm sorry, I've got to bail. Grover is awake and needs me. Sorry, it feels like I literally do nothing anymore except take care of him."

"I'm sorry. Do you need me to come back and help?"

"Haha, could you imagine you and Ro both here right now? I'm good. What I'm saying is that I have a lot of free time, so if you need me to do some digging or research stuff, I can do it. I don't know if I'm as good as your mysterious internet stranger friend, but I can do my part," Hyacinth offered.

"Thanks, Hy, I appreciate you. I really do."

"You be careful out there."

"I will. Give Grover my best."

"I will."

"And Rowan."

"Yep."

"Bye, Hy."

"Bye, Pais."

Paisley put her phone down, pulled out her laptop, and flipped it open. It was time to finally dig into the details of

Derry's sister's death.

The news of the death was easy to find. As soon as she put the town's name in the suggested searches were:

Howling Ivy Indiana burned body

Howling Ivy Indiana murder

Howling Ivy Indiana serial killer

Howling Ivy Indiana missing children

Howling Ivy Indiana dead kids

Howling Ivy Indiana burned alive

Howling Ivy Indiana worst place to live

Howling Ivy Indiana Real Estate

Paisley clicked the first suggested search term and was given pages upon pages of results. A lot of local news sites, but some national pages covered the death as well. The top link took her to a clip from a local newscast. A man sat at a news desk looking like every basic newscaster on TV.

"Tonight's main story is the continuation of the story that has been on all of our minds and hearts the last two days," the basic newsman said. "The disappearance of one of our most vulnerable residents. We go now to Rachel Wright, who is on the scene of this grisly discovery. Rachel?"

The video cut to a woman in a black and white houndstooth waistcoat. Her dark black hair was swooped down over her forehead, then gathered and pulled back into a ponytail. Large, dark-framed glasses rimmed her eyes. Her brow furrowed as she held her earpiece, listening to the suit in the studio.

"Thanks, John," she said and looked directly into the camera. "Officers believe they have discovered the remains of a missing girl in a tragic situation that has been haunting King County since Lydia Knot disappeared from the Fourth of July Celebration two nights ago." She paused before taking a deep breath and pushing on. "And John, search crews have been combing the area since then and found nothing. But today, it seems, a gruesome discovery has been made in this tragic case."

"Rachel, do you know if law enforcement has any leads on

who committed this heinous act of violence?"

"John, officers here have told us that it is an ongoing investigation, and that the public would do good to stay alert. And ask that anyone with information about the crime come forward."

"So they don't have anyone in custody just yet?"

"No, it would appear they are still searching for anyone who might be involved."

"Can we assume that since the body has been located that this is the end of it, or should we be concerned about more missing children?" he asked. His smug face trying to look interested.

"John, I think it would be very dangerous to make any assumptions at this point. The community should be aware of everything going on around them, and keep an extra close eye on their children until the police can wrap this up, and we are confident that they will do just that."

The video ended with John in the studio going on about how his thoughts and prayers were with the child's family.

Paisley clicked back over to her search and found another video from around the time when Lydia Knot's body had been found. It was the same news anchor, Rachel, but she was at a desk this time. Paisley opened the video.

"The medical examiner said that they were having trouble positively identifying Lydia Knot's body, as her father was unavailable to assist. Sources close to the investigation have told us that the girl's older brother, Darius, was contacted and was able to provide some evidence that the body found was, in fact, that of his little sister, Lydia. Those sources say that the body was so badly damaged that a physical ID was impossible, but that items at the scene, and articles of clothing on the body, belonged to Lydia." A photo appeared on the screen, and the chyron identified the child as Lydia Knot, age seven. She was a beautiful little girl with blond hair and blue eyes. In the photo, Lydia sat between Derry, who seemed at least a year younger in the photo, and a large kid, who Paisley would assume was

Patch. Possibly-Patch took the photo in selfie mode of the group.

The thought of how hard it must have been for Derry to have to identify his sister's body made Paisley's stomach twist, and she thought she might throw up.

"This is the last known photo of Lydia Knot. Taken just about an hour before she disappeared. Authorities are saying that there is a possibility that the madman responsible for this crime may still be a threat to the community. He may be laying low and waiting to see the response from law enforcement, or he may be finished with his work here and moving on to somewhere else to victimize another community. In any case, law enforcement officials urge everyone to be on high alert until this killer is brought to justice."

The camera jumped over to John, who was sitting at the desk with Rachel.

"Rachel, is law enforcement at all worried that this grisly crime is related to the string of young girls who have been murdered over the past six years?" he asked.

"At this time, it is too early to make any assumptions about a connection between this crime and the horrible serial murders of those children. Law enforcement has asked the public to hold off on dangerous assumptions until further investigation."

"Sure," John began. "It's just that looking at that photo of that little girl I can't help but be reminded of all the little blonde-haired, blue-eyed girls who have been kidnapped and murdered in the region in the past six or seven years. Am I right? How many are we up to now, like ten or fifteen in half as many years?"

The video ended as the camera jumped back to Rachel, anger and disgust on her face.

After the video ended, another suggested video appeared. *Burning Body - King County Murder.*

Paisley clicked the video, and to her horror, it was exactly what she hoped it would not be.

19

Howling Ivy didn't have much, but what it did have in abundance was abandoned buildings. Thousands of them. Houses, stores, and factories. Everywhere you turned there was the skin of some long-forgotten purpose, shed and left to decay. Not only did the buildings look terrible, but they gave the more desperate individuals in the area a safe space to commit any number of questionable acts.

One such desperate individual was Danny Humphries. Danny was a courier, as they called him. A low-level drug dealer who acted as the middleman between the actual drug dealer and their customer. Someone who didn't know enough to be a threat to the dealer and would only ever carry enough to get a possession charge and not distribution if arrested. It was a job that was often given to those who were addicted to something, but not the drug they carried. Danny's drug of choice was heroin. The Big H. He rode the needle. And if you offered him even enough of it to spike once, he would run packets of meth all day.

Like many of the couriers in the area, Danny was experiencing homelessness. You could argue whether the homelessness contributed to his criminal activity and addiction or if the activity and addiction contributed to his homelessness. Still, spent most of his nights in the abandoned shoe factory near the center of the old industrial district. It was deep enough in the area that he was unlikely to be seen coming or going. It was big enough that he could hide if he needed to, and there were a lot of old machines there that he could tinker with to stay busy.

Each morning, there would be a small bag with the first two deliveries and the meetup locations for them, and two small portable phone chargers waiting for him to pick up at one of a few predetermined locations. Then he'd run the first two and wait for text messages about where to pick up and where to drop off the day's deliveries. Occasionally, there would be a few bucks and a small bundle of what he wanted for himself. That was enough to keep him going.

That morning, he waited for the texts when he heard something from the back of the building. Normally, he would avoid going out onto what used to be the manufacturing floor. It was too big and too open to feel comfortable, but from the sounds of the echo, the noise he heard was coming from there.

Every door in the place was rusted and made an awful noise when opened, so Danny jammed a metal rod into one of the garage bay doors to hold it open just a foot off the ground so he could move quickly without alerting anyone nearby. He dropped down on his stomach, shimmied underneath the roll-up door, and slid onto the manufacturing floor.

Daylight peaked through broken windows and reflected off ancient dust. Danny pressed himself against the old machines strewn about the floor like dinosaurs after the ice age.

Wet slapping sounds stumbled around the machines, and Danny froze. It wasn't the first time some bum had wandered in and started pissing all over the place, but now he considered this place his home, and he wasn't about to let someone disrespect it. There were a few improvised weapons around, more to threaten than to attack, and he settled on a long metal pipe leaning against a machine. To ensure that no one else would attempt similar disrespect, Danny decided to record the incident with the cell phone and show it around. If enough people saw it, he would ensure that everyone knew that this building was spoken for. He pulled the cell phone out, opened the camera app, and hit record.

"I'm about to school this mother fucker about whose building this is." He lifted the metal pipe and waved it in front of the camera.

The sound of the liquid stopped, and Danny knew if he were

88

to catch the perpetrator in the act, he needed to move.

"Let's do this," he said and swung around to confront the mysterious pisser. But there was no one there. Only a pile of rags lay on top of a duffel bag. The pile was soaking wet. A line of liquid ran from it to an open door on the far side of the floor. It was then that Danny could smell the familiar scent of kerosene, the same thing his grandmother used to heat their house when he was a kid.

It was too late to react when the fire came racing in from the doorway, heading for the dripping pile. His instinct was to run, but something about the pile made him hesitate. Had it moved? Danny stepped toward it but was met with a blinding flash and a wall of heat as the pile exploded into flames. The phone clattered to the floor, throwing the fire out of view and pointing up to the ceiling instead. Shrill cries followed, hanging in the air with the smoke filling the cavernous space.

20

Paisley pushed her laptop off her legs and across the couch, trying to create distance between what she had experienced and herself. However, the video had not stopped, and the screams now filled the small faux farm living room where she sat.

"Oh, God," she said. "What the fuck?"

The screams ran around the room like mad children tearing at the loose edges of Paisley's heart and mind. She kept expecting them to stop, but they only became deeper, more gut-wrenching sobs of the person holding the camera. She leaned over and flipped the laptop closed, choking the sounds and bringing cherished silence to the room once again.

Within seconds, she unlocked her phone and typed a message.

ParanormalOrNot - *Are you there?*

ParanormalOrNot - *Hello?*

WhyItHurts - *Hey, what's up? Sorry, I was just getting out of the shower. Are you okay?*

ParanormalOrNot - *You're in law enforcement, right?*

WhyItHurts - *For simplicity sake let's say that I am. Is everything alright? Are you in trouble?*

ParanormalOrNot - *Is it illegal to post a video online that contains murder?*

WhyItHurts - *Oh my God, did something happen?*

ParanormalOrNot - *I found a video regarding the investigation I'm working on and I need to know if there is a possibility that it is real.*

WhyItHurts - *Is it on a credible site?*

ParanormalOrNot - *I honestly didn't check. I sort of stumbled onto it and then freaked out before looking into it.*

WhyItHurts - *What was it?*

ParanormalOrNot - *I think it was a little girl being burned alive...*

WhyItHurts - *Was it something you came across or was it sent to you?*

ParanormalOrNot - *I found it.*

WhyItHurts - *Send me the link?*

ParanormalOrNot - *I will, but I don't want to open it just yet to get it. Give me a few minutes.*

WhyItHurts - *No worries. Take your time and breathe. Tell me about the case.*

ParanormalOrNot - *Well I thought it could be just a simple hoax, or maybe, at worst, an actual ghost or something. But this seems like it could be much more serious.*

WhyItHurts - *One second... okay. According to your last live stream I'm putting you in Indiana, looks like maybe Schneider or Frye?*

ParanormalOrNot - *Wow, close. I am in Howling Ivy. I think Schneider is the next town over. How did you know that? I don't think I mentioned it on the live.*

WhyItHurts - *In one of the streams from the airport, the announcement said welcome to Indiana. There is only one airport there that flies directly from Kentucky, and given the time of your Tweet from there, you had to fly direct. Then you streamed for a few minutes from the car, and even though the image was reversed you could tell the sun was setting, and judging by the shadows from the East the car was heading North East. You tweeted that you made it into town about two hours after you posted about the car arriving. So, traveling in that direction, from that airport, there are only a few places you could have gone.*

ParanormalOrNot - *Wow. Well, you're not wrong. But what if we were taking connecting highways and changed directions?*

WhyItHurts - *Looking at the highway maps, there were really only two possibilities in your direction. And a quick search of traffic conditions showed that one would have taken you a different direction, with construction just a few miles from the airport, so you would have likely gone due east first, then turned north. So, it narrowed the field of where you could be.*

ParanormalOrNot - *You're a terrifying person, did you know that?*

WhyItHurts - *You sound like every guy I ever dated.*

ParanormalOrNot - *You will have to teach me your wise ways of investigation.*

WhyItHurts - *You've already got it. You're just selective as to when you see it. I'm only looking for the things that are there and I know will give me answers. I ignore everything else. It's easy when you're not in the situation. Everything I just did took like five minutes and anyone can do it. You just need patience and practice.*

ParanormalOrNot - *That is probably how that fuck Courtney found out where Hyacinth lived.*

WhyItHurts - *You're probably right. But knowing what region you are in, I've looked up local news that could lead me to the case you are working on, and I believe I have found it.*

ParanormalOrNot - *Okay, Captain Creepo, what do you have?*

WhyItHurts - *Well there is a nationwide manhunt and a tragically long list of little girls who have been kidnapped and killed. Tell me that isn't what you are working on...*

ParanormalOrNot - *Not on purpose!*

WhyItHurts - *Jesus, Paisley.*

ParanormalOrNot - *I thought it was just an EVP. I didn't know that someone had been murdered.*

WhyItHurts - *Well the disembodied voice had to have come from somewhere...*

ParanormalOrNot - *I just really wanted to help this kid debunk that voice. Especially now that he thinks it's his little sister. I couldn't have known that the sister was murdered.*

WhyItHurts - *Darius Knot thinks that the voice he claims to have caught on recording is his sister, Lydia?*

ParanormalOrNot - *Yes, how do you know them?*

WhyItHurts - *Google.*

ParanormalOrNot - *So what do I do?*

WhyItHurts - *Get the fuck out of there.*

ParanormalOrNot - *And ditch the kid?*

WhyItHurts - *I don't want to seem callous, but yes. I just watched the video that I think you are referring to. The one with the kid at the warehouse and the bag?*

ParanormalOrNot - *Yeah.*

WhyItHurts - *It looks like the video is legit. It was removed from YouTube, Facebook, Twitter, TikTok, and just about everywhere else with community guidelines. Looks like it's being hosted on a private server at the moment. It sounds like it may be linked to the other cases. This could be even more serious than we think.*

ParanormalOrNot - *I haven't done a lot of research into it yet. None, actually.*

WhyItHurts - *You didn't look into this stuff at all before you went out there?*

ParanormalOrNot - *I wanted to go in with nothing so that I could make some good videos about the whole discovery process. I thought it would make for better content.*

WhyItHurts - *Can I be painfully candid with you?*

ParanormalOrNot - *Yeah...I guess so.*

WhyItHurts - *You need to decide if you are a content creator who investigates the paranormal, or a paranormal investigator who makes content.*

ParanormalOrNot - *What's the difference?*

WhyItHurts - *One of them is much more likely to get you or someone else killed.*

ParanormalOrNot - *Ouch.*

WhyItHurts - *I'm sorry. As an investigator myself, I've been in some rough situations. One of which left one person dead and me damn near, and it was because I was unprepared. After what happened in Grey Water, you proved what was more important.*

ParanormalOrNot - *Grey Water was a mess.*

WhyItHurts - *Grey Water was a learning experience. You adjusted on the fly and saved lives. But you don't want to walk into another trap.*

ParanormalOrNot - *I wanted something easy this time.*

WhyItHurts - *No, you didn't. You wanted to tell yourself you wanted something easy, and hoped it would be bigger.*

ParanormalOrNot - *I don't know about that.*

WhyItHurts - *You purposefully avoided everything about the case. Even though the first result you get when you search the name of the podcast or either of its hosts, is information about the murder. You had to have seen it and chose to ignore it. Including the fact that Darius Knot* and Steven Simply were both suspects.

ParanormalOrNot - *I may have seen the briefest headline. But not that they were suspects. I didn't know about that.*

WhyItHurts - *So the big question is, why?*

ParanormalOrNot - *Why what?*

WhyItHurts - *Why did you pretend that you didn't know.*

ParanormalOrNot - *I wasn't pretending. When the stuff popped up, I decided that I didn't want to know, so I didn't read anything. I didn't know if it was unsolved, and I didn't know the boys were suspects. When I heard the EVP I Googled his name to see if he was a trustworthy person. The first thing I saw was a headline saying his sister's body had been found. So, yes, I did hope that the voice he heard was his sister. But I didn't want to know anything else. So I stopped looking.*

WhyItHurts - *Okay. But why?*

ParanormalOrNot - *Why what? Why did I stop looking? I wanted to be able to shoot the whole thing for the show.*

WhyItHurts - *Did you film yourself watching the video?*

ParanormalOrNot - *Well no, but that was because I was just doing that now and I wasn't expecting that.*

WhyItHurts - *Can I tell you what I think?*

ParanormalOrNot - *I'm pretty sure I know what you think. You think that I avoided the information and took this investigation because it is dangerous and I wanted to be able to justify taking it to everyone else even though that last one almost got me killed.*

WhyItHurts -*No, I think you did it to justify it to yourself.*

ParanormalOrNot - *Why would I need to justify it to myself?*

WhyItHurts - *Am I wrong?*

ParanormalOrNot - *I just want to help. And when I saw it was a little girl I couldn't ignore it. What if she needs help?*

WhyItHurts - *Honey, you don't have to justify it to me. I just want you to be safe. And the best way to do that is to admit what you are.*

ParanormalOrNot - *And what am I?*

WhyItHurts - *You're a paranormal investigator who creates content.*

ParanormalOrNot - *Sigh.*

WhyItHurts - *Let me take a hard look at this video and dig around a little more, and I will let you know what I find. For some reason, the case files are not online. But I came across a single crime scene photo that appears to have been taken by the first officer on the scene, and he sold it to the media. I'm sending it over.*

ParanormalOrNot - *You sure you don't mind?*

WhyItHurts - *I literally just sit around all day researching weird shit on the internet while my assistant does everything but wipe my ass for me. So, this will fit perfectly into my schedule.*

ParanormalOrNot - *Thank you. I appreciate you. Seriously.*

WhyItHurts - *Be safe. xoxo*

Paisley reluctantly studied the photo of the crime scene. To her relief, it did not show an up close picture of the burned victim, just the debris laying around it. There were things around that could be clues, but it was hard to tell. WhyItHurts made it sound so easy to just look at something and pull details from it.

What didn't belong? Nothing really seemed out of the ordinary to her, but she felt too sick to continue looking, and she certainly wasn't ready to watch the video again. At least not right away.

21

The diner was much busier with the breakfast rush than the day before when Paisley first went in. It was filled with an older crowd that looked like they had become part of the establishment or had always been on those stools, and the diner had magically sprouted out of the ground around them.

Khalida was standing at the lectern when Paisley entered.

"Well, if it isn't Derry's friend! Will he be joining you today?" she asked, giving Paisley a wink and a slight nudge with her elbow.

"Good morning. Yes, it'll be Derry, his friend, and I, thank you," Paisley said.

"Oooh, Patch is coming? I better get back there and tell Evan to throw some extra hashbrowns on the griddle and make another batch of batter. Come on now." Khalida snatched three menus and started down the aisle past the crowded tables.

There were two spots where they could have been sat. One was a cleared-off four-top table in the aisle between the booths and the counter. The other, and the one Khalida chose for them, was a booth all the way in the corner. Khalida stopped in front of the table and placed the menus in the center before inviting Paisley to sit. She did. She sat on the outside edge facing the door so she could see when the boys came in. It also provided her with an opportunity to set an indiscreet camera so that she could catch a shot of the boys walking up the aisle.

Once she sat, Khalida slid one of the menus from the stack in front of Paisley.

"Can I get you anything while you wait?"

"No, I'm okay, thank you. I'll just wait until they get here. Should be any minute now," Paisley said, checking her watch.

"Now, if I know those boys, and I think I do, Derry would have been here twenty minutes ago, but he's probably sitting somewhere waiting for Patch to get ready. So if you're starving, you should eat because it'll be a while."

"Hmm, maybe coffee then?"

"You got it," Khalida replied and was off in the quick walk mastered by servers and nurses.

Paisley took the opportunity to set up a miniature camera on the floor in the corner next to the booth and aimed it up the aisle. Using the Bluetooth connection with her phone, she could frame the shot perfectly and even watch the live view as she recorded.

Twenty-five minutes after the agreed-upon arrival time, the door to the diner opened, and a giant walked in.

Paisley watched as Derry popped into frame and looked around. He spotted Khalida behind the counter and she pointed to Paisley. Then, as soon as Derry saw her, he said something and then was blotted out by what could only be described as a train in human form. The lumbering figure turned toward Paisley, pushing Derry back behind him, and started up the aisle, dominating the frame of the camera. He had to have been at least six-foot-seven or six-foot-eight, shoulders back, arms swinging like the giant broken cables on a suspension bridge in a disaster movie. Customers pushed in their chairs or stood and moved so the figure could pass as he was easily wide enough that his sides brushed the chairs next to the tables in the center and the sides of the booths simultaneously.

Even though he was arguably the largest human Paisley had ever seen in person, no one else's head turned other than those who had to move out of his way so he could walk. They accepted the boy like you would accept a celebrity in your small town. You point and look for a while but eventually get used to them.

"Paisley Mott?" a youthful voice that could not possibly have come from the titan in front of her asked. The voice lumbered the same way the man did, stretching out her name so it sounded like "Paaaaays Lee Mott."

"You must be..." Paisley started but was quickly interrupted by the towering man.

"Steven Simply," he said and swung a hand nearly the size of a toaster toward her to shake.

She attempted to wrap her hand around the large mitt but could barely even bend the first digits around his hand.

"You can call me Patch. Everyone does," he said. Then, with the force and grace of trying to slip a truck tire into a dishwasher, he turned and threw himself into the empty seat across from her. The table shifted and moved, pushing Paisley into the backrest of her own seat.

Patch grabbed the table like the steering wheel of a bus, pulled it into him as close as he could, and settled in.

"You good, buddy?" Derry asked.

"Yup, I'm all set," Patch said, yanking a menu toward himself.

"Hey, Miss Mott. Er, Paisley. Sorry about that. It didn't spill on you, did it?" Derry asked, pointing at the coffee cup and saucer that Paisley collected from the bench beside her.

"Nope, finished this one already," she said and tipped the cup upside down.

"Oh good," Derry said.

Paisley reached down and scooped up the camera before sliding down the bench so Derry could sit on her side.

"You don't mind?" he said, pointing at the seat.

"No, please?" Paisley said, sliding a menu in front of the empty spot.

"Thank you." He plopped into the seat next to her.

"I'm so fucking hungry," Patch said from behind his menu.

"Dude," Derry said as a thud bumped from under the table.

"Damn, man, why'd you kick me?" Patch said, lowering menu.

Paisley got her first really good look at the boy's face. And that is what he was, a boy. He was the largest person she'd been in the same room with, but he was still just a boy. Soft red skin streaked down across his cheeks. He had a tiny button nose that would have looked more appropriate on a toddler than on this giant. His soft blue eyes looked on the verge of tears as he looked at Derry. But the shocking thing about his face, and the thing that Paisley couldn't stop looking at, though she wanted to, was the boy's mouth.

Patch's jaw hung open, showing the few teeth that still remained in the boy's head. They were few and very far between. At a glance, Paisley could only count five, three on the bottom and two on the top, not counting any molars she could not see. Those few crooked, pitted, and chipped teeth stood like battered troops on a battlefield where both sides had suffered devastating loss. Each one appeared both discolored and translucent. There was yellow, red, and green, all pitted with holes. They rested in a black mound that looked more like tar than gums.

"You're not supposed to curse in front of Miss Mott, remember?" Derry said, answering as to why he kicked Patch beneath the table.

"I just said fuck."

"Yeah, and you're not supposed to say that. It's a curse," Derry said.

"Oh, my bad. But you ain't need to kick me."

"I'm sorry, buddy. I didn't mean to. Just on edge. You okay?"

"Yeah, it didn't hurt. You kick like a girl," Patch teased.

Another thud came from under the table, this one a little louder.

"Ayyyyyee," Patch moaned, reaching for his leg. "Why'd you kick me again?"

"I didn't," Derry said.

Patch looked at Paisley and she gave him a big grin.

"Like a girl," she said.

Patch threw his head back and cackled, putting the mess that was his mouth on full display.

"It's the teeth," Derry said as Patch finally calmed down.

"What?" Paisley asked.

"The teeth. That's why they call him Patch."

"Yeah," Patch added, settling against the table. "Cause they look like Sour Patch Kids." He added a grin that might have been charming had he cared for his teeth.

"Really?" Paisley asked. The assumption that someone would embrace such a trait in that way felt disingenuous.

"Some things you just can't help. And Patch has a lot of other stuff working against him in people's eyes. So he owned that one," Derry said.

"And now people can't make fun of me for it. I'm Like Eminem in that movie The Green Mile," Patch added. The lisp with which the boy spoke now made sense, and Paisley was slowly getting more comfortable looking directly at him when he did.

"Eight Mile, buddy," Derry chimed in.

"Oh, yeah, Eight Mile. Fuckin' love that movie." Then Patch busted out an awkward rap that sounded nothing like the original song. "Mom's spaghetti is ready. Mom's spaghetti is ready. Sweaters already, Barney and Betty."

"That makes a lot of sense," Paisley said once it looked like Patch had completed his verse.

"Straight bars, pal." Derry reached across the table and offered Patch a fist to bump. Patch tapped it with a pineapple-sized fist. Then to Paisley, he said, "It's sort of how, like, in your vlog you talk about the anxiety and how much it affects you. You discovered a probable obstacle and turned it into a stepping stone instead."

Khalida appeared from nowhere and moved up next to the table.

"Hey, gentleman. And how are we this fine morning?"

"Hey, Lida," Derry said, looking up at her but keeping his face down. "Your hair looks nice today."

Khalida patted the back of one of the solid puffs that held tight like moons in orbit around her head.

"Well thank you, young man. And might I say you are looking handsome yourself today," she said, flashing a smile that caused

Derry's whole face to match the crimson color in Patch's cheeks. "Did y'all want a minute or do you know what you want?"

"Pancake train," Patch said, flipping the menu up without looking at Khalida. He had a smirk on his face that looked like he had just called checkmate on some unbeaten opponent.

Khalida leaned back and yelled over her shoulder to the kitchen. "Choo-choo!"

The chef in the kitchen popped his head up in the window with a quizzical look, but upon spotting Patch, he nodded and gave a thumbs up.

"What is a pancake train?" Paisley asked.

"Well, it starts with a giant stack of fifteen pancakes on a tray, topped with butter, syrup, chocolate chips, whipped cream, and bacon bits. Comes with hash browns and sausage links on the side," Khalida answered in her practiced way.

"Starts with?" Paisley asked.

"The pancakes are all you can eat. They just keep coming," Patch said.

"Choo-choo," Derry said as evenly as possible.

"Someone needs more than fifteen pancakes?" Paisley asked only half rhetorically.

"Patch once ate thirty-one," Derry said with pride, giving his friend a nod and receiving one in return.

"Thirty-one pancakes? They are like silver dollar pancakes, right?" Paisley held her hands up, making a small circle and showing it to first Patch and then Khalida. Patch shook his head.

"Full size," he said.

"The big, fluffy ones," Khalida added.

Paisley opened the menu in front of her and saw the pile of pancakes pictured. It was impressive.

"My boy is going for the record," Derry said.

"The record?"

"The current record is thirty-eight," Khalida said.

"And, if you eat all fifteen, plus the sides, the meal is free,"

Patch said. Paisley looked down at the menu again and saw nothing about that listed. She looked up at Khalida to confirm, but Khalida just gave her a knowing smile and shrugged her shoulders.

Paisley nudged Derry with her elbow. "You ever ride the pancake train?"

"Me? I can barely ride a pancake car, let alone train. And for twenty-five dollars, I can't afford not to finish them."

"We'll take three," Paisley said, swiping Derry's menu, adding it to hers, and handing them up to Khalida.

"Um, I don't..." Derry started.

"My treat," Paisley said. "Oh, and would you mind, on mine, having all the toppings on the side?"

Derry and Patch looked confused. Then realization materialized on Derry's face.

"Mine too," he said. This doubled the confusion on Patch's face.

"That way when you take home the leftovers they aren't soggy," Derry said, glancing at Paisley for verification.

She nodded and winked.

"Leftovers?" Patch laughed.

"Drinks?" Khalida asked.

Derry looked around the table.

"Orange juice all around? Or do you guys want something else?" Paisley asked.

"Works for me," Derry said.

Patch just gave a nod and thumbs up.

"You sure?" Khalida asked. "Because I think I have a question to ask."

"Oh no," Derry said. "Not now."

"Do it!" Patch said, pumping a fist.

"Do what?" Paisley asked.

"Ask it," Patch added.

Khalida folded her arms and smirked.

"Please don't," Derry said, slipping down into his seat.

"Well, you see, sometimes they get milkshakes when they're

both here, and I have to ask a specific question when they do," Khalida said.

"Oh? And what is that question?" Paisley asked.

"What has two thumbs," Khalida started.

Derry raised his thumbs and pointed them at himself reluctantly.

"And gives you diarrhea?" Khalida finished.

Before Paisley could ask what the answer was, Patch rolled toward Derry, nearly flipping the table, pulled him across it, and started tickling him.

"A dairy attack!" the boy yelled, flailing about.

Derry kicked and pushed, laughing hysterically, unable to push the much larger boy off of him.

The other restaurant patrons gave judgmental looks and rolled their eyes.

"Okay, okay, that's enough, stop!" Derry cried.

Patch let up and sat back. He was sweating, his face was red, and he was laughing.

"Every time, man. Every time," Derry said, wiping tears of laughter from his eyes and trying to straighten his hair.

"Got to love a good *Derry* attack," Khalida said, bopping Derry on the head with the menus.

"Oh, do you? Do you, Lida?" Derry said sarcastically.

"I do. I'll have it all out in a jiffy," Khalida said, pivoting and yelling, "Choo-choo times three!" as she went. A few folks from surrounding tables glanced over at the group. Some in confusion, a few in annoyance, but most with curiosity.

"She seems fun," Paisley said.

"Khalida is the best," Derry said.

"Word," Patch agreed.

"So, Patch, tell me about yourself."

"What do you want to know?"

"Anything, everything. Who are you?"

"I'm Patch."

"She means like where are you from, what do you like to do, stuff like that," Derry said.

"Oh, I'm from here. I like to play video games. And I like to hang out with my boy, the legend, Derry. That's about it."

"Have you ever been out of Howling Ivy?"

"Yeah, I been on the school bus and stuff. Like for football games in other places."

"Do you play football?" Paisley asked. It made total sense that he would.

"Yeah, I play the o-line, mostly left tackle."

"Patch has made All-State all four years. No one can get by him. He's like a moving wall out there," Derry said. The pride he had when he spoke of his friend was endearing.

"Wow, that's amazing. Are you on the team too?" Paisley asked Derry.

"Derry? Playing football?" Patch laughed. "That'd be hilarious."

"No, I don't play. Not my thing. I do like to go and watch Patch play though. So I go to a lot of games."

"We do everything together, me and Derry. He's my best friend."

"That's great. Is that why you two started the podcast?"

"Nah, we started it because my dude likes to talk, and he's way too smart to just be talking to a bum like me," Patch said. "So he talks to the audience."

"You're not a bum," Derry said.

"Derry wanted to do this podcast because he realized he could..." Patch started.

"Here it comes," Derry said.

"Dude, don't interrupt the story," Patch said.

"No, our ten tons of pancakes are coming," Derry said and pointed at Khalida who balanced all three large platters on one arm and carried three glasses of orange juice in the other hand but walked casually as if she had been doing this for a hundred years.

"Here you go," she said, skillfully sliding the plates onto the table.

"Thank you," Derry said, helping move the plates to their

proper positions as they came in.

"Can I get y'all anything else?" Paisley checked with the boys to see if they needed anything, but Derry was shaking his head and Patch had somehow already devoured a few pancakes.

"I think we're okay, thank you," she said.

"Well, you know where I'll be," Khalida said, then touched Patch on his shoulder. "I'll get another stack going for you." She returned to the kitchen.

"Okay, please continue," Paisley said.

Patch looked across at Paisley and held up a pancake on his fork.

"Don't worry about it, buddy," Derry said.

Patch lifted the fork higher in a small salute.

"So what my friend here was saying was that we started the show because people around here kept saying that they were seeing things, and we wanted to get to the bottom of it," Derry said.

Patch looked across the table at Derry with an eyebrow raised, not willing to slow on the battle he was currently waging on his pancakes. Paisley clocked the look but did not acknowledge it.

"What sort of things were people claiming to see?" Paisley said, pouring syrup on a single pancake she had separated from her own tower.

"Spphhider mahn," Patch said through a mouthful of food.

"Spider-Man? Like the superhero?" Paisley asked.

Patch shook his head.

"No, like a man who turned into a giant spider," Derry clarified.

Patch nodded and pointed his fork at Derry.

"Someone claimed to have seen that?"

"A few people have claimed to see it," Derry said.

"Really?"

"Here you go, hun," Khalida said, seemingly appearing out of nowhere to drop another stack of pancakes on the table near Patch and stroll away.

105

"I love you!" Patch called after her.

"I'd really like to get a full setup and get this recorded if you all don't mind saving or repeating some of the good stuff." It would make Paisley's life much easier to cut the footage together if it was shot with a proper setup and not over mountains of pancakes.

"I'd say we could go to my house, but my dad is probably home, and he doesn't like having people there when he's there," Derry said. "Patch doesn't live far from me; his grandma has a house just outside the park."

"Nah," Patch said. "Bridge."

"Oh, we can't do Patch's, his grandma has Bridge today," Derry explained.

"What about a nice park? Somewhere quiet," she asked.

Derry nodded and stuck a forkful of pancakes into his mouth. He chewed intently, swallowed, drank juice, wiped his mouth, and then answered. "We've got tons of open space around here. We could go out to one of the abandoned buildings or something and film? Might be cool."

Paisley shifted in her seat. Her mini camera and microphone would be picking all of this up, and she could only think that if something happened to her and someone reviewed the footage of that moment, they would wonder if she'd learned nothing in Grey Water Ridge.

"I think it is better if we stay closer to town. Somewhere well-lit. It's better for the shot," she said.

"Of course, obviously. That makes sense," Derry replied.

"Hmmm," Paisley thought. She really wasn't interested in letting them know where she was staying. She didn't know them well enough just yet. "Is there a library or something we could use? Maybe reserve one of their meeting rooms for an hour or two?" Paisley asked.

"You know, the library isn't a bad idea. There isn't ever anyone there," Derry said.

"'Cept you," Patch added.

"Yeah," Derry agreed.

"You think the librarians would let us use it if there isn't anyone else there?" Paisley asked.

"Oh, there isn't a librarian. Someone just goes by and opens it in the morning, then returns to close at night. They don't invest enough money into it to staff it," Derry said.

"It should work," Paisley said, looking to Khalida and signaling that she was going to need a box.

22

"I don't remember my real mom and dad," Millicent explained to Squeakers, who sat just a few feet away from her.

Squeakers inched closer, his nose twitching as he sniffed the air around the small corner of crust that Millicent offered.

"It's okay, you can have it. I saved it for you. He doesn't bring me a lot of food, but you can have some when he does," she said.

The mouse had visited often, but this was the first time Millicent had food to offer. It closed the distance and took a nibble of the crust.

"Alisha and Matt weren't my real parents, but they took care of me," Millicent explained as Squeakers finished eating.

"They're dead now. I see them sometimes when I'm asleep."

The girl sat back onto the sleeping bag, adjusting the chain absentmindedly.

"I see a lot of people when I sleep."

23

Images of Boyd Gunnerson flashed in Paisley's head. She stumbled, falling into Patch, who was very sturdy, even while carrying her bags. He put his free hand on her shoulder.

"You okay?" he asked.

"Yeah, just got a little dizzy," she said, stepping up the single step and entering the library.

The cramped room was set in a single-story building near what must have passed for downtown in Howling Ivy. Dusty shelves lined the walls, but very few books occupied them. A few old, dark, hardwood tables and matching chairs filled most of the space.

"This is the library?" Paisley asked. The *Library* title seemed generous. The place lacked books. There were no magazines in sight. No computers.

"Yeah, it isn't much," Derry said. He walked over and wiped the dust off one of the tables near a window.

"Is this where you normally sit when you come in?" Paisley asked.

"No, I normally sit over there." Derry pointed to a table in the corner next to the History Section. "I just figured if you're recording, you would like the window light."

Paisley nodded and then looked back to the lonely table.

"Wi-fi," Derry said.

"Huh?" she responded.

"You're wondering why I come here," he said.

"Oh, right, wi-fi," Paisley said, putting it all together.

"I can get enough wi-fi from my neighbors to do some stuff, but it's way faster here. So I come here to upload the podcast to the internet most of the time."

"Where are all the, um," Paisley started.

"The books? Gone. Anything that was in here that could be sold online was taken. They'd have taken the wi-fi router too if it wasn't locked up." Derry pointed to a small metal cage near the table in the corner.

"Ah, closest to the wi-fi," Paisley said.

"Bingo," Derry replied.

Patch set the bags down on the table. Paisley opened them and started taking out her recording equipment.

"You sure you're still good to tell me the juicy gossip after setting the new record on pancakes there, big guy?" Paisley asked.

"41!" Derry yelled and fist bumped his friend.

"Yeah, I'm g to g," Patch said.

"G to g?" Paisley asked.

"Good to go," Derry explained. "It's a gaming thing."

"Got it. Well, let me get this all set up and I'll be g to g for you to tell me all about Spider-Man," she said.

24

Sweet smells of melting cheese, cooking meat, and baking dough mixed in the air. Patch leaned against the prep counter in his regular rotation of dipping pepperoni in the pizza sauce, and then shoving the dripping mess into his mouth.

A light flour dust coated him from head to toe. The once-white *Fat Slice* uniform shirt Patch wore was a tapestry of yellow, brown, and red stains. An apron was slung low on his hips like a gunslinger's belt, but looked as if something on his hands required wiping, it ended up on his shirt instead.

"I'm telling you, bro, there are fucking zombies here," he said between mouthfuls of saucy pepperoni.

"You really believe in that stuff?" the assistant store manager said as she pulled a pizza from the oven and dropped it into a box on the cut table before expertly slicing it. She tossed it onto a rack overhead. "Nate, run's up!" She shouted into the back of the store before turning her attention back to Patch.

"Of course I do," he said.

"But like, zombies?"

"Yeah, I know a guy who said he saw one. Said it wasn't like the movies though."

"Right. I think that podcast is getting to your head," she said, then looked toward the back room and shouted again. "Nate, the order is ready! Let's go!"

"He's probably taking a shit," Patch said. "Or jerking off. I'll go knock on the door." Patch shoved a few more pepperonis into his mouth, wiped his hands across his shirt, and headed toward the back of the tiny hole-in-the-wall pizza place that served as the only pizza joint in town.

Patch knew Nate wasn't in the bathroom. Odds were he was

out back hitting his pipe before the run, and if he was, Patch was hoping to catch him while he was still out there. He knew from experience that if he caught him in the act he was likely to let him hit it a time or two.

When Patch rounded the corner, the bathroom door stood wide open, and the light was off. He grinned and made his way around stacks of folded pizza boxes, bottled pop, and canned tomato sauce to get a clear view of the back door. Just as he suspected, the door was propped open by an empty pop crate.

Patch pushed the door open, careful not to move the crate and lock them out. The comforting pizza aroma shifted to a sharp chemical smell. His heart raced.

"Nate, you motherfucker, are you back here hitting that shit without me?" Patch said as he burst into the employee parking lot that the pizza place shared with the bar next door.

"Shhhh," Nate, a balding, sickly-looking man, said.

"Wh-?" Patch started before Nate grabbed him by the shirt and pulled him to where he had been ducking down behind a dumpster accompanied by two other men that Patch presumed had come over from the bar.

The men hunkered down and their sweaty bodies smelled of alcohol and ammonia. Patch gagged.

"Shut up," one of the men said.

"What's going on?" Patch whispered. The first thing to go through his mind was that Nate had either pissed off a dealer or he had hit on someone's wife, as they snuck out the back of the bar to have a smoke and a fuck, again.

"There's a goddamn monster over there," one of the men said. He wore a mechanic shirt that identified him as working for the local auto body shop.

"Is it a zombie?" Patch said and tried to look around the dumpster.

Nate pulled him back.

"No, it's something else. I never saw nothin' like this before," Nate said.

A screeching sound signaled that something had slid the

dumpster that sat behind that bar.

"What the fuck?" Patch said. He had moved that dumpster once when he and Nate were playing a joke on the guys at the bar. They got a few folks to help pull the dumpster in front of the back door of the bar to block it. Then Nate gave a guy ten bucks to set off a smoke grenade that Patch had found in a car at the salvage yard. They laughed when the people tried to get out the back but couldn't. But he remembered how heavy that dumpster was, and it wasn't on wheels. It was steel. and whatever was pushing it around must have been massive. "You think it's a bear?"

"Hell no. It don't look like no bear," the other man said. "Looks like a fucking demon is what it looks like."

"I gotta see it," Patch said and stepped out from behind the dumpster.

He stared in disbelief. There was nothing there. After a few seconds, a man walked out from around the far side of the bar. He was tall, plain-looking, dressed in a polo and khaki pants. He noticed Patch. The two stared at each other for a moment before Patch called out to him.

"Hey, you see a fucking demon over there?"

The man looked around.

"No. Was there one here?" he shouted back.

"I guess so," Patch responded.

"I suppose it left." The man shrugged.

"Must've," Patch said. He turned to look at the men cowering behind the dumpster. "Get up guys. The thing's gone."

The other men stood, as best they could, and dusted themselves off. They looked over at the plain-looking man. "You didn't see it?" Nate called out to him.

"The demon?" the man called back.

"Yeah, he was just over there."

"He?" the man questioned.

"Well I didn't see its dick or anything, but I guess it was a boy," Nate reasoned.

113

"There isn't anything over here now, girl or boy," the man in the khakis yelled back.

25

"So then the guy wearing the polo just kind of fucks off, and we are all like, what the hell, man," Patch said, adding a confused look and putting his hands up with a shrug.

"Wait, so you didn't actually see the spider thing?" Paisley asked.

"Well, no, but Nate did, and he said it was huge like its legs were taller than he was, and he isn't as tall as me, but he's taller than Derry," Patch pointed at Derry as if Paisley had forgotten who he was and how tall he stood.

"The only witness to this thing was a guy who was on crack," Paisley started.

"Meth," Derry and Patch corrected.

"Sorry, a guy who was high on meth, and two drunks from the bar next door?" Paisley clarified.

"Yeah, but Nate wouldn't lie," Patch insisted.

"He lied about the fire in the bar," she retorted.

"Well, yeah, but... but that was a prank, and it was funny," Patch said.

"It wasn't just them," Derry said. "Some other people claimed to have seen it a few years earlier out by the highway. After that there are a couple of stories, not sure how credible they are, about seeing it here or there."

"I'm not questioning if they would lie, and I'm not trying to shame them for their choice of extracurricular activity. I'm just saying that all three of the *witnesses* in that story were operating with ability impaired," Paisley said. "That wouldn't even be admissible in court."

"We know that the spider demon isn't all that impressive since no one has, like, photos of it or anything," Derry said.

"Oh, it's a demon now?" Paisley asked with a wink.

"That's just what we call it," Patch added.

"We know that isn't the big fish," Derry said.

"No, it's a spider," Patch added.

"Right, I mean it isn't the big fish we used to tempt you to come out here," Derry corrected.

"I came for the EVP. That being said, if you had a picture of the spider-man then you can just call me James Johnson," Paisley said and added finger guns to emphasize her joke.

"Who?" Derry asked.

"James Johnson, you know, the guy from Spider-Man who is always trying to get Peter Parker to get photos of Spidey," she said.

"Um, you mean J. Jonah Jameson?" Patch asked.

"Is that his name?" she asked.

"Yeah."

"Patch loves comic books," Derry said, adding the smile he often had when talking about his friend.

"Well, comic book movies," Patch corrected.

"I'm a movie buff, thanks to my dad, but I lean toward the older stuff we watched together," Paisley said. She tapped on the desk. The worry that she may have come all that way for nothing hit her.

"Tell me about the EVP," she said.

The words hit Derry and he flinched like he'd got caught doing something wrong.

"I'm sorry, that was abrupt," she apologized.

"No, it's okay. I'm sorry," Derry responded.

"It's hard for him to talk about," Patch said.

"I'm sorry. It seemed so fluid on your podcast when you talked about it, so I just assumed it wasn't a huge deal," Paisley apologized.

Derry slumped in his chair but he sat forward, stretched, and leaned to rest his forearms on the table.

"I guess it's time to tell you the story of the day my sister was taken," Derry began.

26

"Give me that, butt munch," Derry demanded as he took a glow stick necklace from Lydia and started twirling it so fast that it looked like a shield in the late dusk.

"Hey!" Lydia cried and began punching her brother in the arm. At nearly seven years old, her big brother Derry was more than twice her size at a little more than twice her age, so her shots didn't bother him.

"Steve, hey Steve," Derry called to his friend who was at the concession stand.

"Wha'?" the larger boy said as he turned trying to balance three snow cones. As usual, he wore a dirty white t-shirt and the red bandanna he'd favored to keep his floppy hair out of his eyes at his job at the pizza place and the job at the yard.

"You see a mosquito around here," Derry yelled. "Because I think I just felt one land on my arm."

Lydia leaned back and punched him one more time for good measure, holding back a giggle.

"Whoa, dude, you look like Captain America!" Steven said as he stretched out a hand that held two of the snow cones. Derry and Lydia both took one as Steven nibbled at the ice with teeth that had already started to rot from the few years of drug use and the lifetime of sugar that never really saw a toothbrush.

"Thank you, Steven," Lydia said as she licked the frozen treat.

"Thanks, man, but I thought you said you wanted a waffle cone?" Derry asked, sampling the treat.

"Yeah, but they are three bucks each," Steven said.

"Oh, how much did you have? I think I got fifty cents I could have gave you?" Derry said, reaching into his pocket and fishing around.

"I had three bucks," Steven said.

Derry stopped fishing for the quarters he thought were in his pocket, remembering he had given them to Lydia for the glow necklace tucked under his arm. He handed it back to her, and she spun it in her free hand, trying to get the same result that Derry had.

"Why didn't you get it?" he asked.

"Snow cones are a buck each. This way I could get one for all of us," Steven said, fighting the brain freeze that came with trying to eat the frozen treat too quickly.

"Well, thanks, man, you didn't have to do that," he stretched out his hand in an invitation to fist bump, and Steven took the opportunity.

"Of course, bro."

"You're the man," Derry said.

"You're the man, Steven," Lydia said. The red and blue food coloring from the snow cone gave her a purple ring around her mouth.

"Of course, short stuff," Steven said, sticking his fist out for her to bump. She smiled, her face lighting up for the last time in that dying light. She balled up her tiny fist and pressed her knuckles against Steven's.

"Where should we sit to watch the fireworks?" Derry asked, eating his snow cone.

"We could sit over on the lawn by the courthouse, but there's lots of people over there already," Steven said.

"Yeah, then we have to deal with the crowd when we try to leave, and my dad said we had to be home right after the fireworks, so the quicker, the better," Derry said.

"He didn't want to come," Lydia added.

"That's not it. He just doesn't like the noise," Derry said. Their dad had service-related PTSD, and the fireworks were not good for him.

"Yeah," Patch said. "I overheard the guys at the yard asking for volunteers to work on the Fourth since it was the holiday.

119

Your dad said he'd pick up the shift since he wasn't working on the trash truck. He'd do it as long as it was just calls away from downtown Winnie was going to take the city stuff, so your dad didn't have to be anywhere near the noise. That's when I told him he could bring you to the yard since I was working the day shift, and then I'd bring you here and take you home."

A high-pitched whistle rose above the crowd of more than three thousand people who had gathered to watch the Fourth of July display at the city park in Howling Ivy. It wasn't an overly impressive display, but other than Santa setting up in the library for two nights in early December, this was the only holiday event the town put on. So, they tried to make it worthwhile.

A bang followed the whistle and light filled the dark sky. A sizzling sound accompanied a rainstorm of glittering lights as the crowd let out a collective "oooh," followed by applause.

Derry looked back to make sure that even at the far edge of the park, closest to the road, Lydia still had a good enough view of the fireworks.

"This good enough?"

"They are so pretty!" she said, not answering his question directly but he nodded in agreement as if she had.

"Steve?"

"Huh?" Steven asked, not turning his face away from the slow building of explosions.

"This spot cool?" Derry asked.

"Oh, yeah, dude, totally."

Derry looked back again, and a smirk, the last he would crack for over a year, peeked up at the corner of his mouth as he watched the most beautiful thing he had ever seen. Not the bright, vibrant colors perforating the night sky, but those colors instead reflected on the soft face and in the beautiful blue eyes of his baby sister. It would be the last time he would ever see her.

"Look at that one!" she said, and pointed at the heart shape that fell apart as it sprinkled back to Earth.

Six minutes later, the finale began, and fast paced explosions thundered across the sea of people before him. Derry could feel the excitement, as well as the shock wave, in his chest. He looked over and Steven was gone.

His brows dipped.

"Where did Ste..." he began, turning to ask Lydia if she had seen where his best friend had gone.

She wasn't there.

Derry stood at the edge of the park, searching across the street. It was empty. Everyone in town was at his back and it felt like the entire world in front of him was a hole.

27

Tears soaked the sleeve of Paisley's shirt as she dabbed at her eyes. She reached up to turn the camera off but paused with her finger on the button.

Across the table Derry sat with hands crossed at the wrist in front of him on the table, head low. He struggled to look up at Paisley. Patch sat next to him, his hand resting on Derry's shoulder. His face was red and wet. He looked at Derry.

"I'm so sorry, dude," he said.

Derry patted the hand that sat on his shoulder.

"I know, buddy. I know," he responded.

Paisley pulled her hand away from the camera and adjusted in her seat.

"Are you okay to continue?" she asked.

Derry lifted his chin to her. She was crying, Patch was crying, but Derry was not. His face was slack, his body defeated. His eyes may have been red, but he wasn't crying.

"Sure," he mumbled.

"How about you?" she asked Patch.

"Yeah, I'm okay if he's okay," Patch said, still not taking his eyes off Derry.

"We can take a break if you need one," she said.

"No, I'm okay," Derry said. He sat up and wiped his eyes.

"Okay, thank you. I just want to get as much down so I can do some preliminary edits and figure out the direction of the investigation and story if that is really okay?" Paisley said.

Derry gave a thumbs up.

"Patch," Paisley started, "when Derry was telling us about the day his sister disappeared, he mentioned that, when he turned, he noticed you were gone first, and then noticed that she was gone. Would you want to talk about what happened?"

Patch took his hand off Derry's shoulder and put it in his lap. His shoulders slumped and he looked like a dog after someone found a trash bag ripped open in the kitchen.

"Is it okay, dude?"

Derry nodded.

"The fireworks was going off, and they were pretty cool and all, but I've seen enough of them. So, when I looked back and seen that Lydia couldn't see very well, on account of everyone else being so tall, I was going to lift her up and put her on my shoulders, but when I turn she's gone. But I look around and see her walk around the corner way down the end of the street."

Concern poured over Paisley's face.

"Was she walking with someone?" she asked.

"It looked like she had someone's hand, but they was already around the corner and my eyes aren't great. I'm not too fast but when I saw that, I ran," Patch said. His voice hitched and fresh tears crept from his eyes.

"You ran after them?" Paisley asked. "The man who was taking Lydia?"

"I couldn't catch up. I fucking tried." Patch looked at Derry as if apologizing again. "I fucking tried."

"Why didn't you tell Derry before you ran after them?"

"I just started running, I was scared. I tried to yell back, but he couldn't hear me over the fireworks. I just had to go."

"Derry said that when he turned around he didn't see either of you?"

"Patch ran all the way down Main Street to Fifth," Derry said.

Paisley didn't look over at Derry, she just kept her eyes on Patch, who wasn't making eye contact. He stared at his hands.

"Patch?" she said.

"Yeah," he replied, lifting his head just enough that he could make eye contact with her for a brief second.

"What happened on Fifth and Main?" she asked.

"When I got there they were gone. I looked everywhere."

"Were there cars? Did you see anything?" Paisley asked.

"There were cars everywhere. That's just it, someone must have been waiting, cause there wasn't any open spots since everyone was watching the fireworks," Patch explained.

"What did you do then?"

"I saw a cop car and tried to run to catch them to tell them, they didn't stop but I kept running. I ran so far I almost threw up."

Paisley looked back over to Derry.

"What were you doing during all of this?"

"I was looking for them. I went to the concession stand, the bathrooms, and looked around, but by then the fireworks were over and people were everywhere."

"I tried to find him to tell him, but I couldn't," Patch added.

"I walked over to the Sheriff's Office and told the guy at the desk," Derry continued. "He called the Sheriff and she said we had to wait at least twenty-four hours to report her missing."

"That's bullshit," Paisley said.

"Yeah," Derry said. "I called the yard and told my dad. He was upset, so Winslow drove him over to pick me up and then drove us home."

"Who's Winslow? You've both mentioned him."

"Winnie, he owns the salvage yard Patch and my dad work at."

"He's a good dude," Patch added. "Lives up on the hill overlooking the yard."

"Why didn't you call Derry and tell him what happened?" Paisley asked Patch.

"I don't have a cell phone," Derry answered for him.

"And why didn't you call him from the Sheriff's Office?" Paisley asked Derry, nodding toward Patch.

"I tried, but it went right to voicemail."

"My phone died when we were taking pictures," Patch said. "I didn't even have it to take video of the fireworks for my grandma. But as soon as I got back to my car I plugged it in and called the cops."

"They tell you the same thing about the twenty-four hours?" Paisley asked.

Patch nodded.

"When we got home Patch was sitting on the steps," Derry said. "My dad tried to hit him, but Winnie stopped him. Said it wasn't Patch's fault."

"And your dad listened to him?"

"Winnie's as big as a house. If my dad didn't listen to him he'd have just picked him up and carried him inside."

Information mixed in Paisley's head like a potion. She stirred it around trying to find a thread that would lead to the next question.

"I read that they haven't caught the person responsible," she said, pausing to allow for either to contradict her. They did not.

"They haven't found anything. Not a single trace," Derry said. "And it seems like they stopped looking." His head had sunk back down.

Paisley clicked the camera off.

"Are we done?" Derry asked.

"Maybe just for today, if that's okay?" Paisley said.

"Yeah," Derry said, again wiping his dry eyes. "I'm really sorry. I've talked about her so much since then you'd think it would be the easiest thing in the world to talk about, but it's pretty tough still, I guess."

"Well, if you find a way to get over that particular type of pain, let me know," she said.

Derry raised his head to look directly at her. Those light blue eyes stunned her for a moment.

"Because of your mom?" he asked. "Or because of the people in Grey Water Ridge?"

"Little of both?" Paisley answered, unsure. "Maybe a lot of both?"

"I'm sorry," Derry said. Finally, after all of that a tear appeared to be settling on the lower lid of his eye.

"It hasn't been easy. It feels impossible to think of anything else sometimes," she said.

"Yeah," Derry replied.

28

Millicent focused on drawing out the blanket that replaced the sleeping bag. She held the corner with one hand and pulled to make a straight line on the cement floor. Then she pushed her hand into it and curved it around, bending it to a ninety-degree corner. She continued this process over and over, carefully crafting shapes.

"Okay, Squeakers," she said to the mouse. She reached out with a small piece of cheese she'd torn from her lunch and showed it to Squeakers.

The mouse stretched out its neck to sniff the cheese, but she pulled it away before it could nibble it.

"Not yet. You've got to get through this maze if you want the cheese." She placed the cheese in the middle of the makeshift maze she had made. It was actually just a single path with a few turns, but it was the best she could do.

She lowered her hand in front of the mouse, and it approached, sniffing the fingers that had held the cheese.

"Come on. Get on."

The mouse didn't comply with the request, but Millicent was able to usher it over to the entrance to the blanket maze.

Squeakers did okay with the maze, but in the end he just climbed over the blanket walls when he could sniff out the cheese.

"Hey, that's cheating!" Millicent laughed and immediately regretted it.

A creak above her head signaled movement, and she held her breath, waiting for the basement door to open.

"Get out of here," she whispered to Squeakers as she balled up the blanket and tucked it behind her. "Go on."

She brushed at Squeakers with her hand and the mouse ran.

Millicent sighed with relief as the mouse made it safely out of sight before the basement door opened.

29

The grocery store was exactly as one would expect in that sort of town. A town big enough it once attracted the large chain stores, but now so poor that it couldn't afford to keep them up. Shelves were crooked, old fluorescent lights flickered, and chipped floor tiles outnumbered those that were whole, but even the ones that were whole were worn and scuffed beyond recognition. The store felt ripe for the apocalypse.

Paisley was anxious about being in a new place and picked up on all the cosmetic issues, as well as the structural ones. A large chunk of concrete missing from the footer of one of the load-bearing pillars in the middle of the aisle ahead of her caught her attention. She noticed the cart she had grabbed and was now pushing bumped every other step, meaning it likely had something stuck to one of its wheels.

She just wanted to get some provisions to last her a few days and get back to the rental. The driver who picked her up, a professional-looking man in his fifties, was kind enough to wait for her. This helped as she wouldn't have to haul all her bags into the store, but it made her nervous, leaving her gear in a stranger's car. She tried to hurry but the hyper-focus did not help.

The hair on her arms stood up as she overheard part of a conversation at the end of the aisle.

"I'm pretty sure that's her," a woman said.

Paisley glanced up, hoping not to see the woman looking at her, but she was. There was a mountain of a man standing next to her.

"You sure?" the man asked. His voice was low and rumbled down the aisle toward Paisley.

"Yep, that's her. She's the one that's been talking to that

Knot kid," she said.

The man looked away from Paisley and back at the woman.

"Gerry's boy?" he said.

"Yeah, that's the one." The woman pointed at Paisley. "That one there. She's been asking that kid about his sister. You know he does that radio program with that other kid, the stupid one."

"Steven ain't stupid," he said.

"Dumb as tits on a bull," the lady said. "But they been talking about his sister, and that lady come to do a news story, is what I hear."

"Is that what you hear?" the giant said, looking back up at Paisley, who was very obviously just standing there listening to the conversation they knew she could hear.

"That's what I hear," the old lady said.

Without breaking eye contact with Paisley, the giant walked her way.

Paisley's dad used to enjoy watching professional wrestling when she was little. They would sit every Monday night and watch it. He'd sit on the floor in front of the couch, and Paisley would lay on the couch with her head on his shoulder, occasionally adding in a head lock or elbow drop for good measure. One of her favorite wrestlers was a man called The Big Show. He was seven feet tall and had a huge beard that made him even scarier. The man coming up the aisle, who shook the ground with every step, seemed to be a carbon copy of that wrestler. If the man didn't have a full head of hair, it would have been plausible that it was him. Paisley froze.

"Hey," he said, closing the distance between them. He had to lean down to put his hand on the side of her cart. He was older than the wrestler looked when she watched it. He had gray in his beard and hair. If Paisley had to guess she would put the man in his late forties or early fifties.

"Hey," she said back, as confidently as she could muster in the face of a living boulder.

"You the news lady?" His voice was so deep and heavy that it was impossible to tell if he was angry or annoyed. He just sounded like if a bass drum had conscious thought.

"If I say no, are you going to take that bundle of logs you call a hand off my shopping cart?" Paisley shot back.

The man seemed taken aback. It was unlikely that he was ever sassed in such a way. He lifted his hand and looked at it, then looked back up Paisley.

"It's called a clap-back," she pointed out. "It's when you meet a stupid, or seemingly stupid, question or remark with a vaguely insulting response."

"Seems rude?"

"As rude as a human traffic circle walking up to a woman, alone in a grocery store, and putting its grime-covered mitts on her cart and demanding her identity?"

"Uh," he started.

"See? That was another clap-back. Want to try again from the beginning, this time without the out-of-context questions?" she asked.

"I don't think I like your tone," the man said. He stood up straight and puffed out his gigantic chest. He wore overalls, and Paisley wondered where they ever found enough denim to cover him.

This was a move she'd seen a million times from a million men, certainly never one this large, but a million nevertheless. It was done to remind her that she was a tiny woman. To put her in her place.

"Whelp, this has been fun," she said, backing her cart away from the man. "But I've dealt with enough hyper-masculine men this year to fill a monster truck rally sized bag of fuck off, so I'll be seeing you."

The man reached down and put his hand back on the cart. She tried to pull it, but it was as if the man's hand had driven it straight into the tile and sealed it there. She couldn't even turn it in his grip.

"Hey, man, keep it," she said. She let go of the cart, turned, and walked away. She listened for the sound of him coming after her. She wasn't going to be caught off guard. She dropped her hand into her bag and wrapped it around the taser. The good thing about him being so tall was that his balls would be the perfect height for a good tasing.

"My daughter was the first to die," the deep voice rumbled after her.

Paisley stopped. She turned around and went back into the aisle to see the man still standing there with his hand on her cart.

"What did you say?" Paisley asked, not getting any closer.

"My little girl, Heather. She was taken first." His face was pulled up in an attempt to hold back emotion.

"I'm very sorry to hear that," Paisley said. She was conflicted. On one hand, she wanted to be sympathetic to what was obviously a painful situation, but she also hated how this man made her feel.

"I don't think we need someone coming in here and poking around, digging up everybody's hurt feelings," he said.

Paisley took a few steps closer so she didn't feel like she was shouting.

"I'm not trying to stir up any sort of feelings, mister. I'm here to help a kid who asked for it. That's all. I'm not here trying to dig up anything. Just trying to help the kid come to terms with losing his sister," she said.

"I don't think you should be here."

Paisley looked around, surprised the conversation had not drawn an audience.

"With all due respect, I don't give a shit what you think about me being here," Paisley shot back.

"You really don't know who you are talking to," the man said. His head tilted forward, and he lowered his brow. Then he gave the cart a small shove to the side so it was no longer between them.

"I know enough," Paisley stated.

"Yeah? And what is it that you think you know?" he asked, putting his hands on his hips and tilting his head back to look down his nose at her.

"I know you're an oblivious jerk, and your wife over there," Paisley pointed down the aisle behind him, "looks embarrassed to be seen with you."

"That woman isn't my wife," he said, shaking his head as if she had ruined her credibility.

"Not the old bag of moth balls that was in my business a minute ago, that lady," Paisley challenged, pointing past him. "The one that looks like she's seen one too many days with your ridiculous ass."

The man turned to look and see who she was pointing at, and the second his head was turned she made her move.

By the time he turned back around he was looking at an empty aisle and she was halfway to the waiting car.

"Thank you," Paisley said to the man in the front seat as he drove away.

"Sure thing. Did you get what you needed?" he asked, looking back over the seat, seeing that she hadn't brought any bags out with her.

"No. Apparently, the giant at the top of that particular beanstalk was not happy with my presence," she said. She looked out the back window to see the man filling the entryway to the store.

The driver saw the man in his rearview mirror. Realization softened his expression. "You met Winslow Peck, did ya?"

Paisley turned back toward the driver.

"That's Winslow Peck?"

"You heard of him?"

Paisley didn't answer. She just looked back out the window at the man who was burning holes in the car with his eyes as it drove away.

They grew them gorgeous in Grey Water Ridge. In Howling Ivy, they grew them big. Real fucking big.

30

The town passed quietly in the dark as the car slipped through Howling Ivy with very little traffic. The driver hadn't said much since leaving the grocery store. He didn't ask where she was from, where she had been, how her day was, or anything else. He had the destination and seemed content with that.

Happy with the silence, Paisley pulled out her phone to check the notifications she had been neglecting all day in favor of giving attention to the boys and the investigation.

There were a handful of notifications, but the two that stood out were from Hyacinth and WhyItHurts. She checked Hyacinth's first. It was a message asking her to call her when she was on her way home.

"Sir?" Paisley said to the driver.

His eyes, which Paisley could already see in the rearview mirror, looked up to meet hers, but he said nothing. He just raised his eyebrows. "Do you mind if I make a phone call?"

"Not at all," he said, turning down the soft music that Paisley hadn't noticed until then.

She clicked on Hyacinth's icon and hit call.

She answered almost immediately. "Pais?" Hyacinth said. Her voice was a little hurried but didn't sound concerned. Which meant she was excited but not in a bad way.

"Hy, sorry it took me so long to get back to you. I've been on the investigation all day. What's up?"

The driver's eyes flicked back to Paisley when she said it was an investigation.

"Okay, so you aren't back to your rental place yet?" Hyacinth asked.

"Nope. On my way there now."

"Well, okay, you need to stay on the phone with me until you get there, okay?" Hyacinth requested, eagerness in each word.

"Uh, okay, what's going on?"

"Nothing, just a little surprise."

"You're not going to be standing there when I get there, are you?" Paisley asked, hoping that she would pull up and see her friend standing there.

"I wish, but I'm still stuck here," Hyacinth said.

"So what is the surprise?"

"You'll just have to see when you get there. Now, tell me about your day, and stop trying to get me to spoil the surprise."

"Well, the boys are really nice. Though I suspect there are a lot of things they're not telling me," she started.

"Oh, like what? How old are they?" Hyacinth asked.

"Derry, I think he's sixteen, he's the one whose sister died..."

"Dead sister? Oh shit."

"Yeah, she was murdered and he believes he caught the audio of her calling his name on a recording." Paisley noticed the driver look back again. This time, his eyebrows were lower, more suspicious than curious.

"Oh snap. Do you think it is the real deal?" Hyacinth asked.

"I don't know, I don't even know if I believe in the real deal," Paisley answered.

"What? You don't believe in ghosts? Aren't you a paranormal investigator? Isn't that pretty important to the job?"

"A healthy disbelief is important to the job. I can't just believe everything I'm told," Paisley said.

"But like, ghosts are obviously real, right?"

"Well, maybe, but then Patch, the older of the two, who is eighteen, also told me that there was some sort of spider monster thing walking around," Paisley said.

"It's a demon," the driver interrupted. "I've seen it."

"Hyacinth, hold on a sec," Paisley said, holding the phone down and clicking the speakerphone button. "Okay, sir, can you say that one more time."

The driver glanced up at Paisley in the rearview mirror, then turned over his shoulder and saw the phone. Paisley saw his face shift as he mentally calculated whether Paisley was fucking with him or not. "It isn't a man, it's a demon, and it's terrifying," he started.

"I'm sorry, what?" Hyacinth said from the speakerphone.

"It's the driver, Hy. He saw the spider demon," Paisley managed without cracking too much of a smile.

"Oooooh, right, the spider Demon, obviously, sorry, continue," Hyacinth said.

"It was maybe half a dozen years ago, or so. I was hauling log back then."

Hyacinth interrupted. "I'm sorry, hauling log? Is that a euphemism?"

"No, he means he drove a truck that hauled timber," Paisley answered and the man nodded.

"Oh, like in Final Destination? Yeah, fuck that," Hyacinth said.

"Yeah, like that," Paisley said.

"Final Destination?" the driver asked.

"Well, Final Destination Two. It's a movie about death catching up to kids with some wild, graphic death scenes. One of which involves a log truck," Paisley explained.

"Yeah, with the star of my dreams when I was growing up," Hyacinth said.

"Sawa?" Paisley asked.

"Sawa," Hyacinth confirmed.

"He wasn't in that one, just the first one, the best one," Paisley said

The driver looked back at her.

"Oh, sorry. We got distracted," she said.

"Sawa will do that to you," Hyacinth added.

"Anyway, I'd leave from Howling Ivy with the cab, drive over to Gassien to pick up the timber. Haul that down to Newnum, pick up some milled board, and haul it out to Herrick. Then bobtail back up and park at my place here, then drive up the next morning to do it all over again."

Paisley listened as he recounted the route and could not help but think about how people love to tell a story if you let them.

"What's bobtail?" Hyacinth asked when the driver paused.

"It's when you drop your trailer and just drive the semi truck with nothing attached," he said.

"Oh, thanks," Hyacinth responded.

The driver continued his story. "I was driving back up late that night, and there usually isn't anyone out on the road at that time, except for maybe a few other truckers and such, but you have to stay on high alert because that's when deer and such'll dart out in front of you. So I'm rolling up the highway, probably about thirty miles outside of Frye, and a good hour until I get back to Howling Ivy, and I come up over this hill, and I see something out of the corner of my eye moving quick as a flash up ahead out in this corn field. I already got the high beams on, so there ain't much else I can do but slow down and try to see what it is. So I stop, throw my hazards on, grab my spotlight, that thing is at least a hundred thousand lumens, and I climb down out of the cab. Now, I'm not one to just stop in the middle of the road, especially right after a hill."

"Because people will come up over it and not have time to stop if they aren't paying attention?" Paisley asked.

"Yeah, and that particular hill is pretty bad. I've almost hit a few deer right there. Heck, that night, there was debris on the road, so I'm thinking that the thing I'm seeing out there in the field might be a hurt deer since it certainly doesn't have the shape and movement of any deer I've seen."

Paisley leaned in, propping the phone on the back of the passenger seat.

"So, I'm out there, and I get the light, and I'm trying to get a good spot on the thing, but as the light hits it, it leaps, must have been fifteen feet straight up, but it's moving so fast that it's in and out of the light in a split second. My first thought, with the way that it jumped, was that it looked like a squid, but then the way the legs hung down during the jump seemed sort of rigid. I thought maybe it looked more like a crab."

"A crab?"

"Hush, Paisley. I want to hear the rest," Hyacinth said.

The man didn't miss a beat and continued right where he'd left off.

"And boom, it's off, you know? Moving through the field at a wild speed, so I hop back in my rig and start hauling butt up the road trying to catch up to it, but it's moving faster than the truck is. Then, all of a sudden, it darts out in the road, cutting across about thirty feet in front of me. And I have to tell you, if that thing wasn't moving a hundred miles an hour, I would be shocked. Because it just flew across there. Moving any slower and I'd have pancaked it. I tried to slow down to watch where it went, but it was gone, didn't see it again. Heard a few folk tales that say it's been seen, but that was my only time seeing it."

"Did you get a good look at it with it moving that fast?" Paisley asked.

"Oh no, it was just a blur. I tried selling the story to the news, you know, but no one wanted it. I found a picture once, a blurry one, that sort of looked like the thing I saw on the road. I have it at home on my computer, but if you give me your email address I can send it to you."

"Paisley," Hyacinth said, "do not under any circumstance give your email address to the crazy man who just said he saw a giant, demon spider in a cornfield."

Paisley laughed. The driver did not, but Paisley could see in his eyes that he was smiling.

"Hey now, I can still hear you," he said.

"I'm sorry, sir, what was your name?" Paisley asked.

"I'm Mike," the driver said.

"I'm Paisley, and this, on the phone, is Hyacinth."

"Wait," Mike said. "Hyacinth, like in Hyacinth Bloom?"

"Jesus," Hyacinth said on the phone.

"And Paisley, dang, I can't remember. I'm sorry," he said.

"Mott," Paisley said.

"Right, Mott, dang, Mott. Paisley Mott and Hyacinth Bloom. What are you doing out here? Are you looking for the spider thing?"

"No, Mike, I'm out here just looking into some other stuff, but it would be great if you didn't mention that I was out here to anyone. Not everyone knows me, but almost everyone heard about what happened, so it would be better to not call attention to it if you don't mind?" Paisley asked.

"Oh, yeah, no problem. Can I tell my wife? She and I watched the whole thing on the internet. She follows both of you now."

"Yeah, but please ask her to keep it on the down low until I'm all finished, if you would?"

"Course, course. If you want, I can write my number down when we get to where you're going, and you can decide if you want me to send you the photo," Mike said.

"That sounds perfect, Thanks, Mike," Hyacinth said.

"Yes, perfect, thank you... what the fuck?" Paisley said in disbelief.

"Are you home?" Hyacinth asked. "Do you see it?"

As the car pulled off road and started up the long dirt drive, even in the dark, it was easy to spot the bright yellow beast that sat in front of the rental.

"Is that what I think it is?"

"It is! When you told me that you couldn't get a rental car, I decided to hire someone to drive it up there."

"Oh my God, Hyacinth, I don't even know what to say."

"You without it is like the Scooby Gang without their van," Hyacinth said.

"The Mystery Machine," both Mike and Paisley said in unison.

"The delivery guy said you weren't there so I told him to leave the keys under the driver seat," Hyacinth said.

The car stopped and Mike scribbled his info on a receipt and handed it to Paisley.

"Mike, thank you so much. I appreciate the ride and the

information. I'll message you if we need to see that photo. Five stars, my friend. Five stars," Paisley said, opening the door to get out.

"Bye, Mike," Hyacinth yelled.

"Thank you, it was great meeting you. Best of luck with whatever brought you up here," Mike said before the door closed. He drove off, and Paisley turned to look at the Hummer.

"Hyacinth, holy shit. I..." she stopped. The emotion caught her off guard. She wasn't used to anyone other than her dad, caring so much about her to know what she needed even before she did. And the Hummer was exactly what she needed. She'd felt trapped, claustrophobic, and lost since arriving in Howling Ivy, and having the vehicle that was so instrumental and connected to the events in Grey Water Ridge made her feel powerful and confident.

"I love you, Pais. I literally owe you my life. Giving you a car is the least I can do."

"I appreciate it. Thank you so much, Hy, really. I can't tell you how much this means to me. Are you sure you won't need it before I'm done out here?"

"Pais, listen to me, it's yours. I want you to have it. We'll take care of the paperwork when you get back." Hyacinth paused, "I mean, assuming you are coming back here when you are done..."

"Yes, I would like to, if that's okay?" she asked, her chest heavy with emotion.

"Of course, of course."

Paisley stood for a moment, admiring the Canary Yellow Hummer H2. It was bigger than any vehicle she ever wanted to drive, but there was something about it, this one particular that she loved.

"What am I going to call it?" she asked.

"What do you mean?" Hyacinth responded.

"You've never named your car?"

"No, have you?"

"I've never not."

"Well, what do you want to call it?"

Paisley thought for a minute, reliving everything that had got her to that moment. Thinking about why the vehicle was so important to her.

"Gunner. Short for Gunnerson," Paisley said.

Hyacinth was quiet for a moment, likely holding back the same tears Paisley was.

"For Boyd?" Hyacinth finally asked.

"For Boyd."

31

Hyacinth sat with her elbows on her desk, head in her hands, and stared at the blank screen in front of her. The usual creativity that flowed through her had turned viscous and refused to come.

Her marketing business suffered since the events that left her clinging to life. She hadn't completed a single project on her own, and the few folks she managed remotely had wrapped up their projects and were waiting on more.

But that work wasn't coming as Hyacinth stopped checking her email to see if there was more business. She opened her email once since that day and saw that there were requests to work with her because of what happened, and she didn't want anything to do with that. She wanted that to be as far from her mind as possible. So she just stopped looking.

Email wasn't the only thing she had stopped. Her social media accounts blew up with new followers, story requests, and comments of support. Her impressive follower count went up by four times in the first week after the incident. Headlines read: "Beautiful Heiress Escapes Death," and "Internet Celebrity Bound and Gagged," and the one she liked the least, "Heroic Sheriff Who Sacrificed Himself to Save His Girlfriend in Critical Condition."

She wasn't mad at Grover for trying to save her, and she wasn't mad that he missed the clues about Hollis; everyone did, including her, which bothered her a lot, but she was angry that now, when she needed him most, she had to be the strong one. When would she get to break down?

Rowan, who had suffered through all of this, as the accused for most of it, hadn't taken any physical damage from it. She had hoped that he would be there to help her, but instead, he disappeared for a while and then showed up to take care of Paisley. There was no question that Paisley needed support, too, but Rowan was her brother, the only one she had left, and she needed him.

The town was a mess. The church was without a head. The Sheriff's Department was without a head. The two things the town counted on the most, decapitated in one fell swoop. And for some reason, Hyacinth felt responsible for figuring it out.

The bottle of pills she was given to help with the pain called to her like a siren from their place in the medicine cabinet, where they sat unopened. Addiction hadn't ever been a problem, but only because she never did anything that would allow her to be an addict except work. She knew she was predetermined to suffer addiction. She had the gene. Her father was. Rowan wasn't, but that was because his genes were just a little different and he just never had to worry about that sort of thing. The physical pain had all but gone, but the emotional weight continued. At what point would it be too much?

Hyacinth picked up the phone and called the mental health emergency number that her therapist had given her for the third time in as many days.

32

Paisley sat in Gunner's driver seat. The soft leather of the steering wheel felt like comfort and strength in equal measure. She'd spent the better part of an hour there, messing with knobs and buttons, and programming the digital assistant. She selected a voice that was softer and quieter, not exactly like Boyd's, but close enough for Paisley. Combined with renaming the software in the recognition settings she was ready to test it out.

"Hey Gunner?" she said.

"Hello, Paisley," Gunner responded in his not completely robotic voice.

She wasn't sure exactly what she wanted to ask, but she wanted to talk to it. Talk to him.

"Um, what's the temperature right now?" she asked.

"Right now, the weather in Howling Ivy is partly cloudy and forty-six degrees Fahrenheit. Today, expect a high of fifty-eight and a low of thirty-eight."

She had adjusted the seats several times to get them back to where she had them in Grey Water Ridge. She was just about to accept that it was time to go inside when she remembered the receipt in her pocket.

"Gunner?"

"Hello, Paisley."

"Open messaging app," she said.

"Messaging app open. Who would you like to message?" Gunner asked.

Paisley gave the number on the receipt and then requested the photo.

"Gunner, message WhyItHurts,"

"Messaging WhyItHurts. Transcribing now," Gunner said.

Paisley spoke and Gunner transcribed. She was able to follow along on the large screen on the dash, but she did enjoy having Gunner's gentle voice read WhyItHurts side of the conversation to her.

WhyItHurts - *Did you get a chance to comb through the video?*

ParanormalOrNot - *Yeah, it took me a while, and I had to turn off the sound after a few viewings, but I watched it.*

WhyItHurts - *So, you saw the bag move before the screaming started?*

ParanormalOrNot - *Yeah, I saw that. I had hoped that maybe the screaming was coming from off-screen somewhere, but whoever was in that bag was still alive when they were set on fire.*

WhyItHurts - *According to the reports filed this video was entered into evidence in the death of Lydia Knot. So, it appears that your friend's sister was murdered in that video. With some digging, I found the location of the building and the name of the person who shot the video, who is also a suspect in the case, one Mr. Daniel Ryan Humphries age 26. He is currently serving time in the county jail for different charges. This was the last body accounted for in the serial killing and murder case. And since there hasn't been reports of another child taken, or another murder, it is officially cold.*

ParanormalOrNot - *Might be good to pay him a visit, if that's possible.*

WhyItHurts - *You think he knows something he hasn't told law enforcement?*

ParanormalOrNot - *I want to ask him about the camera.*

WhyItHurts - *I think he shot it on his phone. It was listed as evidence. This video would have never made it out had he not been broadcasting.*

ParanormalOrNot - *No, I mean the video camera.*

WhyItHurts - *What video camera?*

ParanormalOrNot - *In the video you can see that there is a camcorder laying on the ground just to the bottom left of the frame.*

WhyItHurts - *Let me look...*

ParanormalOrNot - *Well, that camera isn't present in any of the crime scene photos. Which means it likely disappeared before the cops got there, right? And the only person who had access to the scene was the kid filming.*

WhyItHurts - *Well I'll be damned. You are absolutely right. I can't believe I missed that. You think the kid took the camera?*

ParanormalOrNot - *Worth a chance to ask. Maybe there is evidence on it.*

WhyItHurts - *Great catch!*

ParanormalOrNot - *Thank you! Also, did you see the guy?*

WhyItHurts - *What guy? There was a guy?*

ParanormalOrNot - *Wait, you didn't see him either?*

WhyItHurts - *What guy??? Hold on...*

ParanormalOrNot - *The guy in the doorway.*

WhyItHurts - *The door to outside?*

ParanormalOrNot - *Yep.*

WhyItHurts - *I'm looking right now and see nothing. The door is only visible for like eight frames and I've looked at all eight and seen nothing. What are you seeing that I am not?*

ParanormalOrNot - *Aww, the student becomes the master and the master becomes the apprentice, ah?*

WhyItHurts - *Teach me, oh master Jedi.*

ParanormalOrNot - *You told me to relax and look for what I wanted to see, right? Not to look at what was there, but to look for the information that would give me the information I need.*

WhyItHurts - *I don't recall saying that, but if that is what you took from it, wonderful.*

ParanormalOrNot - *Well, I wanted to see out that door, so I tried to find a way to do it for every frame of the video, even when the door wasn't visible. So I moved forward, frame by frame. Until I saw it.*

WhyItHurts - *In the kerosene pool!*

ParanormalOrNot - *In the motherfucking kerosene pool.*

WhyItHurts - *I see him! Only for two frames or so, but he is there in the reflection of the kerosene! He looks pretty big! Do you think the police have seen this?*

ParanormalOrNot - *I have to imagine that they have. This video has been passed around the dark web a lot and you know how internet sleuths can be.*

WhyItHurts - *I can put a call into the department and find out if they've seen it yet.*

ParanormalOrNot - *Thank you. You're the best.*

The photo from Mike the Driver came back just as Paisley ended the call with WhyItHurts. As she expected, it was worthless. It showed a dark road with a blur that could have easily been a low-flying owl as it could have been a giant spider demon.

33

Scattered clothing littered the floor, and an old, bare futon mattress lay pushed against the far wall of the small space with Derry strewn across it. A ragged blanket wrapped tightly around him as if he had grabbed an end and rolled into it. Light from the old box television flickered like a dying lightning bug, spitting weak flashes that cast shadowy figures onto the walls from the stacks of junk piled haphazardly around the room. Four figures danced across the back wall with the movement of the light. Derry watched these figures as his eyelids filled with lead and he found it impossible to keep them open.

Directly above his bed, the shadows jerked to music that played through the headphones tucked into his ears. His dad had found an old portable CD player and brought it to Derry, who got it working again, using a few spare parts from items he had collected and an AC adapter power cord. Thanks to the fact that no one really kept them anymore he had a very impressive collection of old CDs by way of the dump.

Shadows undulated to the last few bars of "Supernova Goes Pop" by Powerman 5000 and then to silence before grooving to the heavy beats of "When Worlds Collide." Derry watched in amusement as the dancing shadows couldn't keep up with the pace of the rock songs that were years older than he was. Sleep was close and he could feel that he would not make it to the end of the song. He blinked a long, unmotivated blink and looked at the shadows as if to say goodnight. A fifth shadow had joined the quartet and was gyrating on the fake wood panel above his head.

Once-heavy eyelids peeled open watching the new, taller, wide shadow. Instead of swaying with the light it crossed his room, passing in front of the other shadows. The loud music that pumped into his head turned to noise as his brain struggled to make sense of the unsettling figure behind him.

If it was a burglar, they picked the wrong house as they had nothing. Whoever it was, Derry did not want them to know he was awake. He lay in the fetal position with his hands close to his face. He pulled the cord of the earbuds, plucking them from his ears. The sound nearly muted with the single soft tug, but he could still hear the thick drum beats from how one of the buds landed on the mattress near his face.

The four shadows danced where they had been all night, but the fifth slipped slowly away. The stacks that cast the shadows could only be a few feet tall, yet the shadows they cast went halfway up the wall. The fifth stretched even higher before shrinking and creeping toward the TV, then closer to Derry. The shadow took shape and was nearly as sharp as his own against the wall. The silhouette was smaller than he thought it would be, and the closer it got, the more certain he knew who it was. Derry closed his eyes tightly, wanting the shadow to vanish but not willing to look to see if it had. Behind him, a hand, pale and delicate, reached out for him.

"Please," a voice whispered.

Derry tensed, squeezing his eyes shut and hoping the moment would end.

There was nothing and then a familiar sound broke through. It was the banging of the steps against the side of the trailer. His eyes shot open and all the shadows disappeared, replaced by the light pouring in through the window. The motion light from the front porch was on. The metallic sound of the key hitting the lock on the front door jolted Derry out of bed.

The door to the trailer opened and his father stumbled in. The light in the hallway popped on and he watched as his old man stumbled past his door on the way to his bedroom in the back. He thought about calling after him as he went by. He thought about telling him about what he had seen, what he had heard. Depending on how drunk or high he was he would get one of two kinds of response from him. He would either be cruel and tell him that he wished he had died instead of Lydia, or, if he was really wasted, he would be sweet and tell him that he loved him. The latter was worse because he knew it was a lie.

He listened as he went into his bedroom and closed the door. The sound of him kicking off his work boots and falling into his bed limped down the hall. He stood there, not moving, until he could hear his gentle snore. Then he laid on the floor in the hall, being sure to leave space for his dad to make it to the bathroom if he needed to, and fell asleep. He didn't see the figure floating at the end of the hallway, watching him sleep, and wishing she could rest, too.

34

Patch bound up the loose steps leading up to Derry's door. He'd been making that trek nearly every day for years. He wasn't one for running, but there he was excited about getting over there to see his buddy.

Derry had been his best friend since the day they had met. Not that there was a lot of competition for the job. Patch had not only been the largest kid in his class, but the largest kid in his entire school. By the time he was in the eighth grade Patch had already surpassed all of the kids at the school in height, and all but Winslow Peck in town. Winslow was seven feet tall and Patch was pushing six-foot-eight. If Winslow, Winnie, to those who loved him, which was nearly everyone, was the type to mess around on his wife, which he was not, many would say he was Patch's real father.

Patch had been a four-year starter as a Howling Ivy Coyote on the offensive line. He just had to stand there and push. He would wait for the quarterback to tell him which way to shove people on each play. It wasn't just the fact that he weighed nearly twice as much as the other kids at 385 pounds, but that carrying that much weight is one hell of a workout. Patch built up a lot of muscle in the tree trunks he called legs. He didn't fit the typical football lineman personality. If you asked any of the other kids on the team or even his coaches, they would tell you that Patch was too soft for the game. He worried about hurting people. A few colleges called him to try out and after just talking to him for a minute or two, they realized he would be a bad investment.

That was how the world saw Steven Simply. The boy they all just called Sour Patch, or Patch for short. A name he earned from the kids at school when his teeth started falling out early on. His diet of nothing but sugar-filled foods, soda, and the all too often hits from the pipe his mother shared with him before his grandmother finally kicked her out, was surely to blame. Steven had been eating a package of Sour Patch Kids one morning at school, and had just put a handful into his mouth. He reached forward and smacked the kid in the desk in front of him, which just happened to be Bryce Tiller, the starting quarterback of the football team. The same Bryce Tiller that had to tell him which way to push kids in football games. Bryce turned around to see what sort of nonsense the kid was getting into this time. When he looked at Steven, the kid had chewed the candies to the point that they had become a multicolored blob in his mouth. He stuck the blob to his teeth, making it look like a mouth guard, and smiled at his quarterback.

Bryce later recounted the story to the rest of the football team and told them that he couldn't tell the difference between the disgusting, sticky goop and the few remaining teeth that Steven still had in his head. And that was how Steven Simply became "Sour Patch." The nickname didn't bother him much. It bothered Derry a lot more, but Derry didn't have the size, the skill, or the influence to turn that particular ship. Instead, he embraced his friend's moniker and shortened it to Patch. After a few months of shouting "Patch!" in the halls and painting the revised nickname on a sign to hold up at football games, everyone seemed to follow suit and he became just Patch. The lovable giant everyone liked, but no one really wanted to be friends with.

Patch hit the front door to the trailer and pushed it open. This was the morning routine. Derry would get up early and unlock the door so Patch could just come in when he got there. The routine hadn't changed since Derry's sister disappeared. Before, Patch would come in and help Derry get his sister ready. Patch had watched hours of videos about braiding hair just so that he could do Lydia's. Sometimes, if Patch had enough left over from either paycheck from the pizza joint or the salvage yard, he would bring a flat package of frosted cherry rolls, or a sleeve of mini donuts. On days he didn't have money he would come over with a few slices of bread to pop in the toaster Derry had salvaged from one of his dad's dump boxes.

Even though Lydia was gone, and he didn't need to get there earlier to help, he still showed up at the exact same time. No sense in upsetting the system and calling attention to the person no longer there. It was the only time Patch was ever on time for anything.

"Hey, buddy," Derry said as Patch lumbered into the room, exhausted from the hustle across the street and through the trailer park.

"Sup," Patch wheezed as he dropped into an old recliner that was once yellow or gold, but dirt and use clung to it, making it an unsightly brown tint. Derry had been heading back toward the hallway when he stopped. He didn't turn toward Patch. Instead, he just stared down the hall.

"I had a dream last night," he said.

"Yeah?" Patch answered, failing to push the recliner back and flip out the footrest. "Was it the one about the girl at the Goodwill that gots the one eye and big boobs, again?"

Derry turned to look at Patch.

"That was your dream. Not mine."

"Well, yeah. But it was so good that I thought maybe you'd want to see it." Patch gave up trying to recline the chair and flipped his ludicrously large feet onto the busted sofa.

"No, man. No. I don't want to see it."

"Why not? Her boobs are like out to here," Patch said, holding his hands up in front of his chest, then looking at them and moving them a little farther out.

"I've seen that woman over at the Goodwill, and her chest is nowhere near that big."

"How do you know it was the same girl?"

"How many women do you know with one eye that work at the Goodwill?" Derry asked.

"Well, I don't know."

"So I'm pretty sure that her chest isn't that large."

"Okay, but in my dream it was."

"I'll accept that in your dream they were that big if you accept that in real life they are not."

"What was your dream about, if not a ridiculously-large breasted woman with one eye?"

"I thought I heard Lydia again," Derry said.

Patch swung his feet back onto the floor, sat up, and leaned forward.

"In your dream?" he asked.

"I think so. Because I saw something too."

"Was it her?" Patch stood. His head was just a few inches below the ceiling. Normally he hunched over. It was his default posture so people weren't so intimidated around him, but when his friend was upset, he stood upright, fully engaged.

"I..." Derry started, then just nodded his head.

Patch was on the other side of the room but closed the gap with a long stride and wrapped his friend in his arms.

"I'm sorry, dude," Patch said and squeezed. "Tell me about it."

Derry pulled himself free and sat on the arm of the couch.

"I was laying there, listening to music, and I had the TV on. I saw something. It was like she was standing behind me. I could see her shadow on the wall. I knew it was her, Patch. I freaking knew it was her, and I was so scared that I couldn't even turn around. I couldn't turn around and look at my own sister."

"Why not?"

"I was afraid she would..." he paused, sniffled, and continued. "I was afraid she wouldn't look like herself. That she'd be..."

"Burned up?" Patch finished for him.

Derry nodded, tears glimmering in his eyes.

"I'm sorry, dude." Patch dropped to his knees, the trailer, if not the world, shook and he took his friend into his arms again. Derry put his head on Patch's shoulder.

As tall as he was, Patch had never had anyone hug him and place their head on his shoulder. This was a first for him. His friend was hurting. He did the only thing he could think to do,

154

something he had seen in movies his whole life, and he put his hand on Derry's head, which nearly covered it completely.

"What the fuck was that noise?" a voice pierced the relative quiet.

Patch looked up and saw Derry's dad standing at the end of the hall. Gerry Knot was only 35 but looked like he was in his mid-fifties. The years hung off of him like old newspaper stuck to a chain link fence in a windstorm.

"What gay shit are you two doing out here and why the fuck is it so loud?" he growled.

Derry pushed Patch back and stood up. He said nothing, he just looked up at his father.

"What are you out here banging around?"

Derry's head dipped, but he still said nothing. Patch stepped in front of him.

"I'm sorry, Mr. Knot. I was being stupid and horsing around. Derry was trying to get me to stop, but I'm sort of a boulder, as my grandma says."

"Boy, you're a whole ass mountain," Derry's dad said.

"Yes, sir," Patch replied.

"Well, shut the fuck up. I had to work late. I don't want you boys out here making all sorts of fucking noise," he said. Then, he turned and disappeared into the dark room at the end of the hall, slamming the door behind him.

"You okay, dude?" Patch asked.

"Yeah."

"Finish getting ready. I got something for us," Patch said, reaching into his jacket pocket and pulling out a sandwich baggy. He held it up and showed it off to Derry like it was drugs. Two slices of thick bread were tucked into the baggy.

"Is that brioche?" Derry said, raising his eyebrows.

"It's bread," Patch said, looking at his friend sideways. "I'm going to make us some toast, my dude!"

"Thanks, Patch." He patted his friend on the arm before moving down the hall to finish his morning routine.

"Course."

* * *

Minutes later Derry came out into the living room with his jacket and backpack on.

"You look like you're on your way to your first day of kindergarten or some shit," Patch said, holding the toast up to Derry.

"Is that ketchup?" Derry asked, smelling the sweet toasted bread.

"Yeah, you didn't have butter or anything," Patch said.

"Thanks, man." Derry took a bite. "You know, tomatoes are actually fruit. So ketchup is technically jelly."

"Sick."

35

Blurry figures merged as Millicent opened her eyes. The man stood over her, his expression jagged from frustration. He held a hammer.

"Why don't you just go?" he said. "I don't understand."

"I want to go home," Millicent said.

The man threw the hammer and it banged off of a shelf somewhere across the basement. A light brown blur darted beneath the dryer. Squeakers stealthily moved from the dryer to the washer, and then behind the man.

"I'm just done with this!" the man yelled and went up the stairs.

Once she heard the click of the door lock, Millicent sat up and reached out. Squeakers, as they normally did, ran across the floor and climbed into her hand.

"Were you trying to protect me, Squeakers?" Millicent asked, pushing her face close to the mouse so they could nuzzle nose to nose.

Banging came from upstairs as voices rose.

"You have to get rid of her," the woman's voice said.

"You don't think I have tried?!" the man roared.

"We have to get out of here," Millicent said to Squeakers. "I think he's going to kill me."

36

In the cramped confines of the visiting facility Paisley sat across from Danny at a small metal table bolted to the ground.

A guard stood at the far end of the narrow cinder block room. Additional metal tables separated the guard from where Paisley and Danny sat, but she was confident that the guard could cover the distance without issue if something happened. In movies and shows, the inmates would be led into the visitation area wearing shackles, but he just sat across from her, free to move about. She surprised herself with a feeling of gratitude that he wasn't restrained. She wasn't afraid. Danny wasn't a violent criminal. He had just been arrested on drug charges a few too many times. And from what she understood, he had been cleared of any connection to the murders other than interrupting one.

Danny was a thin man with lots of random tattoos, thinning brown hair that hung ragged around his head, and a barely-there beard and mustache combo that looked more like it was drawn on. He wore the standard tan jumpsuit that was commonplace on TV, yet it looked more like nurse's scrubs than it did prison attire. He sat leaned back with his arms crossed as if he didn't give a shit about anything or anyone.

"Who the fuck are you? You the new attorney? You're kind of young, aren't you?" Danny asked. He was putting on an accent. Not a regional one, but more of a social one. The kind that represented a thug to someone who perhaps only ever saw one in the movies.

"If I am?" Paisley asked.

"If you are what?"

"If I am your lawyer? What then? Is that the impression you want to make to the person who is supposed to be fighting for

158

your right to due process?"

Danny sat up, uncrossed his arms, and put his hands on the table.

"Are you?" he asked. His voice had returned to a less caricatured version of a gangster.

"I'm sorry to say that I am not," she told him. "I'm just an investigator looking to help solve a crime."

"The girl?" Danny said, leaning back in the chair but keeping his hands on the table.

"Yes, Lydia Knot. I understand you were there the night she died."

"It's always the girl, man. Why don't anyone ever come talk to me for me? You, the cops, the hot fed lady. Y'all only ever want to talk about her, the girl. She's dead. There isn't anything you can do for her, but someone could help me. I'm still here." Danny patted his hand against his chest for emphasis.

Paisley wasn't allowed to wear her camera into the jail, so she tried her best to remember everything since she couldn't analyze it all later.

"I'm sorry, Danny. I think we all just want to avoid what happened to her from happening to anyone else."

"He's done, man. He killed that kid and ran off, and no one has seen or heard from him since. He's done," he said.

"And I don't think you get enough credit for that."

"Huh?"

"I don't think you get enough credit for that. You scared him off. There was nothing you could do to save that little girl. You going into that room when you did stopped that man from doing it again. At least for a while. We want to catch him before he gets the nerve to try and do it again."

"I burned my hands trying to get her out of that bag, you know that?" Danny held up his hands. Burn scars stippled across his palms and down his wrists.

"I didn't know that."

Danny crossed his arms again, but this time, it wasn't as if he was trying to show he didn't care. This was a position of pride, but not wanting to show that he needed the validation.

"So you're a cop?" he said, raising the corner of his mouth in a flirtatious smile. "You look too young to be a cop."

"No, Danny, I'm not a cop. But I am an investigator," she said.

"Oh like a P.I. or some shit?"

"Yeah, the some shit part," she said, leaning back and mirroring his body language.

"I told the cops everything I seen, so I don't know what I could tell you."

"I have two questions, and that's it. Will you answer them for me?" She leaned forward and put her arms on the table, hoping that he would follow along. It was a trick she had picked up on criminologist's Tiktok. He did. He leaned forward resting his forearms on the metal table.

"Okay," he said. "Ask your two questions."

"Did you see the man before he ran out?" she asked.

"I told everyone, I didn't see him at all. I was too busy trying to get her out of the bag."

"Okay, second question. What happened to the camera?"

Danny's whole body seemed to perk up.

She looked over his shoulder checking to make sure the guard was not within earshot.

"Yo, what camera? I don't know what you are talking about."

"In the video you shot, there is what appears to be a video camera. But it wasn't in the crime scene photos and it wasn't listed in the items recovered from the scene. So what happened to it?"

Danny contemplated his answer.

"Damn, man. I don't know what you are talking about," he said.

"I think you do."

"My dude must have dropped it, okay? But it was broke. I snatched it up to see if I could get somethin' for it. Not like he needed it. And, like I said, it was broke. So I stashed it so I could try to move it later. Damn, I knew I should have taken it with me that night."

"Where is the camera now?" she asked.

"Still stashed," he laughed. "I been up in here since that next morning. My reward for stopping a killer was to throw my white ass in jail. At least they let me watch one last fireworks show before they took my freedom. Fucking fascists."

"Well, it is my understanding that, when they caught up to you, you had quite a few warrants out for your arrest anyway that had everything to do with the sale of illegal substances and nothing to do with Lydia Knot."

"Yo, man. Can you stop saying her name and shit? That fucks with me," he said, putting his head in his hands. "They wouldn't have caught me at all if I wouldn't have gone to the hospital the next day cause the pain in my hands was too much."

"You didn't turn yourself in?"

"Nah, I'm not an idiot."

"So how did they know where to find her?"

"I don't know, man. They said they found her and were looking for who did it. I had to show them the live stream to prove it wasn't me."

"Will you tell me where you put the camera?"

"Nah, I don't think I'm going to be rattin' myself out like that, even if you ain't a cop."

"You said you were going to try and sell the camera, right? Let me buy it from you. How much were you expecting to get for a broken video camera?"

"Thousand dollars," Danny said, but even he couldn't help but to chuckle at the number.

"Seriously though, how much?" she asked again.

"It doesn't matter. It's not like they're going to let you just reach across the table here and hand me a wad of cash. And even if they did, they sure wouldn't let me keep it."

"Well, clearly if you think it is worth a *wad of cash* we have very different ideas of how much a broken camcorder is worth," Paisley said.

161

"Ha, you right, but still, money doesn't do me any good unless you want to put something on my books for commissary." This wasn't a question. He was just pointing out that he was limited.

"What do you mean, put it on your books?" she asked.

"I mean, you can give the prison money and I get credit in this little store here where I can buy overpriced noodles, or flip flops for the shower, and shit."

"Oh, okay. How much would I have to put on to get the location of the camera?" she asked.

"Shiiiiiit, lady. You sure you ain't no cop? You're pretty good at this. Okay, how about five hundred? That'll set me up in peanut butter crackers and Hershey bars until I'm out of here."

"You sure you aren't in here for robbery?" Paisley joked.

Danny laughed and nodded his head in approval.

"That camera isn't worth five hundred dollars," she said.

"No, maybe not, but it isn't the only thing in my stash, ya dig?" he said.

"I won't take anything else. I promise."

He did another check to make sure the guard wasn't listening but leaned in just to ensure they couldn't hear anyway.

"There are things in there that a middle class white lady like yourself would probably not appreciate finding. So as I'm sure you wouldn't take anything, I'm sure you would probably take the time to pour bleach or some shit on it, then it's worthless to me."

"Ah, I see," Paisley said. This is not where she thought she would be. Sitting in prison, negotiating with a drug dealer about not stealing the drugs that were currently hidden with a camera that could have evidence of a string of grisly murders.

"So you see my problem?" Danny asked.

"That is a predicament." She thought for a moment. "Okay, tell you what, I'll put a hundred on the books for you if you tell me where the stash is."

"A hundo? You think my stash is that worthless?"

"I think given my risk in this investment, yes. It's been

months, we don't even know if it is still there. And I can't guarantee you'll tell me the truth anyway. So I could just put the money on the books and then come up empty handed."

"No one would find my stash, trust me, it's still there. And I don't lie," Danny said.

This Paisley actually believed.

"And what about my risk?" Danny asked. "What if I tell you and you run out of here without putting the money on the books? What then?"

"Okay, fair point. Here's the deal. You tell me where the camera is, and I will put a hundred on the books now. When I am doing that, I will get the number of the admin so that if or when I find the camera, I can call and put on another hundred. Seems like a pretty good deal. What do you say?"

"But what's protecting me if I tell you and you don't stop and put the money on the books and instead just go raid my stash?"

"If I walk out of here and don't put the money on the books, you just walk over to that guard there. You tell him that the lady that was in here is on the way to a stash, that you all of a sudden remember the location of, and will soon be in the possession of illegal narcotics. Then I'll be sitting right here next to you." She smiled, leaning back in her chair with earned pride.

"Haha, damn, lady, maybe you should be my lawyer," he said. "Deal."

37

The factories contrasted the afternoon sun, casting the facades into shadow. The lumbering towers stood like giant headstones, marking the resting place of some long-past relic.

Finding the shoe factory was easy enough and, when she pulled up in front, the place looked more than deserted, it looked void. Void of color, of life, of everything. The building aged faster than those around it, which were also old and rundown. Could a traumatic experience age a place the way it does a person?

"I'm taking you with me," Paisley said as she popped her headphones in.

"Smart," Hyacinth said in her ear. "Which is to say that nothing about this is smart, but at least you're showing some sense of awareness while you mosey on into an abandoned factory that you know exactly two things about. The first, a known drug dealer operated out of it. The second, what was the second thing? Oh, yes, someone was violently murdered there."

Paisley stepped out of the car with her backpack and had the live stream going through a pin of a black cat with a knife in its mouth, and she knew that Hyacinth was also watching it, though there was a delay, so she kept her on the phone as well. She also assumed that WhyItHurts was watching, though he had not responded to her last message saying she would be going out there.

"Wait," Paisley said, reaching into her backpack for her flashlight. Then she removed one of her earbuds and put it in her pocket. "Only one headphone. Situational awareness, you know?"

"Smart," Hyacinth agreed.

Danny's instructions were fairly simple, and Paisley recited them as she walked.

"On the west side of the building, there is a ramp that goes up to dock E," she said. She had parked directly in front of dock E, so she followed the ramp up. "Look for a piece of plywood on the bottom right of the locked roll-up door."

"Is that it?" Hyacinth asked, knowing that what she saw was a few seconds behind but still trying to be helpful.

"Yep, I think so," Paisley said. "Then he said I have to pull it back, and I may need a hammer."

Paisley pulled on the board and the dry plywood turned to something akin to dust in her hands. It crumbled, revealing a square vent roughly two feet by two feet. Paisley knelt down and shined the flashlight into it. The beam went down a long way before hitting a wall that appeared to have passages on both the left and the right.

"He said I'd have to crawl about half the length of a football field, then I would want to turn right..." Paisley stopped. She wasn't allowed to take anything in to write down the directions, so when she got back to Gunner she typed them in her phone and sent them to Hyacinth.

"The message says left," Hyacinth said.

"No, I think he said that whatever I did I was *not* to go left, right?" Paisley asked, starting her crawl into the tunnel.

"I don't know, I wasn't there. I'd say you have about half a football field worth of crawling to figure it out though."

"Funny," Paisley said.

The air in the tunnel tasted flat, and Paisley worried that if she breathed too deeply, it could poison her.

"Hyacinth?"

"Yes?"

"Can air expire?"

Hyacinth laughed on the other end of the phone.

"Um, I don't think so."

"You mind just giving that a quick Google search and finding out? Because this shit tastes way past its expiration date."

"Yeah, let me get right on that, on my computer, so the NSA thinks I'm the idiot when they check my search history."

"Okay, which way?" Paisley asked.

"I don't know. All I can see is the ground. What do you see?" Hyacinth replied.

"Oh, sorry about that," Paisley said, pointing her pin down the right corridor and then the left, illuminating them the best she could. She waited a moment for the feed to catch up. "So, which way?"

"Paisley, the feed is breaking up. I think the signal is getting weak. I can still hear you just fine on the call, but I think we are going to lose video streaming. Yep, there it went, it's frozen."

Paisley's anxiety mounted, and knowing that no one had eyes on her pitched it up another degree. She held it together but worried that if she didn't get free of the tunnels soon, she'd really panic. She examined both directions with her light and then closed her eyes. She replayed the conversation with Danny in her head.

"Pais?"

"One sec," Paisley said, not opening her eyes. The more her nerves escalated, the clearer her memory.

She was there in the jail with him. She started to talk with Danny's accent.

"Okay, he said *crawl through that tiny ass tunnel for about half the length of a football field.*" Paisley said, talking to herself in Danny's voice.

"Then I said I didn't like football, and he said, *but you seen a fucking football field before, right?* And I said yes."

"Then he said that *it was half that fucking long. Then when you get to the end you go...* blank, *now don't forget that, because if you go right you'll be crawling around in there for days.*"

"So left. *Then when you get to the end you go left, now don't forget that, because if you go right you'll be fucking crawling around in there for days.*"

Then she was back in the tunnel on her hands and knees, her voice was hers again. "Left, we go left."

"Then let's go," Hyacinth said.

Paisley had barely moved when a shrill, piercing screech assaulted her ears.

"Jesus, what is that?" Hyacinth asked. Paisley could just barely make out her voice.

"I don't know, but it sounds like it's in here with me."

She looked back and saw the dying light of the sinking sun. She could head back that way, but whatever was in the tunnel with her sounded like it wasn't far and that it was closing in.

"Shit, I don't know which way it's coming from," Paisley yelled. She hoped that Hyacinth could hear her. She needed guidance. Mercifully, the screech broke. Like keys on a deathly typewriter, clacking sounds ticked up the tunnel, proceeding a low, ghostly moan.

"Can you hear that?" Paisley whispered.

"I can," Hyacinth whispered. "It sounds like a spider?"

"What?!" Paisley blurted before catching herself and quieting. "What? Why would you say that? Jesus, and why are you whispering, you're not the one stuck in a fucking coffin waiting for death to come around the corner?"

"Sorry. I just mean, it sounds like when a tarantula taps the glass..."

"Hy, shut the fuck up about the tarantula at this particular moment, will you, please? I'm in a bit of a situation and I am actively trying not to shit my pants."

"Right. Sorry, girl. Let's get you out of there."

Paisley started to retreat toward the entrance, but something grabbed her.

"Oh, god!"

"What?!" Hyacinth cried through the phone.

"Fuck." Paisley sighed with relief. "Nothing. My backpack got caught on the ceiling of the tunnel," Paisley said.

"Pais?" Hyacinth said. After a beat, "Paisley?"

"Yeah." She was trying not to hyperventilate with the sounds of something moving closer to her in the tunnel.

"Take a deep breath and listen. Listen to the sound. Listen

for the sound once, and then listen for an echo. The sound will come first, even if by a split second. When you hear it, move the other direction," Hyacinth said.

Without question, Paisley did as Hyacinth said. She took a deep breath and let it out.

The moaning sounded winded, tired. Then the clacks. It was the clacks. It sounded like there were so many of them, but it was just the echo.

"Right," Paisley said. She crawled as fast as she could in the opposite direction, away from the sound.

"Go!" Hyacinth cheered.

The screech erupted, seemingly spurred on by giving chase. Paisley's palms slapped the rough concrete, propelling her forward. The sound filled the tunnel behind her, building pressure like Paisley was a bullet and the tunnel was the barrel of a gun.

One turn, then a short straightaway. It took no more than a minute of crawling, but it felt like an eternity, before she came to a dead-end.

"Jesus, a dead-end," Paisley yelled over the deafening sound coming toward her.

"Oh shit," Hyacinth said.

The fear in her voice came through the line and hit Paisley in the gut. To have someone who loved her so much was not lost on her. And if she died there, with her friend on the line, she would be-

"Fuck me to tears," Paisley yelled as she interrupted her own thought. "It goes up!"

Paisley reached the end of the tunnel and threw the flashlight and the backpack through the opening above. Then she spun around, dropping to her butt so that she could make a move to stand up. The screeching stopped.

"Paisley?" Hyacinth asked.

"Shhhh. It's here."

The hair stood up on Paisley's arms. She couldn't see what was in front of her. She could just hear its presence. Its breathing. Labored and thin. The light she had thrown overhead did nothing to illuminate the horror that stood a few feet away. It smelled dirty, and old.

The thing in front of her, agonized and strained for oxygen. She tried to calm herself, to be prepared for anything.

Still in Paisley's ear, Hyacinth held back screams in fear for her friend.

Click, clack. Click, clack. Click, clack.
The thing crept in closer.

38

Hyacinth sat in her kitchen, behind the dark screen of the laptop on the table, her phone to her ear, listening as her friend sat helplessly in the dark, some unknown creature preparing to attack. She wanted to talk to her and scream for her, but Paisley had urged her to be quiet.

A noise came from the doorway, and Hyacinth jumped, covering her mouth and bottling a scream.

"Oh no, I'm sorry," Grover said, rushing to her as best he could in his condition.

Hyacinth held her finger to her mouth, quieting Grover. He must have seen the worried look on her face because he whispered to her, his mouth making exaggerated movements, the sound nearly inaudible.

"Is everything okay?"

Hyacinth just shook her head.

"Paisley?" he asked in the same quiet way.

Hyacinth nodded. She tried not to cry.

Then, something happened.

The screen on her laptop fluttered and there was light. The feed was back. The feed was dark, but Paisley must have been getting enough signal to broadcast again.

Grover's face contorted and he tilted his head as if it would help him identify whatever was happening.

Click, clack. Click, clack.

The sound through the speakers caused Hyacinth's hair to stand on end.

The screen shifted again. The camera was trying to auto-focus on something in the dark.

"Paisley," Hyacinth whispered. "The camera is back. You

have to move right now. Go."

The camera focused. Light reflected off of two orbs, floating in the darkness, colorless and dead. They moved forward.

"Fuck," Paisley shouted.

There was a commotion, but it was impossible to determine what was happening. The loud screech returned. It grew overwhelmingly loud, and Hyacinth had to pull the phone away from her face.

Audible shrapnel tore through the phone.

"Paisley!" Hyacinth screamed.

The delay was agonizing. She knew in a moment she would see something.

"Fuck," the feed echoed.

Hyacinth and Grover watched as the world spun incoherently for a few seconds. He put his hand on her shoulder and she, without realizing it, had grabbed it.

The camera leveled out as it was clear that Paisley had made it out. The screeching was muted and sounded underground. Paisley turned, and Hyacinth could see that she was in a garage of some sort.

"Is that a loading dock?" Grover asked.

Hyacinth did not respond. She just listened to the horrible sounds from the phone and watched Paisley on camera. The two did not match up. The sound on the phone stopped abruptly, and was replaced with thin, agonal breathing.

Paisley picked up the flashlight. The sounds stopped as soon as she shined the light into the hole.

"Mother fucker," Paisley said. It must have been loud enough for the microphone on the pin to pick up, but not the earbud.

Paisley tilted the pin down to capture what was in the hole. There, just a few feet below, was a very large opossum. It looked up at the camera, revealing the earbud that it munched on.

"You there?" Paisley said through the phone.

Hyacinth hit the speaker button.

"Paisley, what the fuck?" Hyacinth said, before bursting into hysterical laughter.

On screen, Paisley pulled the other earbud from her pocket and put it in her ear.

"You there?" Paisley said before Grover muted the laptop.

"That was intense," Hyacinth finally said when the laughter died down.

"You're telling me," Paisley said. "I'm pretty sure I clenched my butt so hard that I will be pulling underwear out of my ass for at least a month."

"Haha, Paisley, just wanted you to know that you are on speaker phone, and Grover is here now, he was very worried."

"Hi Paisley. Glad you are okay. Sorry about your underwear," he said, giving Hyacinth a wink.

"Well, hello, Grover. I hope you are feeling well. Thank you for almost witnessing my tragic demise," Paisley said. Then added, clearly distracted by something else, "motherfucker."

"What?" Hyacinth and Grover asked in unison.

"Look," Paisley said, and paused, waiting for the video to catch up.

Hyacinth and Grover watched as Paisley turned toward a source of light. It was a doorway. She walked toward it. It led outside. As Paisley approached, the camera adjusted, and there, just a few hundred feet away, sat Gunner. His yellow body bathing in the sun.

"Wait, you mean?" Hyacinth started.

"Yep, that little shit was fucking with me," Paisley said.

39

With the sunlight slowly slipping away, Paisley hurried to finish out the instructions and hoped they hadn't contained more erroneous nonsense. She had followed the instructions that had her climb up on a piece of machinery, shimmied across a gantry crane, and dropped into a small crows nest overlook. She scanned the production floor of the abandoned plant and thought about all the people who must have once worked there. Thousands, likely. And this was one of the smaller factories that lay dormant there. How many people had lost their livelihood when the town shuttered up? How many of them couldn't escape to a different life?

"Pais, how on earth do you plan to get down from there?" Hyacinth asked through the earbud.

The narrow metal staircase that originally served the little overlook had all but disintegrated.

"Well, he didn't tell me how to get down, he just told me how to get up here," Paisley said. "I'll figure that out after I find the camera."

"Is it up here?" Hyacinth asked.

"He said move the file cabinet." There was a file cabinet up there, but it was large and looked difficult to move. She grabbed the front and tried to pivot it out of the way and was surprised with the ease at which it moved.

Beneath the cabinet was a hole, as Danny had promised. The hole was no more than eight inches wide and a foot long.

"He said to reach into the hole and feel around until I find a rope," Paisley said, shining her light into the dark. The light bounced off of something.

"Is that an electrical wire?" Grover said. He had remained mostly quiet during Paisley's adventure, minus telling her twice that she should leave and notify law enforcement that she had the whereabouts of potential evidence in an open investigation. And that she was actively participating in a breaking and entering and trespassing situation.

She had, of course, ignored him.

By the time Hyacinth and Grover had seen what he thought was an electrical wire, Paisley had already grabbed it, thanks to the delay.

"Well I sure am glad that it was not or I'd be catching some volts right now," Paisley said, as she tugged the rope up out of the hole, dragging a tied up garbage bag with it.

"Thank goodness," Grover said.

"I have it," Paisley said.

Paisley took a breath and dumped the bag carefully onto the concrete floor of the overlook.

Even with caution, the camera spilled out of the bag, bounced hard off the ground, and tumbled end over end toward the hole.

"Shit," Paisley yelled, launching herself forward to catch it.

"What?" Hyacinth asked.

"I almost dropped the camera down the hole," she said. "Danny specifically said to be careful because that hole is like an endless fall into the dark. So anything that goes down there isn't coming back."

"Are those drugs?" Grover asked.

"Huh?" Paisley responded.

"There, on the ground. They were in the bag. Are those drugs?" He sounded like a Sheriff again.

Paisley missed that more than she realized. She hadn't known Grover all that well before he was hurt, but she appreciated his presence.

"Oh, yeah," Paisley said, looking at the other contents of the bag. There was an old single burned cooking Sterno, a roll of copper wire, some random junk, and two small bundles wrapped with plastic wrap and secured around the middle in both directions with duct tape. "I guess I should have mentioned that there was the possibility that I would come across some illegal narcotics on this little adventure."

"That's a lot of product, Paisley. You should definitely call the police now," Grover said.

"What product?" Paisley said as she pushed her foot to the packages and gave them a hard shove. The packages tumbled across the floor and disappeared through the hole.

"Now you are tampering with evidence," Grover said.

"I don't know what you are talking about. I was just stretching. Did something happen?"

"Real funny, Paisley," Grover said.

The camera was definitely broken. It took a hard fall.

"Damn, I don't think this is going to do me any good?" Paisley said, holding it up.

"Let me see," Hyacinth said.

"Give it a second," Paisley said.

And in a moment Hyacinth responded.

"Oh, I had one similar to that. It's pretty old. It should have microtapes in it. Can you check? There should be an eject button on top."

Paisley fumbled around with the unit and found what she believed was the button. She pressed it. A small door on the side popped open revealing a small video cassette tape.

"That's it," Hyacinth said.

"But how do I watch it?"

"Well, I'm sure there's a place around there somewhere that can digitize the footage," Grover said.

"I didn't see a Radio Shack in town," Paisley said. "I'm sure Derry could do it, but there is a solid chance that this tape contains footage of his sister's murder."

"I can do it," Hyacinth offered. "Overnight it to me. I have the equipment here."

"Of course you do," Grover said, and a kiss could be heard on their end of the line.

"Awesome, thanks, Hy. You're amazing," Paisley said to the live stream. "Now to get down from here."

Danny had to have gotten down somehow. She went to the opening where the stairs once were, and she could see it. She didn't like it, but she could see it. There was a pole a few feet out that was left over from the stairs. It looked sturdy enough, and she thought that if she could reach it, she could likely slide down it onto the pile of debris that used to be the stairs. She would have to slow herself during descent so as not to risk impaling herself on the mess below, but that shouldn't be too hard. The hard part was reaching the pole. She would have to lean all the way out, and then leap a little to be able to reach it. Missing probably didn't mean death, but it certainly meant serious injury.

"If this doesn't work, delete my browser history," Paisley said.

"Don't do it," Grover replied.

"I don't think I have a choice," Paisley said.

Before she was ready to attempt the jump, she needed to return what was left of the stash. She scooped everything back into the bag, minus the camera and the drugs that were now lost forever. Before closing the bag she discreetly pulled an envelope with some extra cash from her inner jacket pocket and tucked it in before securing it and dropping it back into the hole. A little something for the inconvenience of the lost packages. She was not sure that the few hundred dollars she left would be enough to cover it, but she would call it even for almost allowing her to get eaten by the rodent in the tunnel just for the sake of a joke.

She shoved the file cabinet back over the hole, making sure that it was completely covered.

"Okay, let's do this," she said with sheer determination.

"That looks too far," Grover said.

Paisley grasped what was left of the handrail still connected to the wall, and used it to lean as far as she could out over the gap. Her fingers wiggled just a few inches short of the pole.

"Damn," she said.

"Just hang tight. Call emergency services and the fire

department will come rescue you," Grover suggested.

"Nope," Paisley said. She spun her backpack around to her front and dug in it, pulling out a length of cord. She flipped open a pocket knife, cut off a piece, and tied it around the handrail. "Boom, there."

"What?" Hyacinth asked, waiting on the delay.

Paisley grabbed the cord and used the added length to lean out over the gap even farther and grab the pole. The rest wasn't as agile as she had hoped. When she let go, her foot slipped, and her heart nearly came up her throat. She let go of the cord and grabbed the pole with both hands, saving herself from a horrific fall into scrap metal. The controlled slide went well enough, and with some careful foot placement, she was down and out of the building just a few minutes after returning the file cabinet.

As exciting as the adventure to recover the camera had been, Paisley knew when she edited everything together she would have to be careful to not show locations, or too many identifying things, including the stash spot. The more pressing issue was to find out what was on that tape. Though, had she not, maybe no one else would have died.

40

The salvage yard stunk of grease, rust, and oil, a smell that caused an almost animalistic pulse in Patch's brain. He'd worked at the Hunt and Peck Salvage Yard since before he could drive, and the overnight shift had always been his favorite. There wasn't much to do, other than occasionally drive out somewhere to pick up a car that was in an accident, or get a call from AAA to go out and change someone's tire, or bring them a few gallons of gas. There were nights when he didn't get any calls at all, and he would just hang out in the trailer, watching TV or falling asleep in the chair. It was perfect. The older guys didn't want the shift because it was boring, and they didn't make nearly as much on the pickup bonuses that they got from towing cars and shit.

When he got too bored and wasn't tired, he'd play with the cats that roamed around. Or he would hang out in the yard. Sometimes, he'd sit in different types of cars and wonder what the person who owned that car before had done in it. He didn't want to touch the cars that were in accidents, sometimes brutalized, other times, crushed. Instead, he would stand next to them and just look in. He would lean in, searching for blood on the seats or dashboard.

Patch sat in the trailer, his sock-clad feet up on the massive metal desk that served as the primary place of business for the entire operation. His head lolled from side to side as he fought to stay awake. He stacked a tower of Pepsi cans on the desk. A monument to their failed efforts to keep him awake. He'd let himself sleep, but not before two o'clock in the morning. The chances of getting a call peaked during that time. So, staying awake until then would prevent him from being too drowsy if he had to wake up and do a pick up.

"Fuck," Patch said to the empty trailer. He paced the trailer, downing yet another soda, then added the can to the ever-growing tower.

On lap number three something caught his eye through one of the small windows on the backside of the trailer. His heart skipped a beat. He stopped short. He'd been moving fast enough that by the time his brain registered that there was something outside, he had already passed the window. It had only been a split second, and he couldn't fully accept or process what had been out there, but at the moment, he was too scared to step back and look. Instead, his survival logic told him that he should stay completely still and that maybe whatever was out there would go away and leave him alone. Like it wouldn't see him.

"That's dinosaurs, not ghosts, stupid," he whispered to himself. "Just fucking look. It's probably just a deer that got through the fence."

Patch slid a few feet away from the window, punched the power button on the TV remote with one shaking finger, then flipped out the light switch, throwing the trailer into darkness. A bullet train of light poked through the window cast from the large light pole in the center of the yard. At first, he leaned his large torso, bending at the waist but refusing to put out a leg as a brace, to try and see around the window frame. He could see a bit of the yard but not the area where he thought he saw *something*. He couldn't say what he had seen, just that something was out there. He leaned back, slid his feet a few inches closer to the window, and tried the leaning trick again.

The silence in the trailer welcomed echoes of ticks and pops. For a moment, Patch considered that perhaps fear gave him superpowers, and that he could hear things other people couldn't. Then came the moan from outside, and he wished he didn't have the burden of this power. Cupping his mouth, he scooted away from the window. The moan came again. It sounded like it was right outside. The certainty that if he looked out the window, he would see something terrified Patch and kept him bolted to his spot in the center of the trailer. The

179

sound was stretched and pulled, starting low and going up little by little, the way an old car sounds when started on a subzero morning.

The trailer added its own groaning as Patch tiptoed over to the shaft of light coming through the window.

He held his breath and tilted his head over enough to see where the light had pooled in the dirt.

There was nothing there.

Wisps of dirt swirled in the steady night breeze. It was just the same old empty lot. Toppling soda cans rattled to the floor. He spun on his heels and stumbled backward when he saw her.

She stood behind the desk, one arm reaching out to him, her jaw hanging like a license plate missing three screws. But it was her eyes. Her eyes were dull, ghostly, and ridden with sorrow. Her face was burned and decayed. From the frozen scream she wore like a mask came another moan, dreadful and filled with pain.

"Lydia?"

She was unrecognizable.

He fell backward into the wall, crashed against it, and slid sideways. The trailer shook from the impact, and he rolled quickly, popping up onto his hands and knees to look at her. He hoped she would be gone, but instead, she was closer. Within arm's length.

Pain, confusion, and fear, glimmered in her eyes.

"Lydia," Patch cried. "I'm sorry. Fuck, I'm so sorry." He wanted to look away, but the terror was paralyzing. She drifted closer, and as her mouth released another moan, Patch could see into it. He squinted, looking into her mouth as the grizzled sound of hell came from it.

"What is that?" he asked through his tears.

He flinched as her jaw fell, separating from her face. Dirt spewed forth from the open maw and covered Patch.

"Stop!"

He was cut off by a shrill scream that could pierce heaven and hell. She never broke eye contact with him.

Patch dropped to his stomach and covered his head with his arms, "Go away! Just go away! Please, I am so sorry, Lydia. I am so sorry!"

Then the girl was gone.

41

Squeakers sat on Millicent's stomach as she lay on her back. The mouse had taken to doing this even if she didn't have food to coax it up there. Millicent didn't have any to use if she wanted to. She couldn't remember the last time they had given her food or water.

"I don't know where they went. Sometimes they just aren't here for a while," she said to Squeakers.

As if summoned there was a noise from outside, a distant car door. Millicent sat up, sending Squeakers hopping onto the floor and scurrying away. She looked through the little window and saw two sets of feet coming into the house. One in big, heavy boots. The man's boots. The other in smaller, clean tennis shoes. Millicent knew them both well and was scared of both equally. Though one would hurt her more than the other, the other was just mean, and Millicent didn't like being yelled at or scolded.

The woman's voice was audible in the otherwise silence of the house and came from directly overhead.

"You should check on her. See if she's still down there," she said.

"She's down there. And she'll still be there tomorrow," the man replied.

Millicent's throat burned, and her stomach tightened at the thought of waiting until morning for food or water. She knew neither was guaranteed then, but she hoped. She laid back down, patting her stomach for Squeakers to return, which they did. She fell asleep with the all too familiar pain of hunger and thirst ravaging her small body.

42

Stone pillars stood sentry topped with wrought iron spikes
that held the ornate sign that read: Howling Ivy City Cemetery.
It was unlike any cemetery Paisley had ever seen. The grass was
lush, greener than it should be so late in the season, and
perfectly manicured. Freshly fallen leaves lay among the
headstones. It would be fair to say, by the looks of the place,
the leaves wouldn't be there long.

Paisley navigated Gunner through the open gates and
followed the road into the sprawling cemetery.

Rows of headstones of every size rolled out in front of her
like invitations. Statues of crosses and a few Star of Davids
created silhouettes against the gray and blue sky.

"Shit!" Paisley yelled as she slammed on the brakes, coming
within inches of a man standing on the dirt road.

Paisley threw the vehicle in park and jumped out.

"Oh my god, are you okay?" she yelled, running around to
the man who stood, staring at the monster of a vehicle bearing
down on him. The man was in his mid-fifties by the look of
him. If you counted the slicked-back hairs on his head, you
would find more gray than black. His skin resembled leather
from years of outdoor work and had the wiry muscles that
usually came with it. He reminded her of someone. Maybe an
actor she'd seen, but she couldn't place. His t-shirt, jeans, and
boots looked like he'd already worked a full day even though it
was mid-morning.

"Oh, my. I think I just about had a heart attack," the man
said.

"I'm so sorry. Are you okay?"

"Oh, yeah, I think so. Just a bit startled. You'd think I would
have seen this beast coming from a mile away."

"It is hard to miss."

"Oh, yes, and brightly colored, it is. What kind of vehicle did you say it was?" he asked, pointing at the grill that had come less than a foot from colliding with him.

"Um, it's a Hummer. Hummer H2, to be exact."

"Oh, Hummer, you say?" he asked in a curious way that did not sound like a nearly-pancaked man but more akin to the tone one would use after walking into a car dealership and asking about the newest model on the showroom floor.

"Yes, H2," Paisley said.

The man crossed his arms, his eyes scanning the vehicle in assessment.

"Oh, an H2, yes," he nodded, not looking at Paisley. "And it belongs to you?"

"It does, yes. It's new."

"Oh, this year's model?" he said, pointing down as if to signify that the year was current and present.

"Well, new to me. I think it may be last year's model."

"Oh, yes. Right. Fairly new Hummer, very nice," he said to himself again using the tone that signified he was in the market and Paisley may be selling. "Question?"

"Sure. What is it?" Paisley asked.

"Do these new, H2, you say?"

"Correct, Hummer H2."

"Oh, right, Hummer H2. Do these new H2s not come with brakes standard, or is that something you would have had to pay extra for and just chose not to?" he said furrowing his brow.

Paisley stood with her mouth hanging open. The tone was so stoic that it was hard to tell if he was joking or genuinely upset.

"I'm so sorry. I was distracted by all the statues and such. I wasn't paying attention," she said.

"Oh, they are pretty amazing, aren't they?" he said, waving a hand around at the headstones nearby.

"They are. I'm so sorry, really. I'm so glad you aren't hurt."

"Oh, that makes two of us. Had you run me down and killed me, I don't know who'd dig the hole and roll me in, ya know?"

He smiled at this.

Paisley's heartbeat steadied.

"I really am sorry," she said again.

"Oh don't you worry about that. No harm, no foul. You're the," he paused and counted silently on his fingers, "fifth woman who tried to hit me with a vehicle," he laughed.

"What?" Paisley chuckled.

"Oh, yeah, the first was a Ford truck, then a Honda Accord, a tractor, and then one of those little electric scooters they got over at the Shop N' Save. Those little suckers move!" The man's eyes lit up with delight.

Paisley blurted out a laugh.

"Thank you so much for not hating me," she said.

"Oh, now don't go puttin' words in my mouth," he said with a toothy smile.

"Hey now!"

The two shared another laugh.

"Now that we've hopefully cleared all the near-death experiences for the day, what can I do for you, Miss..." he stared.

"Mott, Paisley Mott." Paisley offered her hand and the man shook it.

"Bond, James Bond," he said.

She giggled.

"Hawke, Stilton Hawke," he said. "You can call me Stil. That's what everyone else calls me, no matter how much I ask them to call me Hawke, which is measures cooler."

"Nice to meet you, Hawke," Paisley said and watched as the first truly genuine smile crossed his face and perhaps carried a small tick of blush with it.

"Oh, the pleasure is all mine, Miss Mott."

"Please, call me Paisley."

"Oh, okay, Paisley. Now that I am more acquainted with you than I am with the bumper of this here car, what brings you out to the city of the dead on this fine day? Meeting someone? Without a reservation I can't get you a table near the kitchen, but I believe I may have something in the bar."

Paisley laughed again, which felt like a guilty pleasure while standing in a cemetery, but she couldn't help it. This man reminded her so much of her dad that she was almost instantly at ease. Though she wasn't naive enough to forget Grey Water Ridge and let down her guard just yet. She'd keep an eye, ear, and camera on this guy. She turned toward him, ensuring that the camera in her pin, a small bear dressed like Gandalf, was pointed in his direction.

"I am actually a bit of an investigative journalist, and I'm out here doing a story," Paisley said. She expected that after she said this, there was a chance he would recognize her, as her face had been national news for nearly two months by that point.

"Oh, you mean you work for the paper?" Stilton asked, folding his arms and shifting his weight to his back foot.

"No, not exactly. I have a YouTube channel."

"Oh... a what?"

"YouTube? The video streaming platform on the internet?" she tried to explain.

"Oh, the internet. Yeah, I never been on that," he said.

"What do you mean, you've never been on the internet? Like, ever?"

"Nah, just not my bag, you know? I'm an old hippie. I spent most of my time outside working, so I don't have much time for all that technology."

Relief flowed through Paisley as she mentally called off her pre-programmed responses she had for questions people always had about her situation in Grey Water. She wouldn't have to answer questions about Hollis or Hyacinth or explain what she thought about the possibility of a sasquatch roaming the hills above that town.

"Well, Hawke, I can tell you, that is great to hear, if I'm being honest with you," she said.

Stilton's face sucked in on itself like he had licked a lemon at the sound of hearing the name again.

"Oh, Paisley, on second thought, would you mind calling me Stil? I think the days of being cool enough to be called Hawke may have passed."

"Sure thing, Stil." She smiled and gave him a thumbs up.

"Oh, yeah, that's better. Now, Paisley Mott, investigative journalist from the YouTube, what can I do for you?"

"I'm doing a story on a local boy, actually," she said.

"Oh, which boy?"

"Darius Knot?" she said. Giving away too much information seemed risky, but seeing as she would need directions to Lydia's grave, it would be pretty obvious who the story was about.

"Oh, this about the ghost?" Stil asked.

"Ghost?" Paisley followed.

"Yeah, his sister. She used to run 'round here sometimes," he said, tilting his head to signify he meant the cemetery.

"I'm sorry, what?"

"Oh yeah, geez, you used to see her once or twice a week, at least." The nonchalant tone with which he spoke was confusing, bordering on alarming.

"What do you mean?" She leaned in closer, leading with the pin to capture what he was saying. It would have been an ideal conversation for a full camera setup, but this could prove to be even better off the cuff. Plus, someone who had never been online could not understand what she was trying to accomplish.

"Oh, she came 'round a lot. Which isn't unheard of, but there are some things that I found strange about it," he said, nodding his head as if agreeing with himself.

"Wait, it's strange that she shows up, or there is something strange about how she is showing up?"

"Oh, showed up, I haven't seen her in a while. There was always something strange about her when she did."

"You'd think that the whole ghost thing would be the strange part," Paisley said.

"Oh, really? You realize where you are currently standing, don't cha?" he asked.

Paisley looked around at the surrounding grave markers and

then back at Stil.

"You know, Stil, you make a hell of a point. If it isn't normal for it to happen here, where would it happen?" she posed the question as a hypothetical, but got an answer anyway.

"Oh, well that's just it. Ghosts don't normally show up where they're buried. They show up where they died. Not always, but that's been my experience. Cemeteries are usually pretty ghost-free."

"Stil, you are one interesting man, you know that?"

"Oh, I don't know. I just been around a long time is all."

"Any chance you'd want to be interviewed on camera for this project?" Paisley hoped that calling it a project instead of an investigation might give her a better chance of not scaring him away.

"Oh, I don't know. I'm not really one for being on TV," he said.

She could have lied. She knew that. Without him knowing what the internet was and who she was, she could have told him it would be a quick interview that would likely not see the light of day.

"That's fair. I have a pretty big audience and you'd likely be seen by millions of people, so I understand why it would seem intimidating," she said.

"Oh, millions?" he asked.

"Yeah. I know a lot of people are waiting on my follow-up, so I think the views are there."

"Follow-up to what?"

Paisley paused, reeling back into herself and mentally slapping her own wrist for bringing it up, especially with someone who wouldn't have known anything about it if she hadn't.

"Two months ago, my friends and I were almost killed by a madman in Kentucky," she said.

"Oh," he started. "Yeah, that sounds about right for Kentucky."

Paisley surprised herself with a laugh. That prompted

another natural smile from Stil.

"We wouldn't have been the first," Paisley added.

"How are you and your friends doing now?" His eyes seemed to grow a size or two as his brows relaxed.

Paisley's breath caught in her chest as she fought to stop her voice from breaking when she spoke.

"To tell you the truth, I don't think any of us are doing as well as we are pretending to be."

"Oh, yeah, that's the thing about trauma. It's like a mask you sometimes forget you're wearing because the only person it's fooling is you."

"I..." Paisley started.

"You got your TV stuff with you now?" Stil asked, flipping his chin up toward Gunner.

Paisley nodded.

"Oh, well drive on up to the building and I'll meet you there," he said. "I gotta grab the rake and such but I'll be there in a sec."

"Are you sure?" Paisley asked, feeling the adrenaline she got from her work starting to kick in.

"Oh yeah, it'll be fun. I ain't never been on TV. First time for everything," he said before retrieving his rake. "Just park out front. The door's open, but if you wait, I can help carry in anything you've got."

"Thank you," she called after him, but he just nodded and continued on his way.

The "building," as Stil had called it, was much more than that. It was an incredible work of art. White block brick held tall pillars ornately designed with flourishes at every corner or peak. The dark green, steeply pitched roof stood out as a sharp contrast to the pale blue sky that this hulking building poked into. It was old, but not neglected. Decades and decades of dirt had penetrated the facade, but it was obvious that painstaking care went into keeping the place up. They didn't look the same, but the gothic comparisons between this building and Raven

Bloom were hard not to make in one's head.

Paisley marveled at the building, afraid to push on the grand door, covered in a mosaic of dark green tiles. She wasn't sure what exactly this building was. Was it a church, an office, a crypt?

Paisley did what she always did when she was unsure. She pulled out her phone, set it to selfie mode, and clicked the live stream button.

"Hey, friends! Just wanted to do a quick check-in and say hello while I had a minute!" She watched the active viewer count go up in leaps and bounds. This was something that she encountered every time she streamed. Everyone was hoping that she would find herself in another dangerous place.

She panned the camera across the graveyard, showing the rows and rows of beautifully lined headstones, then stepped back to cover the building. Comments started to roll in.

"That's awesome!"
"Whoa!"
"We have one like that at the cemetery near my house."
"Can you go inside?"

"Pretty amazing, right?" Paisley asked the audience. She flipped the camera back around and saw her face fill the screen, accompanied by the rolling messages. "The guy that I'm waiting for works here at the cemetery and claims that a spirit has been seen wandering the grounds here on multiple occasions." A comment caught her eye.

"Didn't u learn ur lesson last time? Ur gonna get urself killed."

"Well, yes, I did learn a pretty valuable lesson last time. Which is why I am much more prepared than I was before." She smacked the bag over her shoulder, which she knew had things that could supply some sort of protection in case she needed them.

"Oh, sorry for taking so long. I should have taken the gator down there, would have been a lot quicker," Stil said as he came up the hill toward Paisley.

Without turning the camera toward him Paisley asked, "Are you okay with being on a live stream?"

"A what?" he asked.

"A live stream. It's basically like live television. I've got a lot of people watching me right now, would you like to say hi?"

"Oh, sure. I can say hello," he said, running a work-worn hand over his hair and pressing it down. This move changed nothing.

"Okay, friends, it's time to introduce you to a new friend to add to the bunch." Paisley tapped the screen to flip to the rear facing camera. Stil's face filled the screen. "World, Stilton Hawke, Stilton Hawke, say hello to the world. Say hi, Stil."

"Oh, can they see me?" he asked, looking around the camera at Paisley.

"Yep, and you're looking pretty sharp," she said, giving a thumbs up.

"Oh, what should I say?"

"Well, why don't you tell our friends what you do here at the cemetery?"

"Oh, well, I cut the grass, rake the leaves. That's what I'm working on today. I also keep everything clean, like the mausoleum here," he said, gesturing toward the building. "And the headstones, and everything else, you know?"

"That's a lot of work, do you have anyone that helps you?" Paisley asked.

"Oh I have a bit, just volunteers, but I'm just part time here," Stil started. He continued but Paisley's eye and attention were drawn to something else. A comment on the video. She tapped it to pin it in place.

"Holy shit, do you know who that is?"

Paisley didn't, and she didn't want to interrupt him to ask, and now she hoped someone in the comments section would just say it. The comments section never fails.

"Who is it?"
"That's fucking Stilton Hawke!"
"The fuck is Stilton Hawke?"

Stilton smiled at the camera again, leaned his rake against the wall, and opened the green tile door. Paisley followed each movement with the camera as if she was shooting a movie. She didn't say anything. She just let Stilton eat up as much time as she could while letting comments come in.

"According to the internet he was a janitor at an elementary school in the 80's and he killed some kid. They found his body behind the dumpster at a gas station just down the street from the school."
"I searched it too, and that is definitely the same guy, but it says he was acquitted on those charges because he had an alibi."

Paisley's hands began to sweat. The footage recorded in her pin would be good if something happened and they needed to search it after she turned up dead, but they wouldn't have seen the comments in the live chat. She also wasn't interested in finding out if she was making the same mistake in trusting another maniac who wanted to rip her apart.

"The light out here is really nice," she said. "Maybe we can record with the building in the background?"

Stil stopped and turned back toward Paisley.

"Oh, yeah, we can do that. You're the director, after all," he said. He swung the door closed, picked up the rake, and headed toward Paisley.

"Excellent," she said to Stil, then leaned in close, hoping that the viewers would know she was talking directly to them. "So, what's the *verdict*?" She laid heavily on this last word to drive the question home. Stil was closing the distance.

* * *

"He looks like a killer."

"I bet he did it. He probably has a skin suit hanging in his closet right now."

"The internet says that the alibi was contested. He wasn't acquitted. The case was thrown out due to what appeared to be evidence tampering. He left town and they never chased him down to charge him."

"So am I okay?" she asked.

"Oh, I think you are just fine," Stil said. He was almost within striking distance of the rake if he decided to swing.

"I'd run."
"Get out of there."
"If that's me I'm runnin."

"As long as you are happy with this spot?" Stil said, stopping in front of the camera and turning back to look at the building to see if it was a good angle.

"I, uh, I think that it'll be okay," Paisley said to everyone who could hear her. She turned the camera back to the front-facing mode. Everyone watching would see her face now.

"Be careful!"

"Sometimes you just have to trust your gut and go for it. And if it's a mistake, I'll be prepared," she said.

"She has her pepper spray and a taser. Don't forget who this guy would be fucking with."

Paisley saw this last message and noticed it was from WhyItHurts. Having their confidence in her helped, and she knew that once she stopped recording, they would likely switch over to the live feed from the pin camera.

"Well, everyone, I'm going to shut it down, set up the camera, and get the scoop on what's going on out here. And my friend,

Stilton Hawke," she said, flipping the camera around and getting a nice closeup of his smiling face, "is going to let us in on some of the spooky things that happen around here at night."

"Oh, well, a lot of them happened during the day," he said, never losing his toothy grin.

"Even more intriguing! Until next time, friends! Mott, out!" Paisley tapped the button to end the live.

"Was I on the internet?" Stil asked.

"Yep, and thousands of people saw you talking to me, so, you know, that's pretty cool."

Paisley's watch buzzed and she glanced at it. It was from WhyItHurts.

"Got you on the feed from the pin. Small delay, but I'm here."

Paisley held her hand out in front of the pin and gave a thumbs up. Stil didn't seem to notice, and if he did he didn't say anything.

The camera, tripod, and microphone were up in minutes, and Paisley was ready to roll. Stilton stood on the road leading up to the building, and it loomed over his shoulder in the shot like kaiju ready to attack.

"Ready?" Paisley asked.

"Oh, I'm a little nervous, but I think I am ready," he replied.

"You're going to be great. When I press this button, you just say hello, your name, and where you work. Then I'll ask questions, alright?"

He gave her a thumbs up and Paisley pressed record.

"Oh, hello there. I'm Stilton M. Hawke, and I have been the groundskeeper here at Howling Ivy City Cemetery for, oh, I guess it's been about thirty-odd years now."

"Mr. Hawke, as the groundskeeper does that mean you also dig the graves?" Paisley asked.

"Oh, please, call me Stil, unless you have to call me mister for the show?" he asked, looking around the camera at Paisley.

"No, sorry, Stil. Do you also dig the graves?"

He looked back down the lens of the camera. "Oh, yeah, we just prefer not to call ourselves gravediggers now. The name has just gotten such a bad reputation. And we don't spend nearly as much time as we used to doing it. Tools have made it much easier."

"What sort of equipment do you use now?" Paisley asked, trying to loosen him up for the big questions. She had learned that once you get people talking about things they know a lot about, they are a lot more comfortable telling you things they may not otherwise.

"Oh, well, now we use shovels." He mimed digging with a shovel.

"Shovels? That's the upgrade? What did you use before, your hands?"

"Our teeth," Stil joked, biting at the air, turning his head, and then pretending to spit out dirt.

Paisley surprised herself again with a laugh.

"Okay, goofball. You got me. I'm going to have to keep my eye on you," she said.

"You think digging the grave is bad, you should see when we have to exhume them." He gagged and pretended to vomit.

Paisley laughed again. She would eventually ask him about the ghost sightings, and he would recount, in detail, the first time he saw the girl.

43

Clouds draped the sky, and the headstones cast faint but present shadows. A weak breeze pushed through the cemetery and Stilton leaned back and took it in. The heat on a July afternoon in Indiana was no joke, even with the overcast skies.

Stilton rode along the grassy mounds on the back of his riding mower. He took great pride in caring for the cemetery. He felt like caring for the dead was one of the most noble professions he could have. After working for a school, and having a less than excellent experience, he found Howling Ivy and City Cemetery. It didn't pay much, so he had to take other odd jobs around town, but he appreciated the calmness of the dead.

Stilton mowed in a criss-cross pattern. He liked the diagonal look of the grass when he was done. Though the wind would quickly wipe away the pattern, he enjoyed it for a few hours.

As he turned the mower toward the front corner of the cemetery, where the newer bodies had been buried, something caught his eye.

Stilton would be the first to tell you that he wasn't the most observant person in the world. He was used to things existing in his periphery, so the movement didn't immediately draw his attention. He just went right along mowing. As he passed stones, he would recite the names of those buried beneath. He knew every single one. He'd made it a mission to be able to recall each of them, and when he could, he started to try to remember the dates of death as well. Maybe someday he would get the birthday too, but for now he was just working on the death.

People have a way of lumbering when they walk, but the thing that moved between the stones did not. It floated like a

196

mylar balloon caught in a draft. Wisps of air, not quite dust, but more opaque than air, descended across the grass. The formless fog hung over into Stilton's path and stopped. He pulled the break on the mower bringing it to a halt no more than fifteen feet from the anomaly.

"Oh, now what do we have here?"

It did not respond with any sort of language, but instead, it slowly rotated as if swirling into a funnel cloud, then slowly dissipated.

Stilton sat on the mower for uncounted minutes, staring at the spot where he had seen it, and he had no explanation as to what it could be.

44

"So, it was just like a little smoke in the air?"

"Oh, sort of. It was hard to tell that first time," Stil said, as he looked back and forth between Paisley and the camera.

"So, you did see it more than once?"

"Oh, I saw her a few times. Yeah."

"Her? You call it 'her'. If it was just a shapeless mist, how can you be sure it was a 'her,' or even that it was a spirit at all?" Paisley's voice was soft and encouraging so as not to make him feel like he wasn't being believed.

"Oh, cause I seen her a few times after," he answered.

"And she wasn't just a wisp?"

"Oh, she was a little more than that a few times, but the way I really know who she is is because I seen her come out," he said with a touch of pride.

"Come out?"

"Oh, of her grave."

"Wait, you saw the thing come out of a grave?"

"I did. Yeah."

"Whose grave?" Paisley asked knowing what he was going to say before he said it, but hoping that he wouldn't anyway. When things lined up like that, they felt too real. It all already felt too real, too big. She felt too small for it. Like someone else, someone more qualified, should be asking these questions and getting these answers.

"That poor girl that got burned, Lydia Knot," he said.

The care in his voice did not go unnoticed. Paisley took a deep breath, exhaled, and then took another.

"You saw this thing, this spirit, come out of Lydia Knot's grave?" she asked.

"Oh, yeah, I did, a few times."

"And where does it go? What does it do?"

"It just sort of came out, floated down the hill, and disappeared."

"But you're sure it was a ghost and not, like, some sewer gas pipe releasing steam or something?"

"Oh, ha. No, nothing like that. They don't have anything like that running under the cemetery, on account of the bodies and such."

"Right, on account of the bodies and such. Have you seen any other ghosts around here?"

"Oh, around here? No, they don't often come 'round here. Ghosts mainly stay near where they died unless they can find their way back to a place that was important to them or to see someone specific, but then it's just temporary."

"You sure do know a lot about ghosts," Paisley pointed out.

"Oh, I've studied them for a long time," he said.

"Studied them? That must be hard without using the internet."

"Can I tell you a secret?" he asked, leaning in close but making sure he was still close to the camera and microphone.

"Of course," Paisley said, leaning in as well.

"Books," he said, then leaned back and smiled.

Paisley burst out into a belly laugh that lasted the better part of a minute. When she could finally speak, she did what she often did and dropped a quote from one of her favorite movies to watch with her dad.

"I read it... in a book," she said, quoting Ben Stiller in the movie *Dodgeball.*

"Oh, I learned a lot about them. For instance, do you know why people see old-timey ghosts all the time, and not current-day ghosts as much?" he asked, completely missing her joke.

"Well, I assume it is because we were all correct about Prince being the literal embodiment of Christ, so they didn't start going toward the light until after he died?" Paisley joked.

"Oh, um, Prince, that's the 'November Rain' guy?"

"*Purple Rain*."

"Oh, right, *Purple Rain*, good record," he said. "But no, I don't think that was why, didn't he die in the '90s or something? Maybe the 2000s?"

"Hmmm, you know, you're right. I can't tell you the last time I saw a ghost depicted wearing sweatpants with one of the legs rolled up or coveralls turned around backward, which would be scary, but for a whole different reason," Paisley rambled.

"Oh, why would they be wearing clothes backward or their pants like that?"

"Wouldn't we all like to know? The '90s were a weird time, man."

"Were you even alive in the 90's?" Stil asked.

"Hey, man, am I asking the questions here, or are you?" Paisley said, looking comically offended.

"Oh, you're right," he said, trying to match her comic timing and failing. "The reason is that spirits only really stick around when they need to for unresolved things, which there were a lot of back in the day. They also manifest more fully over time. So someone that has only been dead for a few weeks might only be a wisp or something, but someone who's been dead for like fifty years may look almost normal."

"No shit?" she followed.

"None," he answered.

"Interesting. So what about when they talk to you?" she asked. It wasn't meant as a trick question or anything. She genuinely wanted to know what the odds were that Derry actually caught the voice of his sister on that recording.

"Oh, that's more tricky because they aren't using normal vocal cords like us. They can push air, and sort of touch things, so they do that with air. They remember doing it, so when they talk, or what we would consider talking, they sound like they did when they were alive, you know?"

"So if I was recording with my phone, and, let's say Robin Williams was here, and I caught him on the recording, it would sound like Mork from Ork was standing here next to me doing a bit?" she asked.

"Oh, Mork from Ork? How old are you again?"

"Old enough to know to be offended by that question."

"Oh, fair. That's fair," he said, raising his hands in mock surrender.

"My dad loves that stuff," Paisley said. "If we weren't outside working we'd be inside watching old movies and TV shows. We watched a lot of his old favorites."

"Oh, he sounds like a fun dad."

"He's the best." Paisley leaned out from where she was sitting next to the camera and looked into the lens. "You hear that, dad? You're the best. Now stop lying to everyone and telling them that I'm just taking a gap year and I'll be going to school to be a doctor, would you?"

"Oh, was that your plan? To be a doctor?" Stil asked.

"Um, no. But my mom was a social worker, and they both always thought I'd grow up to want to help people and, like a lot of parents, thought I was smart enough to be a doctor for some reason."

"Oh, but it wasn't for you?"

"No, I love people, but I don't love school. You know what I mean?" she admitted.

"Oh, yeah, I was the same way. That's how I ended up cleaning floors and raking leaves for a living."

"Yeah, I get that, but times are different now. You know?" She didn't want to get in a debate with Stil over the differences, but she also didn't love the idea of having her life choices compared with his.

"Oh yeah, they really are. And you don't seem to be making a lot of the bad choices I made," he said, wringing his hands.

"I don't think caring for people is a bad choice."

"Oh, I did always like taking care of people. Especially the kids." That last bit hung in the air like a pigeon feather sans bird.

"Don't beat yourself up. Most people would give anything to know where they wanted to be and what they wanted to do.

You seem mighty good at what you're doing." Paisley gestured to the perfectly manicured grass around the cemetery.

Stil looked around and admired his own work.

"Oh, I guess I never really thought of it like that. Thank you."

"Of course. I'm sorry that anyone ever let you feel like caring for people, living or dead, made you less valuable than anyone else," she said.

"Oh, you really think so?" he asked, his chin lifting as if the angle would hold the tears that threatened to form in his eyes back from falling.

"I do. Not everyone is meant to be a doctor, or a therapist, or a teacher, or a librarian, social worker, firefighter, artist, musician, or groundskeeper. We are all blessed with talents and it's our responsibility to find them and use them to benefit the world around us. No matter what those talents are. And you've done that, Stil. Sounds like you've been doing it your whole life and you didn't even know it. Thank you."

"Oh, thank you." The words came out stalled and labored, like they had to be pushed through mud to get there.

45

Hyacinth sat in her usual spot at the small table in her kitchen. She had all of Raven Bloom, her Gothic mansion, and she chose to sit at the small table in the kitchen.

She sat with her eyes closed, listening to her own breath and focusing inward, the way her therapist told her to when she was feeling overwhelmed.

She felt buried. She felt as if she couldn't make headway no matter what she did. Her laptop sat in front of her, sputtering, with the cables running from it. It appeared to be on life support. She was digitizing the video for Paisley, and meditated while she waited.

"Hey, gorgeous."

The deep voice shook her, even though she immediately recognized it as Grover's. She jerked, opening her eyes, and nearly tipping backward out of her chair.

"Jesus," she blurted, trying to steady the coffee cup she almost kicked off of the table.

"Oh, God, babe, I'm so sorry. I didn't mean to scare you," Grover said. He put his hand on her head and ran his fingers through her red hair. She loved it when he did that. It was intimate and reassuring to feel his strong hands so delicately touching her.

"It's okay. I'm okay. I don't know why I jumped like that."

"Trauma response, my love. You've been through a lot, and I need to be more careful. I'm sorry." He leaned down and kissed her head.

"I just can't seem to kick it, you know?" she said.

"I know, beautiful. It'll take time. We will get there." Grover kissed her head again and walked over to the counter to get himself some coffee.

"Here, you sit. I'll get it." She jumped up and rushed around him to beat him to the cupboard.

"I've got to start taking care of myself a little bit." He followed her to the cupboard, where she was already pulling out one of his favorite coffee mugs. He walked up behind her and put his arms around her, and trapped her in. She stopped and allowed herself to enjoy it. She felt his hand slide up her arm, slipping into her hand, and taking the coffee mug.

"I just don't want you to rush it," she said. She held the cup for a second before giving in and letting him take it.

"I know, my love. And I am getting there, thanks to you. You're my Wonder Woman."

Hyacinth turned around to face him. Just looking into his big brown eyes made her heart swell. He had lost a lot of weight since that day at Hollis's cabin. His once chiseled features had given way to a more angular face that was equally as beautiful.

She ran her hand over the few days of beard growth on his dark skin. For so many weeks, she had to look down at him in a bed. For a few of those weeks, he was intubated. He couldn't talk, and she really couldn't see his face. Even though he could communicate with a keyboard and a text-to-audio device, she still missed him. She missed his voice. She missed his laugh. She missed him holding her. She missed looking up at him the way she was then.

"I was so afraid I was going to lose you," she said.

"You saved me," he replied.

"Then why do I feel so weak?"

"Because you've used everything you had to save me, and save Rowan, and Paisley," he said.

"Ha, Paisley doesn't need saving. That woman's a tank."

"No, she saved us, but after that, she needed you. She needed you to remind her who she was, to hold her up, and to push her forward. And you did. You're a badass." He leaned down to kiss her forehead.

"It's getting harder even though everyone seems to be doing

better." She leaned her head into his chest, careful not to press too hard. She could feel the scar, from the wound that nearly took him from her, through his thin cotton shirt.

"Why do you think that is?" he asked.

"I told Shawna about it in my session the other day. She said that I'm struggling because I jumped into caretaker mode as soon as everything was over, and I never had time to process. Considering everything that happened, she thinks that I may just need time to grieve, reflect, and heal myself."

"Shawna's a good therapist." He wrapped her up, squeezing her in a little tighter.

"She is." She leaned back and looked up at his face. "So what do I do? Do I sit on the couch and binge watch baking shows and Lord of the Rings until I feel better?"

"Will that make you feel better?"

She thought about it for a moment and then shook her head.

"Can I make an observation that you can run by Shawna at your next appointment?" he asked.

"Of course. But if you make a comment about sex being the best medicine, I may have to poison your coffee."

"I think the reason you're struggling right now is because, for the first time in your life, you aren't in control of what is going on."

Hyacinth's face bunched in confusion. "What do you mean?"

"It started with Hollis. He literally took control away from you. And since then you've been stuck here caring for everyone else."

"I want to take care of all of you," she countered.

"I know you do, my love. But it wasn't your choice. I know had it been, you would have chosen to. But it was sort of just dropped in your very capable lap," he said.

"So what am I supposed to do about that?"

"That's just it. I can't tell you that. I think you need to think of something and just do it. Anything. Take a vacation-"

Hyacinth cut him off. "But you..."

He continued. "I'll be fine, my love. I'm up and about, and

we've got the nurses and the doctor. Plus Rowan is around."

"Sometimes," Hyacinth interjected.

"Well, sure. But I need to start taking care of myself. So don't figure anyone else into your decision. You just do you, babe." He kissed her head again.

Hyacinth made a pouty face that she hoped conveyed how much she did not like the fact that he was likely correct. She turned that pouty face up to him and he kissed her outstretched bottom lip. She allowed it to melt into a real kiss.

When the kiss was over she leaned back to look him in the eye again.

"And what if the thing I want to do is crazy?" she asked.

"Do it," he said without hesitation.

"What if I want to go ghost-busting with Paisley fucking Mott?" She bit her lip in the way she knew he found adorable.

"Well, that's one idea," he laughed.

"A pretty good one, if you ask me. We both know I could only be gone for a few days, but I could go out and help her, then come back quickly."

"I assumed that was what you'd want."

"Why do you say that?"

"Because you can't stay away from it."

"I most certainly can," she said, faking insult.

Grover did not respond. He didn't need to. Hyacinth just stared at him. Then she turned and looked at the computer that was working to pull footage of a grisly murder.

"That's fair," she said. And as if taking her cue, the computer chimed, signaling that the first video was finished. It was the oldest on the tape, with a timestamp that was over seven years old.

"Looks like it's ready," Grover said, turning to go to the laptop.

"Just one," she said.

"One?" He sat down in the chair next to Hyacinth's.

"Yeah, that tape was damaged. So I couldn't just play it straight across and pull it. I had to use a scrubber, which luckily my dad had in the basement."

"I don't know what that is," Grover admitted.

"It runs the tape through it over and over and over. It focuses on pieces of individual frames to collect every usable pixel. It's a similar process to what Hollywood does to remaster film, I think."

"That sounds time consuming," Grover said.

"It is. It identified thirteen different time codes, so there are thirteen clips," she said.

"Lucky number thirteen."

"Each clip takes a few hours, but it looks like the first is done." Hyacinth handed Grover the freshly prepared cup of coffee and sat down. "We'll just send them over to Paisley as they finish."

"At this pace it could be a few days," Grover said.

"Yeah, but maybe there's nothing on here that'll be helpful and it won't matter," she replied.

Hyacinth hit play on the finished clip.

"Jesus." Grover leaned forward. His investigator's eyes sharpened.

"Oh no. No, no, no. No. God." Hyacinth buried her face in Grover's shoulder, not wanting to look.

After a moment, she turned so that she could just barely see the screen.

The two watched in terror.

"No!" Hyacinth yelled as she jumped in her seat.

"We have to give this to the police," Grover said.

"We have to send it to Paisley first."

"No, this needs to go to law enforcement."

"We can send it to her and the police at the same time," Hyacinth agreed, avoiding the screen even though the video had stopped.

"What has Paisley gotten into?" Grover asked.

"I don't know if I want to know."

Hyacinth could feel that Grover wanted to tell her that she couldn't go help Paisley if she wanted to. She knew he would offer to go, if he could. But she also knew that he knew that he couldn't say any of those things.

Hyacinth sent the video.

46

The light in the video was dark, but the scene was easy enough to make out. It was a workbench. The old style with pegs that hold projects in place. It wasn't some handmade chair, or a cheap cutting board, that was stuck to the table in the video. A body. A child. She wore a tattered dress, and someone pulled a burlap sack down to conceal her face and tied her wrists and ankles to pegs on each of the narrow ends of the table. It had a striking resemblance to the medieval stretch torture rack.

The girl laid still as stone. Was she unconscious? Dead? A shadow poured over her. Someone was in there with her. It held there for a moment. It was hard to tell whether the video froze or the figure stood incredibly still.

Ten seconds.

Twenty.

Thirty.

A minute passed, and finally, there was movement, not from the shadow, but from the child. The light, harsh everywhere else, but soft on her skin, swept over her as she tried to turn her leg. She was waking up. The bag masking her face rustled. Or something inside it did.

A flash of light lit up the room and the bag jerked to the left, away from the shadow.

"Oh!" Paisley screamed and put her hands over her mouth. Her brain had processed the information, and she knew what had happened before she was able to logically think about it. Blood seeped its way across the bag as if to prove her right.

Paisley slammed the laptop closed. She gripped at the sides of her face and squeezed. The laptop sat on the edge of the coffee table, taunting Paisley to open it and take another look.

She pulled a cushion from the couch and slammed it on the machine, hoping to silence the invitation to watch it again.

"What the fuck?" She pulled her hands down from her mouth. "What the fuck was that? Did someone just shoot that girl?"

Paisley got up to pace. Her eyes darted around, not knowing what they were looking for but knew there had to be something. Her mind was like a sailor thrown overboard and lost at sea, bobbing up and down, hoping to spot something that would save them.

Her cellphone.

"Hyacinth," she said to herself and ran for the phone. Hyacinth saw the video and warned Paisley when she sent the link. She would understand, and Paisley couldn't handle knowing this alone. It was too heavy a burden.

The photo she used as Hyacinth's contact photo in her phone, a shot of Hyacinth flipping the bird, a slice of pizza hanging from her mouth as she hid behind the refrigerator door, was on the screen and her thumb hovered over the call button.

"I can't." Hyacinth would take her call. She would be worried, immediately invested. She would support Paisley in whatever way needed. And she'd drop everything to do so. That's what Hyacinth did. She took care of everyone. She was everyone's savior. Paisley couldn't pile this on her.

Paisley sat at one of the perfectly cliché mismatched chairs that surrounded the farm table. She opened the messaging app and clicked on WhyItHurts.

ParanormalOrNot - *I know it's late, and I realize I don't really know where you are, so I don't know what time it is wherever that is, but I need you. Are you awake?*

Paisley waited a few minutes before setting the phone down. She put her head in her hands.

A notification chimed from her phone. She jumped, but her reflexes were as quick as her fear response and she snatched the phone up.

WhyItHurts - *Paisley, I'm sorry. I was away from my phone for a moment. Is everything okay?*

ParanormalOrNot - *No.*

ParanormalOrNot - *Shit, I don't know.*

WhyItHurts - *What's wrong?*

ParanormalOrNot - *Did you see the video where I went and found the camera?*

WhyItHurts - *I did! Very impressive stuff!*

ParanormalOrNot - *Hyacinth sent me the video. She managed to digitize it. It shows something really fucked up.*

WhyItHurts - *What is it?*

ParanormalOrNot - *I think it is a murder.*

WhyItHurts - *Are you sure? Did Hyacinth see it?*

ParanormalOrNot - *It certainly looks like murder. She watched it and so did Grover.*

WhyItHurts - *Is it Lydia Knot?*

ParanormalOrNot - *No, it isn't her, but she said there are more. They are just taking a long time.*

WhyItHurts - *Can you share it with me?*

ParanormalOrNot - *I'll send you the link.*

WhyItHurts - *Thank you.*

ParanormalOrNot - *No, thank you.*

WhyItHurts - *Paisley?*

ParanormalOrNot - *Yeah?*

WhyItHurts - *Are you alright?*

ParanormalOrNot - *I don't know. I'm really hoping you are going to tell me that this thing is obviously fake and that it's one of those blood pack things and it's just bullshit.*

WhyItHurts - *I hope so too.*

The videos came six to eight hours apart. Paisley watched them as they came in, but there was no way to prepare for what she would see.

47

Millicent felt like she was flying. She tried to open her eyes but couldn't. She fought sleep as the man carried her up the stairs. The pounding of his boots synchronized with her throbbing hunger pangs.

The sun in the room caressed Millicent's slightly upturned face. Her skin soaked up the warmth. Her eyes twitched and opened, burning from the sunlight and then adjusting enough to take in the beautiful sight. The room wasn't anything special but she couldn't focus on anything anyway. She was just amazed by the rays of light that poured through the windows. She raised an arm to try and grab them.

"Dammit!" the woman yelled. "I thought you said she was dead!"

"I thought she was this time," the man said.

The disappointment in his voice was heavy. Millicent wished she was dead too.

Her stomach turned as the man whirled around and took her back toward the stairs.

"I'm sorry," she croaked through her dry lips.

The man stopped, one foot on the top step of the basement.

"Please forgive me," he said, and pitched Millicent forward.

A combination of her reduced weight and his strength sent her into the angled ceiling above the stairs before she ricocheted off and fell down onto the steps below. Her shoulder hit first and snapped with an audible pop. Her head thudded against the step below, and everything went black.

48

In the second video, the workbench had been wiped clean of the blood, but deep crimson stains remained. Paisley had a hard time focusing. She kept seeing the child on the table from the first video, the cheap burlap sack jerking like it had been tugged. The blood soaking it. The sound of the bang. The horror of watching a child murdered.

It twisted her stomach in knots.

Something moved in the darkness just outside the frame, casting shadows as it had in the first video. Shot from the same angle, too. There was no way to know how much time had passed, but judging by the time between disappearances, she assumed months had passed.

Something abruptly pierced both the frame and silence. A child was thrust onto the table, eliciting a scream. Paisley was unsure if it was from the video or had come from her.

The child looked roughly the same age as the young girl in the first video, but it was hard to tell with the ambiguous clothing. The body lay still. The possibility that this was the same body as the last video floated into the ether. Maybe this maniac had shot the little girl, cleaned her up, changed her clothes, put a different sack over her head, and then used it for another of his sick videos. The body didn't appear stiff or frozen. Paisley heard the shallowest of breaths.

"It's a different child. Is it a little girl?" she asked the tape. "Is it a little blonde girl, you fucking serial killer?"

As if responding, a gloved hand ran a knife underneath the back of the child's shirt, pulling up so as not to nick the skin. When the sides of the shirt fell away from the razor-sharp blade, a few golden curls of hair could be seen slithered out from under the sack.

"You motherfucker," Paisley shouted. "Fuck."

She stood and paced back and forth, her eyes locked on the computer screen. The inner struggle to watch or not watch the video was eating her alive. She didn't want to see another child hurt. She didn't want to witness more killings. But she needed to see if there was something that could help. The videos had also been sent to law enforcement, but would they see what she could see?

The blade, so careful to not cut the child when removing the shirt, pressed against her skin, highlighting the subtle movement of her breath.

Slowly, the hand turned, and the tip of the blade pivoted and found purchase, slipping under a few layers of skin and drawing a bloom of blood.

One of the child's hands twitched at the pain. Her head moved, and a meek voice rose from the bag, but before it could plead for mercy, before it could cry for help, before it could do anything, the wielder of the knife arched it downward and plunged it through the child's back. The horrifying realization of Paisley's gift revealed that the knife caught briefly on a rib. Then the blade rotated, absent of any torque from the hand holding it, likely rolling to slide between that rib and another. The knife hesitated again as it hit the bone on the other side, the sternum, and the sound the child made, like a birthday balloon after the party had ended and the clean-up began, meant the knife had punctured her lung.

Paisley squeezed her eyes shut, but the sound did not stop. The wheezing and agony. A sucking sound as the knife came free. A blast of that restricted air as she was stabbed again. She couldn't. She wouldn't listen to anymore. She wanted to reach out and slam the laptop shut, but couldn't risk opening her eyes and seeing the screen. She covered her ears, but the sound found her. She drowned it out with her own screams.

49

Leaves blew in circles, slithering into the library like a snake uncoiling to strike as Paisley pressed the door open. The room still held that book smell, which again recalled images of Boyd; she wondered if the smell of old books would ever not evoke guilt for potentially causing the death of a kind man who wanted nothing more than to help her.

Derry followed Paisley and Patch into the library.

"You okay?" Derry asked, lifting the camera bag off of Paisley's shoulder.

"Huh?" she replied.

"You were sort of staring off into nothing," Derry said. He set the bag on the table. "Want me to get this set up?" he asked, patting the equipment.

"Oh, um, sorry. Yes, please."

"Of course." Derry unzipped the bag and pulled out gear. He handed it to Patch, who stared at it quizzically.

Paisley wasn't sure what was next. Investigations seemed easier in Grey Water Ridge. There she just went where the information was. Here, she hoped the library would provide that. But it wasn't as easy as looking up information on who would benefit from a string of high-publicity murders. Who benefits from a little girl dying? Or from multiple little girls dying? Why would that person want to record those killings? The thought conjured visions of the knife being pressed into the child's skin.

"Camera, too?" Derry asked.

Paisley flinched when he spoke.

"Sorry. I didn't mean to startle you," he said.

"It's okay. Sorry." She didn't want to bring up the videos yet.

She didn't know everything she needed to know about the boys just yet. "I just need to send a couple of quick messages, so if you could set the camera up, too, that would be great."

Patch held up a thumb. He hadn't really said anything since she met up with the boys on the street and came in, but she herself hadn't been in the most talkative mood, so who was she to judge?

"We got you," Derry said, pulling a tripod from its bag.

Paisley tapped her messaging app and started typing.

ParanormalOrNot - *You around? I'm having a bit of a crisis.*

WhyItHurts - *I'm here. What's up?*

ParanormalOrNot - *I'm struggling with this. This all has to be connected. Derry's sister, the girls on the videos. The podcast.*

WhyItHurts - *What is bothering you about it?*

ParanormalOrNot - *In Grey Water it all seemed to make sense. Someone wanted to draw attention to the town so they killed people to draw attention. But these videos were private. They hadn't even downloaded them. It isn't like the sicko who is killing these girls can monetize them or anything. So who benefits? Why am I here?*

WhyItHurts - *Is that why you are there? Did you go there to solve these murders?*

ParanormalOrNot - *Well, no, but I'm here and I want to help.*

WhyItHurts - *But that isn't why you went. So currently you're chasing two rivers.*

ParanormalOrNot - *Better than chasing waterfalls.*

WhyItHurts - *You're a dork.*

ParanormalOrNot - *So what am I supposed to do? I came here to help this kid determine if the voice on his podcast is his sister or not.*

WhyItHurts - *So you've determined the voice is a ghost?*

ParanormalOrNot - *Well, no, but if it is then I need to figure out if it is her. I assume it is real and I assume it is her. You saw the guy at the cemetery. He's seen her a number of times.*

WhyItHurts - *Investigators don't go off assumptions, Paisley. You can have a hunch you need to prove, but don't let the hunch be the proof.*

ParanormalOrNot - *Ugh.*

WhyItHurts - *What?*

ParanormalOrNot - *I hate it when you make sense.*

WhyItHurts - *Sucks for you as that seems to be my whole personality.*

ParanormalOrNot - *Yeah, and it annoys the shit out of me.*

WhyItHurts - *Again, you sound like every man I've ever dated.*

ParanormalOrNot - *So what is it that I need to solve? What's step one?*

WhyItHurts - *Again, what drew you out there in the first place?*

ParanormalOrNot - *I wanted to help the kid determine if it was his little sister or not.*

WhyItHurts - *I thought your show was called Paranormal Or Not with Paisley Mott. Not It's Paranormal Now Let's Figure Out Who It Is.*

ParanormalOrNot - *You're really bad at names.*

WhyItHurts - *You know what I mean.*

ParanormalOrNot - *So I can't just assume that it is a ghost. I can't really prove that it is a ghost, so I have to remove all other possibilities.*

WhyItHurts - *Right.*

ParanormalOrNot - *Well that isn't nearly as entertaining.*

WhyItHurts - *Good thing you are an investigator who makes content and not a content creator who investigates...*

ParanormalOrNot - *Ugh.*

WhyItHurts - *Be careful out there. Whoever is killing these girls, they've been doing it a long time without getting caught. If they catch wind that you are on their trail, they could get angry.*

ParanormalOrNot - *Maybe I should only mention the voice on the podcast when doing the lives.*

WhyItHurts - *Might be wise.*

ParanormalOrNot - *Okay, I will be careful not to show anything about the serial killer stuff until it's all said and done. That's not a sentence I ever thought I would say.*

WhyItHurts - *And yet it isn't the first time it has applied.*

ParanormalOrNot - *I need a new hobby.*

WhyItHurts - *Be careful out there, Paisley.*

ParanormalOrNot - *You know me.*

WhyItHurts - *Precisely my concern.*
ParanormalOrNot - *I'll message you later. Thank you.*
WhyItHurts - *Be safe. xo*

Paisley put her phone away as the boys put the finishing touches on the setup.

"How does this look?" Derry asked, in his eager-to-please way.

"Looks perfect." She stared into the distance; what WhyItHurts had said floated in front of her, blocking her from seeing anything else.

"Derry?" she finally asked.

"Yeah?"

"Are you certain that the noise you heard was your sister's voice?"

"It was Lydia, for sure."

"On the podcast you didn't seem to want to state that you knew it was her," she pointed out.

"Yeah, I didn't want to make it a statement because I like the idea of people making up their own mind, you know?"

"It's her," Patch added without looking at the two of them.

Paisley crossed over to the large boy who was sitting with his elbows on the table and his face in his hands.

"How can you be so sure?" she asked.

He looked up at her. His eyes were red.

"I've heard her voice a million times. I still hear it in my dreams. It's her." Patch stated.

"I'm sorry, Patch," she said and touched the boy's shoulder.

"It's her," Derry added. "Promise."

"I believe you. But for the sake of the investigation, I have to eliminate as much doubt as I can."

"You can just listen to her," Patch said, pulling out his phone. "Do you have the episode downloaded? Can you play just the voice?"

"I think so," Paisley said. She retrieved her phone, clicked the podcast app, and saw that she was still right at the end of the episode. She hit play, and the boys' voices filled the room.

"See ya."

"Later."

"Derry?" the voice called.

The voice came through. She'd listened to it a hundred times, but this time it sounded more like a little girl than it had before. The hair on her arm stood up.

Patch held up his phone and hit play on a video. It showed Derry, a little younger, sitting on the couch in his living room, the phone clearly held by Patch who sat in one of the chairs across from him.

"Shhh," younger Derry said, as he maneuvered a video game control through the air as if the movement provided better control of the unseen character he controlled. "You'll wake up my dad."

The camera panned to the tv. A muted video game flashed wild lights and colors. The camera panned back to Derry on the couch, and then to the hallway behind him. A white figure stood in the darkness. Then a little clarity. A dingy pajama shirt seemed to float in the darkness. It was a little girl. It was Lydia. She stepped forward, a stuffed bear in her hand. She had been jostled awake by the noise from her brother and his friend.

"Derry?" Lydia said.

Paisley's breath made a fist in her throat. Something was there, something about the voice. It caught in her mind like a fish hook and pulled, tearing at a memory that refused to come.

"Play it again," she said.

"Don't," Derry said, putting his hand on Patch's, pushing the phone down. "Please, I don't want to hear it."

"Okay, Derry, we don't have to. It's okay," Paisley said. "Let's just do the interview, okay?"

"Okay," Derry said, as he pulled a chair up next to Patch and sat, leaning his head on the boy's arm and patting him on the back.

Paisley started the camera and focused it on the two of them.

"Tell me what you know about the other murders," Paisley

said.

Derry and Patch sat across the table. Sweat beaded their brows, and they both squirmed in their seats.

"We've already done your introduction, so now let's jump into some more serious stuff. Is that okay?" Paisley asked.

"I don't have to talk about Lydia again, do I?" Derry asked.

"Not until you want to," Paisley answered.

"Okay, thank you." He wiped the sweat on his forehead with the back of his hand.

"Derry, as the host of the popular show, The Simply Knot Paranormal Podcast, can you fill the viewers in as to what sort of wild things happen here in your home town of Howling Ivy?"

Derry took a deep breath and gathered himself.

"Thank you, Miss Mott. Yes, the town of Howling Ivy is pretty wild. We've had a number of unexplained incidents over the last half a dozen plus years, and the frequency of those incidents is increasing."

"What are some of the things that residents have claimed to see?"

"Well, one of the things that folks have claimed to see, fairly frequently, is ghosts," Derry said.

"Ghosts? Well that's not nothing," she replied.

"There have been a number of sightings out at the cemetery."

"Happens a lot out there," Patch added.

"Oh, interesting. Have either of you ever experienced a haunting?" Paisley asked.

"I've had experiences that I can't explain, but I would be hesitant to call them hauntings," Derry said.

"I saw a ghost at the graveyard. Does that mean it's haunted?" Patch asked.

"Haunted just means there's a spirit present," Derry answered.

"Oh, then yeah, that shit is haunted," Patch said. "Oh!" He

looked at the camera.

"It's okay," Paisley assured him. "You can cuss. It isn't live, so I can edit it if you need me to. But I'll likely be leaving that shit in."

"Fucking excellent," Patch said.

"Fuck yeah," Paisley answered. They turned to Derry. He looked up at them and registered what they were waiting for.

"Oh. Sorry... um...but." He said after a short pause.

"You're really bad at cussing, you know?" Paisley said.

"Yeah, I've been told."

"So, ghosts in a cemetery, that checks out. What else?" she asked.

"Well, we told you about the spider thing," Patch said.

"Ah, yes, the spider man that you didn't actually see, but the guy that I was stuck alone in a car with, in the middle of nowhere, claimed to witness firsthand." The snark in her voice was very apparent.

"Okay, what about the zombies?" Patch countered.

"Zombies?"

"And the aliens," Patch continued.

"Ghosts, giant mutant spiders, zombies, and aliens right here in Howling Ivy, huh?" Paisley tried to hide the true level of her skepticism, but let a little show to encourage the debate.

"Ghosts, yes, I think I can vouch for that. But the spiders, zombies, and aliens I can not," Derry said. It wasn't often that he seemed annoyed by his friend, but there were cracks starting to show.

"So we've talked a little about the ghosts and the spiders, tell me about the zombies and aliens," Paisley said with practiced professionalism.

Paisley could see that the older boy understood more than she thought he did. He picked up on the cues Derry sent. Paisley had read that kids with traumatic family lives often develop a better-than-average ability to read behavior, even if they don't realize they are doing it. The book said that they were so used to watching closely to see if the people around them were going to hurt them that they became natural radars for people's bad intentions.

"Yeah, the alien and zombie stuff was just what Lida, the lady that works at the diner, told us, right dude?" Patch asked Derry, clearly seeking approval.

"That's right. She said there were people who had died and came back. And when we asked how, she laughed and said they were probably aliens," Derry responded.

"Wait, so the zombies are aliens?" Paisley asked.

"No, they aren't zombies, just people that were dead and somehow came back," Derry clarified.

"She said they might be aliens," Patch interjected as if he had just remembered this really important piece of information. "Or time travelers."

"Oh, yeah, I forgot about that. But she didn't say *time* travelers. She said *dimensional* travelers," Derry corrected.

"I'm sorry, they are what?" Paisley asked. She understood the concept he was trying to explain but wanted him to expand on it for the audience who would be watching this down the stream of time somewhere.

"She said, like, what if there was a hole in space and time, and there was a dimension just like this one on the other side, that you could theoretically have multiple versions of the same person across multiple dimensions," Derry said.

"I didn't get that part," Patch said.

Derry turned to him, and the tone of his voice was one that only a best friend could muster.

"Remember in Avengers: Endgame, when they are talking about going to other dimensions and seeing themselves?" he asked.

"Oh, the multiverse," Patch said.

"Exactly, buddy," Derry said, clapping him on the shoulder.

"So which is it?" Paisley asked. "Zombies, aliens, or dimension-hopping time travelers?"

"None of the above. It was just Lida being funny," Derry said. It was obvious he thought the world of the woman by the way he sat up when he talked about her.

"Did she say she saw something?" Paisley asked.

"Nah, she was asking everyone at the diner if they had seen something like that. If they'd seen someone who died come back," Patch said.

"Like a ghost?"

"Like just alive again. It was weird," Patch continued.

"But why did she want to know that? And why did she think you two had seen something like that?"

"She was asking us if-" Patch started but was cut off by Derry.

"She wasn't asking us. She was asking Lydia," he said.

Paisley held her follow up question. Why would Khalida need to ask Lydia that question? What is the connection? Could Khalida have known that Lydia would be a target? She thought back to the videos. Could the person in them have been Khalida? She didn't think so, but she hadn't actually seen the killer as they were always in full sleeves and wearing gloves.

"Why would she be asking Lydia?"

"She was asking all of us, but she was staring at Lydia the whole time," Derry said.

"That sounds very weird. Did she ever mention it after that day?"

"She mentioned it a few other times, but never really pressed like the first time. More of just asking if we'd seen anything weird for a while. But she stopped," Derry said.

"When?" Paisley asked.

Neither of the boys answered, but the silence was answer enough.

"Okay," she continued. "What do you know about the girls who disappeared?"

"The girls before Lydia?" Patch asked.

"And any after," Paisley added.

"There weren't any after," Derry said. His head hung a little lower.

"She was the last?"

Derry nodded.

This was a touchy subject; and she didn't want to risk Derry closing up.

"How much time passed after the last one but before Lydia?" Paisley asked.

"A couple of months, maybe half a year," Derry replied.

"Was that always the space between the deaths?"

"Yeah," Derry replied.

He looked defeated. She hated doing that to him. Some things that just didn't add up, but maybe she could get answers elsewhere and then return to Derry when she had more edges to pull up.

"How are you feeling?" she asked.

"Me?" Derry asked.

"Yeah, you. You doing okay?"

"I don't know. This is a lot harder to talk about with someone else, you know?" His voice caught in his throat.

"Why don't we call it a day?" she replied and started reaching for the camera.

"That's it?" Derry asked. "I don't feel like we are any closer to knowing what is going on."

Paisley sat back in her chair. Derry's voice warbled when he spoke and the idea of continuing seemed cruel.

"I just don't know what else to do without more information. I don't know what to ask. I'm sorry."

"I got an idea," Patch said, raising his hand.

They looked at him.

"We could get one of those We G boards," he said.

"Huh?" Paisley grunted. "You mean Ouija board?"

"Is that what it's called? I just thought it was like *We G,* like we ghost or something."

"That could be interesting," Paisley said, then looked at Derry. "What do you think? Would you be okay trying something like that?"

Patch shrugged.

And that was enough for Derry. "I guess so," he said.

"What the heck, let's give it a try. I've got a few things to dig into but I will find a board before the next time we get together, okay?"

"What do you have to dig into?" Derry asked.

"You know, just the whole thing, really. I feel like I don't know the history, and I want to be respectful about it all. So I want to get what news and such there is, then have you two fill in the details. Does that sound alright?" she asked.

"Thank you," Derry said.

"For what?" Paisley asked.

"Caring."

50

The video quality of the third video was better, brighter, but the workbench was the same. The wooden top was pitted from tool marks and stained with old blood, the color of deep rust.

The camera did not move as another plank of wood slid onto the work surface. The plank had two large eyebolts attached to the edge of one end.

Paisley watched in horror as a child was carried in and laid on the slab. The child wore an adult size t-shirt that fit more like a nightgown. The same burlap style bag hung over her head and blonde curls twisted their way out from underneath.

It was impossible to gain any information from the person manipulating the child as they never showed their face, their arms fully covered by a black shirt, and wore rubber gloves.

One of the gloved hands reached into frame and lifted the girl's hand, palm up. Without warning, a tool entered the frame, pressed into her hand and there was a *thwack*. Once released, it left a small metal circle. The child jerked and screamed. In quick and terrible succession, the tool pressed against the girl's wrist, popping and leaving another similar circle, but now, that circle, along with the one in the hand, oozed. The girl screamed again trying to free her arm. The circles tore the flesh, spitting blood with each tug. The torturer repeated this process again and again and again. Five welts between her bicep and her hand. Blood seeped from each.

Her free hand shot up to the sack over her head but a gloved hand caught it, shoving it down. The killer stretched out across the table and slammed the tool down into the open hand of the girl. Bile rose in Paisley's throat as she got a clear look at the nail gun just before it bit into the girl again. She choked it back, holding a scream in with it.

Four more pops as nails buried themselves through the girl's right arm. The poor child sank her fingernails into the wound, clawing at the metallic infestations, but it was useless. Her right foot was yanked down and pressed against the board and a nail was driven through the top, flattening what arch she had, then another, and another. Her left foot was placed on top of it and the process repeated.

Paisley punched the mute button and was mercifully thrown into the relative quiet of the room, minus her own sobs.

A chain ran through the eyebolts, and the slab was pulled away from the table, leaving only the workbench in frame. There was hope that the video would end there, but disappointment was followed by horror as the camera jerked and tilted upward to reveal the tragic image of the board, now suspended in air, and the girl crucified upon it.

The child fought the pain and wrestled the spikes restraining her. Blood speckled the camera lens when her left foot popped free. She used the foot to plant on the board and try to push away. But her fight was not long-lived as a brilliant flash of light lit the room and a red rose of blood bloomed from a fresh hole in the sack. The body went slack and hung there in the center of the frame, before the camera went dark.

51

The muffled rain outside drummed steadily like tiny hands trying to break through to rescue Millicent from her hell.

She sat against her post, her dirty clothes hung in tatters around her. The chain around her waist had to be tightened as she had lost a considerable amount of weight.

Creaky hinges signaled the opened door and were followed by the familiar sound of the man's boots on the wooden stairs. Millicent would count them every time he came down. Fourteen stairs in all.

"Hey there," the man said. "I brought you some different clothes." He walked over to her. He had the usual plate of food in one hand and a folded stack of clothes in the other.

She always wondered how he was able to walk down there without hitting his head on the ceiling, but he never did. He did manage to smack into the light once, and the bulb broke. It cut his head and he yelled a lot. She thought for sure he was going to kick her, but he hadn't. She noticed now that the cut was gone, no scar.

Millicent struggled to smile at him.

He handed the clothes down to her and she took the small pile.

"Here's your supper," he said, placing the plate of food on the ground next to her. It was tacos. Sometimes it was pizza, sometimes sandwiches, sometimes hamburgers or hotdogs. "And I brought you something special," he said, pulling a plastic bottle from his back pocket and twisting off the cap.

A hiss escaped the bottle and the memory of sugary soda filled Millicent with joy. She smiled, a real smile.

He handed her the bottle.

"I hope Sprite is okay. It's all we had." He waited for her to respond, and when she didn't he turned, crossed the basement, and climbed the fourteen stairs.

Once the door was closed and locked, and she was once again alone, she held the green plastic bottle to her lips and tipped the sweet liquid into her mouth. The flavor exploded and the sugar rushed through her veins. She leaned back against the post, stretched out her legs, and took another sip. She picked up one of the tacos and unceremoniously ate it in just a few quick bites. She washed it down with another sip of the soda, wiped her hands on her dirty dress and lifted the clothes to see what he had brought her.

The jeans looked like they would be too big for her, but she thought she would grow into them. The shirt had the character of Ben 10 on it. And there was a three-pack of boys' underwear, also too big, and a five-pack of tube socks, which she was very happy to have given how cold it got in the cellar. She carefully held the plastic bottle cap between her fingers, filled it to the top with the sugary liquid, and placed it on the floor beside her. She ripped a piece of the tortilla off one of the remaining tacos and set it next to the cap and waited.

It wasn't long before Squeakers snuck out from his hiding place behind the dryer to have his supper and enjoy the soda treat with their friend.

52

"Okay, so the longer someone is dead, the clearer they will show up?" Paisley asked. "So, how long after you buried Lydia Knot did it take to see her"

Stil sat in a lawn chair across from Paisley. The cemetery building once again loomed behind him. He mulled over his response.

"Oh, well, that's tricky because she only formed a few times, and that wasn't for very long. Just a few minutes at a time."

"But shouldn't she, after all this time, appear more solid?"

"Oh, yeah, but she ain't like the rest, I suppose. I don't know why, but she ain't. Maybe she just didn't want to be here? Maybe she was lost? Or trapped? You know, like in those movies where they got to find their bones and what not, and put them in hallowed ground?"

"You think that's the case? Isn't her body already in hallowed ground?" Paisley asked.

"Oh, yeah, sure enough she is. Yep. Right here in the cemetery. So maybe it's something else? Maybe it's because the murder ain't been solved yet?" he suggested.

"But how would she know?" This was something that she always wondered about TV and movies. If the spirit was following the person solving the murder, and if they were helping them, then they would know the murder had been solved. Otherwise, how would the spirit know?

"Oh, I guess maybe she'd just know." Stil seemed a little defeated by this. Not because she had tricked him into admitting his logic was flawed, but disappointed in himself since he hadn't thought of that. "I guess they wouldn't."

He looked around the cemetery, his eyes rolling over the vast sea of stones.

"Are you okay?" Paisley asked.

Stil faced the cemetery. Something was eating at him.

"Stil?"

"What if they're all stuck?" he asked. "What if there are poor souls just wandering around trying to figure out what's next, and they don't know that they've been vindicated or avenged or whatever?"

Paisley looked around the cemetery, too. So many headstones. So many bodies. So many spirits?

"Maybe that's why they always show the person going back to the cemetery to talk to the headstone? Maybe they are telling the spirit," Paisley suggested.

"But what if they didn't?"

"Well, Stil, what would you do?"

"Oh, what would I do about what? If I was murdered and I didn't know the killer was caught?"

"No. What would you do if I solved the murder of that little girl and all the little girls he killed before? What would you do?" she asked.

Stil hesitated. He looked over in the direction of the grave and then off in the other direction as if he was trying to see something else. A place or a time far away.

"Oh, I'd tell her, I guess. If I could, I'd walk over to where she's buried with a handful of flowers. I'd sit right next to her, place the flowers above her, and tell her that this whip-smart young lady from the internet has given rest to her everlasting soul."

Paisley sat with the weight of his comment. She knew if she tried to speak she would fail.

What if she could offer that? Not just to Lydia Knot but to the other girls the killer had taken. What about future victims? How many souls, living and dead, could Paisley save? WhyItHurts's message came back to her. She was an investigator first. And the case was more important than the story.

"I'm going to find him," Paisley started. "And you, Stil, are going to get to tell her just that. Will you do that for me?"

The look on Stil's face told a story. His face sank as if making a big decision. One he had been contemplating for a long time.

"Oh, yeah. Yes. I mean yes, of course, thank you," he said.

"Stil?" Paisley asked, after a moment of letting them both release their emotions.

"Oh, yeah?"

"Tell me more about the little girl you see?"

53

Murky fog, like sweat, descended upon the cemetery, gravely reducing visibility. Sunrise was more than two hours away. The likelihood of it burning the fog away in time for Stil to dig the hole he needed for the service the next day was next to nothing. He'd have to dig the hole and drop in the liner, and that was an all day project. He needed to get started on time.

Normally, when a hole needed to be dug, he would roll out of bed, make his coffee, and get to the cemetery by four o'clock in the morning. That morning, with the fog, was no exception.

He loaded all the tools needed into the trailer, hooked it up to the backhoe, and started the trip down the hill toward the new section of the cemetery.

Stil parked the machine, jumped out, and grabbed his metal detector. He passed the unit over the ground a few times and was rewarded with the pinging beep that told him he had found the lot marker. He cleared away the overgrown grass above it and checked the number stamped on the stainless steel marker. Then, checked against his paperwork.

"Lot 217, plot number one," he said, returning his clipboard to the cab.

"Oh..." he looked up, and there, in the fog, was a figure. Not a solid form but much clearer than the last time he saw her, assuming that it was her as she stood beside the same grave. The figure looked back at him. She appeared to be a young girl of about six or seven, though it was hard to make out any features. She wore a dress that looked too small. He remembered that dress. He had seen it before when he was helping prepare the little girl's body for burial. It was the little girl who got burned to death. She stared at him and the horror of seeing her body, charred and unrecognizable as a human being, came flooding back to him. He remembered the funeral director telling him about trying to get that dress on her without just breaking her damaged body apart. About how hard it was to even tell what was an arm and what was a leg because the body was burned just shy of the point of cremation. Had they had it their way, they would have just fired up the incinerator and finished the job, but her dad said no. He didn't want her cremated. He wanted her buried so that when he died, he could be buried near her. He'd even sold his car to put a down payment on the plot next to hers.

"Hey," Stil said to the figure as she stood or floated; it was hard to tell, especially in the fog. Her form was hard to see as certain parts were more translucent than others.

She didn't have eyes, but the darker areas where her eyes should have sat on her pale face seemed to be facing him. He couldn't escape that encroaching vulnerability felt when someone is watching.

"I'm just going to set about to get this new hole dug, if you don't mind?" he said to her.

The spirit moved a little closer and tilted its head as if looking to see what Stil was looking at.

"Oh, that? That's the marker. They make them out of metal, so we can use this here detector to find them when the grass gets too long, or there is snow on the ground and such," he explained, holding up the metal detector as if his audience was a class full of kids and it was show-and-tell.

The face angled back up to him.

"Oh, okay. So then after I find the right lot, I check for the plot number on my sheet. Then I measure over from the marker to make sure I'm digging in the right place." He whipped out his tape measure and pulled a few measurements. He took a screwdriver from his back pocket and stuck it in the ground to mark his spot.

"Then I get my jig." He pulled two eight-foot boards and two four-foot boards from the trailer. He made quick work of laying them out and joining them at the corner. "Now I measure again." He hopped around the edge of the setup, snapping off a quick measurement with his tape measure. "Now I dig it up!" He hoisted his spade shovel. He paused, awaiting a response from the spirit.

None came.

"Oh, I'm just joshin'," he said. "I'm not going to dig this thing by hand. I just use this to dig the outline, then pry up the sod."

When he looked up to see if she was watching his technique, she was gone.

"Huh. I must be pretty boring. Or there's a sale on sheets at the Walmart." He laughed at his own joke. Not because it was funny but because he knew it wasn't.

Stil continued on with his work. He peeled up the sod in squares and stacked them neatly next to the trailer. Then he jumped in the backhoe and began removing the dirt.

As he neared completion, he got out of the machine, grabbed his shovel, and jumped in the hole. The ground was still fairly soft as the frost hadn't yet hit, so it made for a quick job of squaring the hole and preparing it for the liner.

At five-foot-seven, Stil was not a tall man, and his head was lower than the rim of the six-foot hole he had dug. So, as he shoveled, he had to toss the dirt up and out of the hole. During one of these tosses, he saw her again. She stood above the hole looking down on him. She was still translucent, still incomplete, but she was there.

"Oh, hey there," he said. "Sorry if I got you with the dirt."

She floated around the side of the hole as if trying to get a better look.

"Right now, I'm just trying to square everything out. I make them four-feet wide by eight-feet long so that the grave liner, that's the concrete box that the casket sits inside of, we want to make sure that slides right down in here. Then I'll put dirt around it but make sure none gets inside. It's got holes and such, so the dirt and the water will get in, but the weight of the earth put on top won't make the casket collapse once we put the concrete lid on." He jumped up with one foot on the side of the hole to push himself up and out.

She floated out of his way but observed his every move.

Once he was clear of the hole she floated down into it. Stil watched her descent, something about it was both sad and beautiful. He looked over the edge to see her as she reached the bottom. She rotated until horizontal as if this was her space. He stared down at her, and she stared back up at him.

Then she screamed.

The scream was piercing. It ripped through him, tearing all other emotion out of him and leaving only terror. Stil stumbled backward and tripped over his shovel, falling back into the pile of dirt and nearly hitting his head on the backhoe bucket. He scrambled to his knees and crawled back to the hole, but by the time he arrived at the lip of it, the screaming had stopped, and she was gone.

54

"And this girl was Lydia Knot?" Paisley asked.

"Oh, yeah, it was her," Stil pressed.

"How can you be sure?"

"She was the only little girl buried over there. Other than her, it was all adults. The last little girl killed before that was over on the south side with the others, 'bout six or eight months before Lydia."

"The others?"

"Yeah, the other girls that got killed. They all ended up on the south lawn. But that side was full, and Lydia ended up over here on this side. That's how I know it was her. She's the only one we buried over there."

Stil pointed down the hill to where the backhoe sat. There was a fresh hole and a pile of dirt.

"Is that a fresh grave?" Paisley asked.

"Oh, yeah. Old Laurie Stevens, from the high school, taught there for forty years. She lost her battle with cancer. God rest her."

"Is she in there now?" Paisley turned back to Stil.

"Oh, no. I was just digging the hole. The service isn't for a few more days. Just prepping it."

"So once she's in, you just push all the dirt back into the hole?"

"Oh, no, like I was telling the girl, you got to put the vault in. Then, the casket. Then the cap. Then you can pack what dirt will still fit."

"There's extra dirt?"

"Oh, yeah, we just take the extra back out and dump it near the woods," Stil said, pointing toward the tree line.

"I guess it never occurred to me that there would be a surplus of grave dirt," Paisley admitted.

"Oh, like they always say, beware of anyone with piles of excess dirt. Could mean they dug a grave."

"Is that what they say?"

"Oh, well, if they don't they should. It's good advice."

Paisley looked back out over the cemetery. How many trips down the hill to get rid of dirt did it take to fill such a large place. She turned to Stil, remembering that line of questioning that brought her there.

"How many of them are there?" Paisley asked.

"Oh, how many what?" Stil asked, not following.

"How many little girls have been killed?"

"Oh, there's twelve, with Lydia it's thirteen," he said.

"Thirteen children dead?"

"Oh, yeah. Sad isn't it?"

"And they are all buried here?"

"Oh, no, only nine here. The rest are in other cemeteries, just depends on where they lived."

"So how long has this been going on?" she asked.

"Oh, the first one was about seven or so years back, I'd say. Then they were pretty consistent after that. A few have been local, a few a county or two over."

"All the same person?"

"Oh, from what the Sheriff says, it was."

"So Lydia Knot was the last, correct?"

"Oh, well, the last I've heard of at least." Stil smiled as if to say that he would know if someone else had died.

"Why? I thought they hadn't caught him yet," she asked.

"Oh, no, they haven't, but he messed up with the last one. He got caught on video tape. So the theory is that he's probably hiding out somewhere, waiting for the heat to die down and maybe he'll do it again."

"Heat? It's been more than a year. Sounds like he was doing it every six months or so before."

"Oh, yeah, well we can hope he's done, but we just don't

239

know."

"And they are certain it is the same guy?" Paisley asked.

"Oh, yeah, I'm pretty sure that's what she said," Stil replied.

"Who said?"

"Oh, Jackie. She said that it was definitely the same guy, and that he was most likely from one of the neighboring towns."

"Who's Jackie?"

"Oh, Jackie Peck, she's the Medical Examiner. She covers all of King County and has seen most, if not all, of the victims, even the ones that don't get interred here. Her daughter was the first, you know?"

Paisley tripped over that dropped piece of news.

"Wait, what?" she asked.

"Oh, what?"

"Her daughter was the first?"

"Oh, yeah, went missing nearly eight years ago," he said.

"Peck? Shit, the giant, that's Winslow Peck, right? The guy that owns the junkyard?"

"Oh, yeah, that's her husband. Do you know Winnie?"

"I met him once, at the grocery store. He threatened me," Paisley said.

"Winnie threatened you? That doesn't sound like him," Stil replied, a confused look now plastered on his face.

"Well, sounds like the Winnie that you know and the asshole who tries to intimidate women are one and the same."

"Oh, I'm sorry. I didn't mean to make it feel like he didn't. Not at all. It's just disappointing. He's normally a gentle giant, you know?"

"Yeah, well he's lucky I didn't tase him in the balls," Paisley said.

"Oh, ouch. Yeah, he is very lucky. I'm sorry if I upset you. I certainly didn't mean to question you." The confused look had slid off of his face and was replaced with one of regret.

"Thank you, and I'm sorry I snapped at you."

"Oh, you don't have to be sorry. I'm just out of practice talking to living people I guess," Stil said with a laugh.

"Well I think you're pretty darn good at it," Paisley replied, pointing at the camera, "and I suspect they will think so too."

Stil flushed and smiled.

"You think so?" he asked.

"I do," Paisley said. "Now, back to this connection. You're telling me that Winslow Peck's wife was the coroner on her own daughter's murder?"

"Medical examiner, but yeah, I think she was pretty new back then, but she covered it."

"She's been the Medical Examiner the whole time?"

"Oh, yeah, I think so," he said.

"You think she'll talk to me? Even after the awkward instance at the grocery store with her husband?"

"I could give her a call and tell her you're a friend. I'll see if I can smooth things over. Just know there will be things she likely can't say, but there may be some info you can use for your show." He pointed at the camera. "And you may just find out that none of it is as interesting as it seems."

"Would you do that? Would you call her?"

"Sure thing," he said.

"Well that may be my next stop today," Paisley said, hitting the stop button on her camera.

55

The man wasn't often angry. When he was, he would
sometimes come into the basement and talk to her. Sometimes
he hurt her.

It was hot in the basement. Millicent leaned up against the
pole, flicking a small balled-up thread to Squeakers and waiting
as he pushed it back over to her before she did it again.

A few toys the man had brought lay around, but she wasn't
interested in those. He told her he found them in cars that
people abandoned or wrecked. She didn't like it when he talked
about that. It reminded her of the night he brought her there.
The night Alisha and Matt died. They weren't her real mom and
dad, but they might as well have been. She remembered the fear
as the big truck pushed their car off the road. She could
remember the pain as she came out of the car and hit the
ground. Then there was darkness until she woke up and heard
the man.

Her memory of all the things that had happened had been
fading, but what she could remember was the pain. That she
could not forget. She thought about the pain of the car
accident, and she could feel it. She could feel all the pain the
man and the woman upstairs had inflicted on her since she
arrived. There were no permanent reminders of the abuse on
her skin, but she could remember how each one felt.

His boots beat across the floor above her, and as hungry as
she was, she hoped he didn't come down. She'd gone hungry
plenty of times since being there. She had gotten used to it. But
the thirst, that never went away. Water conservation had
become very important, just in case he didn't come down for a
few days.

Metallic clicking sounds signaled his coming, which

Squeakers took as a cue to leave. The door swung open, and he came down the stairs carrying a bowl and her water bottle. He looked upset.

"I don't know how long we can keep doing this," he said, handing her the bowl full of sliced peaches in syrup.

Her eyes scanned his face for the look he got before he unchained. This meant pain.

"They got people out there asking a lot of questions, and if they come around here, and they find you..." he paused and took a drink of water from her water bottle, spit it out, looked at the bottle as if he thought it was something else, and then handed it down to her.

"Well, if they find you, I don't know what I'll do," he continued. "You know if I try to explain, they won't believe me. They'd probably think I'm some sort of pervert, you know?"

The peaches looked soft and sweet. Millicent plucked one of the slimy things from the bowl with her fingers and sucked it into her mouth. The second the sugary fruit hit her lips, she was thankful that he had come. Even if he was to hurt her tonight, she was glad to have the fruit.

"You'd tell them, right?" he asked. "You'd explain everything and just tell them that I was trying to do the right thing. And that I'm not some sicko or pervert. You'd tell them that, right?"

Millicent wiped her sticky fingers on her shirt. A dirty rag of a thing that, even though it was a size too small, hung off of her skeletal frame.

"Dammit," he said, and kicked at the ground.

The sound and proximity caused Millicent to drop the bowl of peaches. It clattered to the ground, managing not to break but spilling the fruit onto the floor.

"What the hell?" the man yelled, stepping back away from the slowly spreading syrup.

The peaches slithered through Millicent's fingers as she tried to pick them up. Finally, settling on cupping her hand and dragging it across the floor to push them back into the bowl.

"I'm going to have to figure something out. What we've been

doing just isn't working. I think it's time I start thinking about what to do with you, once and for all." He turned and went back up the stairs. He looked back at her as he went. She stopped scooping and met his eyes. He shook his head and continued up the stairs, locking the door behind him.

Millicent slipped the dirty peaches one by one into her mouth, looking over at the dryer, hoping Squeakers would come back. She had no idea how long she had been there, but she hoped she wouldn't be there much longer. She wanted to be with Alisha and Matt.

She wanted to be dead, like them.

56

Not every building in Howling Ivy was dirty, though they all looked it. The City Building was one of the few that, though it had a sepia tone to it, was very clean. It was easily the tallest building in town at four stories, but it would still look minuscule next to the abandoned factories that littered the land outside the town limits.

Paisley pulled open the heavy wooden door and entered the lobby. Stamped, polished concrete floors reflected the light from all the windows that lined the front and side walls. It looked well maintained, but as nice as it seemed, it was surprising that no one staffed the small desk near the entrance. Instead, there was a sign that said *"Please sign in"* next to a guest book.

Paisley grabbed the provided pen and filled out the line with her name and phone number. Then, in the column that asked who she was there to visit, she just wrote *"coroner."*

The board next to the elevator listed where everyone was located in the building. *Jackie Peck - Medical Examiner* was in the basement. Paisley punched the elevator button.

The coroner's office was not exactly what Paisley expected. She'd seen enough shows and movies to think that the woman would be standing in a lab with bodies all around. Instead she was greeted by another small waiting area with another unattended desk. Instead of the fancy polished concrete, the floors down there were dressed with the flattest carpet Paisley had ever seen, worn by decades of people walking over it, and she was sure that it was a thread's width from ripping through to the cement underneath.

The desk sat right in the middle of the room, facing the

elevator with nothing but a bell on it. Paisley tapped the bell and flinched with the surprising volume of its ring.

A head poked up and glanced through a window in a door at the end of the hall that read *Authorized Personnel Only.* The face disappeared before Paisley had a chance to wave.

A few moments later, the door opened and a woman came through; her hair, at the pretty stage between blonde and white, was pulled back into a ponytail. She wore comfortable clothes and shoes, the type one would wear if they stood for long hours of the day.

"Hi," Paisley said as the woman approached.

"Priscilla Mott?" the woman said, stopping in front of her and extending her hand.

"Paisley," she said. "Paisley Mott."

"Paisley, like that pattern?"

"Exactly." Paisley shook the woman's hand.

"Jackie Peck. Stilton called and said you might come by."

"Yes, I hope that's okay?"

"Sure, hon. I probably can't say much, but I'm happy to tell you what I can," Jackie said.

"Thank you so much. Honestly I was a little nervous about coming by," Paisley said.

"Nervous? Why? I don't bite."

"Well, after the slightly awkward introduction to your husband the other day, I was a little worried you wouldn't be interested in me bothering you." Paisley surprised herself with the candor, but she knew the camera in her button was recording and that, at some point, people would likely see this interaction. So, she wanted to stand up for herself.

"Yeah, I'm sorry about Winnie. He told me he ran into you. He's got a heart of gold, he just thinks in a straight line a little too much, if you know what I mean?"

"No, what do you mean by that?" Paisley asked, unsure how thinking in a straight line equated to harassment and intimidation.

"He doesn't always consider how things will be taken. He

just says what's on his mind, and doesn't put any thought into how it might make other people feel. Just sort of says and does things. But he never means any harm, promise. He just got a little ahead of himself. And when it comes to our little girl, Heather, he wears his heart right there on his sleeve." She put her hand on Paisley's arm. "I'm real sorry, hon. He's a big oaf, and if you don't know him, he can be scary as hell."

Paisley nodded. This made sense, but didn't make it okay.

"Thank you," she said. "I appreciate the explanation. It's no excuse, but at least I understand a little better."

"I promise, get him when he's not caught off guard, and you'll see the sweetest man you've ever met," Jackie said.

"Well, I truly hope I get that opportunity," Paisley responded. She wasn't planning to forgive the man just yet, but digging that grave any deeper at that moment wouldn't get her any closer to the answers she hoped for from the woman in front of her.

"I'm sure it could be arranged. We could have you over to the house for supper while you're in town. We could invite Stilton. He hasn't been by in a while. And he just loves my spaghetti."

The thought of going to that man's house was not appealing, though it was hard to deny the value it would add to both the investigation and the story. She'd feel better if Stil was there. That doesn't mean she would go without taking precautions, of course.

"That is a very generous offer, and I think it would add a lot to my..." Paisley paused. She could say it was a story and give the woman the idea that she was doing investigative journalism, but that wasn't what it was. It was bigger than that. She didn't want to just report the facts of a situation. Anyone could do that. She was there to help.

"A lot to your what, hon? Your internet show?" Jackie asked.

"Sorry, no, to um, to my investigation," Paisley answered.

Jackie's posture stiffened.

"Investigation?"

"Yes, I'm looking into a voice that one of the local boys picked up on his podcast. It's something known as an electronic voice phenomenon," Paisley explained.

"An EVP, I'm aware of them, but I didn't know someone captured one. Was it Derry?" She seemed to be easing again, but it was very possible it was a forced reaction to not come across as defensive.

"Derry Knot, yes indeed. They believe it's the voice of his younger sister, Lydia, who was the victim..." Paisley was interrupted.

"I am all too aware of who she is, and her significance to my office, and my family, ma'am," Jackie said.

"Oh, I'm so sorry. I meant no disrespect. It is an occupational hazard to overly explain myself to viewers, so I find myself occasionally doing it at the wrong time. Please forgive me?" Paisley's eyebrows sank along with her shoulders.

"I understand. I guess I'm just sensitive to the whole thing since my Heather was first, and Lydia was last."

"Last? Do you think there won't be any more? Is there a lead?" Paisley asked, hoping the quick question would lead Jackie to spill more information than she wanted to share.

"No, I just mean that she was the most recent," Jackie said.

"But there is reason for hope, right? The murders were happening fairly regularly, one or two a year, and it has been what, a year and a half since the most recent? Does that mean there's a chance it's over?"

"We don't know. There are so many unknowns," Jackie said. She leaned against the desk and sighed.

"Do you think it was all the same person, or do you think there was a copycat?" There would be a lot that Jackie wouldn't be able to say in an official capacity, and Paisley was a complete stranger. But sometimes people enjoy sharing information they shouldn't, especially with strangers.

"That's very, very unlikely," Jackie said, crossing her arms.

"With such a high-profile case, you'd think it would be fairly likely, wouldn't you? I mean, I don't know, I'm just an amateur investigator, not a coroner or a detective, so I'm just guessing."

"Medical Examiner," Jackie corrected.

"Right, I'm sorry. I'm embarrassed to say that I don't understand the difference between the two," Paisley lied. She did, in fact, know the difference. She just hoped Jackie's explanation would give her a look into the woman's psyche, even if just a little.

"A coroner picks up and transports a body. They do all the paperwork and work with the cadaver, but no medical training is required. A medical examiner is a board-certified physician in Forensic Pathology. We do the investigations, determine cause of death, and such. It's a big job."

"Wow, that's, wow, that is a much different job. Thank you for the clarification. So, Stil told me that you've been the cor..., I'm sorry, the medical examiner on all of the cases, is that true?" Paisley asked.

"Yeah. Even the ones that weren't in Howling Ivy were still in King County, which made them my problem."

"But same killer, for sure? Not a copycat?" Paisley rushed.

"No, the same method was used in all of..." Jackie stopped herself.

"All except the last one, correct? Lydia Knot was burned to death." Paisley knew she was pushing, and maybe it was too far, but if she let Jackie regroup, she may be less inclined to answer the questions.

"Since you seem somewhat familiar with the case," Jackie said, "I can assume that you know that the murder was interrupted by a drug fiend hiding in the building, and that it was very likely that the ritual had not been carried out to completion."

"Ritual?" The word hung between them like smoke.

Jackie studied Paisley's face. She was making a decision. Did she accept that Paisley had won this round and answer this one last question as her prize, or would she shut down?

Jackie nodded.

"Yeah, the others all had another piece to them, but I can't talk about what that piece is. It's classified since it is still technically an open investigation."

"I totally understand and respect that. I wouldn't want to jeopardize anything. I just want to understand, and if possible, help."

"Help? Hon, this has been an open case for years, and I have on good authority that we have most likely seen the last of the killings. So poke around with the EVP all you'd like, but I formally request that you stay away from the murder cases so we can do our jobs." Jackie pushed off the desk and stood up straight.

The woman was a shorter than Paisley but still had an intimidation factor about her. Paisley thought about the viewers and resisted taking a step back.

"How about tomorrow night for spaghetti?" Jackie asked, patting Paisley on the arm and stepping around her. She turned a quarter turn back toward Paisley. It was a very clear sign that the conversation was over, but she wanted to push for more.

"Tomorrow sounds wonderful, thank you," Paisley said.

"Great." Jackie pointed to a business card pinned to a cork board near the elevator. "My cell number is on there. Text me and I'll send you the address."

Paisley looked at the card and then back at Jackie, but she was already going through the *Authorized Personnel Only* door.

57

Groceries sat in bags on the counter in Paisley's rental, waiting to be put away but neglected while she tried to pull at the thread that floated at the edge of her subconscious. The only items removed from the bags were a container of grapes that sat, picked over, and dripping water onto the table from her half-assed job of rinsing them, and a Ouija Board.

She unpacked her camera and laptop bags. Once the laptop was set, she plugged the camera in and began scrubbing footage.

There was something about the video Patch had played on his phone. Paisley hadn't been in full-on anxiety mode, or else she would have caught whatever it was for sure, but whatever it was snagged that part of her. She didn't have the video, but she had video of the video, and she hoped that either the camera she had set for the interview or her pin camera caught it.

"Gotcha," she said, stopping on a frame of Patch holding his phone up to her. Luckily the camera had racked focus onto it, and she could see it fairly clearly, with a slight zoom in.

Patch panned side to side, going from Derry to the game and then Derry again. He looked so young. Then the camera panned back to the hallway and the figure that stood there in white. Paisley's palms began to sweat when she saw Lydia. She knew that the girl in the video was alive, but her appearing like a spirit in the hall was hard to ignore.

Paisley scrubbed forward slowly, one frame at a time. The girl looked tired as soon as she stepped into the light. Paisley's mind was fully engaged. The girl stepped forward on her left foot, keeping part of her weight on her back heel - a classic trait of someone who is used to retreating from danger. As she opened her mouth she squeezed her bear tight against her chest.

The sound was off, but Paisley watched as she mouthed *Derry* one frame at a time.

"Fuck me."

Paisley slid the slider back, turned on the volume, and watched the last part of the clip again.

"Derry?" Lydia said from the hallway.

Paisley's arm hair stood up. She skipped back.

"Derry?"

"You've got to be shitting me?" Paisley asked herself. "He didn't?"

Paisley isolated the name and exported the audio, then opened it in her editing software. She did the same with the podcast audio, pulling the EVP from the original clip. She had played the section Derry claimed was his little sister's voice so many times. She had tried so hard to prove it was something else. She had pitched it up, pitched it down, slowed it, sped it up, everything. She was convinced that it was Lydia Knot's voice. And now it was confirmed. It was her.

She lined the two clips up and overlapped the meter, they matched perfectly. She hit play, letting both sounds go at the same time.

"Fuuuuck," she said.

She placed the original sound clips one right after the other, then the overlapped version, and saved it. She sent it to Hyacinth, then called her.

Hyacinth answered on the first ring.

"Pais! I was just picking up my phone to call you! I'm bored as shit, and all Grover wants to do is talk about movies. I swear to Christ if the two of you weren't cut from the same cloth."

"Hey, Hy, um, sorry about your boyfriend, but I've got a thing I need you to listen to. I just sent it to you."

"What is it? Is it scary or gross? Because those are the only two things I can imagine you sending me. Is it the sound of that turtle trying to fuck the rock again? I don't want to hear that. I fell for it once; it won't happen again."

"Twice, actually, remember? Once when we were in the

hospital and then again at breakfast the day I made the bomb-ass omelets," Paisley said. "But no, it isn't that."

"It's not the damn goat screaming again, is it?" Hyacinth asked.

"You have to admit the goats are pretty fucking great. But no, it isn't. Will you just listen real quick? I don't want you to have any context."

Hyacinth was quiet other than her fingers gently tapping her phone screen. Then, there was nothing for a moment. Paisley thought this meant Hyacinth had her headphones in since the taps were quiet, and there was no sound when she presumed she was playing the audio clip.

"Uh, okay, I listened to it," Hyacinth said.

"And?" Paisley asked.

"And what? It's the same thing over and over. Sounds like a kid, a little girl, maybe. Is that the voice he heard?"

"Does it sound like the same girl saying the same name over and over, or does it sound like the exact same clip?"

"It sounds like the same clip three times."

"Dammit. I should have known," Paisley said.

"Known what?"

"One is the clip from the podcast, the one he said was captured while recording. One is a clip from a recording of the girl before she died that his friend had on his phone. The third is the two overlapped to show that there is absolutely no difference in them whatsoever."

"Oh! You think he faked it?" Hyacinth asked.

"I don't know. It sure sounds like it."

"Paisley Mott, uncovering the mysteries of the universe!" Hyacinth cheered.

58

The fourth video was quick but no easier to watch. The pulley system that had been used to hold the crucified body of a child had been repurposed to serve as a makeshift gallows. A noose had been hung through the pulley and lowered down to where a girl sat in the dark. The burlap sack draped over her head had been reused and had ghostly stains from bloody encounters with children before. It was not removed as the noose was stretched over her head and tightened around her neck. The child pulled away, but her hands had been tied in front of her and tethered to her ankles.

A sharp jolt brought her up, and her thin body stretched as she was lifted from the cement floor where she sat. Her body convulsed but took a relatively short time to stop moving.

After watching the lifeless body dangle motionless for a moment, the video ended.

Paisley was thankful for the quick and easy death of this particular child.

59

The library looked very different after dark. The incandescent bulbs dangled from fixtures that must have provided little light to the vacant space. It was the perfect setting for the task at hand.

"Did you find one?" Derry asked.

"Shockingly, or maybe not so shockingly, they had one at Walmart. It was in their board game section," Paisley said, pulling out the Hasbro version of the Ouija Board. It looked so commercial and disappointing. It wasn't like the boards seen in movies - thick wooden boards with ornate letters and a pointer that looked like it was straight out of a creepy oddities shop.

"That doesn't surprise me, actually," Derry said.

"But with the board games?" Paisley asked.

"Where would you put it?" Derry asked in return.

Paisley thought for a second, then responded with a smile. "The phones."

Derry registered the joke immediately, but not Patch. Confusion sharpened his otherwise friendly expression.

"Why would it be with the phones?" Patch asked.

"Think about it, dude," Derry said.

"With the phones?" Patch asked no one directly.

Paisley held her hand up to her head and mimed a phone. It did not help.

"Calling the other side..." Derry started.

"Oh! Because you are calling the ghosts," he said, slapping a hand against his forehead.

"Because you're calling the ghosts," Paisley said.

Patch didn't laugh; he just nodded as if important information had been imparted to him, and he finally understood.

"Are we sure we want to do this?" Derry asked.

"It seems like a logical next step," Paisley said. She had decided to wait to see if she could figure out why he would fake the voice on the podcast before accusing him. He may not open up as much once he knew she was on to him. "We need some solid evidence that the hauntings are real."

Candles purchased from the dollar store down the street illuminated the cheap board, and the whole scene more closely resembled game night when the power goes out rather than an attempt to make a connection with the dead. The library was dark, save for the cheap candles. Shadows glitched against the walls in the flickering light, causing the movement in the peripheral to seem unstable.

The board rested on the table, facing Derry, and candles lined along the top. Paisley and Patch flanked the sides. The trio sat looking at the board with trepidation. It was a moment Paisley could not have prepared herself for. She never assumed that she would be sitting in an empty library in the middle of the Rust Belt with two teenage boys, using a board game she bought for thirteen bucks at Walmart, trying to contact a kid who was burned alive in a duffel bag. What a weird life she lived.

"What do we do now?" Patch said. his arms hung at his sides as he sat in the chair, trying to avoid eye contact with the board.

"Well, let me just read the instructions," Paisley said, flipping the booklet out. "If desired, set the mood by dimming the lights or turning them off. Check." She pushed one of the candles with her finger. "Before using the board, wipe it with a dry dust cloth to remove dust and moisture." She ran her hand across the board as if wiping away anything that might be there before continuing.

"The board is brand new, so I don't think we have to worry. Now, sit opposite another player or gather around the board if more than two are playing." She looked around the table at Derry and Patch and nodded her approval. "Set the board either on the player's laps or on a small table between, and within reach, of the players. Additional players are encouraged to look on and take notes." Paisley stopped and looked up from the instruction booklet. "I think we will be okay without note-takers; what do you think?"

"I could take notes. What if we miss something?" Derry asked.

Paisley reached over and rested her hand on Derry's, just off the board. "Derry, I know talking to ghosts is old hat to you, but this shit is all new to me. So I strongly suspect I will remember every word that the dead decide to share."

Patch barked a laugh, and Derry followed.

"Okay, you're right," Derry said with a smile. "Plus, you've got the cameras going." He nodded toward the camera on the tripod that captured the whole scene.

"Now, where was I? Ah, yes, set the planchette in the center of the board."

Derry moved the cheap plastic pointer to the center of the board.

"Place two fingers *lightly* on the planchette," she continued.

Derry placed his first.

"Come on, dude," he said to Patch. "It's okay."

Patch reached slowly across the table and placed two fingers on the triangle. They both looked at Paisley.

She wasn't sure why she was hesitant. Was it trust? Did she trust that the boys weren't going to sabotage the outcome? The cameras might help, but she couldn't guarantee that she could detect foul play.

"Fuck it," she said and reached for the planchette.

A spark of pain, as if she had touched a cactus, pricked her finger. She gasped, pulling her hand back. The boys jerked their hands away as well, but everything happened so fast that she couldn't tell if one of them had thrown the piece of plastic or if she had, but it flew across the room and crashed against the wall.

"What the heck?!" Derry yelled, jumping back from the table.

"No way," Patch said. He didn't move away, but he pulled his hands back.

Paisley leaned away from the table but managed not to leap from her chair.

"Is everyone okay?" she asked.

"What was that?" Patch asked.

"Was it one of you?" Paisley asked.

"Wasn't me," Derry said, picking up his chair and scooting it back to the table.

"Not me," Patch said.

"Everyone's okay?" she asked again.

"I'm okay," Derry said. "Patch?"

"Yeah, I'm okay," the big man said.

Derry nodded.

Paisley got up from the table to retrieve the planchette. She stood above the plastic triangle, staring it down. She nudged it with her foot, and when she was satisfied that nothing would shock her again, she knelt and picked it up.

Minus a small crack in the plastic, the piece looked okay. The window in the center of the pointer was intact. She held it up close to inspect it further but saw nothing suspicious.

"Okay, let's call that a false start and give it another go," she said, sitting back down, placing the planchette in the middle of the board, and gently resting two fingers on it, trying her hardest to make it look like she wasn't terrified.

"You want to try again after that?" Patch asked.

"Sure, why not?" she asked.

"Um, because some ghost or something basically just told us to GTFO," Patch said.

Paisley looked to Derry for translation as she didn't speak fluid Patch yet.

"Get the f out," Derry said.

"Yeah, like, that's coming through pretty clear with throwing shit across the room, right? Like we all accept that was some fucked up shit, right?" Patch cried. He waved his hands around the room.

"We don't know what that was," Paisley said. "True investigators don't make assumptions."

"True, but they do make theories, and I think Patch's theory is pretty solid," Derry chimed in.

"Thanks, dude," Patch said, reaching out to high five his best friend.

"Course," Derry replied, slapping the large hand.

"It is a good theory, and what do scientists do when they have a theory?" Paisley asked.

"Well, they would... um, study that theory," Derry said.

He knew the answer. Paisley could tell he knew what she was looking for but was playing coy.

"They would test their theory," Paisley said. "Many, many times. And they would do that by observing something, creating a theory or hypothesis, and then repeating the test over and over again to see how external changes affect it." She smiled and put her fingers dramatically back onto the planchette.

Derry looked at Patch, raised his eyebrows, and tilted his head toward the board. Patch shrugged and placed his fingers across from Paisley's.

"Fine, I guess we can try again," Derry said. He sat down and stretched out to touch the board when suddenly, he lurched his hands back, grabbing his fingers.

"Oh my god, Derry?" Paisley yelled, leaping out of her chair, but Patch was faster. The big man was up and standing next to Derry before his chair hit the floor.

"My finger," Derry hissed through clenched teeth.

"Let me see," Patch demanded.

Derry obliged. He slowly lifted his hand, careful not to bump or move it too quickly.

"Don't touch it," Derry warned.

"I won't, man, just let me see what happened," he said.

Derry lifted his hands a little more, his left cupped over his right. He slowly removed the hand to reveal what he had been protecting.

"How does it look?" Derry asked Patch, pressing his extended middle finger, which had no visible sign of injury, up to Patch's face.

"Oh, dude, fuck you," Patch said. He laughed and shoved Derry so hard that the smaller boy nearly fell.

Paisley laughed and flipped Derry off. Patch joined in.

"Excuse me, madam, I am a child, and that is hardly appropriate," Derry said, trying to restrain a laugh.

"Well it's this, or shove that game board somewhere dark and full of terror," Paisley replied. This brought about more laughter from the group.

"Okay, if we're going to do this, we should do this," Derry said. "Enough of your games."

Patch flipped Derry the bird one more time for good measure. He kept the finger extended alone while he lowered it onto the planchette. Then, once it was settled, he extended his index finger to join it. The other two followed suit and placed their middle fingers on their pointer first, then allowed the index to join.

"What do we do now?" Derry asked.

"The instructions just say to concentrate," Paisley started, "then we ask it a question."

"What kind of question?" Patch whispered.

Being the avid film buff she was, Paisley had seen this play out a thousand times on-screen, so she knew what question to start with.

"Spirit, are you with us?" she said.

Both boys inhaled as the seriousness of what they were doing spattered onto their faces like a man standing behind the victim of a sniper's bullet.

"Dude, you moved it," Patch accused, flailing back but careful not to remove his fingers.

"It's moving," Paisley said in disbelief.

"That isn't you?" Derry asked neither of the others in particular.

Scratching sounds marked the slow, laborious movement beneath their fingertips. It looped once, picking up speed as it went, and stopped first at the top left corner on an illustration of a sun wearing a wicked smile. Next to the sun was the word *yes*. Then the planchette crept to the top right corner of the board, settling briefly on a crescent moon wearing a face in profile. Next to the moon was the word *no*.

The triangular piece glided across the middle of the board, creating a figure eight.

"I think that means it's ready," Paisley said.

"Ready for what?" Patch asked.

"A question," Paisley replied.

"You should do it," Derry said to her, only glancing up to meet her gaze before he refocused on the board and the mysterious plastic piece beneath his fingers.

"Is there someone here?" she asked.

"Yes," the three said aloud as the disk in the middle of the planchette centered itself over the word.

"Who are we talking to?" Paisley asked.

"T-I-F-F-A-N-Y," they said together.

"Tiffany," Patch certified.

Paisley looked at him, "Do you know a Tiffany?"

"Yeah," he replied.

Derry and Paisley exchanged glances, awaiting more information.

"And?" Paisley finally asked.

"And what?"

"Who is she, buddy?" Derry asked.

"Tiff? She's this chick that used to work at the pizza place," he said, looking back at the board in confusion. "But it can't be her."

"Why not?" Paisley asked, nearly regretting it as the words came out of her mouth.

Patch wore a stern expression on his face. "Because I told her never to text me at this number."

There was a moment where nothing happened. The world

appeared to cease moving through time and space. Finally, Patch's face contorted and he spit out a laugh.

"You fucker," Paisley blurted. She let go of the game and leaned back to hold her stomach while she let loose a rip of uncontrollable laughter.

Patch allowed his laughter to avalanche into full hysterics, putting his hands over his face as he coughed the sound into them.

The fit continued until Paisley noticed that Derry wasn't laughing. She looked at him through tears and saw that he had both hands on the planchette, which zipped around the board.

"Derry?" she said, sitting forward.

The boy did not respond. He was busy reading the letters under his breath.

"R-T-L-E," he said. His hands stopped as the piece came to a rest at the bottom left corner of the board.

There was a black drawing there of a group playing with an Ouija board. Phantom hands reached in from the sides holding a planchette, but the only person playing that could be seen was a woman whose hands were not on the game at all.

Derry's hands traveled again with the piece as the minuscule window revealed another face behind the woman. This one looked like the disembodied head of a child. The planchette spun in a circle and came to rest on the head. Then it did it again. And again, highlighting the child's face over and over.

The hair on Paisley's neck stood up as if a cold finger had run across the skin there.

The planchette jerked itself free from under Derry's fingers and swept itself quickly across the words *GOODBYE* on the bottom of the board. Then, it flung itself up toward Paisley. She screamed as the thing flew past her head. If it had been aimed at her, it would have hit her as she was not quick enough to move out of its way, but it wasn't. Instead, it struck something behind her and fell to the ground. Only there wasn't anything there. It struck thin air.

"What the fuck?" Patch said, jumping to his feet. His eyes

were fixed behind Paisley. Derry fixated on the same spot.

"What is it?" Paisley asked, her voice nearly unable to pry itself from her throat. She couldn't turn around. Even if she wanted to, she felt paralyzed.

"There isn't anything there," Derry said. "Well?" He sounded unsure.

"What is it?" Paisley asked again.

Patch took a step forward as Derry came around the table and stood directly behind her, his lower back pressing into her shoulders as if shielding her from something.

"What is happening?" she said.

"I don't know," Derry said. His voice sounded distant.

"Whoa," Patch finally said, shaking his head as if he had been in a trance. "What the fuck was that?"

Paisley turned in her seat, then stood to see around Derry. There wasn't anything there.

"I want to get out of here," Derry said.

"Dude, what was that?" Patch asked.

"What was it?" Paisley asked again.

This pulled Derry out. He looked at her as if he hadn't seen her a moment before.

"I don't know," he said. "It looked like a mirage."

"Was it a ghost," Paisley asked.

"We should get out of here," Derry pressed, turning and clicking one of the lights off. "Please?"

The look of fear and sadness in his face was impossible to ignore.

"Of course," she said. She moved to turn off the cameras and realized that there was one pointing directly at her. It would have captured whatever it was that the boys saw. She clicked it off and packed it away, knowing she might not be ready to see what was there.

60

The rental was quiet as Paisley spread her equipment out on the table. She hooked up her laptop to dig into everything that had happened with the Ouija board. Her first thought was that the boys had somehow played a trick on her. With the very strong possibility that the voice on the podcast was a fake, anything was on the table.

She had trusted Derry. She'd go as far as to say that she liked the kid. But if he was lying, and he tricked her into coming out there, what was his end game? The connection to Grey Water was obvious. Her stomach knotted at the thought. She had been led to Grey Water like a calf to the slaughter by someone much more charismatic and convincing than Darius Knot.

As the computer loaded the footage, Paisley leaned back in her chair and rubbed her fists against her temples. Thoughts moved around in her head like flies trapped between a window and a screen.

She picked up her phone, clicked into her streaming app, and hit the live button. She covered the camera with her thumb, casting the stream into darkness as she watched the viewer count rise. Once it was over a thousand, which was less than a minute, she uncovered the camera.

"Hey, friends!" she said to her audience. "I know I haven't been streaming live much, but I'm in the middle of an investigation, so it's a bit tougher right now. There isn't much that I can share, other than that things are pretty intense right now."

Comments rolled in.

KelpMe - *What's the story?! Another murderer??*
WhyItHurts - *You be careful out there.*

DexterDog - *Where is this one at?*

"I can't really talk about it. There are things that I'm finding that don't fit the investigation as I knew it, so I'm trying to sort it all out, ya' know? I really just..."

She paused. It was overwhelming. She wanted to have something to share, but there were still so many unanswered questions, and she wasn't sure how to get it all organized in her head. She was failing. She was failing Lydia Knot. She was failing all the other girls that were killed. Panic arose in her chest. She watched comments scroll by as she sat frozen, staring into the camera.

Djradmaddi - *You can do this. I know you can. You're Paisley Mott.*
DexterDog - *@djradmaddi is right! You are Paisley Fucking Mott! You got this!*
WhyItHurts - *We are all here for you.*

"Thank you all so much. It really does mean the world to me that you all support me so much. I needed that. I can't tell you much, but I can tell you that tomorrow I am having dinner at the home of the man who verbally attacked me and tried to intimidate me at the grocery store, his wife, the coroner, and the gravedigger because there is never a dull moment in the life of Paisley Mott, am I right?" Paisley could feel her heart rate beginning to slow.

A message went across the screen and Paisley tapped to hold it so she could read it a few times.

Hybloom - *I'm so proud of you. I love you.*

"I love you, too. Thank you," Paisley said to the audience, but Hyacinth would know it was directed at her. "Talk to you all soon. Mott out."

Paisley set the phone down. The anxiety amped up the focus on detail, but the audience, and the calm that came from them, helped her organize it. It was a cycle that she was trying to get used to and hoped to master.

She started the footage and began to scrub forward to the point when they were at the Ouija board.

Paisley stopped, and the video played. She and Patch had been laughing and missed what Derry had spelled out.

"F-I-N-D, find," he said. Then the planchette did a little spin, presumably to signal the end of a word. Paisley wondered if Ouija board operation was just something all ghosts understood. Was there a class? Was it like Beetlejuice? Was there a guide to the afterlife? Was it common to do the little circle between words? She had so many questions. " T-H-E, the. Find the." another spin. "T-U..."

"Derry?" Paisley said in the video. Derry just went on reading.

"R-T-L-E," Derry said.

The planchette moved to the bottom of the board, but Paisley was no longer focused on that but the spot behind her in the video. Something was there. At first, it looked like the reflection of a car's headlights going by. But when it didn't shift, just grew more opaque, she could make out shapes. Figures.

"Oh, oh fuck!" Paisley hit the spacebar, stopping the video. Her timing had been perfect. The planchette had just lifted off the board and was flying in her direction. Behind her, looking over her shoulder, was a group of young girls. They were still transparent, and most faded below the shoulders, but their faces hung in the air behind her like haunted dreamcatchers. It was impossible to tell for sure, but they all seemed to have light-colored hair and were roughly the same age. Paisley hit the spacebar, and the video played. The planchette bounced off the stoic face of the young girl just over her shoulder.

"What the fuck is happening?" The calm Paisley had pulled from the livestream was gone. Replaced with an empty feeling of isolation and terror.

She felt herself slipping into a valley of dread, but she managed to save and export the clip. She dropped it in the cloud folder so Hyacinth and WhyItHurts could see it.

Moments later her phone rang. It was Hyacinth.

"Jesus Christ, Paisley. Did you catch what I think you caught?" Hyacinth asked as soon as Paisley answered.

"I don't know. How did they do it? I get how they faked the voice, but how did they fake this? How could they do this? This is my video. They haven't had any access to it. There's no way that it's edited. It had to be a practical effect. How did they do it? Hyacinth, how did they make those kids appear there?" Paisley was speaking in bursts.

"What if it isn't fake, Paisley?"

"What do you mean? Do you think it is real? It can't be real. People don't just catch real live ghosts on camera." Her heart was racing. The sweat in her palms greased the phone, and she wiped them on her pants, putting the phone on speaker. She leaned over it.

"Well, no, they aren't real live ghosts, because if they were alive they wouldn't be ghosts," Hyacinth joked.

"What?" Paisley asked. "No, I just mean... oh, dammit, fuck you for joking at a time like this." Against her best judgment, she chuckled.

"Pais, there are things in this world that don't make sense, but it doesn't mean they don't exist." She sounded more serious than usual.

"What do you mean? Are you saying that you genuinely believe in ghosts?" Paisley asked.

Hyacinth seemed like the grounded-in-reality type. She always came across as skeptical, so the idea that she would believe in ghosts did not fit the narrative Paisley had for her. The thought made her uneasy.

"I believe in a lot of things. I think it's good to keep a cynical eye on all of this, especially after the voice thing, but I also think it's a good idea to leave a little room to suspend your disbelief because there's a lot to the world that we can't see."

"I just..." Paisley started. It wasn't like she hadn't believed in ghosts. She did. She went to the lighthouse in Jigsaw Bay, where she filmed her first viral video, looking for a ghost because a mother was struck by lightning and died there. Then, the woman's heartbroken fiancée took his own life there shortly after. The rumors of their spirits occupying the place were abundant. She wanted to believe that if there were ghosts, there was a Heaven. Because if there was, there was a chance that her mom was somewhere happy and not just reliving being stabbed in the stomach and thrown from a cliff every night like she was in some horror novel.

"Pais?" Hyacinth asked, pulling Paisley back to the conversation.

"Oh, sorry, I just, I am just having a hard time wrapping my head around this. How are you so calm?" Paisley asked.

"I've been introduced to some pretty weird things."

"Have you?" It wasn't that she didn't believe Hyacinth. It was just that she seemed like the type to be above all of that.

"My mom was into some wild shit before she died. And then there's dad's side of the family."

Before Paisley could follow up, her phone lit up as a notification came through. It was WhyItHurts. Paisley tapped the screen.

WhyItHurts - *Message me as soon as you can. There is something you have to see. You could be in danger.*

"Shit," Paisley said.

"What?" Hyacinth asked.

"I have to go, but this conversation is to be continued. I think you owe me answers."

"Is everything okay?"

"I don't know. If not, then I will let you know."

"Do you need me to come out there?"

Paisley's brain stopped racing and froze on that question.

"Come out here?" she asked.

"Yeah," Hyacinth said. "I couldn't be gone long. Just two or three days at most. Grover is doing well enough that he'd be okay with just the nurse. And Rowan is here if he needs him."

"Oh, Rowan." Paisley's voice drifted off. She had almost forgotten about Rowan. Was it a good sign that she was not focusing on someone who may be unavailable? Not through any fault of either of them, but because she may never get past how much he looked and sounded like Hollis. Or was it a sign that the trauma was not allowing her to think of things that could potentially make her happy? She didn't know, but now that Hyacinth had said his name, she wondered if he would be on her mind.

"Yeah, he's been helping out since my little breakdown," Hyacinth said very nonchalantly.

"Breakdown? What happened? Are you okay?" Paisley asked, not forgetting about WhyItHurts or Rowan, but the parallel thoughts of them froze in her head.

"Yeah, I'm okay now. I just freaked out a little the other day. I'm still processing everything that happened, and, like I said, I haven't had time to really sort through it myself. I needed a break. So Rowan dropped everything to help."

"He's a good guy," Paisley pointed out.

"Yeah, Paisley, he is. And that good guy really likes and misses you. If I have to listen to him ask me one more time if I've heard from you, I'm going to kill him. I need a break, girl."

"I don't know that coming out here is a break, but of course, I would love to have you." Paisley's phone lit again with another message from WhyItHurts. It was an image attachment. "Crap, I have to go, but I will call you back. Sounds like we have a lot to catch up on. Give Grover and Rowan hugs for me."

"Okay, Pais. Please be careful out there. I worry about you."

"It sounds like worrying about everyone is maybe your problem, Hy," Paisley joked but worried the truth in the joke was too large.

"Look who's talking," Hyacinth retorted.

"Touché."

"Talk to you later."

"Love you," Paisley said. She wasn't sure it was the right sign-off, but she meant it. Talking to Hyacinth had climbed the comfort ladder and was there at the top, just below calling her dad.

"Love you, Pais. Be careful."

"I will."

Paisley was trying to open the message before the screen had the chance to change. She worried that if she didn't just dive into whatever it was, the other thoughts would creep in, and she may be unable to sort them.

Paisley was confused when the photo opened. It was a mugshot of a man that appeared to be in his thirties. He was vaguely familiar.

ParanormalOrNot - *Who is this?*

WhyItHurts - *Here...*

Another image came through; this one was a screenshot. It looked like a court document that had been scanned. Paisley poured over it.

"Fuuuuuck," she said to herself. It was becoming her catchphrase.

WhyItHurts - *I took the liberty of searching for the guy from the cemetery when everyone said they recognized him. A lot of what they were saying was not true. There was a murder, but he wasn't in town when it happened. They just accused him because of a conviction a few years earlier.*

ParanormalOrNot - *Are you telling me that in the early 90s Stilton Hawke was convicted of felony abuse of a minor?*

WhyItHurts - *It appears so. And because it was a small town before computers were really used for all of this, there isn't a ton of information about the case. The victim's identity was redacted from these documents before they were uploaded because it was a minor.*

ParanormalOrNot - *Did this asshole sexually assault a child?*

WhyItHurts - *I tried to search for that too, but the registry only goes back to 1994.*

ParanormalOrNot - *Dammit, and I was starting to think this guy was a sympathetic case. Turns out he might be a fucking murderer.*

WhyItHurts - *Whoa, Paisley, slow down. I didn't show you this for you to jump to conclusions about the investigation. It was just to show you who you were going to be having dinner with. The big guy, Peck, has already proved that he is aggressive, and the wife seemed sketchy. I assumed that this Hawke guy was your safety net. You trust him, so you thought he'd keep everything even at dinner. I just wanted you going in with as much info as was available.*

ParanormalOrNot - *It just seems a little too coincidental, don't you think? I have a habit of falling for men's bullshit.*

WhyItHurts - *Let the evidence alone create the narrative of the investigation. Only facts can lead the case, not coincidence. We know nothing else about the conviction. I will look into it and see if I can peel anything back. I just want you to be safe over there.*

ParanormalOrNot - *Thank you. I appreciate you. I just need some time to digest all of this, and see if I can get some idea of the chain of events, and where everyone stands, you know?*

WhyItHurts - *I do. I understand very well.*

A loud thump burst the silence in the rental and Paisley jumped. It repeated.

ParanormalOrNot - *There is someone at the door...*
WhyItHurts - *Of the Airbnb? Do you have a weapon?*
ParanormalOrNot - *I've got my taser.*
WhyItHurts - *Get it out. And maybe a knife. Camera on. Be careful. Call 9-1-1 if you don't feel safe.*

Paisley took the advice. The knock came at the door again.

"Who is it?" Paisley called out as she grabbed the taser from her bag, a knife from the kitchen, and clipped on one of her camera pins, a shark wearing a cowboy hat and throwing a revolver. The camera peered out of his little black eye.

"Paisley Mott?" a woman's voice came through the door.

Paisley waved her hand in front of the pin camera and then looked at her phone. After a few moments she saw the message.

WhyItHurts - *Got it, you're live. Be careful. Sounds like a woman?*

"Yeah, sounds like it, but trust me, I will cut a bitch," Paisley said quietly to the camera on her shirt, then swiped the knife a few times in the air. Half for the person she knew was watching the camera and half for practice. As the blade swung far right, her attention landed on the tall, narrow, window next to the door that looked out onto the porch. Paisley had pulled the small curtain draped in front of it to the side that morning to let the sun in and had apparently not returned it to its place, as she could see a woman waving at her through the window. They made eye contact. The woman smiled.

"I've been made," Paisley said into the camera.

"Miss Mott, you don't need the knife or the stun gun. We are federal officers. We just need to have a quick chat with you," the voice called back through the door.

"The feds!"

Paisley returned the knife to the counter but kept the taser. She opened the door a crack.

"Can I help you?" she said through the slit. Her foot was positioned as a doorstop, and she hoped that it would stop anyone from just pushing in, but she wasn't prepared to bet her life on it, so she held the taser at the ready so that the first person through the door was catching volts.

Just like in the movies, the credentials were the first thing Paisley saw as the door opened. "Special Agent Haley Quinlan, Federal Bureau of Investigation," Paisley read out loud. She tried her best to angle the camera high enough to catch the credentials.

"Yes, ma'am, that is correct," the woman said. "Special Agent Haley Quinlan, this is Special Agent Theodore Prince. We came to ask you a few questions, if you have a moment?"

The woman's appearance was off-putting. It was similar to how Paisley felt about seeing Hyacinth for the first time. Typical beauty standards were not something Paisley ever used to judge anyone, but when someone looked like they stepped directly out of hair and makeup on a big Hollywood movie and into real life, she took note.

The woman wore a black suit with boxy shoulders. The jacket was perfectly fitted, and though Paisley knew nothing about tailoring or fashion, she assumed the jacket alone probably cost more than the average person's monthly paycheck. Or maybe she just wore it in such a powerful way that it felt like it. Her platinum blonde hair was cut short on the sides and brushed back.

Paisley's anxiety played its little trick, and she could see that the perfectly tailored jacket didn't leave any room for a gun, so perhaps it was tucked into the back of her waistband. Or maybe the man standing behind her was carrying enough firepower for the both of them.

"Question," Paisley stated.

"Yes?" the woman asked.

"In what world are those shoes practical for your line of work?" Paisley asked.

Their faces followed Paisley's finger and trailed down to look at the woman's shoes. She was wearing black high heels.

"Like, you have the full on vibes of a super villain," Paisley pointed out.

The woman laughed.

"I will take that as a compliment. As for the shoes, I'd like to ask *you* a question." She folded the credentials and slipped them into her jacket.

"Um, okay," Paisley said.

"If you dreamed of something your whole life. You thought about it day in and day out. You worked hard toward it. You trained and studied every free minute of the day. At night, you would lay in bed and think about it. It became who you were. And let's say you busted your ass, proving to everyone that you were the best of the best. Now, let's say you got everything you ever wanted, right?"

"Okay..."

"Then some man told you how you had to dress for it. You'd be pretty pissed, right?"

Paisley thought about it for a moment, conceded the point, and nodded.

"This makes me feel good about myself," Quinlan said.

"Is this who you wanted to be when you were little?" Paisley asked.

"No. This is better."

The two looked at each other. The scales in Paisley's head were weighed whether to be impressed or annoyed by the answer.

"May we come in?" the woman asked before Paisley could decide. "We won't be but a minute."

Paisley didn't say anything. She just stepped back, letting the door swing open. The woman stepped inside, clearing Paisley's view of the man behind her.

The man stepped forward to enter and Paisley raised her hand to stop him.

"Let's see em?" she said.

He stopped and held his credentials up. He cocked an eyebrow as if to say that it was unnecessary to check, but Paisley wasn't going to let just anyone in.

"Special Agent Theodore Prince," she said. She stepped back and allowed him to enter.

He was a little shorter than the woman he had come with, with a narrow build. He had his head shaved, but Paisley could see the slight stubble already starting to peek through his scalp. The man would likely have a full head of hair if he allowed it to grow out. So, his bald head was a choice. Perhaps to try to look more intimidating. He wore no facial hair, but the stubble from his head grew in on his face at the same rate. Maybe he just liked the symmetry of it all. The midnight navy suit he wore looked tailored as well but wasn't anything like the one the woman wore. He definitely looked more like what she expected a federal agent to look like.

"That's me," he said, stopping in the middle of the living area and looking around as if some sort of information he had been searching for would spring out and present itself to him.

"So your name is Teddy Prince?" Paisley asked.

"Yes, ma'am," he responded.

"Sounds made up," Paisley said.

"All names are made up," he responded.

"Yeah, but that one sounds like you *just* made it up," Paisley said. It sounded weird coming out of her mouth. She normally wouldn't push against authority in such a way, but her emotions were inflamed. She had just seen what could very well be a group of ghosts standing behind her on footage she recorded and then found out that a man she trusted was a convicted child abuser and a possible suspect in a series of brutal killings of children. Then, out of nowhere, the FBI showed up. She struggled to keep it all together, so humor and defiance were the weapons she drew for that particular encounter.

"Well, I didn't," the man said. He seemed a little annoyed, but didn't want to break the professionalism.

"Miss Mott," the woman said before Paisley could say anything else. "We don't want to take up too much of your time. We just have a few questions, if you don't mind?"

Paisley walked to the table and closed the laptop. She stood with crossed arms.

"Ask away," she said.

The woman looked from Paisley to the laptop and back.

"Miss Mott, we understand that you are in Indiana investigating a series of murders that are of interest to the Federal Government. Can you pl-"

Paisley cut the woman off.

"No, I'm sorry, I am not here investigating murders. I am here talking to a teenager about perpetrating a hoax against his podcast listeners. That's all."

Quinlan turned to look at the man who was now taking a

mental inventory of everything on the table. She looked back to Paisley.

"We were led to believe that you have been investigating the disappearance and subsequent murder of a number of girls in the area. And that you have contacted..." She held her hand out toward the man who handed her a small notepad. She checked it. "Darius Knot, Steven Simply, both minors, I would add. Winslow Peck, Jacquelin Peck, a government employee, and Stilton Hawke. Have I missed anyone?"

"I have talked to all those people, yes. But not to investigate a murder."

Paisley's watch vibrated, signaling that someone was messaging her, but she had placed her phone face down on the table and could not sneak a peek to see who it was.

"So it is a coincidence that you have spoken to four separate people who were, at one time or another, suspects in one or more of the murders that have taken place in the area?" Quinlan asked.

"Pretty coincidental," the man added.

"Easy, Ted," Paisley said, shooting him a raised eyebrow.

Paisley's watch buzzed again and she fought the urge to look at it.

"Miss Mott, we are not accusing you of anything. We are just asking questions because we could use some help, honestly," the woman said.

"Help?"

"This case has been open all these years and we don't seem to have any real leads. We were just hoping that a fresh set of eyes would spot something we missed." Quinlan gestured at herself and then the man.

"But why ask me? I'm just a streamer."

The woman smiled. The life in her eyes made her look like she'd seen everything there was to see, and had spent lifetimes doing it. There was something there. Something deeper.

"Because, Miss Mott, we know who you are. Who you really are. We've studied the Grey Water Ridge case. We know what happened in the hills there. We know about the preacher," she looked down at the notepad, "Hollis Grimm. We know what he did. We know a lot more than was publicly available."

"What do you mean?" Paisley asked. She could feel herself getting frustrated. She didn't want anyone talking about that, especially someone who wasn't there and only saw it as some distant crime that happened to someone else.

Quinlan sighed and looked at Prince, who nodded once.

"Miss Mott, we know everything," she said.

"What is everything?" Paisley gripped the taser tightly, but with her arms crossed, she hoped it wouldn't be noticeable.

"We know about Hollis's stepfather leaving him all of the property in the town," Quinlan said. "We know about the shooting at the Main Street Dinner. We know about," she checked the notebook, "Boyd Gunnerson's communication with someone related to this case here. We know his mother, Sylvia, asked you to come out here. Or, rather asked the brother of the man who tried to murder you and your friends to ask you to come out here. Which makes one think that there may be a close relationship between the two of you." She looked serious, but she delivered the list with the tone of someone who had had a lot of these types of conversations over the years.

"My private relationships are none of anyone's god damn business," Paisley said. Her watch vibrated again.

"No, Miss Mott, they are not. You are correct. I just point it out to show you we are on the same side. And we have done our homework, so we know who we are working with." Quinlan took a step closer, and Paisley took an equal step back.

"Any of the records could have been pulled," Paisley retorted. "And the stuff about Boyd, you could have asked his mom. None of that proves anything other than you two might be the most well-dressed stalkers ever."

The woman lowered her head in contemplation.

"Miss Mott, I say this with zero judgment. I say it with one purpose: to prove to you that we have inside information and can support each other, do you understand?"

The look in Quinlan's eye caused Paisley to pause. The woman knew something.

"Say what?" Paisley asked.

"We know that you had a physical relationship with Hollis Grimm that was consummated just days before the pinnacle of the attack," she said. Her face grimaced as if using that information caused her some sort of heartburn.

Teddy Prince didn't flinch.

"What the fuck?" she finally said. "Fuck you."

Paisley hadn't told anyone about her and Hollis in the church. So Hollis must have told someone, and that person told the fucking FBI. Her watch vibrated again.

"I'm sorry, Miss Mott. It is just important to me that you know we are legitimate, and that we can help you, if you help us." Quinlan took another step closer.

"You said this would only take a minute," Paisley rotated her wrist to look at her watch. The messages were from WhyItHurts. She could only see a clip on the most recent one.

WhyItHurts - *Don't say anyth...*

Paisley took a step forward and grabbed her phone off the table, opening it and reading the messages.

WhyItHurts - *I will see what I can dig up on these two.*

WhyItHurts - *I can't find anything on them, but that isn't unusual for federal agents.*

WhyItHurts - *This seems fishy. I don't like it.*

WhyItHurts - *Oh, fuck this lady!*

WhyItHurts - *Don't say anything to them. Tell them that if they really want to work with you, they can share what they've got first. Then, when you're ready, if you want, you can share what you've come up with. But I think if they don't have a warrant, or if you aren't under arrest, they need to fuck off.*

* * *

278

"Miss Mott?" the woman said, pulling Paisley's attention from the phone.

"Stop with the Miss Mott shit."

"I'm sorry," the woman said. "Paisley."

"If I'm not under arrest, or if you don't have a warrant, then I would like for you to leave. You can send me over any information you would like me to review. And if I find anything that I think will help your case, I will share it, but I don't feel like this is a conversation I would like to continue at this point." Paisley stepped back and signaled toward the door.

"I'm sorry for taking up so much of your time, and I am sorry for upsetting you," the woman said as she walked by and headed for the door. "I just really want to find peace for these young girls."

The man followed but said nothing. The woman stopped and looked back at Paisley.

"Please, Paisley. If you know anything about these girls, or have seen anything weird regarding this case, I would really appreciate you sharing."

Something rubbed up against Paisley's memory like a cat trying to get attention.

"What do you mean anything weird?" she asked.

"Pardon?"

"You said to tell you if I see anything weird. What do you mean by that?" Paisley asked.

"I meant anything out of the ordinary," she responded.

Remembering what the boys had told her about what the woman at the diner said, Paisley asked, "You mean like aliens, time travelers, zombies, or a giant fucking spider?"

Quinlan paused as if, in the bank of normal answers she had, the answer to this question had yet to be programmed.

"Got it," Paisley said, not giving her the chance to respond. "If I see any of those, I'll give you a call."

The woman shook her head as if clearing the bug that froze her on the last question. She pulled a card from her inner pocket and handed it to Paisley.

"Please call me if you come across anything that you think can help us find the girl," she said.

Paisley took the card.

"What girl?"

The woman just looked at Paisley. There was frustration in her face.

The man touched her arm and the two turned and left without saying anything more.

61

Thoughts swam through Paisley's head. She tried to catch one and focus on it, but she couldn't seem to pick just one thread to pull. Her phone buzzed.

WhyItHurts - *Well that was very unusual.*

ParanormalOrNot - *Right? What the fuck?*

WhyItHurts - *I don't know if I trust these two. Something isn't right about them. I thought they would be there about the videos, but they didn't seem to know about them.*

ParanormalOrNot - *I didn't want to bring it up if they didn't. Did you hear what she said about "finding the girl?"*

WhyItHurts - *I didn't catch that, but I am glad you did. Do you think the killer has taken another one and since the body hasn't been recovered they think she may still be alive?*

ParanormalOrNot - *You would think that it would be big news if that was the case. You would think that law enforcement would want every possible eye on it if there was a chance she was still alive.*

WhyItHurts - *I am looking now, but there doesn't seem to be anything local to that area. But I will dig around. Give me a bit, and I will be back. But keep the taser close by.*

The thoughts still swirled around in Paisley's head. Too many leads. Too many things that didn't connect. She needed to take better notes. Or get one of those big cork boards people on TV always put pins on. Connecting the dots. She could really see the value of those now. She would do her own version of the cork board. Her own secret trick to piece things together. Knowing she couldn't livestream any information about what she was doing, especially now, she decided to record her pontificating about the case. Then, she could drop it in during the edit as a nice piece of exposition. That should help her make some connections.

She stepped back and looked at the camera setup, lifting the phone she used as a portable monitor. She had the perfect amount of blur in the background. You could tell it was a cute little farmhouse kitchen behind her, but it was blurred enough, so viewers could not make out any defining details.

"So, here we are. Facing some difficult questions in this investigation." She paused for a moment. So many things went through her head, including the thought that she wouldn't cut the pause. She would leave it in to show the dramatic tension she was experiencing.

She finally looked up into the lens.

"I think I saw real ghosts today," she said. "Not in person, but on camera. It's sort of a hinge point for me here. Because of what I saw, I have to start looking at things with a wider scope."

She would edit in clips of her setting up the Ouija board here but not show the clip of the ghosts. She would save that.

"I came here because of a scared kid." She held that thought. She realized she hadn't made a final decision on Derry's credibility. She hadn't proved he had lied, but it was hard to deny he had.

"He's a good kid. When I listened to his podcast and could hear his sister, rest her soul, calling his name, I had to help. That's how it all started. Now I'm out here, and things are evolving. His sister was kidnapped and burned alive, and he claims that she's reaching out from beyond the grave to speak to him. It would be easier to write him off, but there are other claims from locals that they have seen her, too. The gravedigger claims to have seen her coming and going from her plot in the cemetery."

"Whether I believe the voice is real or not, at the moment, doesn't really matter because there's reason enough to believe that something is haunting the people of Howling Ivy, Indiana. Maybe multiple somethings."

Paisley took a deep breath, unsure if she wanted to talk about the videos.

"This area has been plagued by a serial killer. Twelve victims over eight years. And there's been a lull. Lydia Knot, the voice claimed to be on the podcast, was the final victim."

Paisley stood up and took a quick lap around the room before sitting back down in front of the camera.

"I've come across a series of videos that I believe show the brutal murders of these poor children. And they are brutal. Horrifying. I wished I hadn't watched them, but I needed to see if something had been missed that maybe I could see. What I saw were innocent little girls being tortured and killed. But something happened with Lydia's. Hers was interrupted. Caught on camera by someone else. We've sent these videos to law enforcement, so I hope it helps them reopen this case, but we haven't heard anything from them."

Paisley took another moment. The videos had taken a toll on her, and even thinking about what she had seen caused her stomach to knot. She didn't know how to explain the horror, or even if she wanted to try, but she wanted to convey the pain that the girls had suffered.

"I've only watched a few of the videos, but more are coming. I anticipate that they'll get worse. The ones I have seen thus far have shown children shot, stabbed, and crucified. Who crucifies a child? A fucking child." Paisley rubbed a tear from her eye and wiped it thoughtlessly on the table in front of her. "And one hanged. You'd think after the others, a hanging wouldn't be as bad, but the way the child just accepted it and didn't seem to fight..."

Paisley looked off toward the corner of the room and took a few deep breaths.

"I have so many more people to talk to, but I don't know if it'll get me anywhere. There's the server at the diner. She was asking the boys some interesting questions that didn't seem to mean anything. Then these feds just showed up at the door, and it sort of sounds like they are asking similar questions. So maybe she is worth talking to." She hadn't planned on interviewing Khalida unless it was to get some background on the boys that might make for good filler. Things were different, though, and took a turn she hadn't expected.

"Tonight, I'm doing something exceptionally stupid," Paisley started again, changing gears just a bit. "A few days ago, a mountain of a man accosted me in the grocery store. I thought I was going to have to tase him, but I managed to slip away. Then I met his wife, the town's coroner, and she invited me over for spaghetti. And let me tell you, I could use a good home-cooked meal, but I am obviously very weary. I had agreed when she offered to invite the local gravedigger, who you would have all met by now, who seemed like a very upstanding guy. But, as I found out today, turns out he may be a viable suspect for the murders based on a criminal history we have just uncovered. Now, I'm not saying that one mistake leads to another, and I don't know the details of that case, but this is the man that I hoped would be the peacemaker between the big man and myself. But I'll go and have the cameras rolling the whole time."

Now that she had laid it all out it didn't seem as overwhelming. She would go to the dinner and hopefully not be crushed by the giant hands of the ogre, and she would try to ask some good questions that could help her out. She would also eat enough spaghetti to choke a large dog or a small to medium horse.

Then she would deal with Khalida.

62

The man came down the stairs with a sad look on his face. He carried a long green dishrag in his hands.

Millicent pulled against her chain, moving around the post. The man would hurt her again. Sometimes, it wasn't too bad. Other times, she couldn't remember it all, and when she woke, she was missing chunks of time, but she wasn't sure how much. She had reason to be scared. She knew the man didn't like it when she showed fear. It made him sad; sometimes, if he got too sad, he hurt her worse.

He stopped a few feet in front of where she hid behind the post.

She tried to not look scared but failed. She shook her head as tears plucked at her eyes.

The man flinched as if the gesture stung him. She saw anger flash across his face and knew she had made a mistake. He stood, the dishrag still in his hand.

Millicent tried her hardest to stop the tears and force herself to smile. It may have been convincing had her bottom lip not quivered.

The man's face was a confusing mess that was hard for the young girl to figure out.

"I have to do something, and you just have to deal with it," he said.

He stepped forward and grabbed her with one meaty fist, palming her entire forearm.

She pulled in protest, but any sort of refusal of his commands or acknowledgment of what he was doing at all was met with anger and a more severe punishment.

"Stop it," he said, jerking her by the arm.

There was a sharp pain and a pop. She cried out.

"Shut up," he said, stuffing the dishrag into her mouth and wedging it back with one thick finger. "You stop it right now. We've got someone coming over in a couple of hours, and you need to be quiet."

Millicent tried not to fight back, but the pain was so bad that she couldn't help it. She did the thing she knew she should never do. She used her free hand to scratch at his face. The skin on his cheek gave way under her nails and she had a rush of victorious pride for a fleeting second. That feeling was short-lived.

"Dang it!" the man yelled. The hand that covered her face and the rag shoved her hard enough that the back of her head bounced off the post she was chained to with a quick *thud*.

Pain shot through her skull like lightning and lit up in her eyes. The world darkened, and again, she hoped it was for the last time.

63

"Oh, that's Basil," a voice said from behind Paisley.

She tensed and turned to see Stil. Paisley stood outside the gates of the Hunt and Peck Salvage Yard. She was early for the spaghetti dinner and thought she would shoot some B-roll outside the place that seemed to operate at the heart of some of this story. A cat wandered out from between two of the cars and approached the fence to greet her. The cat was black except for its white stomach and a few white spots on its head.

"I'm sorry?" Paisley said, trying to hide her surprise and unease. She now knew things about this man that made him potentially dangerous. Or, at the very least, a person of interest in the missing children. She wasn't ready to damn him yet, but she felt like until she knew more, she needed to be careful around him.

Stil walked up next to her, and she scooted sideways as he approached, creating a decent gap as he knelt next to the gate. He stuck his fingers through petting the cat with his index and middle finger.

"Oh, her name, it's Basil," he said again. "She showed up a while back when her mommy wandered in and dropped her litter in the back of a smashed-up old car over there." He nodded into the yard. "Momma and most of the rest moved on, but ol' Basil and her sister here stuck around."

Paisley looked around. "There's another cutie around here?"

"Ginger likes to hang out near the office where she can get attention. Basil here is usually pretty shy. She only likes the best sort of people. There's the proof. He pointed at the cat meowing at the fence in Paisley's direction.

"Ginger and Basil? Who named them, the Spice Girls?" Paisley asked.

"I did," Stil said.

"You a big fan of spices, Colonel Sanders?"

"Oh, no. I named this one Basil on account of the spots here that remind me of basil leaves." He scratched the white spots on top of her head.

Paisley cocked her head to the side and squinted.

"I guess I can kind of see it."

"The Regal they was born in had Virginia plates. So I named the other one Virginia, but I started calling her Ginger since she's also a pretty little orange thing."

Paisley looked at him trying to figure out if the answer was really thoughtful or just silly.

"Did you name the others spicy names before they left?" she asked.

"Oh yeah. We had Salt and Pepper, of course, and Cinnamon."

Paisley couldn't help but to laugh. "And what was the mom's name?"

"Oh, Brenda," he said with a deadpan delivery that made Paisley laugh even harder.

"You have to be kidding me?" she said.

"Oh, kid? Like the goat we have?" he asked. He looked around the yard as if to spot it.

"A goat?" Paisley asked. She knew enough older men and could see that this was a setup for a joke, so she tried to beat him to the punchline. "What's his name, Billy?"

"Oh, no, he's much too sophisticated a goat for such a basic name," he said.

Before she could get the punchline the sound of a door opening came from up on the hill. Winslow Peck stood staring at them.

"What the hell ya'll doing over there?" he yelled down to them.

"Oh, we'll be right there," Still called back.

"Well, hurry the hell up," Winslow yelled before disappearing into the house.

"Guess we better get up there," Stil said.

"Guess so." Paisley turned to give Basil one last pet, but she had run off as soon as Winslow had come out.

Stil had already started walking around the fence to get to the house on the hill.

"Are you just going to walk then?" she called after him.

"Oh, yep. You can drive up if you want, but I suspect I'd beat you there," he called back.

"Well, crap," she said and darted after him. When she caught up they walked side by side for a beat before he spoke.

"So what was the sophisticated name you gave the goat?"

"William," he said.

Paisley spit out a hard laugh and doubled over.

64

Millicent struggled to open her eyes. Sounds banged around in her head, a symphony of pain. Her hands were taped behind her back. She tried to shift her weight and pull herself into a sitting position.

The peeling sound her hair made as it ripped from the pool of drying blood made her want to throw up. The rag was still in her mouth, held in place by a knotted rope around her head. She leaned back against the pole and tried to breathe.

She could hear someone upstairs. She wasn't sure who it was, but it was a voice she didn't recognize. She couldn't make it out, but it sounded like a woman. She sounded happy.

Millicent tried her hardest to scream, but the pain and the gag combined were too much. She had to do something. This could be her only chance to signal someone.

A tiny noise caught her attention. Little footprints tracked the dried blood over to where Squeakers sat, just a few feet from her. He sniffed at the air the way he did when he wanted her attention. She was not foolish enough to think that the mouse could help her get someone's attention, but he seemed to want to help.

She shifted her weight toward Squeakers, but as soon as she did, the little mouse ran back behind the dryer.

The dryer. It was fairly close, but not close enough to reach. What if she could throw something at it? It could make a loud enough noise to get someone's attention. With her arms tied behind her, that wasn't an option. An idea hit her, and she spun around pushing her feet out from underneath her. The shoes. The man had given her a pair of shoes, even though she couldn't walk much chained to the pole. He told her that it was too cold down there for her not to have shoes.

She used the toe of one shoe to push the other off the heel. It hung limply off the end of her foot. She could hardly distinguish the white hulk of metal in the dim light. Cautiously, she pulled her leg back and swung it toward the washing machine. The shoe went wide, sliding along the concrete floor and resting against the wall far to the left of the machine. The voices above her seemed to quiet down, and Millicent took the chance. She pried the other shoe off and flung it at the washing machine. This time, it was a direct hit. A loud noise ripped through the otherwise quiet basement, silencing the murmurs above her.

"What was that?" she thought she heard the happy woman say. There was another voice; it was the woman who hated her. Then, she heard the man's muffled words. The door opened at the top of the stairs.

Millicent tried her hardest to scream but couldn't make more than a low moan.

"Probably just the raccoon trap I've got set up down here. Darn things keep getting in through the coal shoot and eating all the potatoes down here," the man said as he came bounding down the stairs.

"I'm just going to go down with him," the happy woman said.

"No, you just stay up here. It's filthy down there, and you wouldn't want to mess up that pretty dress of yours," the mean woman said.

By the time she finished talking, the man towered over Millicent. He dropped to his knees in front of her and wrapped his hands around her neck, applying just enough pressure to put her to sleep.

"Yep, just a rodent banging around down here," he yelled back up the stairs.

65

The Peck house wasn't dirty; it actually seemed rather clean despite the knick-knack clutter: a few bears carved from logs, a miniature plaster fisherman, a few lighthouses, and an unusual amount of stuffed bears commemorating various American Historical events. This wouldn't have been alarming if the civil war bear wasn't dressed in gray.

The place wasn't small, but the layout and all the collections made it feel claustrophobic. Winslow had opened the door and invited them in, and before Paisley could turn around to look back at him, she was certain she would see the giant man hunched so he didn't hit his head. He didn't. He walked normally with what appeared to be a sliver of light between his head and the popcorn ceiling. Paisley wondered if the man had ever taken an enthusiastic step in work boots and wiped some of that dated, stippled flourish off the ceiling.

"Hey there," Jackie Peck said, coming around the corner. "Something wrong?" Jackie followed Paisley's gaze to the ceiling.

"Huh? Oh, no, I was just... You have a lovely home."

"Why thank you, hun. Come on in and make yourself at home," Jackie said, waving her hand at the few pieces of furniture that seemed to blend seamlessly into the hectic decor.

Paisley chose the nearest spot, a floral print sofa that could have been identical to the one at Derry's house. She dropped a few inches as she sat and found that her feet could no longer touch the ground. It was as if there was a hole under the cushion.

"Oh, let me help you," Stil said, acting quickly to take her hand and pull her up.

"Sorry about that, hun. That's Winnie's spot, and he's done

warn it down to about nothing," Jackie said.

"Jesus," Paisley said, coming up and dusting herself off. She added a nod of thanks to Stil. "How do you get up from there?"

Winslow responded by dropping into the spot. He looked ridiculous doing so. His legs poked up and over, much like Paisley's had, but his were long enough to sit on the floor.

Everyone watched Winslow for a moment before Paisley finally broke the silence.

"And getting up?" she asked.

"I don't," he said, and smiled.

The group shared a laugh that felt foreign like she was laughing behind enemy lines.

Paisley ended up sitting in a wicker-backed wooden rocking chair.

They anxiously exchanged small talk before dinner. The group, including Paisley, kept changing the subject to avoid discussing what she was doing in Howling Ivy. They had mostly discussed the salvage business. Winslow told her that he took the business over from his dad when he died. They talked a little about how Jackie wanted to retire but that was still a few years out for her. They said nothing about Stil, and he contributed only a few head nods as if authenticating the stories of the other two. Then dinner was served.

The plates were the white with blue filigree that Paisley remembered from somewhere, perhaps her grandparents. Jackie piled a mountain of spaghetti on her plate and topped it with a heaping ladle of meat sauce. Jackie jerked the utensil a few times, bobbing it like she was playing a drum.

"You're not a vegetarian, are you? Shoot, I forgot to ask," Jackie said, still shaking the ladle above her plate. "I got a jar of sauce left in the cupboard still, I can warm it up for you?"

"No, no, this is perfect, thank you," Paisley said, breathing a sigh of relief when the attention and the ladle moved on from her.

"Oh, Jack, you know that I think your spaghetti is just the

best, right? Best in the whole county. Heck, best in the state, I'd bet," Stil said, not waiting for the sauce to settle before he started to twirl his fork into the mass of pasta in front of him.

"Come on, now. It's just jarred sauce and some ground beef," Jackie said, putting nearly twice as much as she had given Paisley onto Winslow's plate, then filling her own.

"This really does look delicious. It's been a while since I've had a good home-cooked meal," Paisley said. She stuck a spool of pasta wrapped around her fork into her mouth and savored the taste.

"Been too busy putting your nose in people's business?" Winslow said in a completely conversational tone, but close enough to still add confusion to the surprise.

"Winslow!" Jackie said, backhanding his arm, letting her fingers graze him.

"What?" he said, looking at Jackie and then to Paisley. "You said I needed to be nice and not say anything right when she walked in. Well, she's been in. She's sat in our chairs. She's eaten our food. She's used my mother's good plates. At what point can I bring up that she's here poking her nose into business that isn't hers and stirring up things that are better left alone."

"Hey, man, I was invited here. To the town and here," Paisley pointed out. "I didn't come into your home trying to dig up anything." She had pushed back from the table and put her hands up. She was ready to drop down and crawl under the table if the big man made a move for her.

"I'm sorry, hun. We just haven't completely healed from our Heather just yet," Jackie said. She put a hand on Winslow's arm as if that would hold him back if he made a play.

Paisley expected Winslow to say something, but when she looked at him she realized that he wasn't looking at her. She followed his gaze and saw that he was looking at Stil, who had stood up and was standing in a way that he was directly blocking Winslow's path around the table to get to Paisley.

"And what in the hell do you think you're doing?" Winslow

asked him.

"Oh, I'm just standing here, keeping everyone honest, you know?" Stil said.

"I ain't going to hurt that girl. Sit down," Winslow said, and Stil did as he was told.

"We just don't like talkin' about Heather," Jackie said, pushing spaghetti around her plate. "And over the last few years, people been showing up here, without warning, asking questions about her but not looking for the person who took her. It brings up a lot of frustration."

"Who else showed up?" Paisley asked.

"Huh?" Jackie asked.

Winslow shot her a look but then continued shoveling food into his mouth.

"Just the usual," Jackie said. "Every now and again, someone will do some true crime podcast or something. Then they show up here, much like you're doing, for comments or something. Then, because the feds don't seem to know what they're doing, they show up and ask the podcast people if they found any new leads. And you know what?"

"What?" Paisley responded after an uncomfortable beat of realizing the question was not rhetorical.

"They never do," Jackie replied. "Not once have they actually helped the case. Instead, they just show up here, ask a bunch of questions that reminds us that our little girl is dead, and that they will never find the guy that did it. And we will never get answers as to why."

Paisley paused while she thought about all of this. She looked down at her plate. She didn't want to say the wrong thing. She wanted to negotiate this as carefully as possible in hopes that she could still salvage some sort of answers that would help her. So far, she had nothing to show for the visit.

"I'm very sorry," she said. "I didn't come here to ask about your daughter. I honestly didn't know that your daughter was a victim until the other day. I am very, very sorry for your loss. I can't imagine that pain, nor would I ask you to relive it."

Paisley stopped and waited until Winslow looked up at her. "Please forgive any unintentional callousness I may have shown toward your daughter or her memory."

The group was silent, all eyes on Winslow. After what felt like forever, he nodded and went back to his spaghetti.

"Thank you," Paisley said.

"So, if you weren't there to ask about Heather, why did you come to my office?" Jackie asked.

"Well, like I mentioned the other day, I am mostly interested in Lydia Knot's case."

"Oh, she came by the cemetery to see where Lydia was buried. So I can vouch for that," Stil said. It was a nice reminder that he was part of the conversation.

Winslow stopped chewing and stared at Stil. Jackie put a hand on his arm and he went back to eating.

"But you have to know that stirring up stuff about Lydia will directly involve our Heather. The two are connected," she said.

"I didn't know there were other victims when I got here, and I don't have any intention to ask any questions about your daughter. I'm only after the answer as to why a little girl's voice is on a recording. Whether that be because someone faked it or someone is trying to ask for help."

"So why were you at her office then?" Winslow interjected without looking up from his food.

"I was hoping to talk about the coroner's report for Lydia Knot," Paisley said.

"Medical examiner," Jackie and Stil said in unison.

"Sasquatch," Paisley said, mimicking their tone.

"Stil is the coroner, technically," Jackie said. "And he doesn't really do anything but pick up the bodies once law enforcement is done with them. Then he brings them to me. The only report he fills out is the one saying where he picked them up and that he dropped them off."

"Wait," Paisley said looking from Jackie to Stil, "you're the coroner?"

"Yeah, I mentioned that I do work for the county, including

296

Jackie," Stil said.

"He works for me too," Winslow interrupted. "There a problem with a man trying to work hard to fill up his time and his wallet?"

"Well, no, I just wasn't aware," Paisley said. She looked back at Jackie. "I was at your office in hopes of seeing the medical examiner's reports for the Knot case."

"Christ," Winslow said, setting his fork down hard enough to shake all the glasses on the table. The move made Paisley flinch, but she hoped no one saw it.

"Why is the report not public?" Paisley asked.

"Do we really have to do this?" Winslow asked, grabbing the edges of the table with both hands.

"It's not public because it's part of an active investigation," Jackie said.

"Can we please talk about something else?" Winslow growled.

"Oh, yeah, that one was different," Stil chimed in.

"Not you, too?" Winslow said, shooting Stil a harsh look.

"Oh, no, I'm just saying, with the video and all," Stil said. "I know the others are unknown, but the public knows the cause of death with Lydia. She was burned."

"There are things that I can't discuss, and there are things I do not want to discuss, especially over my dinner table," Jackie said.

"Right, they were sealed, so there couldn't have been any copycats. It wouldn't make any difference for Lydia's if, one would assume, it was a different cause of death," Paisley agreed.

"Well that's just it. The public doesn't know, and they don't need to know. It would just cause panic and confusion. We don't need that," Jackie said.

"Why panic? Were the murders gruesome?" Paisley asked. She knew what she had seen in the videos but also knew that wasn't public knowledge.

"Dammit, that's enough!" Winslow shouted. "You can stop

talking about this now, or you can all go ahead and get the hell on out of here and let me eat my supper in peace. Your choice."

Everyone was silent.

"Sorry, friend," Stil finally said.

"I'm sorry, Winslow. I meant no disrespect." Paisley put her napkin on the table and looked around to see everyone just staring at their food. "Would you mind if I used your restroom? I just want to take a minute, wash my hands, and come out and try this all again. Would that be okay?"

"Yes," Jackie said, pointing out of the kitchen and into the living room. "Around the corner, down that hall, first door on your right."

"Thank you," Paisley said. She stood and walked toward the hall, noticing that no one was talking, but sure they would as soon as she was out of earshot.

The bathroom was not free of the clutter that covered the rest of the house like a cheap rendition of a Cracker Barrel. There were fishermen, the steering wheel for some seafaring craft, and a statue of a ship captain with his pants down. It appeared that if you pressed down on his cap, he might squirt water out of his exposed bit, but Paisley chose not to find out.

Paisley did her business, trying hard not to make eye contact with a fabric doll with a flat, drawn-on face and red yarn for hair that sat opposite her on a linen shelf.

"What the fuck are you looking at?" Paisley asked the doll. She laughed at the fact that she was talking to an inanimate object but still unconsciously covered herself when she stood up.

There was something very odd, but it was hard to put a finger on. There was too much happening to see patterns or holes in patterns.

Paisley's phone buzzed, it was WhyItHurts.

WhyItHurts - *Been watching, that got tense.*
ParanormalOrNot - *Oh, hold on and I'll turn the camera back on.*

* * *

Paisley reconnected the small wire to the back of the pin and allowed the camera and microphone to start streaming again. She hadn't thought about it the first few times she went to the bathroom with them on, but Hyacinth was kind enough to point it out and delete the footage from the server.

WhyItHurts - *After you mentioned the medical examiner's report I did a little digging. I talked to a contact to see if they could get a copy, but no luck. The log just says, "Physical copy on site." Which means she doesn't upload her reports to the national server.*

ParanormalOrNot - *Well why not? Should that be a law or something?*

WhyItHurts - *It's commonly accepted practice to seal the file during the investigation. It can be kept offline. That way, it isn't made public and doesn't jeopardize the investigation.*

ParanormalOrNot - *So what do I do? I feel like I need to see what they are hiding.*

WhyItHurts - *Could be nothing.*

ParanormalOrNot - *Could be something.*

WhyItHurts - *Well, unless you can convince Jackie over there to let you see them, short of getting the Sheriff to grant access, you're sort of out of luck.*

ParanormalOrNot - *Is that something the sheriff would do?*

WhyItHurts - *For a licensed private investigator, possibly, but sadly, I'm not sure they would for someone claiming to be investigating a ghost on a podcast for a YouTube show.*

ParanormalOrNot - *Yeah, you're probably right. Guess I will just have to break in and steal the Declaration of Independence.*

WhyItHurts - *I am going to pretend you didn't say that. Not because it didn't make me spit out my wine, because it did, but because I can't be privy to anything that might actually be considered a felony.*

ParanormalOrNot - *Well, in that case, you can't come.*

WhyItHurts - *What about the fed?*

ParanormalOrNot - *Huh?*

WhyItHurts - *The fed? The one with the high heels that came to your airbnb. How do you not remember that?*

ParanormalOrNot - *I'm sorry! It was the term "fed". I'm not used to all this high level shit.*

"Paisley? You doing okay in there?"

Jackie's voice came from down the hall, startling Paisley and she dropped her phone in the sink.

"What was that?" Jackie called.

"Yeah, I'm okay, sorry. I just forgot to take my gas pills before eating pasta. You know how that goes," Paisley shouted through the closed door.

"Okay, well take your time," Jackie said.

It didn't sound like she was walking away, but Paisley also didn't hear her in the first place.

WhyItHurts - *It couldn't hurt to ask her if she has access to those records.*

WhyItHurts - *Paisley?*

WhyItHurts - *Hahahaha, your gas pills?! Smooth, girl. Smooth.*

ParanormalOrNot - *Oh, shut up. I'll message the fed and see what she can do. But I don't trust her. Okay, I got to go. Talk later.*

WhyItHurts - *Be safe. Xoxo*

Paisley left the bathroom, half expecting Jackie to be standing there, but she wasn't. Instead, it was just a hallway filled with photos. Most of them were older. There were some with a much younger-looking Winslow with a little girl. Her blonde hair and blue eyes tugged at the part of Paisley that knew each girl was taken because they shared those traits.

"Why couldn't you have been born with brunette hair, little princess," Paisley said under her breath.

One of the photos caught her attention. It was a photo of Jackie with another woman. The woman looked roughly the same age, possibly a year or two older. The woman wore a sheriff's uniform. It appeared to be at some sort of graduation.

"That's my sister, Stacy," Jackie's voice said from the end of the hall.

"Goat nuts," Paisley spurted out and tried not to fall over after leaping sideways at the surprise. "I'm sorry, I don't know why I said that."

Jackie stepped toward her, clearly ignoring what she had said.

"That was the day she graduated," Jackie announced.

"She's a policewoman?"

"She was a deputy." Jackie pointed at the photo. "Now she's the county Sheriff. You might say law enforcement in this county is a family business." Jackie carried a new tone. Sharper.

"Is that right?" Paisley asked.

"That's right." Jackie got a little closer to Paisley. "I'm only mentioning it because it comes across a touch insulting when someone who knows nothing about our town or our people comes in here and starts calling into question the quality of our local investigations. You see what I'm saying?"

Paisley put on her best understanding smile and took a step to the side, creating a little space between the two of them, but gave herself a clear path past Jackie.

"Absolutely, I understand," she said. She walked past the older woman and into the living room. Jackie followed.

"That's good. Let's finish up supper," Jackie said. Her jovial tone had returned.

"I understand very well," Paisley said. The fire inside her lit. "Actually, I think I am uniquely qualified on this subject. But let me get this straight. Small-town children die. No one seems to be able to solve it or really seem to care to solve it."

"Hey now, watch it," Jackie warned.

"Oh, is everything okay?" Stil said, coming into the living room with Winslow close behind.

"Yeah, I was just summing up a situation that I believe I understand very well. So we've got innocent people dying, and I can't express the sadness I feel for your loss, genuinely, but there have been many more, and no one seems to have made any progress on the case. Then, an outsider comes in, and everyone gets their knickers in a twist because she starts asking

301

questions, wants to help, and seems to be making some progress. That sound about right? Because yeah, I think I understand that shit all too well. I've been down that road and it almost got me killed. But you know what?" The question was not meant to be answered, but Stil replied anyway.

"Oh, what?"

"I solved it. I figured out whodunnit," Paisley said.

"Yeah, and look what it got you," Jackie shot back. "You almost died. You got your friends hurt, and they almost died. And, from what I read in the comments sections on your videos, you got a lot of innocent people killed by mucking around down there and showin' off your tits on camera, am I right? That's why that boy went down there and shot up all those people?"

Jackie's voice, filled with vile intent, struck Paisley right in the chest. She couldn't breathe.

"Oh, now, that's enough. We don't need to do all this," Stil said. He stepped forward and put a hand on Paisley's elbow as she stood frozen in the living room. He gently turned her toward the door. "Come on, now. You don't need to be here right now."

Stil led her out the door and walked her down toward the salvage yard entrance without another word.

Paisley stopped, her phone buzzed in her pocket. She knew it would be messages of support from WhyItHurts, or possibly from Hyacinth if she had tuned in. She'd check them when she could.

"What the hell was that?" Paisley asked Stil. She wasn't sure what side of this he fell on. He was kind to her, but she couldn't deny the comparisons to Grey Water Ridge, especially after pointing them out to the fucking Peck family.

"Oh, they are just upset. They've been dealing with this longer than anyone."

Paisley looked back up at the house. She expected to see them coming after her, or at least peeking out the window, but there was no sign of them.

"I just want to help," Paisley said. "I don't want anyone else to get hurt because of me."

She turned and walked away from Stil. She expected him to follow her or try to stop her, but no one seemed to be doing what she expected them to do that night. She felt adrift.

66

Paisley pulled her phone from her pocket. She had a few missed calls from Hyacinth and a bunch of messages from WhyItHurts, but the thing that stood out was a new media file Hyacinth had sent. It was the next video. Her best judgment told her not to open it. That she shouldn't sit alone in her car, especially while she was so angry, and watch the video. But Paisley Mott wouldn't be Paisley Mott if she didn't challenge good sense in favor of getting shit done.

67

The camera pointed down, suspended again. The workbench was gone, replaced by a deep metal trough with a ring welded to the bottom.

A figure clad in black entered. It blocked the camera momentarily, and when it moved, there was a child in the fetal position. As before, a burlap sack masked the young girl. The jean shorts she wore were too big for her, and the torn t-shirt had a clown, maybe Ronald McDonald, printed on it. It was hard to tell with her arms bound in front of her, not just at the wrists but all the way up her forearms, secured with a metal wire. Her elbows touched, the restraints so tight. The thin cable ran through another metal ring that hung between her elbows. The girl did not move as she sat hunched over at the bottom of the tub.

Paisley couldn't help but hope that this child would live. That she would wake up and run. Escape somehow.

The figure in black returned and hooked a metal carabiner through the binding at the girl's elbows, then rolled her over and connected the carabiner to the ring in the bottom of the tub.

"Oh, god, no. No," Paisley said. "Don't."

The figure left the frame and returned with a hose, kinked so it wouldn't spray until it was dropped into the trough.

The water spraying into the tub woke the child.

She kicked and pulled, but she was stuck. She thrashed so hard that the sack came off of her head, and her curly blonde hair swung in every direction. She writhed, fighting to keep her nose and mouth out of the water.

Paisley paused the video. She wasn't able to identify which child it was. She had researched the missing girls, and they all looked similar. Curly blonde-haired little beauties with fair skin. But she wanted to see *this* child's face. It would change nothing. The sacks over their heads felt so demeaning. She wanted to see her face to give her the respect of not dying alone. Even all these years later. It was no wonder these girls were not at rest. She stared at the face. At her eyes. She was so scared.

She played the video.

It took a few minutes for the water to fill the basin enough for the child's head to completely submerge. Then, she couldn't turn for air. She kicked. Convulsed. At one point, it looked like her shoulder dislocated, a flurry of bubbles filled with precious oxygen represented the scream of pain.

She stopped moving. Then a twitch. And another. Then stillness. The girl's head hung motionless. Her hair stuck up out of the water as she knelt in the tub. She was so young. She looked more like a child at home, kneeling next to their bed reciting evening prayers than a lifeless corpse floating in a metal trough in some sicko's basement.

The basement. The fucking basement. When Paisley walked to the bathroom she noticed the hollow feel of the floor. The Peck's either had a basement or a crawlspace. And she was about to find out what was down there.

68

Paisley backed Gunner up just a few feet from the Pecks' front door and jumped out, leaving the driver-side door open. Before she could second-guess herself she knocked.

Jackie answered. It was unclear if the surprise on her face was because they didn't get many unannounced visitors, or because Paisley, the woman who just insulted them and stormed off, returned.

"I did not expect to see you back here," she said.

Winslow entered the living room but did not approach the door.

"Ain't you done enough?" he asked.

"Oh, Paisley, is everything okay?" Stil said and came between Jackie and Paisley.

"I'm sorry, this is embarrassing, and the last thing I wanted to do was come crawling back here, but I left my phone in your bathroom, I think. And as fancy as my car is, it doesn't have the address of my rental saved. I can't get home without it. So, if you don't mind, I'd like to go get it?" Paisley turned sideways and slid between Stil and the doorway. She was glad he had come out because it was doubtful that Jackie would have allowed her to walk right in.

"I'll grab that for you," Jackie called after her as she moved through the living room.

"It's okay, I don't want to put you out," she said as she made it to the hallway.

She only had a second to choose. There were four doors in the hall and she hadn't seen any others in the small house. The bathroom door she knew. The door at the end of the hall, just past the bathroom, was closed, but if she had mapped it out

307

properly in her head, that wall would have gone directly behind the kitchen, meaning there wasn't much room, and the linen shelves were set just a few feet behind that. A closet was likely on the other side of that door. So, her options were the two doors on the left. The front door sat in a nook, which meant it cut into the space closest to the mouth of the hallway, so she assumed that on the other side of the wall, directly across from the front door, was a staircase.

Paisley grabbed the handle to the first door on the left.

"That ain't the bathroom," Winslow called from behind her, but it was too late. She pretended not to hear him and opened the door. She was in and moving before he finished his sentence.

There was a landing and stairs going down to her left. She had made the correct assumption. She flipped the light on and hurried down the steep stairs.

"Hey!" Winslow called from behind her.

She pulled her phone out and held it to her ear as she hit the bottom of the steps. She heard the monster of a man coming down behind her. It was too dark to see. The light from the top of the stairs was not enough to see into the room.

Paisley searched around for a light, but the room lit up before she could find one. Winslow was there. The ceiling was a little lower, and he had to slouch a little to fit.

"Paisley?" a voice said through the phone. It was Hyacinth. Paisley had dialed her number before going into the house, a defensive move.

Winslow stood looking down at her.

"Hyacinth, I am at the home of Jackie and Winslow Peck. I am in their basement right now. If you don't hear from me after this call, just know that this is my last known location."

Winslow continued to stare at her. His face gave more annoyance than anger.

The basement was nicer than the main floor. There was neatly painted drywall where Paisley thought she would see old brick walls. Where she thought she would see cement floors were hardwood planks. An enormous television was mounted on the wall, and a set of recliners sat across from it. In the corner was a narrow door that one would assume housed a water heater and furnace. A stacked washer and dryer unit was tucked away in the opposite corner with a sink and counter built in next to them.

"What are you doing?" Jackie said, coming around Winslow.

"I was looking for my phone," Paisley said.

"Well it appears you found it," Jackie said, pointing at the phone Paisley held to her ear.

"It's nice down here," Paisley said. Her brain was still trying to catch up to the rest of her.

"Winnie remodeled it himself a while back," Jackie said.

"Oh, I helped a bit," Stil said. He had somehow sneaked down during Paisley's meltdown.

"Um, it's beautiful," Paisley said. "I'm sorry." She squeezed between Stil and Jackie and ran up the stairs. She was out the front door and in the car before anyone caught up to her. She suspected they were left standing in the basement, wondering what the hell just happened.

69

"Hyacinth?" Paisley said after clicking the answer button on Gunner's display.

"What the hell was that?" she yelled through the speakers.

"Which part? The part where I made a total ass out of myself and insulted the people that invited me over for dinner? Or did you mean the part where I barged into someone's home and went into their basement without permission? Because things are unraveling a bit. So, I need you to be specific."

"I think you should consider calling it quits on this one, Pais," Hyacinth said. "It's getting a bit out of control."

"You've seen the videos, Hy."

Paisley didn't have to say anything more.

"That's what I mean. This is much more than a kid faking a recording," she argued.

"But why, Hy? Why did he fake it? Why did he try to get me here? What is happening? I saw ghosts. They were real. I believe Stil when he says he's seen her. But why?" Her heart was racing. Her mind swam, flooding with her errors, her foolishness.

"I don't know, Paisley. But maybe you should fall back and regroup."

"Shit," Paisley said. She mentally replayed the evening.

"What?" Hyacinth asked.

"Her sister is the fucking Sheriff," Paisley stated, thinking Hyacinth would connect the dots.

"Oh," Grover said from somewhere in the background. Paisley must have been on speaker phone.

"Yeah," Paisley said.

"We sent the videos to the Sheriff, Stacy Patrick," Grover

explained.

"Oh!" Hyacinth said. "That's why they have been so shitty to you."

"But is it because they know there's evidence, or is it because they got sent footage of their Heather being killed?" Paisley asked.

"If they were involved, and they were covering it up, which, with the coroner and Sheriff involved, it would be easy enough to do, that would explain why they want the records sealed," Hyacinth said, putting things together. "And why they'd be upset that these videos are popping up."

"I've got to get to those case files," Paisley said.

"Paisley," Grover said, "I tried to get access to them, but it said they weren't available on the database, which means..."

"Which means they're hard copies," Paisley said.

"Right," Grover confirmed.

"I'm going to see if I can get the fed lady to get me in there to get them. She seemed eager to break something. Maybe she'd be willing to help me if I send her the videos."

"Just be careful who you trust. That fed lady rubbed me the wrong way," Hyacinth said.

"I'm going to text her and see what she can do," Paisley said.

"All the videos are finished. Do you want them tonight? They're bad. Very bad. I couldn't watch them. I don't think I can. But Grover did and told me about them. It's horrible," Hyacinth said.

"Send 'em." Paisley was upset but more determined to solve the case.

"Do you really think you'll be able to solve this thing with some grainy tapes made by someone who tried really hard to stay off camera?" Hyacinth asked.

"I don't know, but I'm sure as hell going to try."

"I didn't see anything obvious on the videos, but that doesn't mean you won't find something," Grover said. "But Paisley, they are hard to watch. They get worse. Are you sure you want to put yourself through that?"

"I have to see. There's a reason I'm out here and found those tapes."

"Yeah, that reason is that you went looking for them," Hyacinth said. "No one is in danger right now. No one needs saving. Answers, maybe, but what happened to those girls has already happened. It seems like it's stopped now. Maybe we should leave well enough alone?"

That wasn't Hyacinth speaking. That was Hyacinth's fear for Paisley speaking. Yes, maybe there wasn't another missing kid right now. But there could be. The person who did all of it was still unknown. It could be anyone. It could be Winslow; maybe his daughter was an accident, and then the rest revealed his modus operandi. Once a killer succeeds in some methods, and they are sexually or sadistically satisfied, they stick to it. Maybe it was Stil, the man with a history? Or Patch? Or the woman from the diner with the weird questions? It could be anyone. There was no way of knowing until she knew what was in those files and what was on the rest of the videos. Paisley didn't type in the address she needed. She remembered the way. She didn't want to have it saved anywhere because she planned to break the law, and if she learned anything from trying to solve crime, it was how to properly commit it.

"I've got a few more leads to run down, and if things get any thicker, I will back off and regroup," Paisley said.

"Promise?" Hyacinth asked.

"Of course," Paisley said, turning the car toward town.

70

A closing door somewhere in the fog of unconsciousness woke Millicent from her sleep, coma, death? She didn't even know anymore.

She only heard the man's voice above her in the house, and the lady with the happy voice was outside. Weak hands pulled at the pole so she could stand, the weight of the chain felt like it had doubled.

Sometimes, when the man and the mean woman left, she could see their feet. The familiar shoes of the people who hurt her. Every now and then she saw a different pair of work boots. Another man, maybe. At that moment, though, she saw the comfortable shoes of the visitor, the woman with the happy voice, and the smooth black legs that rose out of them and disappeared under a pretty blue dress.

Millicent hoped the woman would stop and turn around. She imagined her turning and catching her eyes, veiled in the darkness. She'd kneel to wipe away the grime on the window and look in to see her, to really see her. She'd yell, plead, she thought. Then she remembered the gag as her jaw clicked. A single beam of moonlight found her and lit the wet streaks that streamed down her soft, dirty face.

She let the chain yank her back to Earth, her dream of being discovered dashed.

A familiar squeak caught her attention and she looked down to see Squeakers sitting at her knee. She put her hand down and the mouse climbed into it. She leaned her head back against the pole and let sleep take her once again.

71

Paisley parked Gunner and walked the block up the street to the Justice Building, instinctively placing her hand over where the pin camera normally was when she reached the door, which was protocol for such tasks. She lowered her hand, remembering that she left the pin in the Hummer. She didn't want any evidence of what she was about to do.

Her eyes scanned the landscape until they settled on the prize. She knelt, hoisted a decorative rock the size of a lunchbox, and hefted it under her arm. She glanced around before ducking into the alley next to the building. A number of windows offered themselves to destruction, but none looked right. Their enormity guaranteed a noisy giveaway if shattered. It was still early, but the sun had gone down. Paisley assumed that a government office would be closed, but she saw lights inside.

She set the rock against the building and left the alley, wiping her hands, hoping that it would look like she had just finished eating and had simply entered the alley to dispose of a food wrapper. Then she skipped up the steps of the Justice Building and pulled on the door, which opened freely.

She strolled right in the front door, without committing a crime and gawked at the still-empty reception desk.

"Really?" Paisley asked the empty room.

She didn't spot any security cameras. She crossed the lobby to the elevators, then decided instead to take the stairs. It would be less of an announcement of her arrival if the elevator didn't ding.

There wasn't anyone in the basement either. That reception desk was empty, too.

"Hello?" Paisley said as she stepped into the reception area.

Nothing. She walked down the hall and glanced through the window of the *Authorized Personnel Only* door that Jackie had gone through. It was empty as well. The door swung in both directions, likely to ease the movement of bodies in and out. Fortunately for her, it wasn't the type that locked. Paisley slipped in, careful not to let the door swing back too hard.

The room was what one would expect from a medical examiner's office. The floors were linoleum, much easier to clean, which explained why all of the surfaces were stainless steel. A counter ran the length of the office on one wall, two tables in the center of the room, various tool carts scattered about, and a desk in the corner.

It wasn't out of place, and it wasn't a surprise, but Paisley froze when she saw the entire wall filled with square metal doors. Like little walk-in coolers all stacked on each other. If you opened one of these you might find a few feet and a toe tag attached to a recently deceased individual awaiting their burial or the crematorium oven.

The hair on the back of her neck stood when a voice bounced down the hall from the lobby.

"Don't forget to grab the bin behind that desk."

Paisley peaked through the small porthole window on the swinging door. A woman wearing jeans and a t-shirt walked through the lobby carrying a rag and spray bottle. A younger man, if he could be called that, as he looked to be in his late teens, followed, pushing a mop bucket.

"I know you don't know what a trash bin looks like, but you'll figure it out," the woman said and then laughed.

"Real funny, mom. Are you going to joke about everything?" the young man asked.

"Probably. Mop that area in front of the elevator while I vacuum, then we'll hit in there. Then we'll be done with this floor," the woman said, waving her hand toward Paisley.

There weren't a lot of places to hide. At least none that were enticing.

"Alright," the young man replied.

"You do know what a mop looks like, right?" the woman cackled.

The sound of a vacuum provided a little cover for Paisley to move, but it also meant she couldn't hear what the cleaners were doing.

"Shit. This is so cliché."

There was nowhere else. There was no closet or cabinet. There was no sheet she could pull over herself while lying on one of the tables. Even if there was, that might work in the movies, but the cleaning crew would likely have to call someone if they thought a body had been left out.

The fridge was three drawers high by five drawers wide. Fifteen choices. She grabbed the door in the middle row, second from the right, and pulled the handle. Something wasn't right. The handle seemed to be broken. It didn't click. The door just opened with a little tug.

"Jesus," Paisley gasped. A set of old and wrinkled feet greeted her. It wasn't a surprise that they were there, just that she had hoped she wouldn't see any. She closed the door softly and moved down one door to the left.

This handle worked properly. It clicked open with some force. It was illogical that this made her feel safer. Not that it was harder to get into the cooler, but instead made it harder to get out. The one she opened before was in the most convenient spot, the easiest to load and unload. That particular door probably saw the most use, hence the broken handle. She would have to remember, when she climbed in, to be sure not to let the door latch behind her, or she would be in real trouble.

She swung the second door open and resisted screaming at the large, swollen feet that greeted her. A paper tag hung from one pale toe and read *Seth W.*

"Oop, sorry, Seth." Paisley closed the door, holding the latch so it wouldn't click too loudly when she released it.

She grabbed the handle of the next door. The vacuum sound stopped.

"Come on," the woman's voice said.

Paisley opened the door. It was empty. She yanked the sled out halfway and climbed on, lying on her back so it was easier to slide herself in.

"Bring the mop," the woman continued, her shadow visible against the wall outside the window.

Paisley slid herself in feet first and then closed the door, making sure to stop when the latch touched, but not enough for it to click.

"All the tables and such get sanitized by the staff. All you need to do is a quick mop, grab the bins, and wipe down the outside of the cooler. Got it?" The woman's voice was muffled but not terribly.

The crack in the door helped Paisley hear them. It also provided enough light to see that the fridges were not contained. It was one big freezer with multiple sleds and doors. She looked to the side and could see Seth's feet less than an arm's length from her face.

"Okay," the young man said.

Bile rose in Paisley's throat. She breathed recycled air, circulating over god knew how many corpses.

"Get that wiped down. I will get the cart, since you didn't think we would need it in here. You must think the bins in here empty themselves." The woman's voice trailed off.

The man sprayed and wiped the outside of the coolers. Paisley's heart hammered so fast that she could feel it thump against the cold metal sled she lay on.

The thin crack of light grew, and the space filled with the face of the young man. The stubble on his face was the kind that young men often don't shave, so it looks like they have more than they do. He wasn't looking at her though, his head turned over his shoulder. He watched to make sure his mother/boss wouldn't catch him sneaking a peek at a corpse. His face fell. They made eye contact. She froze, not knowing if it was out of fear or strategy. She didn't blink or allow her eyes to move even the slightest bit.

"What are you doing?" the woman's voice broke the silence.

Paisley's body tensed.

"Nothing," the teen said.

"You can never, ever open those," the woman scolded. "If they find out you were in here messing around, it's a felony. Tampering with evidence and such. So don't you ever open those doors."

"But, I didn't open it. I was closing it. It wasn't latched all the way. So I was just pushing it closed."

There was silence for a beat.

"Here, you mop, and I'll finish wiping it down. I want to get out of here. It's creepy down here," the woman finally said.

It was torture listening to them bicker out there. She tried to refocus her thoughts, but that proved just as agonizing. She was trapped and would freeze to death before morning when Jackie Peck discovered her. Or, since the sled wasn't in use, it could be days or weeks before she was found.

Paisley laid still, listening to the murmur from outside as she debated what to do.

Knowing that the Sheriff of the town was related to the Pecks made her feel like it could be more than a legal issue if she was caught, and could be dangerous. So she waited for the murmurs to stop. Then she waited some more.

Her fingers started to go numb from the cold. She knew she couldn't stay in there much longer. She had to figure something out. She pushed hard on the door, hoping that it would give and just pop open the way the first door did. The one that had been broken and likely just fixed by affixing a magnetic strip to hold it shut.

"Oh, no," Paisley whispered. It was a way out, but it wasn't a pleasant one. She could always use her phone to call someone, but Hyacinth was not close enough to help. Stil was too close to the Pecks. And she wasn't about to involve the boys, asking them to break the law. She was on her own. She would have to climb her way over to the broken door.

The light from her phone illuminated Seth's pallid skin. His stomach was distended, giving very little room above him for

Paisley to negotiate herself through. The journey over him and out past the body on the sled with the broken door, felt like a quest worthy of a fellowship and a ring.

"One does not simply walk into Mordor," she said, turning herself over and preparing to try to crawl straight across Seth's leg.

She placed a hand on the metal sled behind his knee and then pushed herself forward with her feet, hoping to clear the body without touching it, but the ceiling was too low. She was going to have to slide her body across his legs. She put her phone in her mouth, biting down on it so that the light was facing up as she crawled. She needed both hands to pull herself past the mountain of a man next to her.

Pain rattled in her teeth as her face brushed past the man's knee. She thought, at first, that the man had moved and kneed her in the jaw. She tried not to scream, but lost the battle and the phone fell from her mouth and clanged against the metal, bouncing away from her, cartwheeling and wedging itself between the man's hairy thighs.

The reality of what had happened set in when the phone buzzed again and she realized it had vibrated, first, in her mouth. The light from the LED on the back highlighted the vibration through the man's thigh.

She reached for her phone, but the quick movement, combined with the slippery sled, forced her knees out, and she pitched sideways, landing with her shoulder on his thigh and her face right above her phone. The hand that had been reaching for the phone shot wide, and she grabbed something else. Something softer. Something shriveled.

"No!" She yelled, pulling her hand back and grabbing her phone in one move. The light filled the chamber again as she tugged it free, spotlighting what she had grabbed. She struggled not to scream, because if she did, she would have vomited. And that would be a lot of cleanup. She knew then that she wasn't putting that phone back in her mouth.

She planted her feet against the rail of the sled and pushed, forcing her to slide across Seth's legs. She crawled slowly until her shoulders had cleared him, and then she reached over and grabbed the rail to the sled just past him. The sled that held the old, wrinkled feet, which appeared to belong to an elderly woman.

She tried to use her feet to lift her so she didn't put all her weight on the man beneath her. He rocked and then settled back to where he started. Another good shove and her face was next to the old woman's knee. She worked hard to keep her face from touching it, so she jammed her left elbow into the side of the sled to give her enough balance to push the door open.

The cleaners had turned off the lights. At least she wouldn't have to face the shriveled body she laid on. Small favors, Hyacinth would say.

Paisley needed to angle her way out, so she rotated, pulling herself by the foot of the old woman's sled. Her body pivoted on Seth's legs, and her feet kicked for purchase, smacking against his chest and stomach.

Her foot slipped and slid up Seth's stomach, her shoe pressing hard against him. She waited for the hollow, hard feeling of his breastbone, but instead her foot went past where her mind told her it would stop. The toe of her sneaker dipped lower as if, instead of a sternum, the man harbored a black hole. She jerked her foot back, and her heel caught inside the man's open ribs.

Paisley screamed. She kicked and scrambled, not caring what damage befell the bodies. She had to get out. She needed air.

She flopped like a fish dropped from a net into the bottom of a boat onto the freshly mopped floor of the exam room. She rolled to her back and kicked the door closed. The magnet caught with the thump, and the door stayed sealed.

Paisley lay on the floor, breathing hard. Her phone vibrated next to her. She reached over and clicked the answer button, then the speaker button, without picking up the phone.

"Hello?" Hyacinth's voice finally came through after Paisley said nothing.

"Hey, Hy," she responded.

"You okay? Your camera is off, and I texted, but you didn't respond. I know you were thinking about going to the *place* to get the *thing.*"

"Shit." She forgot about the files. She rolled to her stomach and propped herself up on her elbows, looking around the room.

"What?" Hyacinth said.

"Nothing, I just..." Paisley looked at the desk. It had to be locked. Why hadn't she thought about that.

"You just what?"

"Hold on," Paisley said, standing up and grabbing the phone.

"K," Hyacinth replied. Her jovial tone reminded Paisley that her best friend had absolutely no idea what she had just been through.

Paisley crossed the room to the desk.

"Hy, you don't know how to pick a lock on a desk, do you?" she asked.

"I don't, but Grover might," Hyacinth said. "Need me to get him?"

Paisley tried the side drawers on the desk, and they opened.

"Well, I'll be a son of a bitch." Paisley smiled. "Nope, looks like the law of averages just worked out for me. The drawer was unlocked."

"Did something bad happen?" Hyacinth asked.

Paisley stopped what she was doing and thought about this. How would she even begin to describe what she had just been through? She wasn't sure she would ever be able to. She would like to think she would be able to explain it to a therapist someday, but the legality may be muddy on that one.

"Let's just say that it's been a long fucking night," Paisley said, returning her attention to the drawer.

There were a number of file folders, but the averages were still paying out. The desk only housed active cases, of which there were a few, including the two bodies that she had just become awkwardly acquainted with.

"Ha!" Paisley snorted.

"What?"

"Seth Weiner. His name is Weiner!" Paisley couldn't help but laugh, then looked at the hand that had touched Seth Weiner's weiner and wiped it on the desk.

"Whose name?" Hyacinth asked.

"No one, it's no one. Let's never mention it again," Paisley said.

"Well, I just Googled the name, and there are only a few, and one happened to die of suspected heart failure in Howling Ivy two days ago. Oh god, Pais, was he murdered? Did you know him?"

"We just met," Paisley said dismissively. "Got it!"

She retrieved a thick file from the drawer and laid it on the desk. It was the autopsy reports of the murdered girls from the case, including Heather Peck and Lydia Knot.

"Got what?" Hyacinth asked.

"The medical examiner's reports," Paisley said, closing them and tucking the file under her arm. "Now I need to get out of here."

"You can't take them."

"You don't know what I've gone through to get these."

"No, I mean, if you take them someone might notice them missing," Hyacinth pointed out.

"Shit, and if they find out, and I get caught with them, I'm in possession of stolen government files. Probably a lot of laws broken there."

"I would assume so."

"I'll take photos," Paisley said, and laid the folder out. "I'll call you when I get out of here."

"Be careful," Hyacinth said.

"Oh, you know me."

"That's why I have to remind you. Call me, k? Love you."

"I will, love you, too."

With that the line was dead, and Paisley took pictures of

each page in the file. It was hard not to stop to read each one, but there were so many notes and pictures. The files looked like they had been studied a lot. The pages were worn and crinkled. A coffee ring connected one of the photographs to the paper underneath. It wasn't a clue, just evidence that someone had been looking for the same answers she was.

On the cover of each report was a photo of girls when they were still alive. They each looked so much like the one before and like the next, with blonde hair and blue eyes. Then came the crime scene photos. Paisley snapped the pictures with the flash on and tried to go as quickly as possible, but something was wrong.

"What am I missing?" she asked the nonexistent audience. It was harder to process and see everything when she knew what she was saying would never be heard. She was lost in her head. As much as people made her anxious, isolation was her kryptonite.

72

Paisley made it out of the building easily enough. The cleaners sounded like they were on the second floor, and the door was now locked, but it was as simple as walking out and letting the door close behind her.

When she returned to the Hummer she took off her over shirt and turned it inside out to sit on it so no part of the clothing that touched the bodies touched the car. It would be easier to put it behind her if she didn't think she would have to smell it every time she got in the car. She spent the next few minutes burning through an entire travel-sized bottle of hand sanitizer as she rubbed it on every exposed part of her body. She had never felt so unclean in her life.

She called Hyacinth as she drove.

"Paisley?" Hyacinth said as soon as she picked up.

"Hi, Hy."

"Did you get it?"

"Yeah, I got files. There are crime scene photos, but they aren't the place where the murders took place. The asshole took them somewhere else to dump them. Which doesn't bring us any closer to who did it."

"Do you think there'll be something you can use in there?"

"I don't know. I'll look when I get back. First, I'm taking a very long, very hot shower."

Paisley recounted the events of the evening. Hyacinth was disgusted but slightly amused since her friend had made it out safely. Paisley had to assume she would feel the same way if the gooey shoe was on the other foot.

The shower was long and hot, as promised. She put the

clothes and shoes she'd worn into the small wood stove in the rental. The rubber smell of the shoes burning was gross but a welcome replacement for the smell of the bodies that she worried would be stuck with her forever.

After she was cleaned up and dressed, and the old clothes were nothing more than memory and ash, she set up her camera and transferred the pictures of the documents from her phone to her computer. She sat down to record herself going through them. She wanted to talk through them with the audience so that she could cut the footage in. As the camera light came on, a calm set over her. Her superpower was back.

"Hey, friends," she said into the lens. She spun the laptop to face the camera and showed the image of a report.

"I have come to possess copies of the medical examiner's reports for the murdered children here in Howling Ivy." She turned the computer back toward herself and started to narrate what she saw.

"This is the first reported disappearance in this case, where it all started. Heather Peck. She was taken, and her body was found just a day later at a warehouse outside of town. Says the cause of death was..."

Paisley advanced the page to see the medical examiner's report. A string plucked deep in Paisley's heart when she looked at the photo that accompanied the page. It was a small girl, wearing a yellow dress, lying on the hard concrete floor of some factory. The juxtaposition was jarring. The girl looked like she should be having a nap under the sun in the grass somewhere. Her eyes were closed, and her hands were folded on her chest. She looked peaceful.

"This must have been before the psycho started butchering them," she said. She read the words printed on the sheet next to the photo. "Cause of death was determined to be an overdose of a paralytic. Appears that someone injected it directly into her neck. She must have been one of the lucky ones. If anything about any of this is lucky."

Paisley advanced to the next case file. This one was the same. A small girl with blonde hair and blue eyes, kidnapped, taken to an abandoned warehouse, and shot full of something that stopped her heart. They were all like that, complete with pictures of the girls looking peaceful as they lay on the ground, almost as if they had just laid down and gone to sleep. All except Lydia's.

Were these the same girls she'd seen on the video? Or was it a hoax? Had someone falsified the reports to cover up a more grisly series of murders?

"Was it going to happen to Lydia, too? I wonder if they stage the photos first, then torture the girls? Or maybe the photos are fake? Like Photoshop or something. But then, when Danny Humphries, the kid I had spoken to in jail, interrupted it, maybe he broke the cycle?"

Paisley opened a file on her computer that she used for taking notes and clicked on the tab that said, *Howling Ivy Murder Videos*. Something wasn't right.

"I was right," she said, turning the laptop to the camera. "The dates don't match at all. Even if the dates on the camera were incorrect, the time between the murders should be the same, and they're not. So unless the killer took the girls, faked the crime scenes, then tortured the girls later, there is another string of killings going on here."

She jumped back over to the photos of the medical examiner's files. Lydia's file contained more than just a single photo of the crime scene like the others. Hers had multiple and covered everything left at the scene. Paisley forced herself to look through them. The first photo was the one that had been leaked from the first officer on the scene. She had already studied that photo. The others included multiple shots of the body. Not a single inch of skin remained unburned on her body. Red and black blisters surrounded by the fat under the skin covered the poor child. Flashes of bone peaked out from brittle, cracked flesh that looked more like dried seaweed than skin. The final photo was taken from the door that the killer had fled from. It showed the girl's burned arm stretching from the pile of ash she lay in, appearing to try and reach the teddy bear that lay just a few feet from the pile.

"The report says that Lydia's body had been found burned beyond recognition, and that the cause of death was just that. It's the only report that is something besides this overdose stuff. The report also says that her father was unavailable, so her teenage brother, Darius, was asked to identify her. He did, but she was burned so badly that he had to identify her by what was left of the t-shirt she was wearing and the bear she carried everywhere with her. A bear that was found laying near the burn site. Darius's signature is on the paper." Paisley stopped for a moment and sat in silence.

"Can you imagine?" she asked no one. "Can you imagine being a teenager and looking at something like that? Seeing your loved one like that would destroy you."

Paisley examined the report. There was a section for visitors during the autopsy. Most were investigators, detectives, Derry, and then, the very last line, was Khalida Walker. The woman from the diner.

"What is this waitress doing getting involved in all of this?"

Paisley paused the recording, grabbed her phone, found the number she wanted, and hit call. Nothing lined up the way it should, so she needed to get some answers. And the best way to do that was to get them all together and ask them.

"Go," Patch said from the other end of the line.

"Patch? It's Paisley. You and Derry free for breakfast in the morning?"

73

The metal tub returned to the stage of horror, lined with a plastic drop cloth.

Paisley stopped the video and pushed the laptop away. The videos became too intense and grotesque, and the drop cloth signaled that it would only worsen. There wasn't a point in continuing to watch them. The murderer hadn't slipped up yet and gave away no defining details that would bring her any closer to solving the case.

Paisley thought about Derry, the boy stuck at the center of this and willing to do anything to find out what happened to his sister. She thought about Lydia, the girl whose spirit allegedly frequented the grave where her body was laid to rest. She thought about Patch, who blamed himself for the whole thing. She sighed, opened the laptop, and hit play.

A young girl was placed in the tub. She wore a tank top and shorts and the same burlap sack, stained with blood and dotted with a few bullet holes. Beneath one of the holes in the sack a blue eye opened. The girl thrashed. Screams came from the bag as the child fought, but the killer was too strong. Ropes wrapped around each wrist and each ankle. One was looped around her neck and restrained her, cinching the bag even tighter around her head, pulling the bullet hole closer to her eye. It peered out, looking directly at Paisley, begging her for help.

The sound of multiple block and tackle pulleys, which Paisley had used many times growing up at her grandpa's cabin in the woods of Oregon, rattled as the girl was stretched and lifted out of the tub, suspended by her limbs which were pulled in every direction.

With the force exuded it looked like the intent was to try and pull her apart, like some torture rack, but that wasn't the plan at all.

A familiar whirring sound joined the screams, and a hand entered the frame holding something that Paisley recognized immediately. It brought back memories of Thanksgiving dinner, her dad wielding a similar tool as the one the figure dressed in black held. The figure pressed the electric carving knife to the flesh of the girl's thigh. Blood spurted and then poured as the knife ate through skin and meat, diving to the bone. The wound ripped open as the girl frantically struggled against the ropes, trying to free herself. Her screams drowned out all other sounds. The blade's teeth bit at the bone, vibrating and shaking gore and bits of flesh free. The mess dropped into the plastic lined tub.

The person holding the knife grabbed the girl's leg below the knee, keeping her steady while the electric knife worked through the bone. The girl went silent and her head fell back against the rope wrapped around her neck. It was impossible to tell if she had passed out from the strangulation, from pain, or from loss of blood, but Paisley was thankful that the screaming stopped. However, she could hear the metal against the bone and it made her teeth hurt.

Once the blade grooved into the bone, the leg stopped vibrating and the knife was able to do its work. With a few changes of angle, after a minute, the leg began to pull away. The force on the rope tore tendons, flesh, and muscle from the underside of her thigh while the knife finished on the bone. Once it broke through, the blade severed the stressed connection of soft tissue, and the leg tore away, flopping against the side of the tub before whatever was holding the tension released that pulley, allowing the appendage to drop into the bottom of the tub, now slick with blood.

The body sagged to one side and nearly fell into the tub. The hand holding the carving knife bobbed like drumsticks. Something clicked in Paisley's head as the signal seemed to tell someone else to lift the girl.

"Pull it taut," a voice hissed, and the ropes were yanked,

pulling the girl level again half a foot above the top of the tub.

"Is there someone else? What the fuck?!" Paisley shouted into the living room of the rental.

She clicked back to rewind the video. It was the first time there had been any speaking at all. There was also proof of a second person. This was huge. She didn't know how she'd use it but knew it was a big break.

Paisley listened to the angry-whispered voice a dozen times, trying to find some identifying characteristic, but there was nothing.

Paisley went to the kitchen, her eyes fixed on the drawers, giving them as much distance between them and her as possible. There was a chance that there was a carving knife just like the one in the video in one of those drawers. The thought clenched her stomach, and her throat closed. She shook the notion away, opened the cabinet under the sink, grabbed the trash can, and took it back to the table. She suspected she would need it.

The video continued, this time with the other leg, then an arm. When the girl was left with just one arm, her torso, and her head, the knife bobbed again in that same way, signaling for the body to be lowered. It was. It hit the side of the metal tub and slid down into the mess at the bottom. The hand holding the blade jerked upward, and by the rope around the girl's neck, the body rose straight up, her arm dangling at her side, still wearing her rope bracelet.

Then it happened. Another voice. A deeper voice. Not the one she had heard before. It was quiet, but audible, like it was closer to the camera.

"Forgive me," the voice said. Then, the body was hoisted to just the right height, and the knife was taken to the girl's neck, just below the bag.

The cutter started at the back of the neck, struggling to get through the bone first, and when they did, the head rolled forward. It caught on the rope and what was left of the throat and arteries. The weight of the body pulled against it, and the child's head popped off with a wet slapping sound. The bag was caught between the rope and the top of her torso. It fell forward, spilling the head end over end. It flipped, and blonde curls matted with blood flew wildly. The head banged off the side of the tub and ricocheted in, coming to a rest against a leg.

Paisley paused the video and minimized the player. The photos from the case files were still up. She looked through the girls, hoping to identify which one it was. It was the sixth video, so she went to the sixth girl who disappeared. It might have been her, but it was hard to tell. She flipped back and forth between the video and the photo, but they all looked so similar, and the video was so dark and grainy that she couldn't be sure.

She played the video and it mercifully ended just after.

Paisley leaned over the trash can. She stayed there processing everything she had seen. Hyacinth had told her she may not want to watch them, but she had to. She finally got something from them, and she was determined to watch the rest and try and find something, anything, that she could use.

Paisley watched the videos. All of them. They got much worse. All different forms of torture. A live dissection, of which Paisley would never get the sight of a heart beating in a child's chest out of her head. Videos of bladed weapons gave way to hammers and tools. Then there was the burning. The killers stayed off-camera in all the clips, even the last one. The one where a man, who was in jail, tried his hardest to save a little girl being burned alive in a bag.

74

The diner was busy, but not wildly so, so Paisley did not feel bad about asking Khalida to join Derry and Patch momentarily after they put their order in.

The boys sat on one side of the booth, and Paisley across from them. Khalida dropped into the booth next to her, the way servers sometimes do when trying to create the association in the customer's head that they are friends.

"Thank you all for coming this morning," Paisley said, sliding farther into the booth to make room for Khalida. She used this opportunity to place her bag on the table, which just so happened to be adorned with pins. One of which was a young red-haired man with wings and a sword with a black jewel in the hilt, which, upon close inspection, would look suspiciously like the tiny eye of a camera.

"Of course, thanks for inviting us," Derry said. His innocence was either genuine naivety, or he was very good at masking.

"Pancake trains will be out soon, so I only have a second," Khalida said. "What can I help you with?"

"First things first," Paisley started and then looked at Derry. "Why did you fake the EVP?"

Everyone sat stunned, Patch looked insulted, his jaw hung loose and his eyes narrowed. Khalida looked confused, but Derry looked sad. His head and shoulders dropped and he looked defeated.

"That thing is real," Patch said. "You've heard it. That's his sister on there." The large boy's face turned red.

"Settle down, buddy," Derry said softly. He patted his friend on the arm, and like magic the larger boy settled. "She's right."

"What?" Patch asked. Then it was his turn to look hurt.

Khalida just looked on as if the conversation had no surprise to it at all. She didn't look bored, but she didn't seem surprised.

"How else was I going to get the great Paisley Mott out here?" Derry said, eyeing Paisley, though he answered the question Patch asked.

"I was lied to once to get me to help someone, and it didn't go well. Especially not for the one who lied to me." Paisley's tone was matter-of-fact but not angry. She didn't want Derry to feel threatened.

"It isn't like that," Derry said. "I'm sorry I lied, but I'm nobody. I wanted to ask you for help, but I didn't think after what happened in Grey Water Ridge, you would come based on my word alone." His shimmering eyes appeared truly apologetic, desperate even.

"What do you need help with?" Paisley asked.

"No one cares about Lydia. They stopped looking. And now I'm... I'm seeing her."

"Her ghost?" Paisley asked.

"I think so. They could be dreams, but it feels so real."

"Me too," Patch added.

"You're seeing her in your dreams, too?" Paisley questioned.

"No. They aren't dreams," Patch answered.

"Lydia?"

"I think so."

"And you?" Paisley asked Khalida.

"Me?" she responded. "I haven't seen her, no."

"What's your part in all of this?"

"I'm the waitress," she answered. "And if I am not mistaken, food is up." With that, Khalida was up and off, just to return a moment later with their breakfast. She had brought an extra cup of coffee that she sat behind as she slid back in next to Paisley.

"Now, if you have specific questions, I am happy to answer them," Khalida said. "But if your idea was to put me on the spot and have me open up about the things I've seen, well, that will just not happen. I can't write your story for you."

"Okay, specifics. Why did you go visit the medical examiner after Lydia's body was found?" Paisley asked.

This caught the woman off guard and she sat up. Then she smiled. It was a beautiful smile. The kind that looked like it had been pleasantly surprised a lot of times, and never got tired of it. She and Derry exchanged a glance.

"You trust this woman, young man?"

"I do," Derry said without hesitation. But he looked concerned, perhaps he was surprised to hear that Khalida had gone to the medical examiner after his sister's death.

"Verifying the identity, that's all," Khalida said.

"Why?" Paisley asked.

"I'm looking for someone," she responded.

"Who?" Derry asked, beating Paisley to the punch.

"I don't know."

The bell above the front door rang.

Khalida didn't answer. She just stood up when she saw who came through the door.

"Ah, right on time," Paisley said as the FBI agents that had shown up at her rental spotted them and approached.

Khalida studied Paisley with worried eyes.

"You know them?" she asked.

"Well, sort of. I knew things were too big for me, and I wanted some professional help. So I called the feds," Paisley said. She felt like she had just moved a piece to put her opponent in check. She thought having everyone in one place would help. And if she was lucky, Stil, Jackie, and Winslow would be close behind.

"No, Paisley, they aren't feds, and they aren't here to help you," Khalida said, picking up the butter knife off the table next to Paisley's plate.

"Ah, Lida, so nice to see you," the woman who had identified herself as Special Agent Haley Quinlan said. The woman was dressed as she had been before, and the man that followed her still played the same part of the quiet observer. But something seemed different about them. Khalida's reaction

334

to them made Paisley see them in a different light.

"You shouldn't be here, Vivian," Khalida said.

"Vivian?" Paisley asked.

The woman in the suit and the waitress stared at each other, their eyes like darts. They both ignored Paisley, who slid out from behind the table, but kept a reasonable distance between herself and Khalida, who was clutching the butter knife.

"Miss Mott says she has new information, so I figured I would drop in and follow up," Vivian said.

Khalida raised the knife and pointed it in her direction.

"I told you not to come back here. You've done enough damage to these people."

"These people?" Vivian gestured to Paisley and the boys. "This woman isn't even from here. As for them, I had nothing to do with that one, and I think you know that."

"You need to get out of Howling Ivy, now." Khalida rotated her wrist with grace and confidence. The type of move you would see a master swordsman make.

"And if I don't?" Vivian asked.

"I'm calling the cops!" A man's head popped up in the kitchen window. He had been watching the drama unfold, but ducked back down after yelling.

"They are already here," another voice called from the door. The bell must have sounded, but the tension had masked the rest of the world.

A short woman, about fifty, stepped around the corner. She wore a sheriff's uniform and Paisley recognized her instantly from the photo in the Pecks's hallway. She was older, obviously, but it was her. Sheriff Stacy, Jackie's sister. The one who had received the videos from the killer's camera and said nothing about them.

"Haley Quinlan, FBI." Vivian said, turning and producing the same credentials she had shown Paisley.

"Ha," Khalida snarked.

"You saying you know this woman and that she ain't really a fed?" She asked Khalida without taking her eyes off Vivian.

"You know impersonating a federal officer is a pretty serious crime?"

Everything moved in slow motion to Paisley's attentive eye. In that instant, the sheriff's hand dropped to the handle of her sidearm. Khalida shifted her weight to her front foot. The man in the suit slid his hand into his jacket, and Vivian was the catalyst. She held the credentials out with her left hand, blocking the sheriff's view, and turned sideways. She had a gun. The sheriff wouldn't be able to see it. She would get the draw on her, and though she saw it, Paisley couldn't do anything except yell.

"Stop!" Paisley shouted.

The sheriff and the man in the suit turned toward her. Vivian did not. Khalida did not.

Vivian raised a small, military-looking handgun from under her arm. Then Khalida was there. She reached under Vivian's outstretched left arm and grabbed the right hand with the gun as it went up. In one lightning-fast move, she yanked the hand down under the outstretched arm and twisted it. Khalida stuck out her leg and pulled all their weight and momentum toward it. Vivian flipped, landing hard on the floor. Khalida held the gun.

"Holy shit," Paisley gasped.

Before anyone knew what was happening two more guns were drawn, both pointing at Khalida. The sheriff and the man in the suit.

Khalida held the gun dangling from one finger in the trigger guard.

"I think we need some answers here," Paisley said. "Because I think every one of you motherfuckers is lying about something."

"I think everyone needs to just calm down," Sheriff Stacy said. Her gun was still out, pointed at Paisley rather than Khalida.

"What are you doing?" Paisley asked the woman she'd never met.

"Lower the gun," Khalida demanded. She clicked something

on the side of the gun she held, and the magazine slid out and fell to the floor. Then, with just one hand, she pulled back the slide and ejected the last bullet, causing it to bounce off the table. The boys both moved to dodge it as if it would hurt them. Then Khalida tossed the gun into the booth where Paisley had been sitting, still not breaking eye contact with the sheriff.

"You just keep out of this Lida," the sheriff demanded. Khalida slowly stepped to her left, interrupting the line of sight between the sheriff and Paisley.

"I need everyone to just settle down and put their guns away," Khalida asked in a gentler but still demanding tone. She looked from the sheriff to Vivian, who was getting herself to her feet.

"Put it away," Vivian said over her shoulder, and the man did as he was told.

It was just the sheriff aiming at Paisley, with Khalida standing in her way.

"Thank you," Khalida said, putting the butter knife on the table as another gesture of peace.

"Excuse me, can someone please explain to me what the fuck is going on here?" Paisley asked. As grateful as she was that Khalida had stepped between her and the gun pointed at her, she was still very curious as to why it was pointed at her in the first place. "Is this about going into your sister's basement? If so, I'm sorry, but this seems excessive."

Khalida looked over her shoulder at Paisley and then back at the sheriff.

"You need to come with me," the sheriff said.

Derry attempted to slide out of the booth and stand in front of Paisley, but Patch put his hand on his shoulder.

"She can't go with them," Vivian said to Khalida.

"I don't think you have a say in it," Sheriff Stacy said.

"She called us all here for a reason, and I think we all have the same goal." Khalida looked at Vivian and added, "Basically." She said this last bit with a bit of disgust.

"I think she knows." Vivian nodded toward Paisley.

Khalida turned to Paisley.

"I know what?" she asked.

"Everyone just shut up," the sheriff barked. "Paisley Mott you are under arrest and you are coming with me. Now step around here."

"No," Vivian said, and raised a hand. "She is coming with us."

Paisley had thought everyone would come together and she would piece things together like detectives on TV, but instead everything was fucked.

"No, she isn't. She's coming with me, and if you can prove those credentials are real, then you can have your boss call me, and we can discuss what happens with her after I'm done with her, but I have two dead bodies and a bunch of missing files that say she is coming with me," the sheriff said.

Paisley's head sank. Breaking and entering, theft, and tampering with a dead body. She was in deep shit. The cleaners must have seen her leaving.

"Bodies?" Derry asked.

The disappointed look on Derry's face hurt Paisley.

"No, not like that, kiddo. I didn't kill anyone. I just touched some dead bodies," Paisley admitted. She stepped around Khalida and stood in front of the sheriff, who did not lower her gun. The woman just stood, staring at her, with the gun leveled at Paisley's chest. Something wasn't right.

"Hey, I'm surrendering. We can all calm down. I admit it. I snuck in, but I didn't break in. The door was open. And, yes, I touched the bodies in the fridge, but I had to. I was stuck."

"You were what?" Khalida asked.

"Long story, anyway, yes, I touched them, and I am sorry, it was stupid, but I didn't take the files," Paisley insisted. She was hoping not to have to admit she took photos of them, but if they already knew she touched the bodies, they probably had her fingerprints, and she would be in even more trouble for lying.

"You touched them? That's a goddamn understatement," the sheriff said.

"Okay, so my foot did go into the guy's stomach, but that was an accident," Paisley tried to reason.

"What is wrong with you?" the sheriff asked, tightening the grip on her gun.

"I admit it, I'm sorry. But I did not *take* any files," Paisley insisted again.

The sheriff reached back and wrestled her handcuffs from the pouch on the back of her belt. "Wrists."

Paisley put her hands out but nodded at the gun.

"This is a little much, don't you think?"

"Paisley Mott, you are under arrest for the murder of Maria and David Stanley," the sheriff said, slapping the cuffs on one of Paisley's wrists and then the other.

"Wait, what?" Paisley asked. "Murder?" She tried to pull back, but the sheriff grabbed the links between the cuffs and yanked her close, nearly hitting her in the face with the muzzle of the gun.

"Murder?" Derry and Khalida asked at the same time.

"Miss Mott here was seen sitting in the front seat of her car, a very distinct, yellow truck, trying to clean herself off after leaving town hall last night. When a deputy went down from the office to find out why the cleaning crew hadn't made it up to the top floor, they found the front window broken out and Maria Stanley and her son, David, two members of the cleaning staff, butchered in the lobby. There was blood everywhere. So, Miss Mott, I do not think this is *too much*." The sheriff wiggled the gun before finally placing it back in the holster.

"I didn't kill anyone," Paisley insisted. "They were both alive when I left."

"Wait," Derry pleaded. He didn't seem to have a plan outside of that, but Paisley appreciated the effort. He jumped up from the booth. "Please?"

"Sit down, young man," the sheriff ordered, but Derry remained standing.

Vivian stepped toward the sheriff.

"Listen, I understand what you have to do, and I'm not here to get in your way. So I will stand down, but I request the opportunity to interview the suspect about a different matter while you have her in custody. Would you allow that?"

"I don't know who you are, but you better come at me with something better than those weak credentials if you want to talk to anyone I have in custody," the sheriff said, pulling Paisley by the arm and turning her to leave.

"Tell me what you know, girl, and I can help you," Vivian called after Paisley as she was being led toward the door.

"She won't be talking to anyone but me," the sheriff said, shoving Paisley out of the diner.

"There has been a serious mistake," Paisley pleaded as she went out onto the sunny sidewalk.

"Wait," the sheriff demanded, stopping in front of a pickup truck with lights and sirens, all the bells and whistles. She opened the passenger side door.

"Get in," she continued.

"Wait, what?" Paisley asked.

"Get in," the sheriff repeated.

"You don't have like an actual police car? Or a paddy wagon of some sort? This all feels very unofficial."

"The sheriff gets to pick their own vehicle. I had a Charger, and when it died, the county tried to make me drive some electric piece of crap, but I hated it. It's a giant paperweight behind the station now. I went with the truck instead. I don't normally transport, so I don't need a big backseat. But today, I'm making a special exception. Now shut up and get in."

Paisley reached up and grabbed the handle on the roof, just inside the door, and pulled herself up into the seat.

The sheriff slammed the door and walked around to climb in. Paisley looked into the back seat. It made sense to her now why, even if it was a truck, she wasn't sitting in the back seat, seeing as the truck had a second row that was equal in size to any car. The back seat was covered in file boxes, folders, and loose papers.

"You really don't have company in here often, do you?" Paisley asked as the sheriff slammed her own door.

"Shut it, or you'll ride in the bed," the sheriff said as she started the engine.

75

Large plastic sheets hung from a pipe frame, closing off a large portion of the lobby in the Justice Building. They were just translucent enough for Paisley to see someone mopping behind them. The idea that the remains of the cleaners from the night before were being removed made Paisley choke.

"Oh my god," she said.

"What's the matter? Can't stand to see someone having to clean up after you?" the sheriff said, and pushed Paisley toward the curtain.

"I didn't do this."

The sheriff grabbed an edge of the plastic and revealed the bloody mess scattered across the marble floor. The bodies were gone, but whatever had happened to them, it was gruesome.

"Stop it," Paisley said, trying to pull herself back away from the scene but not so hard that it felt like she was trying to escape.

The woman tugged Paisley back and led her to the elevator.

"I didn't do that."

"We'll see," the sheriff said, pushing the button to go up. "We've got some pretty good sets of prints that don't belong to anyone in this building off of the ransacked office downstairs. And I would bet dollars to donuts that we're going to hit a match on you."

The elevator opened and Sheriff Stacy pushed Paisley in. They were going to find her prints. They were going to find them all over the place. They were also going to check her phone and find pictures of the stolen files. She had no alibi. She was there but had no way to prove she hadn't killed anyone. Her legs went weak, her chest tightened, and she fell against the wall of the elevator.

"Stand up," the sheriff said, pulling her upright like a frustrated mother might a disobedient child. "You'll get the chair for this if I have anything to say about it."

"I really didn't kill anyone."

"You'll get your trial, but for now, you can rot in a cell here, for all I care."

A bell rang as the elevator door opened into a small booking area. The sheriff gave her a push to move her along.

Everything in booking was a blur. It didn't seem real. She had been fingerprinted, frisked, and placed in a holding cell. They'd done everything except strip search her, but she was assured that it was coming as soon as charges were pressed and she was moved to the jail.

The cell she was in was exactly like the ones on TV. It was a small metal walled room, with a big, heavy-duty, window facing a room surrounded by identical cells. All the other cell doors were open and their lights were off. A large table sat in the middle of the room, for recreation or for meetings. There was nothing in the cell but a bunk and a toilet. It was clean, which Paisley was thankful for, but that small bit of gratitude was not enough to buoy her spirits as she sat on the bunk facing the window.

She hadn't gotten the phone call Hollywood told her she should get. The sheriff told her that she would get to use the phone later, but they were trying to collect the evidence from the night before. She could assume this meant the Hummer and the clothes she had been wearing. When they went to the rental, they would find she had burned the clothing in the fireplace, which did not look good.

Paisley laid down on the cot and pulled her knees up to her chest.

"Fuck."

76

A loud bang jolted Paisley awake. She sat up. The thought that it had all been a dream lingered for a second until she saw the source of the noise. A deputy stood outside the sliding door. A few hours earlier, the same officer brought her a tray with a sandwich and a pile of potato chips and passed it through a hole in the door. It was that moment that broke Paisley even further. She felt like an animal in a cage.

"You've got a visitor," the guard said as he swung open the door.

"I didn't know I could have visitors," Paisley said, swinging her legs over the edge of the bunk and standing up.

"Sit back down for me," the deputy said.

Paisley did as she was told and was then handcuffed to a small D-ring on the bed.

"Is this necessary?"

The officer didn't answer. Instead, he just stepped out and let the visitor enter before closing the door and leaving them alone.

"Vivian?" Paisley asked the sharply dressed woman.

"Special Agent Quinlan," the woman corrected. She stood near the door as if Paisley would lunge at her at any moment. She held a black folder as if she could use it as a weapon if called to do so. And by the looks of her, she could do so effectively.

"Right, you really expect me to believe that?"

"You can believe what you'd like, Miss Mott. The fact of the matter is, you're here chained to a bed, and I'm standing here having been let in by the agency holding you. So obviously, one of us is telling the truth, and the other is not."

"Okay, *Agent* Quinlan, what do you want? You here to charge me with more crap I didn't do?"

"No, actually, I'm here to help you."

"Help me? And how exactly will you be doing that?"

"Well, that depends." The woman shifted her weight and crossed her arms, tucking the folder under her arm.

"On?"

"On if you can help me."

"With what?"

"I'm told that you are an incredible investigator, and I have a case that I need help with. You help me, give me some information, and I can see what I can do about all this." The woman waved her hand around the cell.

"What case?"

"The one you're working on. I just want to know what you know."

"I don't know anything. I thought I did, but I don't," Paisley admitted.

"Why were you after those files?"

"I didn't kill those people."

"I know, but why were you after the files?"

"You know?"

"You aren't the type. Now, what did you find in the files? I've looked at them and I can't find anything that points to the killer or anything out of the ordinary about the victims." The woman waved the folder in her hand as she spoke.

"Those are the files?"

"Copies of them," the woman said, holding them up. "You've seen them, yes?"

"Yes, but I just took photos of them at the lab. I didn't take them, and I didn't hurt anyone to get them," Paisley insisted.

"What did you see in them? What am I missing?"

"If I talk to you about this, you'll help me?"

"Yes, just tell me what you know about the case," the woman said, dropping the folder on the bunk beside Paisley. "But you can't discuss our deal with the sheriff. I suspect she has some strong feelings about this. And if she finds out I requested copies of these files, she'll cut off my access to you, and I will not be able to help you."

Paisley thought for a moment before replying.

"I didn't get a lot of time with the photos, but I got enough to ask myself some big questions, and big questions often lead to big answers."

"What questions?"

"Why was Lydia Knot burned alive at the location when the other girls were obviously killed elsewhere and then taken somewhere to be disposed of?" Paisley spread the files out on the bed with her free hand. She plucked the coffee-stained photo of the crime scene off the top and held it, running her fingers over the stain.

"Because it was a copycat," the woman said.

"Is that a question?" Paisley asked.

"Not a question, just a theory."

"Well, I agree with you. I've seen the videos, and the killer definitely killed the girls at a second location, and then-" Paisley was interrupted.

"What videos?" the woman demanded.

"Huh?" Paisley froze. She hadn't told anyone other than Hyacinth and Grover, and Grover had given them to the sheriff, but the sheriff must not have told this woman. Maybe there was a reason for that.

"Videos. What videos?" the woman asked.

"Videos?"

"Yes, you just said that you have seen the videos. Are there videos of the murders?"

"No, I just meant the video from the kid."

"The junkie, yes. It's all over the internet, but you said videos. Are there others?" The woman stood, hovering over Paisley.

"No, I just watched multiple videos where people discuss that video. That's all." Paisley hoped that would get her past the slip-up or at least buy her time to think of a way to get out of it.

"If that's the case, why do you think there was a second location with the others?"

She didn't have enough information to lie properly and didn't want to give away that there were videos of brutal murders until she figured out how it all fit together.

"I'll show you," she said, lifting some of the files and looking at them. "These aren't right."

"What isn't right about them?" the woman said, looking down at the files.

"They don't match. These say that the cause of death was overdose of a paralytic," Paisley said as she flipped through each file.

"That was the cause of death, except for the last one, the copycat. That's who we need to find."

Paisley set the file down and looked up at the woman.

"Why do you need to find the copycat and not the original killer?"

It took the woman a moment to answer.

"Well, if it is a copycat, and we both agree that it is, then the actual killer hasn't killed in nearly two years. So, the copycat is a greater threat at the moment."

"I suppose so," Paisley said, pushing the files around, shuffling them in hopes that they would magically change and show her something she hadn't seen.

"What is it? What do you know?" The woman put her hand on Paisley's shoulder. "It's okay. I can help."

"Why did Khalida call you Vivian? And why were you trying to pull a gun at the diner? Who are you?" Paisley asked, looking up at her.

The woman did not recoil the way Paisley thought she might with the questions.

"Khalida Walker is someone we have been interested in for a *very* long time. I was an investigator on a case she was involved in, and she got to know me as Vivian. That's all. She's upset that I fooled her to get the information we needed."

"And did you? Did you get the information you needed?"

347

"No, we didn't, sadly. We failed in that case, and Khalida Walker continues to get in my way."

"When you came to my house, you said you were looking for a girl. What girl are you looking for?" Paisley asked, throwing the next question quickly, hoping that it would cause her to stumble.

"I misspoke. In my line of work we always have to think of open cases in terms of the next potential victim. I have to assume that there's another one out there, and if I act quickly, I may be able to save her. It helps drive me. It should help drive you, too."

Paisley processed all of this.

"There are videos of the killings," she finally said.

"What do you mean?"

"The video camera."

"What video camera?" The woman crouched down to meet Paisley's eyes.

"In the video of Lydia's death, there is a video camera lying on the ground." Paisley turned, found Lydia's file, and held it up to the woman. "It isn't in this photo."

The woman took the file and stood up. She studied the photos closely.

"I never caught that," the woman said to herself.

"It was easy to miss. I missed it the first few times I looked at the photo."

"Here," the woman pointed to an empty spot in one of the photos. "It's here, isn't it?"

"Yeah," Paisley confirmed where the camera had been sitting in the video.

"We've watched it so many times and never caught that."

"Again, easy to miss."

The woman put the file down and looked at Paisley.

"What was on the tape?"

"The murders," Paisley said. Her stomach knotted thinking about them.

"How?"

"How what? How did he kill them?" Paisley asked.

"How was it filmed?" the woman clarified.

"He did it. The killer. He filmed as he butchered them. All of them."

The woman stood up and paced around the cell.

"I just don't understand why they are lying about it all," Paisley continued.

"What do you mean?"

"They don't match. The videos and the reports. Those girls were tortured."

The woman stopped and stepped to Paisley. Her once accommodating demeanor was gone.

"I need to see them, immediately," she insisted, turning to pace again.

"The sheriff has them. You could ask her."

The woman stopped so abruptly that it caused Paisley to flinch.

"What did you just say?"

"What?"

"She has the videos?" the woman asked, pointing out in the direction of the sheriff's office.

"Yes. We thought it would be a good idea to share them with local law enforcement in hopes that they could help identify the murderer."

"And you didn't think that it was suspicious that the videos show kids being butchered when the reports all say that the kids were injected with a paralytic?" The woman scooped up all the files and stuffed them into the black folder.

"I didn't know what they listed the cause of death as until last night." Something caught in Paisley's mind like a grasshopper caught under a jar.

"Something much bigger is going on here, Miss Mott, and it sounds like you've stepped in it completely by mistake."

"Yeah, that sounds like my move, to be honest with you."

The woman straightened the files and put them under her arm before banging on the cell door to be let out.

"Hey, you said you'd help me?" Paisley cried.

"My advice, Miss Mott, stay here, where you might be safe. There are killers on the loose, and you seem to be in a position to expose them or the people covering for them. So, I'd not tell anyone else what you told me. Just stay here and lay low."

"Lay low? That asshole sheriff wants to give me the electric chair."

"If you're innocent, you won't have anything to worry about, right?"

The door opened, and the woman walked out without looking back. Before Paisley could call after her, the door was slammed shut, and Paisley was left with her scattered thoughts.

77

The sheriff's office looked nothing like they do on TV, which was Paisley's point of reference for most things. This was the second small-town sheriff's office that she'd been in in the last few months, and she noticed a pattern. There weren't people handcuffed to desks awaiting interrogation. There weren't officers clamoring around shuffling papers or eating donuts. Instead, it was quiet and empty.

"We've got some things to go over before I take you over and officially charge you," the sheriff said. "This is as close to freedom as you're ever going to be again, so soak it up." The sheriff pushed Paisley past a few cubicles and toward an office with a nameplate that read "Sheriff Stacy Patrick".

The office was small and well-maintained. Giving the woman a modicum of humanity were a few framed certifications, photos hung on the walls, and a crayon-drawn picture tacked to the wall behind the desk.

"Sit," the sheriff said, pushing Paisley into a wooden chair in front of the desk before sitting in the oversized leather chair behind it.

"Shouldn't I have been given a phone call? I feel like you shouldn't be able to hold me like this." Paisley said, then realized she may need to approach this with a little more care. "Listen, I know how all this looks, but I would never hurt anyone."

"You wouldn't discharge a firearm in hopes of shooting a mister..." the woman looked down at a notebook that lay open on the desk in front of her, "...a Mr. Hollis Grimm?"

"That's different! He was trying to kill my friends," Paisley argued.

"And then you stabbed him in the leg with..." the woman

looked down at the notebook again.

"A hot dog fork, yes," Paisley said before the woman could finish. "But that's because he was trying to kill me, too."

"Miss Mott, you are in a lot of trouble, and the only chance you have of not getting the death penalty is to cooperate."

"There is nothing to cooperate with. I really didn't hurt anyone."

"Tell me about the video recorder you found."

Paisley shook her head. It was a hard turn to go from talking about her being the prime suspect in a double murder to evidence of a string of other murders.

"I had nothing to do with those murders either," Paisley demanded.

"Where did you find the camera?"

"I'd rather not say."

"I've seen the videos. Your friend, Sheriff Northfield," she said, checking the notes again, "sent them. They aren't real. They're fake. Some cheap student film, probably."

They weren't fake. Paisley knew they weren't. She'd seen plenty of very expensive horror movies to know what the effects looked like, and those weren't faked, but if the sheriff, who would be one of the few people in the world who would decide her fate, said they were, then there was a reason for it, and she wasn't going to argue it, yet.

"That's sort of what I thought, too," she said.

The sheriff raised her eyebrows in surprise.

"Oh, you did, huh?"

"Yeah, the blood looked fake, and you can see the actor breathing when they are supposed to be dead a few times," Paisley said. Hopefully, she wasn't laying it on too thick.

"Excellent. Well, then, if we are in agreement on that, there is no reason to question your involvement with that case."

"My involvement?"

"With what you did to those two downstairs, having tapes that may or may not have depicted the ritualistic torture and murder of a child doesn't look good. But since we both know they are fake, there is no reason ever to mention them to anyone again, right? Because we don't want anyone trying to draw you into that."

"No, no reason to bring them up," Paisley agreed.

"Excellent," the sheriff said.

She pulled a packet of papers from a tray. The front of the packet said they were arrest reports, and the sheriff wrote Paisley's name across the top.

Paisley sat quietly, afraid to say anything else without a lawyer and to ask for one since she felt that the lie about the videos had earned her some brownie points.

In the room were photos of the sheriff accepting a few awards and promotions, a few of her at events, and one of her and a little blonde girl that Paisley thought she recognized as Heather Peck, the woman's niece. That explained the crayon drawing on the wall behind her. It was a crude drawing of a little girl with yellow hair waving goodbye to a woman in a large police truck.

Paisley was an outsider, poking around in unsolved murder investigations that were incredibly personal to the local sheriff, and she showed up with these videos that local law enforcement had never seen. Then, she is accused of murder in the same building that the same sheriff occupies. It would make sense if the sheriff would want to punish that outsider to save face for the murders she couldn't solve.

The sound of the phone ringing startled Paisley but not the sheriff. Paisley was used to cell phone ringers but less accustomed to a landline's loud, piercing sound. The sheriff grabbed the receiver, lifting it to her ear with practiced ease.

"Sheriff Patrick."

The person on the other line spoke for a second and the sheriff stopped looking at the paperwork and looked up at Paisley.

"Yeah, she's sitting right here."

There was a break and the punch of a voice from the phone sounded like someone speaking directly, but not yelling.

"Hold on," the sheriff said, hitting a button on the phone cradle before hanging up the receiver. "Okay," the sheriff shouted, "you're on with Miss Mott."

A man's voice came through the speaker. There was a hint of a New York accent, but one that felt withdrawn and not used to imposing force.

"Miss Mott?"

"Yes," Paisley said, raising her voice the way the sheriff did.

"Miss Mott, my name is Shelby Graves. I am an attorney hired by Hyacinth Bloom to represent you," the voice said.

"Shelby Graves, why do I know that name?" the sheriff asked.

"He's the one that refused to represent that asshole billionaire, the one that they arrested for drugging and raping a bunch of women," Paisley said.

"That's it!" the sheriff said. "That was big news. They said you'd have made millions defending him, but instead, you refused, and he went to prison for like twenty years. Why would you pass that up? That's money even if you lose."

"I only defend innocent people," Shelby Graves said. "Which brings us to the case in point. Sheriff, you are detaining my client without proper evidence. The law says you may hold a suspect for 48 hours on suspicion alone. Do you have sufficient evidence to hold my client? If so, I will need a list of such evidence sent to my office immediately."

"We have a witness that says they saw Miss Mott get into her very identifiable vehicle parked near the building, after hours, where the bodies of the deceased were found."

"And?" the lawyer questioned.

"And what? An eyewitness is pretty solid grounds to hold someone," the sheriff argued.

"Are you prepared to sign an affidavit saying that you have an eyewitness who saw my client, Paisley Mott, murder two people? Because I can have one of my assistants send that over to you now if you'd like. If that is not what you are saying, and the eye witness can only testify that they saw my client leave a public sidewalk, get into her legally parked personal vehicle, and drive away, and you have no other evidence, then you are holding my client without cause."

"We have fingerprints collected at the scene," the sheriff said.

"I assume you have vetted all of these prints, ruled out persons that had business in the areas where they were taken from, and then run them through the database, which usually takes 48-72 hours on a good week? Because, sheriff, I have never seen a positive match return as quickly as it does in the movies." The lawyer was calm, but stern.

"Well, no, but I guarantee that they will come back as a match for Miss Mott here," the sheriff replied, her lip beginning to curl like an angry dog on one side.

"Can I be direct, sheriff?" Graves asked.

"Please," she responded.

"Your guarantee means about dick to both me and the eyes of the law. Now, you have every right to hold my client for another twenty-two hours and sixteen minutes on suspicion alone. We both know those prints are not going to come back in that amount of time. If they do, I am going to dig so far up your ass with a microscope and demand that every single person that is part of that process testifies that their system has magical powers imbued by some god of justice that allows them to process them that quickly. So, if you decide to charge her without that evidence, be prepared to have this case thrown out. Or, you could release Miss Mott now with the understanding that she is not to leave the county until those results come back."

"I don't think so," the sheriff said. "I can't have a violent criminal wandering our streets."

"With all due respect, you have a very serious serial killer on the loose in a very embarrassing cold case."

"Hey!" the sheriff started, but the lawyer continued.

"I only bring that up as a way to say that your county is hurting, and rightfully so. I feel for you all, I do, but holding

Miss Mott implies her guilt, and everyone in the county will see that, and then there is no chance of her getting a fair trial. She is innocent until proven guilty. So let her go. She will stay put, and then, if your prints come back with a match, I will drive her to your office myself."

"I don't think so," the sheriff answered.

"If not, I will be forced to ask why, Sheriff Patrick. I will be moved to investigate everything that is happening in your county. Every case will be examined, open or closed, and we will find any and all incidents where you may have ignored the law the way you would be in this case, if you hold my client without proper cause."

There was silence in the room for a moment. The sheriff growled under her breath.

"Fine," she said.

"And my client's vehicle?"

"It is part of a murder investigation. We will be holding it. That is non-negotiable."

"You've had it long enough to process it. I happen to know that it has been cleared because it has been spotted at Hunt and Peck Salvage, which I believe, and correct me if I am wrong, is contracted as the county impound lot. Which, according to ownership records, belongs to your sister, Jackie, and her husband, Winslow. If I am not mistaken, *sheriff*, giving a government contract to family is a bit of a conflict of interest."

Somewhere outside, a dog barked, and a trash truck lowered a dumpster, the noise perforating the moment.

"A deputy will take Miss Mott to pick up her vehicle at the impound lot when she leaves here," Sheriff Patrick said, keeping a leash on her tone like a rabid dog snapping at a passerby.

"Miss Mott, you are free to go, but do not, I repeat, do not leave the county before the sheriff calls you to give you the all clear. Do you understand?" the lawyer on the phone asked.

"I do, absolutely. Thank you," Paisley said. "But what about my other stuff?"

"What other stuff?" the sheriff asked. Her patience had long passed gone.

"My phone, my bag, everything else I had with me."

"We only checked in the stuff that was in your pockets. A phone, keys, which are at impound with your vehicle, and some purple rock," the sheriff said. She seemed happy to report they had nothing else of Paisley's to give to her.

"Amethyst," Paisley said.

"What?" the sheriff responded.

"The purple rock, it's amethyst. It's supposed to help with anxiety."

"You believe in that stuff?"

"My mom did. She gave it to me. So I've kept it in my pocket since. Seems to help." She wasn't sure why she felt the need to clarify or validate it, but she certainly wished she had the stone or an audience to talk to.

"Your stuff is locked up at the front desk. You'll get it on the way out."

"Sheriff, thank you," Graves said. "I look forward to helping you see that my client was not involved and, in doing so, help your efforts to collect relevant evidence to put the true perpetrators behind bars."

"Yeah, okay," the sheriff said. Her shoulders slumped, and she wore a look that met somewhere between furious and confused on her face. She reached over and hit a button on the phone, disconnecting the call.

She didn't move for a few long moments, but pushing wasn't wise.

"Thank you," Paisley finally said.

The sheriff looked up at her without responding. Her eyes scanned Paisley.

"Also, I'm sorry," she added.

"Sorry?" the sheriff asked. Her face contorted into a grimace.

"That I haven't been able to find anything that can help in your niece's case," Paisley said and nodded at the crayon drawing on the wall.

The sheriff winced as if stung, but said nothing.

"I know that I came here just for Lydia Knot," Paisley said. "But this has become something bigger. Heather deserves justice, and I know you want more than anything to give it to her and all the girls."

"You don't know anything about that," the sheriff shot back.

"I know, and I can't imagine how difficult it must be. I never meant to make it feel like I was undermining your investigation. I am very sorry." She was going to be able to walk out of there. There was no reason to turn the screws and cause more pain or frustration for this woman.

The sheriff stood and walked around the desk without a word. When she got to Paisley, she held out a hand, and Paisley lifted her still-cuffed hands to her.

"Don't leave town, and stay where I can find you."

78

The patrol car rolled up to the open gate of the salvage yard after a quiet drive. Paisley tried making small talk, but other than telling her no, when she asked if the officer had a charger for her dead cell phone, he said nothing. She remembered turning the phone off when she turned it over to the deputy at booking, but when she got it back it was dead. They told her that the fed that had gone to visit her had tried to open it.

"Do you know where my car is?" Paisley asked the deputy.

"They should be able to tell you," he replied, pointing at the trailer just past the gate.

"Thank you," Paisley said as she exited the vehicle, paused for a reply, got none, and closed the door. The car was already in motion before the door was out of her hand.

"One star," she said, poking the black screen of her dead cell phone. "So much for innocent until proven guilty." She headed to the trailer.

She knocked once before opening the door and poking her head in. It smelled like corn chips and cigarettes inside the small trailer. Paisley scrunched up her nose, thinking it may be more polite than plugging it, but there wasn't anyone there to see whichever she chose.

"Hello?" she said into the seemingly empty room. "Anyone here?"

She stepped in and looked around. The front gate had been open so she didn't think they were closed. Maybe they were out getting her car for her. She decided to wait.

Paisley moved some things around on the desk to see if she could find a phone charger but she found something better, her keys. The Sheriff must have called and cleared her to pick up the vehicle, because they were the only set of keys sitting on the desk.

"Hello?" she called again. "I found my keys. The sheriff said I could get my car back. I'm just going to go ahead and take it, if that's okay?"

Paisley waited for a response, but when none came, she plucked the keys from the desk and headed out into the yard to find the vehicle.

Darkness stretched across the dirt, casting the place into an eerie contrast from the setting sun that banked off the collection of dust-covered, rusty cars and the shadows they cast. It was scary wandering aimlessly in the massive lot without direction. The occasional breeze would sway a rogue antenna causing a twang, or push an open car door sending a groan across the yard. Paisley's shoulders rose as she walked, the key fob to the Hummer stretched out in front of her, clicking every few seconds, hoping that it would beep the horn when she got close enough.

A noise behind her added to the orchestra of sounds she had inventoried since setting out to find the car. It was gravel. It was light, careful steps.

Paisley whipped around but could see nothing but old cars and the growing darkness creeping up on her.

"Hello?" she called out. The response was what she wanted, as her voice caused something in the shadows to move. She couldn't see it but could hear it move, disrupting the gravel again. "Hey, I know you're over there. Come on out."

The wind held its breath as Paisley did. The yard fell silent. Paisley walked backward, not wanting the thing to move and her to miss it.

"If you're over there, just come out. You're going to look real dumb when you try to jump out and scare me and find out why my nickname is Paisley 'Better Not' Mott, President of the FAFO Mafia. That's right, that's fuck around and find out, in case you were curious."

A hiss came from behind her, and Paisley whirled to look, raising the keys that were poking through her fingers like claws ready to strike. Had she been in a better state of mind, she would have recognized the sound and the shape flying toward her, but she didn't. Instead, she jerked in terror as a small black missile shot across the ground at an incredible speed, forcing Paisley to jump in the other direction. She saw reflective green eyes.

A cat.

Paisley's heart froze for a beat as the fear enveloped her. Not just from the cat, but even in the dark, she could see that had she continued walking backward she would have gone over a drop and fallen God knew how far into a pitch black void.

"Jesus Christ," Paisley said, trying to catch her breath. "You scared the shit out of me, cat. I don't know whether to curse you for nearly giving me a heart attack, or thank you for stopping me from dropping over the edge there."

Paisley searched the darkness, looking for the reflective shine of the cat's eyes among the cars, but did not see them. She looked out over the void. It appeared that, at some point, the yard continued in that direction, but had collapsed into a sinkhole, or perhaps it was an old river bed that finally gave way. Either way, it was deep. Kicking a few rocks off the edge and listening to them bounce a few times off the side before banging off what Paisley assumed was some old car that had either dropped with the ground or been rolled off the small cliff at some point. Either way, she knew that if she fell, she wasn't coming back up. She had to be more careful out there to avoid making that mistake again.

She turned in the direction that the cat ran, along the drop off and, after just a few dozen steps, was rewarded with the first beeps from the Hummer's horn and faint flash of the headlights in the distance.

"Fuck yeah!" Paisley cheered and was met with a soft meow as the cat that had darted past her strolled as cool as could be out from behind a minivan backed up to the edge of the cliff. "Well, there you are. I owe you a debt of thanks."

She knelt and petted the black cat on the small white patch

on its head that looked like a leaf.

"Basil, right?" She scratched the cat for a few seconds before standing. "Well, lead the way." She clicked the button and heard the horn again, watching to pinpoint where the lights had flashed, and began moving that way. "Okay, I'll take point."

Paisley inched through the bramble of cars and trucks, and the cat followed. She was careful to tread slowly to avoid a misstep that could cause a twisted ankle, or worse yet, a trip over the edge and fall into the darkness below.

The vehicles loomed around her like burial mounds, their shape and size hidden by the darkness, only revealed for a fleeting moment when Paisley pressed the button on the fob and the Hummer's lights illuminated the wheeled graveyard. With less than a few hundred feet and a few vehicles in the way, Paisley's focus honed on traversing the labyrinth and clicked the button to identify her path forward.

"Shit!" Paisley yelled as something moved and caught her eye. Just before the Hummer sat an older car with a smashed windshield. It hindered a clear view, especially in the dark, but when Paisley keyed the fob one last time to close the last few feet, she saw something in the beater. A shadow moved quickly. Its height above the seat indicated that it could have been someone's head as they ducked out of sight.

"Hey! Who's in there?" she yelled, the horn blaring as the lights flashed again. The Hummer was backed in, right up to the cliff she'd been following to get there. "Who's in that car? I saw you. Come out!"

There was no answer from inside, but Basil, braver, or just more used to the area, scurried past Paisley and jumped into the broken back passenger side window.

Paisley squinted as the lights flashed, and she stepped closer.

"Well, you must be Ginger," Paisley said, smiling as the flash of the lights revealed another cat curled up on the seat. "You scared the shit out of me."

Paisley reached in and petted the cat that had been following her and then the one she had mistaken for someone in the car.

Had she been more aware of her surroundings, the shadow moving between cars as the lights flashed and footfalls on the gravel hidden by the Hummer's powerful horn, may have been noticed. Instead, it came closer, out-pacing her to the Hummer as if it knew the path well enough to traverse it without the aid of the light.

Paisley reached farther in to pet the other cat when something moved beneath her foot. At first, she worried she had stepped on another cat but was relieved to see it was only a mound of gravel and dirt that was piled between the cars.

A hand emerged from the dark. It dug its fingers into her hair and slammed her face forward into the door frame of the cat's car. She could feel something beneath her left eye crack, and blooms of white took over her field of vision. She tried to push herself away from the car, but whoever was behind her was too powerful; their massive body pushed up against her, crushing her against the car. Her face dug into the remnants of the broken window, and glass ripped at the skin next to her eye as she fought. The hand, still in her hair, pulled back, her bloodied and broken face pointing to the sky, and then slammed it forward again. She attempted to turn her head to avoid damaging her other eye, and took the full force to her jaw instead. Something popped, and her mouth dropped open against her will.

The hand pulled her head back one last time as an arm, bigger than a parking lot bollard, slipped around her neck and began to choke her. The pain and terror subsided momentarily as she accepted the inevitable. She was going to die. She lived the last year of her life for an audience, and now she would die, here, in a junkyard, with the only witnesses being the monster who killed her and two cats named after spices sitting in the back seat of an old car. As her body numbed and the world drifted away from her, she thought first of her dad, and how much he would miss her, and then of her mom, and hoped that she was wrong about the afterlife, just so she could see her again.

"Forgive me, please," a familiar voice whispered in her ear

before her body went limp.

79

"Listen, I really just need to talk to my friend. I drove all night to get here because when I called, no one would let me talk to her on the phone. Isn't she supposed to get one phone call?" Hyacinth asked the man standing at the Sheriff's Department reception desk.

"Yes, miss, she is. But that means she's allowed to make one call, not receive one call," a young deputy explained. Before she could reply, a voice came from behind her.

"Hyacinth?"

Hyacinth turned to see Darius Knot, the kid Paisley had been there to help, standing in the doorway holding a can of Dr. Pepper and a vending machine sticky bun.

"Darius? Er, Derry, right?" she asked. "You know who I am?"

"Of course I do," he replied. "I watched Paisley's series. Also, she talks about you all the time. So I feel like I know you pretty well by now."

"Well it's nice to meet you. What are you doing here?"

"Looking for Paisley."

"Me too. But I can't get anyone to tell me where she is."

"I told you that I am not at liberty to discuss an ongoing investigation," the deputy said. He sighed and leaned forward on the counter.

"Well where's the sheriff? The one who arrested her. I want to talk to her."

"She's out on a call. I don't know when she will be back. But like I told the kid, you are welcome to wait." The deputy signaled to two wooden chairs against the wall near the door. There was a Terry Pratchett novel lying open on one of them.

"How long you been in for, kid?" Hyacinth asked, nodding

toward the chair.

"About an hour. My friend dropped me on his way to work." Derry took a nursing sip of his Dr. Pepper and looked over at the deputy. Hyacinth followed his gaze.

"You really going to make this kid sit here all night and give him no information at all?" Hyacinth asked the deputy. Derry made the best sad puppy dog eyes she had ever seen.

"I told you, I can't talk about the case," the deputy said. "I'm sorry."

"I will give you fifty dollars right now to tell me how long she will be held for or if charges have already been pressed," Hyacinth said.

"I can't."

"Hundred," Hyacinth countered.

"Seriously?" the deputy replied.

"Seriously. Right now." Hyacinth stuck her hand into her pocket and fished around.

"She was released about two hours ago or so," the deputy blurted out.

"What?" Hyacinth and Derry asked in unison.

"A deputy was taking her to get her car at the impound lot, and then..." the deputy stopped himself and gulped hard, as if he could swallow the last two words.

"Then *what?*" Hyacinth asked.

"I really can't say."

"Then what?"

"We got a call there about a fire. A car went over the ridge. Sounds like it was hers. It's really dark out there at night. If they weren't out there with her she—"

"Oh fuck you." Hyacinth threw a bill across the desk at the deputy and turned toward Derry. "You coming?"

"Of course," Derry said, shoving the sticky bun in his mouth and scooping up his book.

80

The flashing lights were visible from more than a mile away, only to be surpassed in brilliance by the fire that licked at the sky from the back of the salvage yard.

"Oh no," Derry whimpered as he saw the flames against the black sky.

"Jesus Christ, no," Hyacinth added.

"There's Patch," Derry said, pointing at his friend who leaned on the hood of his old Toyota, pressing the bumper down nearly to the dirt, in front of the salvage yard.

"What's he doing here?" Hyacinth asked as she pulled the car in, ignoring the two deputies who signaled her to stop and parked next to the sobbing boy.

"He works here." The kid jumped from the car before it was in park and ran to his friend.

Hyacinth got out and circled around the front of the car, avoiding the deputies stomping toward her, and joined the boys.

"What happened? Where's Paisley?" Derry asked Patch as Hyacinth walked up. The smaller boy rubbed his friend's shoulders as if trying to warm him up.

"I got here and went to open the gate to pull in and I heard an engine rev up from somewhere in the back, then I heard a crunch, and loud noise. Then this..." The boy took a deep breath and wiped his eyes, "...this giant fireball. So I think that maybe some kids got in, hot wired something, and were fucking around, you know, like we used to do? So I ran into the trailer and called the sheriff."

"Was it Paisley?" Hyacinth asked, interrupting the boy. Grief-stricken, the boy wailed and nodded.

"No," Hyacinth said. Her legs shook beneath her.

A deputy in a wide-brimmed hat grabbed her arm. He intended to either steady or apprehend her, but she didn't give him time to tell her which.

"Is she okay?" Hyacinth barked at the deputy.

"Who?" he responded.

Hyacinth's face scrunched, and she fought the urge to yell at the deputy with the dumbfounded look. She waved her hand at the pillar of black smoke, slowly giving way to white.

"You folks can't be here," the sheriff called.

"I want to know if Paisley Mott was in that accident." Hyacinth said, matching the sheriff's authoritative tone.

"And who exactly are you?"

"I'm her sister. Now tell me where she is," Hyacinth said.

Sheriff Patrick took a deep breath, exhaled, and removed her hat.

"Miss Mott was dropped off here by one of our deputies to pick up her vehicle from impound. It appears that, instead of checking in at the office, and having someone collect her vehicle for her, she decided to go out into the yard and find it herself. It can be very dark and dangerous back there if you don't know your way. It appears Miss Mott got turned around and drove into a sinkhole that stretches across the back side of the lot. The vehicle dropped about thirty-five feet..."

"No..." Hyacinth gasped.

"Upon impact with some vehicles that had fallen when the sinkhole formed, Miss Mott's vehicle burst into flames and subsequently exploded."

"Did she get out?" Hyacinth asked.

"We have confirmed that Miss Mott was in the vehicle at the time of the accident, but we are unable to recover the body."

"I don't believe you!" Hyacinth cried and rushed past the sheriff. Derry shook Patch loose and went after her.

"You can't go back there," the sheriff said. One of the deputies stepped in front of Hyacinth, and she stopped. "Once the fire rescue team has put out the fire and secured the area, we will recover Miss Mott's body."

"Her body? You don't know that it's her. You don't know that she's dead." Hyacinth turned and pushed past the deputy, who moved to grab her but was waved off by the sheriff.

"I say this with every ounce of compassion I can. It will do you no good to see her like that," the sheriff said.

Hyacinth turned and looked back at the white smoke, billowing up into the sky. Then she turned to Derry. He looked confused, scared, and hurt.

"She can't be," he said, dropping to his knees with a defeated cry.

"I suggest you all head home for the night and let us do our jobs," the sheriff said. "Once we have this all figured out, we can answer whatever questions you have."

"Go home? You want us to just go home?" Hyacinth yelled at her.

"I don't care where you go, but you can't just hang around here." The sheriff turned to address the deputies. "Clear them out of here. This is a crime scene. Take them to jail for interfering if they don't listen."

"Crime scene? You said it was an accident," Hyacinth shouted after her.

The sheriff turned and walked back a few steps to come face to face with Hyacinth.

"Listen to me, I don't know who this woman is, but she showed up here, causing a lot of trouble for a lot of people. I tried to help her by just putting her in a cell, but that wasn't enough. She thought she was above our system. This is what happens when you think you are above the law. You end up making a mistake that gets you killed."

Hyacinth's fists clenched. She was ready to swing when she thought about the conversation she would have to have with Grover when he found out she hit the sheriff.

She shook her head and stood down. Of course, that was what the Sheriff wanted. If she hit her, she would go to jail, and rightfully so. She would be right where the woman wanted

Paisley, out of the way, stuck in a cell. Unable to investigate. But it wasn't illegal to speak your mind.

"You're an asshole, you know that?" Hyacinth laughed.

The sheriff's face expanded as if in a wind tunnel.

"What?" Hyacinth continued. "You look surprised. You shouldn't be. You know you're an asshole."

"I can arrest you for defamation of character. Slander." The sheriff put her hand on her cuffs.

"Slander is when you make a false statement. And I think *when* it went to court, and I would make sure that my very expensive lawyers saw that it did, and I called up all these witnesses, they'd say that you were being an asshole. The judge would certainly agree, given the circumstances. Then it would be on record that you are, indeed, an asshole. So, instead, my new friends and I are going to figure out our next move, and if it involves you, we'll let you know. Kay?" The switch from grieving to false cheer, was abrupt, even to her, but needed in the moment.

The sheriff said nothing to Hyacinth. She just turned and addressed the deputies again.

"They don't go anywhere near the scene."

Hyacinth waited for the sheriff to disappear back into the yard before going to Derry, still on his knees in the dirt. She squatted down next to him.

"Hey?"

Patch joined them. Derry looked up, first at Hyacinth, then to Patch, then back to Hyacinth, but he said nothing.

"Something isn't right about all of this. That lady doesn't want anyone poking around, that's obvious, but why?" Hyacinth asked.

"Because it's a crime scene. She said that," Patch pointed out.

"She didn't want Paisley involved before. That's why she wanted her in jail," Hyacinth continued.

"It's 'cause they said she murdered some people," Patch said.

"Paisley wouldn't have done that," Derry interjected. He

370

stood, refusing Hyacinth's hand when she offered it, but leaned into Patch as he scooped the boy under the arm and hoisted him. "Paisley was a good person. She shouldn't have had to be wrapped up in all of this. This is my fault."

"You can't think like that, kid. Trust me on that one. You start letting other people's choices weigh you down, they'll drown you. Paisley's a big girl; everything she did, she did because she wanted to. You got that?" Hyacinth cocked her head to try and make eye contact with the boy who just stared into the dirt. He met her eyes.

"Thank you."

"Now, I want to know what this woman is hiding. This doesn't add up. Paisley would have never done what she said."

"She would have never snuck in somewhere to get her car?" Patch asked.

"Oh no," Hyacinth said, nodding, "that is actually fully on brand for Paisley. One hundred percent. But she wouldn't have backed off of anything. She's used to driving the Hummer, and she's been driving big vehicles in dark mountains her whole life. That's the part that doesn't make sense to me."

"Won't the investigation show if that is what happened or not?" Derry asked.

"But what if that's what the sheriff is trying to hide from us?"

"That seems like a bit of a leap in logic," Derry pointed out.

"Maybe, but I'm just trying to think like Pais. What would she do? She wouldn't want to miss out on checking something that could have been tampered with, just in case."

"There's a section of fence missing over on the far side, where the sinkhole pulled it down," Patch offered. "We'd have to be real careful, but I bet we could sneak in over there. Depending on where the firefighters are, we should be out of sight."

"They'd see us walk over, though. These deputies are watching us like hawks," she said.

"Thing about hawks," Derry started. "They only watch things

they can prey on. So, if we get in the car and drive away, they no longer have a reason to pay attention to us. We are only prey if they think we will try and get through that gate. We leave and go down and turn down the little access road. Unless they walk out to the street, they shouldn't see us turn."

"Then let's go," Hyacinth said.

"Your car or mine?" Patch asked.

"We'll take mine. I'll bring you back for yours later."

The group started toward Hyacinth's car and she yelled back over toward the deputies.

"This is bullshit, and you know it. I'm coming back with a warrant."

The deputies looked confused but did not reply or follow as she backed out on the street.

"Why would we need a warrant?" Patch asked, as the car took off toward the road on the far side of the yard.

"We don't. I just felt like I had to say something to them so they think they won, or they might chase us down to prove they're in charge."

"Oh," Patch said. "I'm Patch, by the way. I'm a big fan."

The hole in the fence was only a few hundred yards from where the emergency crew was positioned, trying to put out the fire that had spread to what appeared to be about fifteen cars that lay at the bottom of the sinkhole. The fire revealed that the sinkhole itself wasn't exactly a hole. A creek ran behind the yard and the earth had eroded away and weakened to the point where it gave way and fell. The cars along that side had been too much weight, which meant that it was just a matter of time until the next row went as well.

"Be careful stepping near the hole. You don't want to fall," Patch whispered, leading the way through a tangle of brush and a broken fence.

Weeds climbed the cars on that side like the earth was reclaiming them. The tires were all flat and rotting away. Rust spread across the hulls like psoriasis, eating away at the bodies of the cars, leaving holes where metal once was.

Patch stopped behind an old Honda to look across the sea of metal to the ravaging fire. The others followed and crouched down to peer over the hood. Two fire trucks sprayed around the edges, soaking the cars that weren't yet ablaze.

"Why ain't they putting it out?" Patch whispered.

"They are probably trying to control the burn," Derry said. "They know they won't be able to stop the fire at the center, so they let it burn itself out. They get everything else wet enough so it doesn't burn too."

"Where's Blue?" Patch asked. He was clearly listening to Derry, but his gaze was directed at an empty spot near the mouth of the hole.

"Who's Blue?" Hyacinth asked.

Patch dropped down and turned to Hyacinth.

"Blue. The car."

"I'm sorry, big guy, I don't know what you're talking about," she responded.

Patch looked back at Derry who just shrugged.

"Blue is a 1988 Chevy Caprice Wagon. Cracked engine block and front end damage. It's been sitting right there since the first time I ever came back here. It's gone."

"A blue wagon? Like a station wagon?" Hyacinth asked.

"Yeah. One of the old kind, not the lame little hatchback stuff that Subaru makes," Patch answered.

"You mean like that?" Hyacinth pointed past the boys and off into the darkness. The fire did a lot to cast a spray of dancing light into the yard, and Hyacinth could just barely make out a car that looked like it wasn't pushed into a space like all the other vehicles were. The others were lined up, but that one felt out of place.

"Yep, that's Blue." Patch nodded. "You know your cars, lady."

"I wonder if the fire department moved it to get close to the fire?" Derry said, looking back toward the drop.

"Maybe they have a better angle from where they are, I

373

would think. And would they have moved it over there, or would they have pulled it back far enough to be out of the way?" Hyacinth theorized. Something brushed against her hand, and she jumped back. "What the fuck?!"

A dark blur darted back under the car they hid behind and crouched there. It was a cat.

"Ginger," Patch said, extending a hand. The cat slowly slunk from the shadow and rubbed its face against the boy's massive hand.

"Oh, the junkyard cats. I think I remember Paisley talking to one of them." Just saying her name hit Hyacinth like a punch to the stomach, and she recoiled at the painful thought about the fate of her friend.

The cat pushed hard against Patch, then turned and bound back across the dirt clearing between them and the drop. It stopped where Patch said Blue had been, and glanced back at the group cowering behind the car. It meowed and hopped up through the busted window of a totaled sedan. The fire lit the interior. It wasn't alone. There was another cat in there with it. They were both perched on the back of the bench style front seat.

"That seems odd, right? That's odd?" Hyacinth pointed out.

"That's Basil and Ginger. They live in that car. They hang out there a lot," Patch explained.

Something was off. Hyacinth wished she had Paisley's perception of things out of the ordinary, but she couldn't put her finger on it.

"I want to get a closer look." Hyacinth tiptoed toward the front of the car, but Derry's hand on her arm stopped her.

"They'll see you out there, for sure."

The layout of the cars gave Hyacinth decent coverage if she went out the other way, stayed low, and approached the cats' vehicular home from the far side.

"I'll stay out of sight, be quiet, and everything should be fine. I just want to get a look. That's what we came in here for, right?"

Derry nodded, then Patch followed suit.

Hyacinth went around the boys and behind the car, crossing a dirt patch and ducking behind another hulking piece of metal. It took less than two minutes to go from one hiding place to the next. When she made it directly across the dirt road from the car with the cats, she stopped and looked back at the boys. Their heads were fairly well hidden as they peeked around the back of the car, but she could spot them since she knew they were there.

Hyacinth could see up the dirt drive to where the fire truck sat, providing a secondary light source, showing no one was looking in her direction. She was just about to make her move to cross the road when she glanced back to see Derry waving his arms. He was still hidden, but he shook his hands back and forth to get her attention, and thankfully, it worked. She lifted her hands palms up and shrugged. The boy pointed toward the drop.

"What is it now?" Hyacinth said. "Shit." She ducked behind the car and pressed herself against it. There, across the dirt road, just two cars away from the cats, stood three people that were very easy to make out even though it was dark, and they were only visible by the fire. It was the Sheriff, Winslow Peck, and Jackie Peck. Hyacinth knew all three of them from Paisley's video stream, and Winslow would have been visible from space.

She hurried back to the front of the car and hid in the darkness that it provided, peeking around the side to watch the three looking out over the drop. Winslow pointed toward the open space, where Patch said Blue had been, and moved his hand like he was miming a car going out from there and over the cliff. Then he pointed down at the plumes of smoke rising from the drop.

Hyacinth's face went red and tears stung her eyes. She knew what they were looking at, the fiery tomb of her friend. She wanted to scream. To push them away because they didn't deserve to look at her, but she didn't. She stayed hidden. Knowing that was what Paisley would do. She remained there until it was safe because she couldn't jeopardize the investigation. After a few minutes, the group finally walked back toward the firefighters, working their way up the tangle of cars at the bottom of the cliff. She gave them a minute, and then Derry gave her a thumbs up. She made her move.

She walked low and slow across the dirt road, glancing just briefly to ensure no one saw her. When she got to the other side, she lay flat on a pile of dirt between the cats' car and the car next to it, trying to make as little of a silhouette as possible. She looked underneath the car, across the clearing to where the boys hid, and she could see Derry. She hoped he could see her or at least know she would look to them for a sign that she had made it without being spotted. The sign came. Derry's hand reached out from behind the bumper and gave her a thumbs up.

"Thank God," she whispered to herself, putting her hands out to push herself into a crouching position. "Gross." Her hand slid across the dirt through something wet. She stabilized against the car door to stop herself from pitching forward and falling into the small splash of liquid.

"Oil?" she said to herself, raising her hand to her face in the dark. She wasn't sure what oil smelled like, but it was a habit. The sticky substance on her hand did have the faint smell of metal. She wiped it on her pants and stood, noticing the perfect hand print she had left on the car door opposite the cat car. As she stood, one of the cats popped its head out the window to greet her. This one was black with a spot of white between its ears. She was careful to pet it using the dry hand.

"Whatcha doing in he..." She surprised herself with the sound she made. A scream. The loudest scream she'd ever mustered.

She could hear people behind her at a distance, questioning who she was and what she was doing. People called to her, asking if she was okay. But one of the things that would stick with her for the rest of her life, and there were many from that moment, was the speed at which the giant boy ran at her from across the clearing.

"Help! Someone help!" she finally managed to yell.

The boy didn't slow down. He allowed himself to hit the car behind her with full force, turning at the last second to put his shoulder down. The car rocked and the two remaining windows blew out. The door panel he hit bent and the car looked like it had been t-boned in an accident. He rebounded off the car and glanced past her and into the car. When he saw what she saw he did not react the way she had. There was no surprise, just action.

The boy grabbed the door handle and jerked it up, pulling the old heavy door open so hard that it came off in his hand. He tossed it aside. Both cats in the backseat moved as the giant quickly and carefully leaned into the car. When he emerged, he was holding her. He cradled her, bracing her bloody head against his chest.

"Someone help!" the boy roared as firefighters ran toward them. He refused to wait and rushed to them carrying a body.

"Paisley!" she called after her. "Please."

81

"What the hell is that?"

The woman's booming voice woke Millicent. She sat up quickly. She knew if the woman was angry, it was bad.

"What is it?" the man asked.

The woman pointed toward Millicent's legs. She could feel something there, something familiar. It was Squeakers. The little mouse sometimes liked to crawl behind her knees and nestle in when she slept.

"Looks like a mouse," the man said.

"Ugh, like we don't have enough pests down here. We have to deal with mice now, too?" the woman responded.

The man stepped forward, his large body blocking out everything else in the room. Millicent shielded Squeakers from his view for just a second so he could get away.

"Move," the man said, shoving Millicent aside.

"Over there! He ran behind the dryer," the woman called.

The man pivoted and pulled the dryer forward, but Millicent could see that Squeakers was already on the move. Her eyes had adapted to the lower light and had gotten used to watching his speedy journey back to a small hole on the far side of the basement.

"He's gone," the man said, shoving the dryer back against the wall with a bang.

The woman shoved her finger into Millicent's face.

"You feeding that thing? Is that why it's down here? Maybe we need to stop giving you food so you can stop bringing that kind of filth in here." Spit from the woman's lips speckled Millicent's face.

"Come on, now," the man said, pulling the woman back.

"Let's go back upstairs. I'll come down and get the laundry later."

"I'm just so sick of her," the woman said as she was led toward the stairs. "Why can't we just be rid of her. I told you she's a curse."

Once the door was closed, Millicent tried to whistle for Squeakers to come back, but the mouse didn't hear her. She was alone again.

82

Light tore at Paisley's head like a metal hook, scratching the back of her skull and dragging itself around, sinking into her orbital socket and pulling outward. She could only open one eye, and the pain made her regret it. She closed it again. A muffled sound moved close and she tried to open the eye again.

"...sley? Can you hear me?" the voice sounded like it was coming from a steel drum at the bottom of a lake.

She tried to respond but her face hurt when she did and something held her jaw closed.

"Paisley?" the voice said again. Then, as if it was farther away, "Hey! She's awake! Guys, she's awake!"

Her eye opened again, this time it wasn't her doing, and an even brighter light pointed into it. She attempted to pull back against the pain but couldn't move.

"Paisley, can you hear me?" a woman's voice said. "If you can, try and squeeze my hand."

Paisley could feel something in her hand, and then there was pressure. She squeezed. It wasn't much, and she wasn't sure why she was doing it, but she figured it best to comply.

Another voice joined, this one familiar, but she couldn't place it.

"She's awake?!"

Then, there was a voice that grabbed her and pulled her forward toward consciousness. A voice that, with just a few words, started rebuilding the universe that had escaped her. The one she almost left.

"Paisley, kiddo, dad's here."

"Dad?" she tried to force out. She wasn't sure if he could hear her, but she could feel him. His hands on her shoulders.

And they were his. She would know them anywhere. The hands that carried her as a baby. The ones that lifted and brushed her off when she fell off her bike after taking off the training wheels. The hands that held her at the funeral after her mother was killed. They were her dad's hands, and they let her know that everything would be okay.

"I'm here," he said, his gentle hands held her.

She opened her uninjured eye and blinked the prism of light away until the forms standing around the room began to take shape. Her dad was the first one to come into view. He was sitting on the bed with her. Tears ran down his unshaven face. Paisley looked around to see if she could recognize anyone else, and to her surprise, it was coming back to her. The first voice she had heard when she woke had belonged to Derry. He stood in the corner of the room, clearly not wanting to be in the way. There was a woman she didn't recognize but looked like a doctor.

Paisley's breath caught painfully in her throat as she saw the beautiful woman standing at her bedside.

"Hi, Hy," she said and reached for her.

"Pais," Hyacinth said, rushing to grab the hand so it didn't have to travel too far. "Try not to move too much."

"What are you all doing here?" Paisley asked.

Hyacinth laughed and squeezed her hand.

"Am I in the hospital?"

"Yeah, kiddo. You are. But you're going to be okay. You're going to be just fine," her dad said.

She moved her eye back to look at him.

"What happened?" she asked.

"You were attacked," Hyacinth said. "Someone tried to murder you. Little did they know that Paisley Mott is not that easy to kill."

Paisley thought hard, trying to remember, but everything was fuzzy.

"Who did it?" Paisley asked.

"We were hoping you could tell us," Hyacinth said. "You

were at the salvage yard."

Memories started to trickle in.

"There was a cat. No, two cats. Honey and something else, I think," she said, sorting through the images reforming in her mind.

"Basil and Ginger," Derry said from the corner.

"Yeah, that's it," Paisley said. Her jaw ached, and it felt like it was tied shut, but she was able to push the words out.

"Who did this to you. Was it the boy?" Paisley's dad asked.

"Boy? What boy?" Paisley whispered, trying not to move her jaw.

"They arrested Patch," Derry said. His voice had tones of both fear and anger. "He didn't do anything."

"Why would Patch do this?" Paisley raised her hands and motioned to her face and then the room.

"He wouldn't," Derry added. "They said that he was the only one there. They're full of shit."

"Did Patch do this?" Paisley wasn't sure who did it, but she knew the person who did was very big. There were only two people in town that it could be, but Patch was one of them, and Winslow Peck was the other.

"Of course he didn't," Derry interjected.

"We don't know who did it, Pais. Patch was there when we got there, but he was outside," Hyacinth added.

"They said he can get out today because they don't have any evidence," Derry added.

"The investigator was hoping you'd be awake soon enough to tell them if he was or wasn't involved," her dad said.

"Miss Mott needs her rest," the doctor said. "I don't think this is the right time for this. The detectives will be in at some point to get a statement. Maybe it's best if we don't muddy it up with everyone else's opinions in the meantime. I do, however, have private medical information to discuss with Miss Mott, so if you all wouldn't mind leaving the room?"

Derry stood and took two steps toward the door, and stopped. Paisley's dad and Hyacinth weren't moving. Derry looked confused, as if it surprised him that you could refuse to comply with an authority figure.

"I'm not going anywhere. Someone tried to kill my daughter. I'm staying right here," her dad said.

"Same," Hyacinth agreed.

Derry said nothing. He just went back to his chair and sat down.

"Well, that is up to Miss Mott," the doctor said. "I will be sharing some private things. If she wants them shared, then that's up to her."

Paisley wasn't sure what private info could be shared but didn't see anything she could hide from her dad or Hyacinth, unless maybe she was *assaulted* after she passed out, but she didn't think that was the case. She was starting to remember things and was fairly certain that wasn't part of it. Derry was still a relative stranger, but he was harmless enough. It wouldn't be a big deal if he heard about what bones were broken. It would probably hurt more if he was excluded and the only one asked to leave.

"Everyone can stay."

The doctor sighed. It seemed to convey both annoyance and surrender.

"Miss Mott, you suffered a maxilla fracture, the bone under your right eye. Luckily for you, it didn't shatter with the force you appear to have been hit with. You suffered a number of lacerations to your face, but we were able to close them all with simple adhesive, and you will likely experience minimal scarring. You have multiple abrasions and contusions, but your head and face were the areas that took the most damage. We were able to examine your eye, but without you being awake, we couldn't assess the full extent of the damage. Until that swelling goes down, we will not know if there is any long-term damage, so we will continue to monitor that."

"That all sounds promising," Paisley said. She was afraid to look at her own face but she didn't want anyone else to know that was on her mind.

"The best news, of course, is that the baby seems to be doing well," the doctor said, closing the chart she held.

"There was a baby there?" Paisley blurted out.

"The what?" Hyacinth asked.

"Wait..." her dad added.

"Your baby, Miss Mott. The fetus seems to be doing just fine. You went through a lot of trauma, but your baby seems to be just as much of a fighter as you are."

There was silence in the room as everyone processed the news.

"I'm pregnant?"

"Yes, based on the size of the fetus, you are about six to eight weeks along," the doctor said.

Another moment of silence while math was done by almost everyone in the room.

It hit her. Hyacinth must have gotten it at the same time as she looked down at Paisley and a look of both horror and sadness crossed her face.

"Oh, Pais, I'm sorry," she said.

"Pregnant?" Paisley's dad said. His voice quivered.

"I'm okay, dad. Everyone is okay." Paisley put her other hand on her dad's.

"Now would you like some privacy?" the doctor asked.

"Do you mind?" Paisley asked.

"Not at all."

With that the doctor left the four of them alone.

"Dad, Derry, do you two mind waiting out in the hall for just a minute?" Paisley asked, pulling her hand from her dad's after giving it a hard squeeze.

"I'll be right outside," her dad said, kissing her carefully on the forehead, finding a spot where the skin showed between bandages.

Derry didn't say anything. He just followed Paisley's dad out and closed the door behind him.

Hyacinth looked at Paisley with compassion in her eyes and then reached up and wiped a tear from under Paisley's swollen eye with her thumb.

"That fucker always had to get the last laugh," Hyacinth finally said. An unexpected chuckle rumbled out of Paisley's mouth.

"What am I going to do?" Paisley shook her head as if it would've made the realization disappear.

"You'll do whatever you damn well please." Hyacinth looked around at the walls of the hospital room as if she could see through them and into the hearts and minds of the people in the town. "Maybe just not here."

"It was one time," Paisley said.

"I do *not* need the details of any relationship you had with my brother." Hyacinth's eyes went wide. "Oh. Rowan."

"Shit," Paisley said. They didn't need to say it, but they both knew that Rowan would be devastated. He was very fond of Paisley, and finding out that she was pregnant with his brother's baby, the same brother who had tried to kill his own sister as well as the woman he now had feelings for, might break him.

"Yeah," Hyacinth agreed.

"I have to get out of here. I can't deal with this all right now. The person who tried to kill me is the same person who killed those girls. I'm close. I know I am. They wouldn't be trying to take me out of play if I wasn't."

"Out of play?" Hyacinth said. "This isn't a game, Paisley. You were almost killed for the second time in less than two months. We need to get out of here, alright. We need to get back to Raven Bloom, where it's safe."

"I can't leave her, Hy. You know I can't."

"Leave who? Who are you looking for? You're chasing dead girls."

Paisley sat up fighting the pain in her head.

"What if he isn't done? Lydia was the last one, and it hasn't happened since, but there was always a break between murders. So he could be ready to strike again. I need to find him first."

"Paisley, this is all too much like what happened with Hollis. You have to see the similarities?"

"I do, of course I do. I just..."

"You just want to solve this one so you can feel like you're gaining control since you feel like you didn't have it last time?" Hyacinth said, cutting her off.

"I think that is part of it, but I also have to catch this guy so he doesn't hurt anyone else. So what if I'm using my pain to try and stop someone else's. Isn't that what we're supposed to do? Use our pain for good?"

Hyacinth Bloom was a philanthropist. She knew a lot about giving to try and stop people from suffering the way she did. Yes, she came from one of the wealthiest families in the country, but that came with an absent father, and, like Paisley, her mother had been killed. Hyacinth would understand. She just had to look past her fear.

Paisley felt weak. She was healing and, apparently, carrying a child. Even though she was grateful to be awake, all she wanted to do was sleep.

"How long was I out?" she finally asked.

"Not quite two days, now. The doctor said that she thought you might not wake up when we got you in here. We really thought we'd lost you in the fire. Then, when we found you in the car, you weren't breathing. The doctor said you wouldn't have made it to the hospital if paramedics had not been onsite already. They got you going again. They just couldn't get you to wake up."

"Wait, I died?"

"Yeah, but like, just a little," Hyacinth joked. This was how she dealt with pain. It comforted Paisley.

"Whoa, I'm the undead!"

"You look like the currently dead." Hyacinth nudged Paisley's bed with her hip.

The two were quiet for a moment. Paisley tried to digest it all. She'd almost died again. She'd let someone get the drop on her, and she didn't see it coming. She should have known better than to go out into the yard alone. Without an audience or someone to listen while she worked things out on her own, she just couldn't seem to put things together. It felt like her head was full of puzzle pieces, and she couldn't lay them out and put them together without talking it out. Her hand went to her stomach unconsciously.

"It's going to be okay," Hyacinth said.

"You think since I'm a zombie, it is too? You think it'll eat its way out like some sort of fucked up baby vampire thing?" This was a joke, but the thought made her queasy.

"Oh god, if it comes out shimmering I'll stake it myself." Hyacinth mimed holding something in the palm of her hand and then jamming a stake into it.

"Wait, am I a zombie or a vampire?"

"Um, I don't know, but I'll take whatever you are because I'm just glad you're still here." Hyacinth took Paisley's hand and gave it a squeeze.

"I couldn't stop yet. I need to figure this thing out."

Hyacinth held her hand for a moment, sighed what seemed to be reluctant acceptance, and then nodded.

"Then let's figure it out."

"I need something first."

"And that is?"

"An audience."

"Well, Derry grabbed your gear when you got arrested. It's in the car. I can go down and grab some of it," Hyacinth offered.

"No, it's okay. We can just use my phone," Paisley said.

"They never found it. They think it was in the Hummer. We can use mine. It's set up to save to your server, so it should work unless you plan on going live."

"The server, WhyItHurts, do they know what happened?" Paisley asked. She hadn't considered what her online friend would think when she vanished.

"I sent a message through the server like you showed me and let them know what was happening. I said I would update if I heard anything."

"Well, then start recording," Paisley said and tried her hardest to smile. "Hold it horizontal though. This will be cut into the story, not added to the socials."

"Right, got it," Hyacinth said, turning the phone and hitting the record button. "Okay, aaaaaaand, action!"

"First off, hello, WhyItHurts. I will assume that you are watching this and relieved to see that I am alive and, um, well... ish. I've lost my phone, clearly the worst possible thing that's happened to me this week." Paisley paused as if the beat would punctuate the joke. "Okay, so, update," now she was talking to WhyItHurts and the future audience. She could feel the fog in her mind lifting. "Let me tell you what I remember, then we can try and solve this fucking case."

83

Memories of the attack poured in like molten steel, hardening as they hit Paisley's mind leaving the nightmarish shapes in the form.

She had blacked out, and when she came to, someone dragged her the way one would yard waste that you planned to toss into a fire. The memory connected to that of Hollis snapping her leg and tossing her around like a rag doll, but the person who pulled her by her hair felt much, much stronger than Hollis.

Paisley tried to open her eyes, but her face felt numb and unresponsive. She wanted to fight but knew that there was nothing she could do. She didn't have the strength to pull away, even if it meant leaving her hair in their grip. So she played dead, hoping that the damage done was enough.

The Hummer door opened, and her captor lifted and threw her into the driver seat. The jolt was surprising and painful, but Paisley managed not to react. A large arm slid across her and started the ignition. The gear shifter had clicked just once, indicating that it was in reverse. There was movement, but it wasn't rolling. The slight incline stopped the vehicle from rolling directly off the cliff, but that was clearly the idea.

There was a deep grunt of disapproval, and the driver side door slammed shut.

The pain was incredible, and the vision coming through the single opened eye was blurred and distorted. A figure stood directly in front of the Hummer's headlights. He was massive. Not thick the way that Patch was. This man was a giant. It was Winslow Peck. He leaned down and pressed the car backward up the incline. It took force, even with the car in reverse, and he leaned into it.

She had to act. She could hit the brake, but that would only cause him to come around and pull her out, a temporary fix that would end in more pain, if not death. She could try and put the car in drive and hit the accelerator, running him over in the process, but he would likely step out of the way, and she couldn't see well enough to successfully navigate the Hummer out through the labyrinth that was the salvage yard.

His head was down as he struggled to move the vehicle. The sound of the engine beside his head was her only saving grace. Maybe he wouldn't hear her. She had to try.

Paisley dragged herself across the center console and pulled the passenger side door handle. It clicked open, but the sound did not seem to register with Winslow as he continued to push the vehicle back.

The ground felt impossibly hard as she landed on her side, fighting not to cry out in pain and give away her position. Instead, she pulled herself up and slipped silently through the broken window of the car next to her, squirming her way down onto the floor boards, displacing Virginia, the cat hiding there from the sound, and likely the man responsible for it.

Winslow roared louder than the Hummer's engine as he pushed. The headlights streaked across the interior of her hiding place, and if Winslow had been looking at that moment, he would have seen Paisley trying to make herself as small as she could, but he wasn't, and the Hummer's engine revved as the earth beneath the back tires gave way to the drop, and it went over, falling into the night. The crunching sound it made when it landed hurt Paisley's head. The sound of the engine was distant and soon replaced with a crackling sound of fire.

She could hear the man breathing outside of the car, and though she couldn't see him, she knew he would see her if she moved. She hoped the cats wouldn't give away her position, but they were as scared as she was. Basil curled up on the seat and rested her head just a few inches from Paisley's, and the world began to flicker out like a candle burning its last reserve of wick.

She could only hold her head up for a moment before it lolled back on its own. There was something there. Another small face peered out from underneath the seat. Its small, unblinking eyes just watched as she drifted off. Then she was gone, first to unconsciousness, then to death. She fought against the light, her spirit not wanting to call it quits until she heard Hyacinth's voice outside the car. Until then, she could not rest. But hearing her best friend's voice gave her the peace she needed to let go. Luckily for her, she was the only one ready to give up.

84

"Patch ripped the door off the car and pulled you out," Hyacinth said. She held the phone, still recording Paisley recounting the story.

"It was Winslow," Paisley said. "It was Winslow Peck. He tried to kill me. He killed the girls."

Hyacinth stopped recording.

"You know what this means, right?" she asked. "If it was him, then the sheriff has a very good reason to silence you."

Before she could continue, Paisley's dad came in.

"We've got a problem," he said.

"Dad, what's going on?"

"The sheriff is out there, and she's talking to the doctor now, but since you're awake, they don't want you talking to anyone, and they want to take you into custody."

Paisley flung the bed sheet and blanket off of herself and swung her legs over the side of the bed.

"Let's get out of here," she said.

"No, sweetheart, you can't," her dad said, trying to guide her legs back up.

"If they arrest me, then the case is over." Paisley pulled the wires from herself and tried to stand. Her dad put his hand on her shoulder gently, and she stopped.

"We will figure it all out," he said. "They can't pin anything on you since you didn't do anything. We just need to make sure you get your story straight before they come in here."

"It was her sister's husband that did this," Hyacinth said, nodding toward the door that the sheriff could come through at any moment.

"What? Are you serious?" he said, holding Paisley up and

helping her steady herself. "Should we call the feds?"

"Dad, I love you, but I have to get out of here. If it was me, if you were a father whose daughter was missing, and there was someone who could help, you'd want that person to do anything they could, to risk anything they needed to risk, to get to me, wouldn't you?"

Her dad stepped back and put a hand to his mouth.

"You know how close I've come to losing you already? I can't..." his voice caught.

"I know, Dad, but I have to do this. If I stay here they'll make sure that I never get to expose them. Who knows who else may be hurt?"

"Why can't someone else do it? Why can't law enforcement? Why can't she?" he waved a hand at Hyacinth.

"Because, Mr. Mott, none of us can do what Paisley can do. None of us can see what she sees," Hyacinth said.

He looked at Paisley and she nodded, then he sighed and shook his head.

"I'll slow them down. Go out and to the right. They were at the nurses station and they may still be there. If so, you should be able to get out unnoticed. There is a staircase at the end of the hall. I'll slow them down." He reached into his pocket and took out a rental car key. "Take my car. It's a silver sedan, an Altima, I think."

"I've got us covered," Hyacinth said, holding up a fob. "Let's go."

"Take these." Her dad took off his jacket, gave it to her, then unbuckled his pants.

"What are you doing?" she asked, putting the jacket on over the hospital gown.

"You won't make it off this floor dressed like that, let alone out of the building," he answered.

"Where are my clothes?" Paisley asked.

"They said they are evidence and took them," Hyacinth said. "I've got extra clothes in the car. We just need to make it that far."

Paisley's dad slid off his pants, leaving him in his t-shirt and boxer briefs.

"Take them," he said, kicking his tennis shoes toward her. "They're going to arrest me anyway, so I'm sure I'll be in an orange jumpsuit soon enough."

"What? Why?" Paisley asked while slipping on the pants that were too wide and too long, cinching her dad's belt past all of the holes and doubling it up on itself before tying it.

"Because I am going to hold that door closed so they can't get in here. I'm going to buy you as much time as I can. They won't know you're gone until they get through that door. I'm sure they won't be too thrilled with that. I'll get *interfering with an investigation* or *resisting arrest* for sure."

"I can't let you do that," Paisley said.

"Pais, we've got to go," Hyacinth pleaded. She had opened the door and looked out. "They are still over there. Come on."

"Go," her dad said.

Paisley kissed his cheek, and he hugged her.

"I love you," she said.

"I love you. Be careful," he said to her, then to Hyacinth, "You, look after her."

"Yes, sir," Hyacinth said. "Wait." She held up her hand. "Now," she whispered, and walked out the door, moving quickly with Paisley in tow.

Derry saw them and hurried toward them. Paisley made eye contact and signaled for him to slow down. He read the signal and played it cool, following them until he was around the corner, then ran to catch up.

Before they hit the stairs, she heard someone knock on a door. Then, knock again a few seconds later.

"Sheriff's Office, please open the door." It was the sheriff's voice. "Open this door right now."

85

An explosion of pain struck Paisley as they went through the emergency exit at the bottom of the stairs. The sunlight burst through her wounded eye, which she still had limited use of.

Hyacinth tugged her across the parking lot while she tried to hold up the oversized pants. She gave up on the shoes once they were outside, allowing herself to step out of them as she walked.

Hyacinth ushered Paisley into the back seat of an SUV.

"There's some gym clothes and such in that bag," she said, pointing to a duffel bag on the seat. "Use what you can. Derry, you're up front with me."

Derry followed orders and jumped in the front seat while Hyacinth went around to the driver seat.

"We are limited on time, Pais," she said, climbing in and slamming the door. "So it's time to do what you do and figure out how all this shit connects." Hyacinth drove them out of the hospital parking lot.

There hadn't been any deputies running out to stop them. Paisley grinned. Her dad must've given quite the performance. *The lengths that man would go to.*

"How can I help?" Derry asked, keeping his eyes on the road as Paisley changed clothes.

"Here, once Paisley's dressed, aim this at her and hit record," Hyacinth said, handing Derry her cell phone.

The boy took the phone and held it in his hands as if he was preparing to take a portrait.

"Hold it the other way, horizontal," Hyacinth said, and the boy complied. "Where am I going?"

"Just get us out of here. We will figure it out as we go,"

Paisley said, her voice muffled by a shirt raised over her head.

"Got it."

"Okay, ready," Paisley said from the back. She had shed her dad's pants and put on a pair of sweatpants and socks from Hyacinth's bag, and gave up on trying to squeeze into a pair of Nike running shoes that were far too tight. She had also put on a t-shirt from the bag but kept her dad's jacket on over it.

Derry hit the record button and aimed the phone at Paisley, still holding it the way Hyacinth had told him.

"Hey, friends," Paisley started. This would all be edited in, but she wanted to get it all right, and she had some knots to untangle, so she began talking. "We are currently evading the police at the moment. There are things that don't make sense in all of this. Winslow Peck had an alibi. There was no way he could have taken the girls that were kidnapped. He wasn't even in town. Plus, the autopsy doesn't match. The reports say that the girls were given some drug that killed them instantly, but the girls in the videos were butchered. The only one that matches is Lydia's, but even it is weird. Things aren't adding up."

Paisley sat back in the seat. Her mind did its trick. She saw things come together. The clarity she needed from her audience was there.

"The dates don't match," she said.

"What do you mean?" Derry asked.

"The dates. There are time stamps on the tape, and they aren't anywhere near when the girls were found."

Paisley flipped through the files in her head, the mental notes she had saved.

"That's it!" she said. "Derry, Lydia was taken on the Fourth of July, right?"

"Yeah, from the park, during the display," he responded.

"The kid, Danny, the one who interrupted the killer's disposal as the body burned, said that he ran away so he could stash his stuff before going to the cops. Then he said he went and got high and watched the fireworks because he thought it might be his last night as a free man." Paisley looked past the camera, the audience, and directly at Derry.

Derry tried to hold the camera up but couldn't. He let his arm fall onto the center console.

"What?" he mumbled.

"I met with the kid because I wanted to know what happened to the video camera on the ground in his video, but not present in the crime scene photos. He told me he hid it but also that he watched the fireworks that night." There was a heavy pause as this sank in. Then Paisley asked the question that Derry was clearly thinking himself. "Derry? You identified your sister. Are you sure it was her?"

Derry's eyes bloated and his lip quivered.

"It was. It had to be. They said it was her. She had the same shirt on. She had her bear," he whimpered.

"In the crime scene photos, Derry, she didn't." Paisley reached up and put her hand on his shoulder. "It's okay. You didn't know."

"What do you mean she didn't in the photos?" Derry ran his arm across his nose.

"I don't know how I missed it. It's right there. The video and the crime scene photos showed the body. Lydia's clothes and the bag she had been in were gone. By the time the fire went out, there wasn't much left."

"But her bear. She had him when I went and saw her."

"She didn't have him on the Fourth of July when she was taken, though," Paisley pointed out.

"Yeah, she did. I think," Derry responded but didn't look convinced.

"When you and Patch told me the story, you said she was carrying two snow cones, right? Who had the bear? Were you carrying it?"

"Maybe Patch was carrying it?"

"Was he?"

"She had it, I know she did. Because in the truck, on the way to the salvage yard, my dad gave Lydia a ribbon for Bear, and she wrapped it around his head like a bandanna."

"Wait, you were with your dad that morning?"

"Yeah, we rode with him to the salvage yard since he had to work, and since Patch was working at the yard that morning, we just went with him so we could leave from there. It saved Patch the drive back to the house." Trying to remember everything gave Derry some clarity and focus.

"How long were you at the yard before you left?" Paisley asked.

"Just a few minutes, I think. Winnie came in and was really upset. He said there had been an accident in the yard. He smelled like..." Derry froze. "No."

"What?" Paisley asked. "Derry, what?"

The boy hung his head, staring at the seat next to Paisley. He looked like he was peering into another dimension, hoping to find what he needed there since this one didn't have answers.

"He smelled like gas."

"Gas?" There was a beat while Paisley processed. "Oh."

Derry looked up at Paisley, his eyes, that had been filled with tears moments before, were now filled with rage.

"He came in smelling like gas. He told us that there was a car leaking fuel. He yelled at Patch for having kids in the office, which scared Lydia. Patch apologized and we left." Derry's eyes drifted from Paisley's for a moment, then snapped back to her. "The bear. It was on the desk. Patch had set it there and pretended it was typing when Winslow came in. We left it there." His eyes drifted again.

"What else? What else are you remembering?" Paisley knew how the kid felt. The slow viscous pour when memories return. Like a candle coming to full power in a dark room, pushing itself into the corners and exposing the hidden things within.

"When we got in Patch's car, he said that he thought Winslow was being an idiot. He said that Winslow didn't know the difference between gasoline and kerosene."

"Why would he say that?" Paisley asked. She knew why, but she wanted Derry to connect those dots.

"Because Winnie said a car was leaking gas, but he smelled like kerosene. So Patch said that Winnie must have been trying to fill a car with the wrong gas, and that's why it wasn't running."

Everyone was silent. Paisley gave Derry space as he searched his memory for anything else from that day.

"Winslow had the bear," he finally said.

"It's Winslow on those tapes killing those girls. I suspected that early on, but now I have no doubt. But if that wasn't Lydia, who was it?" Paisley asked, not expecting an answer, but she wouldn't have been disappointed if someone had one.

"Derry?" Hyacinth finally spoke up.

The boy looked over at her and wiped the tears on his cheeks.

"Yeah?"

Hyacinth nodded to the phone in his hand. It was still recording but pointed at the seat and then nodded back to Paisley.

Derry looked down at it, nodded, and pointed it at Paisley again.

Paisley looked into the lens and started talking. She knew there were answers locked in her head somewhere, and if Derry could flip the lights on and make them scurry like roaches, she could, too.

"I've watched videos from the camera, seen all the crime scene photos, and read all the autopsy reports, and they don't fit. That wasn't Lydia Knot in that bag."

Derry's breath caught. They had just discussed this, but Paisley knew saying it out loud would affect him. She knew he'd have questions she didn't have an answer to, but she was determined to find them.

"But, just because it wasn't Lydia in the bag," Paisley looked over the phone and into Derry's waiting eyes. "That doesn't mean that it wasn't Lydia Knot who was identified by her incredibly brave brother at the hospital two days later."

Derry's eyes glistened, but Paisley knew she had to keep his expectations down. There were two sets of dead girls now, the ones who had been kidnapped and killed via a paralytic drug, and the ones on the tape. None of the kidnapped girls had survived. That much was obvious as they were all accounted for. There were, however, a lot of questions about Lydia. Paisley needed to get it all out and hoped Derry would be ready. She smiled at him, breaking the flow she had given to the camera, and he smiled back.

"You okay? Need a break?" she asked.

"No, keep going. Let's catch this jerk."

Paisley looked back into the lens and could feel the information lining up to wait its turn to march out.

"It seems that Winslow Peck burned someone alive on July Fourth of this year. Then, two days later, authorities claim that the body was that of Lydia Knot, who was kidnapped hours *after* the discovery of the burned body. It was discovered by a man named Danial Humphries in an abandoned building after interrupting the killer in the act. So the first question is, did they replace the body of the child burned on the Fourth of July with the body of the recently abducted Lydia Knot? Or was the body identified by her brother, the amazing Darius Knot, not actually her? If so, what happened to Lydia? Did Peck take Lydia to use her body to cover up another crime? Was he involved with the disappearance of all of the other girls who had been injected with something lethal, and then left around the dilapidated buildings that haunt Howling Ivy, Indiana?" Paisley stopped for a moment and thought. The two sides of things were getting clearer, but how they were connected was not. "How does Winslow Peck, whose daughter was the first victim, play into the kidnapped girls' deaths? Where are the bodies of the children he butchered on video?"

Paisley paused as she noticed that Derry had taken one hand off the phone, and it was tilting slightly: it was hard to see what he was doing, but the light shining upon his face indicated that he was probably looking at a phone.

"Everything okay?" Paisley asked.

"Oh, I'm sorry. I texted Khalida to let her know we left the hospital and she just texted back," Derry replied, holding up a cell phone to show her.

"When did you get a phone?" she asked.

"It's Patch's. When he got arrested, he told me to hold onto it since he knew you'd need help. He said he'd walk to the diner if they let him go. So I called the diner and got Khalida's cell number."

"How do ya like them apples," Paisley said, giving him a wink. "What'd she say?"

"She said that Patch is still at the sheriff's office. The investigator said they'll let him go only if you clear him. They said they need to hear it from you. But they said the sheriff is on the way to ask you at the hospital now."

"Ha, well, won't they be surprised when they open that door and I'm not there? That's good, though. Maybe we can get him before the sheriff realizes what's happening. That'll put us a few steps ahead."

"I'll let Lida know we are going to get him."

"Perfect! Let's go get the big guy. We've got work to do."

Paisley smiled. She wasn't sure if the smile looked as unhinged as it felt, but everything was coming together in her mind. She had already pushed things when she felt like nothing was happening. She felt it was time to do it again. Derry saw the look on her face and froze. Her eyes went to the phone he had been recording with, and she nodded. Derry wedged Patch's cell phone under the headrest on his seat and used both hands to steady the camera pointed at Paisley. Her voice was solid, stern, and full of electricity when she spoke.

"It's time to kick this nest and see what hornets come out. We're going to the sheriff's office to get our friend and then demand answers from one of the only people who really knows what the hell is going on in this town, or any town for that matter. We're going to go see the grave digger. But first, a shoe store, 'cause your girl's got big feet!"

Hyacinth looked in the rear view mirror to catch Paisley's

gaze.

"I have no idea where that is, I've literally never been here before."

86

Khalida leaned over the diner counter and focused on her phone. The dining room was empty. The last reminders of lunch blew around under the low-hanging ceiling fans that circulated the air.

"Playing your game?" Didi Gill, an older woman who had worked at the diner for at least forty years, said. "You kids just can't get enough of them, can you?"

"No, had to put the game on hold. Just texting with a friend," Khalida replied.

"You know I never could get the hang of those messages. My grandkids use them, but I just ask them to call. It's easier for me."

"Yeah, I remember when we actually had to go over and knock on a door if we wanted to talk to someone," Khalida said.

"Oh, sugar, I'm sure you aren't nearly old enough even to remember corded phones."

Khalida chuckled and set her phone down.

"How old do you think I am?"

"Oh, I'd guess..." The woman eyed Khalida, focusing on the skin around her eyes and neck. "Couldn't be older than twenty-five or twenty-six."

Khalida tilted her head back and let out a single solid laugh.

"I am older than that, but thank you. That's very sweet."

"Well, I never was any good at guessing. These young kids look so much older. My granddaughter is thirteen, and you'd think she was twenty-one. She'd have you believe she was, at least."

The phone on the counter vibrated.

"Oh no," Khalida said, snatching it off the counter to get a closer look.

"What is it? Everything alright, dear?" Didi asked.

"It's my friend. I think he is about to walk into some trouble. Do you mind covering for me? I'm out of here in thirty minutes anyway."

"Oh, you go on and meet up with your friend." Didi added a sly wink that Khalida chose to ignore and not explain that Derry was a child.

"Thank you." She stood on the footrest of the stool, reaching over the counter, and plucked her purse from behind the register. "You mind punching me out?"

"I'll take care of it. You just go."

"Thank you."

Khalida headed for the door wondering what she could say to Derry to warn them of the mess they may be getting into, though she suspected that Paisley may know part of it and is still running head first into it. She didn't like the idea that she was dragging Derry along with her, but knowing Derry, he wouldn't allow her to leave him out.

87

A series of weak squeals brought Millicent back. She sat up, the thin beam of light from the rising sun illuminating the dust. Another squeal, this one louder.

"Squeakers?" Millicent said. She stretched the chain to its length as she crawled on her hands and knees toward the sound.

She saw it. A glue trap had been laid behind the dryer and Squeakers was stuck to it. The mouse's face and front legs were pressed into the sticky pad, the fur around its nose was gone, lost to the glue, and raw flesh pulled away as it struggled to get free. It cried out for help.

"Squeakers!" Millicent clawed at the chain around her waist. She tried to slide it down over her emaciated body but couldn't get it over her hips.

The mouse drove its back legs, the only part of its body not stuck in the trap, pushing the pad toward Millicent.

"Come on, you're almost here." She reached out as far as she could, but the trap caught on the corner of the dryer and stopped. "No!"

The mouse pushed, but the corner of the pad slid under the dryer and wedged against the foot.

"Someone help!" Millicent yelled. "Help!"

The door opened, and heavy thuds crashed down the stairs as the man descended them.

"What is it? What's wrong?" he yelled as he approached.

"Squeakers! Help him!" Millicent pointed at the mouse trap.

"Are you kidding me?" the man yelled. "You've not said a single word to me all this time, and you finally decide to open your mouth, and it's for a stupid mouse?"

The man turned and walked to where Squeakers struggled. He bent and pinched the mouse's tail between a thumb and forefinger that looked like potatoes. He brought it over to her.

"Help, please?" she cried.

The man held the mouse up to his face. He watched the pad do a small pirouette while the mouse fought and kicked. He lowered it to Millicent's face.

Her friend's eyes were black and full of pain. A wash of yellow glue caught one eye and didn't allow it to turn and look at her.

She grabbed for it but the man pulled it just out of reach.

"Please," she begged.

The man looked from the mouse to her. He lowered the trap to the floor, gently placing it on the cement before her.

She reached for it tenderly, not wanting to cause him to panic and get more stuck.

The boot came down hard, just missing Millicent's fingers and the sound of small but sharp pops of tiny bones punctuated the air like someone cracking their knuckles.

Squeakers's skull collapsed and pressed his brains out through his open mouth, catching briefly on the two elongated teeth the mouse had used to nibble playfully at Millicent's fingers. The mess from his mouth landed and stuck to the glue, but the mess from his exploded stomach spurted out, a trail of insides shooting far enough to slap against the cement past the edge of the trap. Small dots of blood hit Millicent's chin and bottom lip.

"Squeakers!" Millicent yelled, throwing herself back against the post. "No! No, no, no!"

The man lifted his foot and peeled the trap away. He examined it with amusement.

"Want to see?" he said. He bent at the waist and held the trap to Millicent's face.

She turned away.

"Look at it," he demanded.

"No," she replied.

"Look at it!"

The man couldn't have seen it coming, which was her only advantage. Millicent swung her hand up, her fingers hooked like a claw, and caught the man's forearm just below the wrist, her nails ripping at the flesh.

"Dang it!" the man yelled, stumbling away from her. He looked at the scratches and then at her, bewildered. "That was stupid."

Millicent tried to back away, but there was nowhere to go. The man approached, holding the trap up. He grabbed her hair, wrapping his fingers tightly into her curls, and pulled her head toward the waiting glue trap.

"I'll teach you to mess with me," he snarled.

"Winnie?" the woman's voice called from the bottom of the stairs. "What are you doing?"

The trap hovered an inch from Millicent's face. She could smell the glue, iron, and putrid, mushed insides. The man held her there for a moment and then let her go. She fell back against her post.

"She scratched me," he said without looking back.

"Maybe it's time," the woman said.

"Yeah," the man sighed, "I suppose you're right."

He stood upright and dropped the trap onto the floor in front of Millicent.

"We've tried long enough," the woman said.

"I'll do it tomorrow," he said. He turned and walked to the woman. He showed her his arm, and she looked back at Millicent with venom in her eyes.

"It'll be good to be done with her."

The two left her there with Squeakers. She lay on the floor, resting her head on her hands next to the overturned trap. She felt awful for her friend but was also jealous that Squeakers no longer had to be in the basement.

88

Paisley slowly took the stairs to the judicial building. The pain in her head had returned with a vengeance. Despite her new sparkling, purple Converse, she was not in any condition to race anywhere.

"You doing okay?" Hyacinth asked, taking her arm and guiding her up the remaining steps.

"I'm okay," she replied. Then, she looked at Derry who was carrying her camera and recording.

"I'm good." Derry moved up the stairs, beating Paisley to the top. He got a shot of her as she reached the door.

"You're pretty good at this," she said. "You better be careful or I'm going to put you on the payroll."

The area where the bodies had been before was now clean, back to normal, minus a single chair that looked to be new. Undoubtedly replaced because its predecessor was covered in unspeakable things. Seeing such a disturbing act so quickly wiped away was unsettling.

"Get a shot of this lobby, will you?" she asked, and Derry obliged, swinging the camera smoothly arching across the entire room at an even pace. "Nice."

A loud bell sounded as the elevator door opened into the sheriff's office. The office appeared empty outside of the single deputy standing at the check in desk.

"How can I help you?" he asked Paisley as they exited the elevator. He was a tall man with broad shoulders and the typical mustache that seemed cliché, even for a small town.

"Yes, I am looking for-" Paisley began but was cut off when the deputy snapped at Derry.

"Put that down. You can't film in here."

Derry looked at Paisley for guidance and she pushed her hand down signaling him to lower the camera, and he did so.

"You don't have to be so aggressive," Paisley said.

"Turn it off," the deputy demanded, paying no attention to Paisley.

Derry flipped the button to off and held it up for the deputy to see. He nodded.

"He's just trying to keep everyone honest," Paisley said.

"Ma'am, I swore an oath. That oath is to serve and protect the citizens and visitors of this county. If I come across stern, it is because I take that oath very seriously. I assure you that honesty and transparency are of the utmost importance to me and paramount to my ability to fulfill that oath. Now, that being said, what can I do for you?"

Paisley dramatically rolled the one eye that wasn't still covered in a bandage. She then looked to Hyacinth who nodded her approval to move forward. Paisley glanced at Derry and raised her one visible eyebrow, not without considerable effort and pain.

"Oh!" Derry said and then nodded.

Paisley smiled.

"Okay, Deputy. Thank you. Now, we are here to pick up our friend Patch." She paused, waiting for the deputy to say that he would get him, or that the investigator needed to see her first.

"I'm sorry, who?" he replied.

"Steven Simply," Derry spoke up.

"Oh, the kid with the teeth," the deputy said, looking down at his computer.

"Yeah. Yep. He, yep. He has some of those, yep yep. That's him," Paisley replied. She turned and gave Derry an apologetic grimace, which drew an awkward chuckle from the boy.

"Looks like the agent in charge of the investigation has requested confirmation from the victim of the assault that Mr. Simply is accused of to assure his lack of involvement before he can be released." The deputy studied Paisley's face for a moment. "I am going to assume that is you."

"You sure you aren't the lead investigator there, Poirot?" Paisley joked.

Derry released a surprising laugh which drew everyone's attention.

"Wait, you know who that is?" Hyacinth asked.

"I do, sorry," Derry said, lowering his head and covering his mouth to mask his giggles.

"I was just pointing out that it looks like someone did a real number on your face," the deputy said.

"Ah, well, that makes it all better, thank you," Paisley quipped.

"You can all come back, but you have to leave your personal items out here," the deputy said, retrieving a plastic tote from under the counter and placing it in front of them.

They emptied their pockets. Hyacinth put Paisley's bag in, which she had been carrying for her, and Derry carefully set the camera into the bin before the deputy pulled it back and set it on a desk behind the counter.

"Nothing else on you?" he asked.

They all patted their pockets and shrugged.

"Come on," he said, opening the door and letting them in.

The group walked through the open area, past the sheriff's office, and back to the holding cells where Paisley had been a few days prior.

"Look familiar?" Hyacinth joked as they entered the cell area.

The floors were linoleum, easy to clean in case someone had an "accident." The same table sat in the middle of the room with the same boring plastic chairs around it. Cells surrounded the room. These were not the typical barred cells, but concrete rooms with metal doors and three quarter inch thick reinforced plexiglass windows.

All the cell lights were off except the one housing Patch. The boy sat slumped on a metal bunk.

"Patch," Derry said, but the other boy couldn't hear him.

"The glass is pretty thick, kid. You'd have to yell for him to hear you," the deputy said and gave his head a flip toward the cell, signaling that it was okay for Derry to go over.

Something wasn't right. Paisley caught a few things. She had spent enough time around law enforcement over the past two months, and she knew that their radios never stopped squawking, even in a quiet place like Grey Water Ridge, or Howling Ivy. In addition to not having a live radio, the man also wasn't carrying the keys to the cells that she had grown accustomed to hearing bounce off the deputies who worked here when she was being held. She also noticed that one of the dark cells was not open all the way. She struggled to remember everything that happened when she had been there, but one thing that was clear was that the door had to stay open if the cell was unoccupied. Paisley assumed it was easier to push someone in if they were being rowdy.

The last thing she noticed was that, other than the door they came through, there wasn't any other way out of the room. And since they hadn't seen any investigator in the outer rooms, there likely wasn't one. The deputy stood in front of the door, blocking their exit. She turned to call "Stop!" to Derry, but he was already at the cell. He banged on the glass, and Patch looked up at him in surprise.

"Hey buddy!" Derry yelled.

"Derry?" Patch replied inaudibly. His face pulled back in horror. His eyes turned to the dark cell with the closed door.

Paisley knew what it would be before the door even opened.

"Derry, get back!" she yelled.

It was too late. The door opened, and the giant stomped out, ducking so he wouldn't hit his head on the top of the door jamb. He wasn't fast, but with his size, he covered so much ground so fast. He grabbed the back of Derry's shirt, yanking the boy toward him. Derry looked weightless in Winslow's arms as he threw a forearm around the teen's neck, putting him in a chokehold.

Patch lunged at the door to his cell, hitting it with the force of a meteor. The walls shook, and for a second, Paisley thought that the boy would burst through.

Winslow flinched and took a step away. Derry dangled in the crook of his arm. The boy's face turned dark red.

"Put him down," Paisley yelled. She looked to the deputy, who stood stoic.

The deputy just shook his head and shrugged.

"You know, you really had me with that whole *oath* bullshit," she said.

"Paisley," Hyacinth called, returning her attention to Derry, who appeared to have lost consciousness.

"Put him down you sick fuck." Paisley stepped forward and raised her fist.

"Now you just wait right there," Winslow said, taking a serrated hunting knife with a foot-long blade from a sheath on the back of his belt. He pressed the tip against Derry's side.

"Stop!" Paisley shouted.

The command was lost among the hammering thuds from Patch slamming against the door.

"Shut up," Winslow yelled at Patch, holding the knife where he could see it.

Patch stopped.

"What do you want?" Paisley asked.

"Is it money? I can give you money," Hyacinth offered.

"I don't want money."

"What do you want?" Paisley asked. "You clearly set all this up so we'd walk into it. So *I* would walk into it."

"I didn't want any of this. Don't you understand that? I never wanted to hurt anyone."

"You're hurting *him* right now." Paisley pointed at Derry. "Look at him."

Winslow looked at the boy and adjusted his arm. Derry's limp body dipped forward with the weight shifting from his neck to his chest.

"Is he breathing?" Paisley asked.

Winslow lifted him up to his ear, not taking his eyes off of

Paisley.

"Yeah."

"Please, just put him down so we can talk?"

"There's nothing to talk about. You've ruined everything, and now I have no choice but to do this." Winslow raised Derry as evidence of how far things had come.

"You killed those girls. That isn't my fault. It isn't his fault. You have to see that." Paisley took a half step forward.

"No!" Winslow roared.

Paisley jumped back, in fear and from the pain that bolted through her skull like a kill hammer through a sheep's head.

"Just one. That was it. I only hurt one. You don't do that. You don't tell me I hurt more than one."

"I saw the videos. I know about all of them. How many were there?"

"You don't know what you're talking about!" Winslow tightened his arm around Derry's neck just as the color returned to his face.

"Whoa, come on, I'm just telling you what I saw," Paisley said, holding her hands up and inching toward the man again.

A bell ripped through the office causing everyone to tense up.

"Not a word," Winslow said, holding the knife against Derry's stomach.

Patch jerked forward in his cell. The boy's soft face was almost as red as Derry's, and tears threatened to fall at any second.

"Everyone just stay here and be quiet," the deputy said.

"Or what?" Hyacinth challenged.

The deputy stopped and stared at her.

"Or I'll come back here and shoot every fucking one of you in the fucking face."

The deputy went back out to the front office.

"I hate to be this person, Winslow," Paisley said just loud enough not to be heard outside the room. "But there are three of us. You might be big and strong, but I suspect we could

413

surprise you."

"I didn't seem to have a problem with you before," Winslow growled.

"You had to sneak up on me before," Paisley countered.

"So maybe I gut this one, then I just have to deal with two of you." Winslow looked back and forth between the two women. "I won't even need the knife. I'll rip you apart with my bare hands."

Patch slammed against the door again.

"I will fucking kill you, you murdering piece of shit!" he yelled. His muffled voice broke as he screamed.

"You shut up, Steven. I know you didn't want to be involved in this, but here you are. I always told you that you shouldn't be hanging out with this loser. I told you he'd get you in trouble. He's just like his worthless dad."

The walls rattled and a chunk of cinder block cracked and fell loose as Patch threw himself into the door.

"Do that one more time, you fat turd, and I'll cut his head clean off, cut you open, and stuff it inside," Winslow promised. "Now, everyone, shut up."

The handle turned and the door opened.

89

The bell on the elevator rang and Khalida stepped off into the empty sheriff's office. She saw no one.

"Hello?"

She stepped up to the counter, looking for a bell to ring for service, but there wasn't one. She saw a tote with a camera and a very familiar bag with a number of silly pins adorning it.

"I'm sorry, the office is closed," a deputy said, walking from the back. Khalida had recognized the tall man with the mustache from the dinner. He never tipped. He just said *you're welcome,* and tapped his badge when he got up to leave.

"Oh, hey, you. Deputy Morehouse, right?"

"That is correct. I'm sorry, the office is closed, and I am in the middle of something. So I'm going to have to ask you to leave."

"What if it's an emergency?"

The deputy looked around.

"There doesn't appear to be any imminent threat. So if you could please leave and call 9-1-1, dispatch will help you," Deputy Morehouse said, pointing at the elevator.

"But..."

The phone on the desk rang. It rang a few times and stopped. Then, it started again almost immediately.

"What the hell?" the deputy said.

The phone rang a few more times, then stopped. Again, it rang immediately after.

"You going to get that?" Khalida asked.

"They need to leave a message or call 9-1-1. The office is closed."

The phone continued to ring.

"Fuck." He picked up the receiver. "Morehouse."

He listened for a moment, his stern face softened.

"Everything okay, deputy?" Khalida asked with genuine concern.

The deputy held the phone away from his head and looked at it in astonishment.

"It's for you."

"What?"

"It's for you."

"Who is it?"

"He didn't say," he snarled.

He handed the phone to Khalida. She pulled the cord so it would reach and then put the receiver to her ear.

"Hello?"

"Khalida Walker?" The voice on the other end of the phone sounded robotic, like the artificial ones she'd heard in social media videos.

"Yes?"

"I need you to listen to me and listen carefully. The deputy across from you is involved in a plot that has four people held hostage in the back of this very office. He is armed and dangerous. Winslow Peck, who I believe you know, is in the back with a knife to a boy's throat right now."

"What is he saying?" Morehouse asked.

Khalida just held a finger up to silence him.

"I told him that I had access to his security cameras, and if he didn't hand the phone over to you I was going to stream them live," the voice continued. "You're in danger. I told him that he was to let you walk out of there. Take the stairs. I've called every law enforcement office in the surrounding counties, and they are sending help, but it is too far out. There is nothing you can do for them right now. The best I can ask is that when you get to the lobby, you pull the fire alarm. Maybe it will cause enough confusion to buy them some time."

"Right," Khalida said. "Well, thank you for that. I appreciate it."

"Be very careful, please. That's my friend in there."

"Yeah. I've got a few of those in there, too," Khalida said, acknowledging the deputy who appeared fidgety and anxious.

"Remember, take the stairs so they can't trap you, pull the fire alarm in the lobby, and then get out of there," the voice said.

"Got it." Khalida looked at the phone and then held it out to the deputy.

"What did he say?" Morehouse asked, reaching forward to take the phone.

Khalida's free hand shot out, grabbing the sleeve of the shirt of Morehouse's outstretched arm. He tried to pull back, but she swung the receiver at him, letting the slack out enough that it wrapped itself around his neck, banging off of his head as it reached its limit. She put her foot on the counter and leaned back, pulling the deputy over and bringing the base of the phone with him. Her shoulder dipped, causing the man to deflect and go face-first into the ground.

She unplugged the phone cord from the base, suspended just over the edge of the counter, releasing the tension on his neck. A gurgle of blood and teeth spilled out onto the carpeted floor as she pushed him with her foot, allowing him to get air.

"I'm just going to borrow this if you don't mind," she said, unsnapping his holster and removing the Glock 22 from his hip. She pulled the slide back just enough to see that there was not a round chambered. She racked the slide and smiled when the brass of the .40 caliber round glimmered as it seated.

Khalida put her free hand on the counter and jumped up onto it. Then, she swung her legs over and hopped down, heading for the back room with the pistol presented in front of her as she had done many times before.

90

The door opened, but there was no one there.

"Morehouse?" Winslow called into the void.

Paisley leaned around the door jamb and was shocked to see Khalida standing there. She had a gun in her hand.

"Hey there," she said.

"Khalida?" Paisley asked. She shook her head, which was admittedly foggy, but this seemed like too weird a hallucination even with a concussion.

"What did you say?" Winslow yelled. "Morehouse?"

"Mind if I come in?" Khalida said, stepping in past Paisley, who was still trying to make sense of what was happening.

"What are you doing here?" Winslow turned when he saw the gun, putting Derry's body between him and the woman who had just come in.

"You really think you're going to hide your big ass behind that little boy?" Khalida asked, leveling the gun at Winslow. Her hand was still, and she held the weapon with confidence.

"I'm sorry, what the hell is going on here?" Hyacinth said, taking the words out of Paisley's mouth.

"Put the gun down, Lida, or I'm going to take this boy's head clean off."

"You aren't going to hurt him, Winslow. You're not a bad man," Khalida said.

"Oh, you have no idea," Paisley added. "What are you doing here?"

"Well, when Derry said you were headed here, I figured I better come down to make sure everything stayed on the up and up. Since the guy that did *that* to you happened to be related to the woman you'd be seeing when you came in here. I wasn't sure if you knew that. I wanted to come check."

"And how did you get back here," Paisley asked. "With a gun?"

"Well, apparently someone is watching it all go down. An eye in the sky," Khalida said, pointing at the camera on the ceiling.

"What?" Paisley said. That didn't make sense. Who could access the sheriff's office cameras that would be on their side?

"Pais?" Hyacinth said.

"Huh?"

Hyacinth tapped the pin she wore. It was a Miniature Pinscher dog wearing a top hat and monocle; inside the monocle was the dark eye of a small camera peering out.

"Must be close enough to the transponder in your bag that it's still sending a signal," Hyacinth said.

Paisley looked down at the pin.

"There's one live on the bag, too," she said. "WhyItHurts."

"Listen, I don't know what that means," Khalida interrupted, "but do you mind if we deal with this situation real quick?"

Small droplets of blood poked out of Derry's neck and swam along the edge of Winslow's knife.

"You might hit me, but I promise you that this boy doesn't live through it." He lifted Derry so that his head lolled back onto Winslow's shoulder, exposing his neck. He had the boy around the chest and used his body to obscure any shot Khalida might have of hitting him in the head.

The room shook and pieces of cinder block jumped from the wall like popcorn from a kettle.

Winslow angled toward Patch's cell.

"You hit that door one more time, and I swear to god I will kill this kid."

Patch backed away from the door and paced. He looked like a bull waiting for the gate to rise so he could charge.

"Everyone just calm down," Paisley said. Even though Khalida showed up and shifted things in their favor, the situation grew more unsettling by the minute.

"Why don't you drop the knife, set Derry down, and go ahead

and hop into one of those cells, shutting the door behind you," Khalida said, pointing the gun at the sliver of Winslow's head that she could see behind Derry. "Law from all over is on their way here right now, and the only way out is in a body bag or cuffs."

"You don't know what you're talking about. I trusted you. We had you over to our house. You ate our food," Winslow said.

"Yeah, and you said there were *coons* in your basement, remember? You think I didn't catch that subtle racism, asshole?" Khalida said. "Was it her? Was she down there? Is she the one that scratched you?"

Somewhere a phone rang. Everyone fell silent. It rang again.

"You hear that?" Hyacinth asked.

The phone rang again, but there was another sound. Khalida must have heard it, too, as she started to move.

Wood splintered as pellets from a shotgun tore away part of the door where Khalida had been standing a split second earlier. She dropped and rolled away as soon as the metallic click of the shotgun being pumped sounded over the shrill ringing. She popped up at an angle so that Morehouse, who stood in the hall with a shotgun, could not see her.

"Come around that corner, and I'll blow what's left of that mustache off of your face," she called, leveling the gun at the new threat.

"Put the gun down and kick it over to me," Winslow said. "If you don't, I cut this kid. You have to ask yourself if you're quick enough to get me before I get you. And whatever happens, Morehouse there comes in and takes care of anything I don't get to."

Khalida turned and aimed the gun at Winslow.

"Come," he yelled.

Morehouse stepped through the door and pointed the shotgun at Khalida. His upper teeth had acted like a buzzsaw when he hit the ground, taking off his lip and leaving it hanging like a bloody caterpillar on the side of his face. The hole that was left was full of broken bits of teeth and gore.

Paisley looked at him as he came in the door and recoiled.

"Looks like someone did a number on your face," she said.

Morehouse pointed the shotgun at her, and she backed up against the wall.

"Hey, keep it on her," Winslow said, taking the knife away from Derry's neck and pointing it at Khalida.

With the knife away from his neck, Derry twitched. Paisley was relieved to have some proof of life in the boy. Khalida's head tilted, indicating she saw it, too. Hopefully, she was the only one.

"I have a question," Paisley said.

"Tell her to put the gun down and then you can ask it," Winslow said.

"He puts down the scattergun first," Khalida said, nodding to Morehouse.

"No," Winslow said. "Just ask your question, but make it a good one because it will likely be your last, woman." He still pointed the knife at Khalida.

"Okay," Paisley yelled. "What has two thumbs..."

Paisley saw Patch's head jerk with recognition. Khalida looked over her shoulder, made eye contact with Paisley, and gave a slight nod. But Derry's right hand was the most important movement. He lifted his thumb ever so slightly.

"And gives you diarrhea?" Paisley shouted.

"What?" Winslow blurted.

A roar came from the cell as Patch launched himself at the door with all his might.

"A Derry attack, you motherfucker!" he yelled.

Bits of metal and cinder block exploded as the door flung open. Winslow started to turn, but Derry took the opportunity and spun his body to face the man's chest. He pushed off with his hands and feet to create enough separation that Derry dropped free when Patch hit the giant.

As soon as Patch hit the door, Khalida dropped back, swung the gun, and fired two quick shots. One struck Morehouse in the chest, spinning his bulletproof vest and tossing him back through the door. The other lodged in the busted door frame, just missing his head as he fell.

Khalida rolled onto her side, trying to get a good shot at Winslow, but the momentum from Patch hitting him had sent both the big men hurtling toward where she knelt.

Patch's foot caught Khalida's leg and the pair tumbled, coming down hard on top of her. The gun spilled out and slid across the floor.

Winslow was on top of Patch and had his hands around the boy's throat, squeezing. Patch tried to punch around the man's arms, but they were too big to get any force, so he clawed instead. With the better angle, Winslow pummeled Patch's face. Seams burst along Patch's cheek and nose, splitting his face like a busted grape.

"Stop!" Paisley yelled and charged the monster, but Hyacinth intercepted her and grabbed her arm.

"Paisley, no. He'll kill you," she said.

Derry ran across the room. Something flashed in his hand, and he swung it downward, catching Winslow on the shoulder. The big man yelled and rolled away, ripping the knife from Derry's hands and sending it skittering across the floor.

As soon as Winslow had moved, Patch rolled to his side revealing Khalida. She held her ribs as she failed to take in any air. Paisley and Hyacinth ran to her. Air pushed from her mouth with a wheeze on every attempted breath.

"I think she has a punctured lung," Hyacinth said.

"We can't move her," Paisley said, trying to put herself between the injured woman and the fighting men.

"Get off me," Derry yelled.

Paisley looked up and saw Winslow on his knees over Derry, choking the boy with one hand as he tucked the other up against the side of his body. Proof that Derry's attack with the knife did some damage, at least.

"Hyacinth!" Paisley yelled, pointing at the gun.

Hyacinth darted to grab it, but Winslow's arm shot out and tripped her. Even injured, the man was deceptively fast. He grabbed Hyacinth's ankle and dragged her over, pulling her across the top of Derry.

Paisley turned to find the shotgun. It was in the hands of Morehouse, who was again standing in the doorway.

"Don't," Paisley said. "Please."

Winslow stopped his pummeling of Hyacinth and Derry. Blood ran down his face. Gashes opened from being hit by Patch and Hyacinth, who had got a few good hits in herself, while trying to cover her face and vital organs from the onslaught of the titan. He looked more frustrated than angry as he spit blood or a tooth onto the floor.

"Everyone just stop for a second," Winslow said, standing up. He wavered at first, then steadied himself. He looked around for his knife and spotted it near the overturned table. "Anyone moves, Morehouse, you cut them in half. You hear me?"

Morehouse grunted his agreement.

Winslow grabbed the knife and went to Patch, who lay beaten and bloody. He rolled the boy onto his back and slapped him in the face with the flat side of the knife.

"Wake up! I want you to see me open you like a coin purse," he said, running the knife down the boy's chest without any pressure.

The bell above the lobby signaled someone else's arrival.

"Who the hell is..." Winslow began, but a knee to the side of his head stopped him. It was Khalida.

She was moving impossibly fast for someone with what appeared to be some serious injuries. Morehouse tried to get a bead on her, but after she struck, she landed, rolled, and jumped up to attack him again. She speared him, shoving her shoulder into his chest and driving him off of Patch. Her speed, however, was no match for Winslow's strength. When they came to a stop, Winslow had her by the throat. He squeezed, and the tendons in her neck bulged around his fingers. He looked over his shoulder at an empty cell and stepped back into the doorway.

"I'm getting sick of you," he said, preparing to toss her into the cell.

"Hello?" A woman's voice came from the lobby.

"We're back here, help us!" Hyacinth shouted.

"I'll get one of you, at least," Winslow said, pressing the hunting knife into Khalida's stomach and then letting go of her neck. Her body weight hung on the knife before skin, bone, and organs gave way and she dropped a few inches. She went slack, and Winslow tipped the blade allowing her to slide off onto the floor. Paisley was grateful not to be able to see her. Winslow stepped out and tugged the door, leaving it when it caught on Khalida's motionless feet.

Morehouse let the shotgun swing down to his side, pointing at the ground. He raised his other hand as if to ward someone off.

"Step back," a woman ordered from the hallway.

"What did she say, asshole? Step back," a man added.

They were familiar but impossible to place given the circumstances. Morehouse backed into the room.

"Who's out there?" Winslow called, wiping his knife on his shirt sleeve and making one final attempt to close the cell door.

91

The gun came through the door first, followed by the woman holding it. It was Agent Haley Quinlan, followed by Agent Teddy Prince. Even though they were not entirely who they said they were, and trusting them at any other point would be impossible, at that moment, anything that would stop Winslow Peck from winning was welcome.

"Everyone, just stay exactly where they are." Agent Quinlan said.

"Thank god," Paisley said, stepping toward her savior.

The woman swung the gun and pointed at her.

"Another step and I'll put you down."

"You, drop it," Agent Prince demanded of Morehouse, who complied, letting the shotgun clatter to the floor.

The room was hot, and the air was thick with the metallic smell of blood.

"Sweep," Quinlan said, and Prince proceeded around the room, calling out each person's condition.

Morehouse did his best to intimidate despite his lip hanging off of his face.

"Adult male, officer, facial injuries. Potential threat," he called out. "Request to eliminate?"

"I'mmm nahh a rheep," Morehouse attempted.

"I think he said he's not a threat. Request to eliminate anyway?" Prince called.

"Hold. Continue," Quinlan ordered. "But if he moves a muscle, you blow his other lip off."

"Roger," Prince called out and continued. "Teen, male, conscious, condition stable."

Paisley felt a sigh of relief at Prince's assessment of Derry.

She had seen the boy attack Winslow, so she knew he was alive, but he was flung off, and it could have been a dying push. He sat up and tried to stand, but Prince touched his shoulder and he slumped back to the floor.

"Teen, male, multiple facial lacerations," Prince said, checking Patch's pulse. "Looks like he's awake."

"Can you get him up?" Quinlan asked.

"Come on big fella." Prince pulled on Patch's hand. "Give me a hand here kid," he said to Derry.

Derry stood, and the two of them managed to get Patch to his feet.

"Come on over here with your friends, both of you," Quinlan said, signaling for Derry and Patch to join Paisley and Hyacinth.

Winslow shifted in the periphery.

"You, on the other hand, move again, and that'll be it for you," Quinlan said, pointing the gun at Winslow.

"Shit," Prince said. "Shit!"

"What?" Quinlan asked.

"We have to get out of here right now!" he called.

Prince stood near the cell behind Winslow.

"What is it?" Quinlan shouted.

Prince looked up at her with genuine fear in his eyes.

"It's Khalida," he choked.

"Is she breathing?"

Prince pushed the unlatched door open and knelt, disappearing behind the half wall.

"Just barely, but she won't be for long. Her insides are all over the floor."

"Fuck!" Quinlan shouted.

"Khalida," Paisley cried. Against her better judgment, she stepped over to where she had a sight line through the door, and to her surprise, the woman from the diner turned her head. Their eyes met and she said one word.

"Run." Then her breath stopped and her eyes locked in place.

"Shit!" Prince yelled.

Quinlan turned and ran out the door, back into the office,

not waiting for Prince.

The group heard the fed impostor crashing through the door to the stairs in the lobby.

Everything Paisley ever knew, everything she thought made sense, was about to change.

The bell above the elevator rang, announcing the arrival of something new.

92

Everyone stood still awaiting whatever was to come next.

"Hello?" a man called from the hall. It was a soft voice, curious but not cautious, as most would be in that situation. "Hello?"

Agent Prince raised his gun and pointed at the door, sidestepping to see out, then leaning back.

"Who is it?" Winslow whispered to him.

"Khalida said to run," Paisley whispered. "Wait for my word, and then we run, got it? Run to the stairs, not the elevator. Got it?"

Hyacinth nodded.

"What about Patch?" Derry asked, signaling to the condition of his friend.

"I'm okay. I'll be alright. She says we go, I'm ready."

Paisley nodded and rubbed Patch's arm.

"Hello?" the voice sounded like it was just outside the door.

"Stop," Prince said.

Footsteps stopped at the door jamb. The tips of comfortable white sneakers poked through the door.

"Who is this, my grandpa?" Paisley tried to whisper, but she must have been louder than intended because the man leaned forward, past the door frame.

"Hello there," he said in that same unnervingly calm voice.

The man appeared to be in his forties, cleanly shaved, with nicely combed hair. His appearance was square and unassuming, but one could imagine that he would be rather dashing with a five o'clock shadow, and a little hair gel. He seemed completely out of place there, like Ned Flanders at a BDSM party.

"Hello," Paisley returned.

"Don't talk to them," Prince shouted.

The man straightened up and entered the room. Just as one would suspect from such a man, he wore khakis and a button-up, short-sleeved shirt.

"With whom should I speak to then?" the man asked. "You?"

"She's gone," Prince said. "She ran off because she knew you were coming."

The man approached, ignoring the gun being pointed at him. "Who did? Who ran?"

"Vivian. She's gone. So just get the fuck out of here," Prince said, lifting the gun just a little higher to prove that he was not afraid to shoot.

The man stopped and took a deep breath.

"She fell here, yes?"

Prince did not respond.

"Where is she?" the man asked.

"I told you, she's gone," Prince pressed.

"No. Not her."

Prince said nothing.

The man scanned the group of injured people.

"And who did this?" He waved his hand at them.

"He did," Prince said, signaling toward Winslow with his head.

"And Khalida?"

"I think that was him too, yeah?" he asked, glancing at Paisley.

She nodded.

"I see. And Khalida is gone now, too? Run away with the other?" He asked of Paisley.

She nodded again. She didn't understand what was happening, but whatever it was, she wanted it over.

"I see. I suppo..."

A bullet popped a hole the size of a dime in the man's face, and his head snapped back. He looked annoyed as another hole joined it. The sound of the gun firing repeatedly was deafening in the small, cement room. Prince fired until his gun was dry. The man stumbled and fell into the hall, landing on his back.

"Now," Paisley said, standing to run, but was pushed out of the way by Winslow as he charged through the door.

The quartet was close behind. They stepped over the body lying on the floor. The center of his face had caved in, and blood and brain covered the carpet below.

"Jesus," Derry said as Paisley pulled him along.

to tell which. His head went farther back, past where logic or physics said it should stop. A low pop sounded like a cough from a closet in an empty house. The man's head fell straight back and bounced between his shoulder blades, coming to a rest like a bag of oranges hung on a shopping cart.

"What the fuuuuck," Patch said, trying to back away but there was nowhere to retreat. A noise escaped the shadows where the group hid.

The man's misshapen body jerked in their direction and the dark spots on the man's chest were finally recognizable. As it walked closer all six of the black circles protruded from the skin, rotated, and pointed at pallets that shielded the group. In the center of his chest, the two largest black circles, the size of drink coasters, peered out. Two smaller orbs sat above each of them. Paisley put her hand over her mouth and pulled hard as the eyes scanned the dumpster.

With the thing distracted, Morehouse took the opportunity to run down the alley. The eyes rotated in their bloody sockets and found the fleeing man. Its body turned in pursuit.

The way it ran was not natural. It ran with its legs straight, moving slower than it should. Then, the legs began to crack like wood planks under a boulder. Slivers of black ripped through the openings and forced their way out, shredding the skin and leaving the flesh in tatters, replacing its legs with bundles of black sticks. The sticks then separated, propelling the thing into the air as they unfolded.

"Holy shit!" Hyacinth screamed. The plan to hideout and await law enforcement evaporated. They had to escape while whatever the thing was was busy.

Paisley tried to run, but Derry froze, gawking at the creature. Its eight legs clacked madly at the ground as the towering thing skittered after Morehouse, catching him quickly and hitting him with one long, black, spined leg. Morehouse fell forward onto the pavement, and the thing came down on him, jamming two legs into his torso, puncturing the bulletproof vest he still wore, and ripping through his chest. Blood spurted up, dousing the black legs in crimson that began to drip from the spines of the legs immediately. Wet smacks beat against the asphalt as the legs hit the ground beneath Morehouse. His body turned as the legs moved, and in a show of horror and strength, the thing reared back, lifting Morehouse into the air and tearing his body in two. It left his head, shoulder, part of his ribs, and a leg on one side, and the rest on the other. Everything that had been inside the man, that made the man, fell to the ground, landing like a cloth sack full of congealed sponges. The thing turned and directed its hellish eyes at Prince, who was the only thing standing between it and them.

Prince lunged forward, grabbing Derry by the arm. Patch tried to grab his friend, but it was too late. Derry reeled forward and crashed to his hands and knees in the middle of the alley.

"What the fuck, dude?" Patch yelled, but Prince was gone, running in the other direction out of the alley.

The thing pitched forward, looming over Derry. The boy's reflection shone in the things black eyes. Paisley felt like she was screaming, but she couldn't tell, as the world seemed full of shrieks from the writhing creature.

The skin below its eyes stretched and ripped like a tent in a hurricane, revealing the ribcage below. Fractures raced across the bone like a fault line before they snapped and popped outward. The bones from the rib cage splintered as a vertical mouth chomped at the air just in front of Derry's face.

The boy scrambled backward, trying to distance himself from the disfigured demon. The being launched itself forward with its back legs and grabbed Derry with the man's hands, which, along with his arms, were the only thing that still looked human, though they now hung off a giant carapace. It stood, lifting Derry into the air. The arms, acting as makeshift mandibles, brought him toward the monster's waiting maw.

"Hey, asshole," Paisley yelled at the thing.

It stopped, and the slimy eyeballs zeroed in on her. It had been so focused on Derry that it didn't hear the silent patrol car turn into the alley. The sun beating on the window made it impossible to make out the figure behind the wheel, but Paisley thought that maybe Prince had a change of heart. All four wheels of the car chirped as the car lunged forward, picking up incredible speed over a very short distance. The thing hadn't heard the quiet electric motors until it was too late.

Paisley took a calculated risk and threw herself forward, grabbing Derry around the waist, ripping him from the monster's grasp, and clearing the path of the car just as it crashed through the legs of the beast.

The thing cried out while it cartwheeled over the roof of the car and came down hard behind it. The car beeped once in reverse and slammed into the thing again. This time, the rear bumper ran up onto the thing's head, lifting the back wheels off the ground, but the front wheels turned, pushing the thing across asphalt, leaving skin and gore in its wake.

The car stopped. The driver got out, swinging the shotgun that Morehouse had once carried, and jerked a shell into the chamber.

"Khalida?" Paisley said, looking up at the woman who, other than a torn and bloody shirt, looked okay.

"Get in," she said. She shouldered the shotgun and unleashed a shot into the thing behind the back tire. She racked another and fired.

As many questions as Paisley had, they would have to wait as she hauled Derry to his feet and shoved him in the backseat of the car, and climbed in with him. Patch sat in the passenger seat, and Hyacinth jumped into the back on the other side of Derry.

"What the fuck?" Hyacinth exclaimed.

"She doesn't have a scratch on her," Derry said in disbelief.

Khalida got back into the car and hit the accelerator. The vehicle dropped as it came off the thing's head and darted forward.

"So, everyone okay?" she asked.

94

"I don't want to be rude here, but what the fuck?" Paisley said, leaning forward against the cage in the backseat of the electric squad car.

"I understand that this is all a bit weird," Khalida said.

"Weird? No, the fact that Maine is the only state whose name has only one syllable is weird. This is fucking insane," Paisley said.

"Is that true?" Patch asked.

"Listen, there will be time to explain everything later, but right now, you've got to break this down for me," Khalida said. "You said that you don't think it's Lydia Knot in her grave, right?"

"It's someone else buried there, or they killed Lydia to cover up someone else's murder," Paisley replied.

"And you think Winslow is the only person that knows the truth?"

"Him and his wife, and probably her sister, the sheriff. And, possibly Stilton Hawke."

"Why would he know?" Derry asked.

"Because he would have picked up the bodies, and he would have buried them. So if there was anything wrong with the timeline or the condition of the bodies, he should know," Paisley answered.

"Well, let's just see what he has to say," Khalida said, turning the car toward the cemetery.

"Okay, now that we have a plan," Hyacinth started, "you were like dead, right?"

"There's a lot to cover, and I promise I will do my best to explain all of this later, but for the sake of time, there are just a few things you need to know," Khalida said. "One, yes, I died, twice in there, actually. And yes, it hurt a lot. Exactly as much as you think it did. It wasn't the worst I've had, but not something I would like to repeat."

Khalida paused to give everyone time to process this information.

"What about Ohio? It's short. O, hi, o," Patch said, counting the syllables on his fingers.

"I'm what's called an Echo," Khalida continued.

"Wait, are there others like you?" Paisley asked.

"Yes, Vivian, the agent in the flashy shoes? She's an Echo as well."

"I hate to move on from the undead situation that seems to be happening right now, but what was with the giant spider man?" Derry asked.

"Man-spider," Patch said, "and I fucking told you, dude."

"That *thing* is called The Neverborn. And its sole purpose is to hunt Echoes."

"Is it dead?" Derry asked.

"Yes. But not the way you want it to be." Khalida swung the car into the cemetery and headed up the hill.

95

The wind came in like waves pressing and rolling over the cemetery hills, causing the leaves previously held tight in the trees to break loose and rain flame-colored flutter down around the group as they stepped from the car.

Derry opened the trunk.

"Looking for something?" Khalida asked.

"First aid kit," he replied.

"Check the front," Khalida said, hitting a button on the key and popping the hood, which concealed another storage area and not an engine since the car was electric.

They had parked near the building, but Paisley looked toward Lydia's grave. The headstones laid out in front of her like pawns in a never-ending game of chess. Spirits waiting for their turn at her.

"How well do you know Stilton Hawke?" Paisley asked over the wind.

"He's a nice guy. He works over at the yard, too," Patch said. He leaned against the car, and Derry cleaned up Patch's face and applied bandages from the first aid kit.

"I talk to him sometimes when I'm there with Patch. And sometimes I see him here when I'm visiting her." Derry nodded in the direction that Paisley was looking. "He's a good guy." His young cheeks were red in the wind, and his eyes teared up. It was hard to tell if it was the wind, Patch's condition, the situation, or the proximity to his sister's grave. Maybe it was everything. It was a lot for a kid to deal with.

"I heard he did some bad things in the past," Paisley said. "You think that could be true?"

"You mean the allegations from that student?" Derry asked.

Paisley turned to the boy bandaging his friend. The boy never ceased to amaze her.

"You know about that?" she asked.

"Yeah, I've got the internet, you know. After Lydia died..." he paused for a second. "Went missing. I looked into everyone in town. I verified every alibi I heard. Ran down every rumor. Everything."

"So even with those allegations, you don't think Stil could be involved?"

"He grabbed some racist kid who was harassing another student. The boy he grabbed tried to hit him, and he put him in some sort of hold."

"A wrist lock," Patch added, grabbing Derry's arm, gently simulating the move.

"But then he was accused of a murder a few years after, right?" Paisley asked.

"That happened before he even moved there. They just didn't have anything, so they blamed him," Derry said.

"He told you that?"

"Yeah."

"And you believe him?"

"I looked up his tax records to see when he started the job at the apartment complex where he worked when the girl was killed. I called the place and talked the front office manager into looking back through the records to see when he moved in. I even searched local newspapers to read about it. It was the girl's uncle. He just didn't get convicted because a cop planted evidence to help the case, and they threw it out. The uncle started blaming Stil when he moved in on account of Stil getting drunk one night and admitting to the conviction from before."

"He's a good dude," Patch said.

"Well, he's a good dude that seems to be right in the middle of all of this. Something isn't right, and he knows about it," Paisley said.

"How can we be sure?" Khalida asked.

"He talks in past tense," Paisley answered, "There's been things he should know, that he says he doesn't. And he knows things he shouldn't. I don't trust him."

Paisley considered all of it. The boys had been through so much already. She wanted to send them home.

"You two don't have to do this," she said.

Derry stopped working on Patch's face and turned toward Paisley.

"Yeah, I do. Lydia was all I had. I need to find out who took her from me and why," Derry said.

"You're too young to have to say things like that," Hyacinth said.

The sadness on Derry's face nearly broke Paisley.

"Tragedy doesn't discriminate based on age," he said. "And the trauma that follows doesn't care. You, of all people, should know that, Miss Bloom. I know we've all suffered different things, but the common thread between the three of us is that we've all lost our moms. You and Hyacinth lost yours to murder, and I'm so sorry for that. I feel like I lost mine twice. Once, when my sister was born, she traded her life for Lydia's. Then I lost her again when someone took Lydia. So I think we all understand why I need to be here."

"And if he's here, I'm here," Patch said, holding his fist out to Derry to bump.

The door to the building opened, and Stil squinted into the wind, looking across the drive and up the hill to where they stood.

"Oh, hello!" He let go of the heavy door and it blew shut. The man rambled up the hill as quickly as the wind would allow and stopped just in front of Paisley.

"Stil," she said, taking a small half-step back as he approached.

"Oh, I am so glad to see that you're okay. I was worried about you. I heard there was an accident at the yard."

"I'm doing okay," Paisley replied.

"Jesus, Steven, what happened to you, boy? Are you alright?"

Stil said, moving past Paisley. "We need to get you to the hospital?"

"I'm okay, Stil," Patch said.

"They do this to you in the lockup?" the gravedigger asked.

"Not exactly," the boy replied.

"Your friend Winslow did this," Hyacinth said. She stepped over to stand next to Paisley.

Stil turned to her as if he hadn't realized she was there.

"Oh, I'm sorry, where are my manners? I was so concerned about Steven here. Stilton Hawke, ma'am." Stil wiped his hand on his flannel shirt and extended it to Hyacinth. She didn't shake it.

"Hyacinth."

"Oh, like the flower."

"It's a plant, actually, but yes."

"Oh, yes, that is correct, but it is a flowering plant, no? And I don't think people are stuck being what they are born as, or what people see them as, but instead what they are capable of becoming." Stil smiled and looked over to Khalida, who was still on the far side of the car. "Oh, Miss Khalida, how do you do?"

Khalida just nodded in his direction.

Stil put his hand on Derry's shoulder. "It's always a pleasure to see you, Mr. Derry."

Derry faked a smile and shrugged Stil's hand off of him.

"I think Paisley was hoping we could talk about some things," Derry said, redirecting his attention back to her.

"Oh?" Stil asked.

"I'm not here to accuse you of anything, Stil, we're just here to ask some questions, is that okay?"

Stil must have concluded that there was no threat because he agreed.

Paisley continued.

"Something isn't right, and I think you know that. You're the gravedigger and caretaker of the cemetery, but you're also the coroner. Which means you pick up the bodies and bring them in for examination, right?"

"Oh, I do, yeah."

"And you work at the junkyard?" Hyacinth interjected.

"Oh, yeah. I do a lot of things, you know. I don't like sittin'
still. I like moving about, working. That's all. So I kind of do
whatever the county needs. Driving the wrecker for Winnie or
the wagon for Jackie."

Paisley caught a laugh before it escaped but couldn't help but
comment.

"Either way, you're picking up dead things off the side of the
road and dropping them off," she said.

Hyacinth spat out a laugh, but Stil just nodded.

"Oh, yeah, I guess that would be right," he said. "Most folks
that pass here in the county are road accidents, so that would
be accurate."

"What about Lydia Knot?" Paisley asked, cutting through
both the wind and the tension.

"Oh." Stil looked at Derry. He hesitated either to protect the
boy or out of guilt. It was unclear at the moment. "She wasn't
in a car accident, no."

"What happened to her?" Paisley asked. Her gaze bore so
strongly into Stil that he could not look away once he met her
eyes.

"She got burned," he mumbled.

"When?" Paisley demanded.

"Huh?"

"When? When did you collect the burned body?"

"I... I don't know the date," Stil stammered.

"Was it July Fourth or Fifth?" Paisley pressed.

"I don't know. I'm sorry."

"Was it Lydia Knot that you buried?"

"What?" Stil stumbled backward as if pushed. "I don't know
why you are asking all these things." He turned and started
toward the building.

"Stil, wait," Derry called after him. "Please?"

The man stopped. His shirt tugged around him in the wind

like a thousand tiny hands trying to usher him away from the questions. He lowered his head and cupped his eyes with a calloused hand.

"We know it wasn't her, Stil," Paisley called to him. "We know there was someone else. Who was it?"

Stil froze like the statues of the dead that surrounded them. He did not respond.

"Who did you bury in Lydia Knot's grave, Stil?" Paisley demanded.

"I don't know," he relented.

Derry tensed and went for Stil, but Paisley stopped him with a hand on his arm. The boy looked up at her. The tears forming in his eyes that had previously been unidentifiable, were now filled with confusion, pain, and a very dangerous splinter of hope.

"We have to dig her up, Stil," Paisley yelled.

He turned and shook his head.

"We can't. Please. We can't."

"We have to. Now," Khalida added.

"Can we just wait for Winslow to get here?" Stil called back. Paisley jerked back.

"Why is Winslow coming here?" she asked.

"Paisley, we should get out of here," Hyacinth said, taking her arm.

"He said that we needed to get our stories straight. He didn't know you'd be here."

"Winslow is a bad man, Stil. You have to help us. We need to see her. We need to see who you buried there," Paisley continued. She was terrified, but she had come too far.

"We can't."

"We have to."

"We can't!"

"Why?" Paisley shouted.

"He moved her!" Stil cried. "He moved her, okay?"

"What?" Paisley asked. "Why?"

"I don't know. Months back, Winslow said he needed to dig

her up. I told him not to. He said I needed to be gone when he did it. Said I couldn't be here. I just came back and filled the hole, but she was gone."

The group stood stoic despite the shock. The wind tore around them as Stil approached.

"There is something that I just remembered," he said.

"What is it?" Paisley asked.

"When I picked her up, Lydia, I mean, they said she'd died earlier that day, but there wasn't no way. She was cold and dry. All of it was," he said.

"It wasn't her, was it?" Paisley asked.

"Did she have her bear?" Derry yelled into the wind. "The one you buried her with? Did she have it?"

Stil thought about it. "I didn't bury her with no bear."

Something struck Paisley's memory. The bear. She knew the bear hadn't been buried, but how?

"Where did it go?" Derry yelled. The boy was taking on something he hadn't before: advocating for himself and his sister.

"I think Win..." Stil started but was interrupted.

A cloud of red mist burst from the center of Stil's face, first mushrooming out in front of him and then caught in the wind and blown back, dousing him in his own brain matter. A distant crack followed, ushered away with the same gust that circulated the mess created by the Winchester .270 round. Stilton Hawke momentarily stumbled around, looking for the right side of his head before falling to the ground.

Derry stood, petrified, gaping at the mess the bullet had left. Paisley grabbed his shirt and yanked him backward behind the car where Hyacinth and Patch hid.

Another bullet exploded the back window of the patrol car. Khalida ducked and worked her way around to them.

"You think it's Winslow?" Khalida shouted.

"I would bet on it," Paisley answered.

Another bullet slammed into the side of the car.

"I saw a flash," Derry said, pointing toward the tree line. "It's coming from there."

"We have to get out of here," Paisley said. She scanned for an exit route and gasped. Winslow Peck, the giant, ran at them.

"Shit!" she screamed as he reached them.

He hit Patch first, shoulder-checking him, slamming him against the front of the car. His hand came down quickly, wielding another hunting knife, not as long as the first but just as deadly.

"No!" Derry yelled as they all watched the knife plunge toward Patch's chest.

There was a blur as Khalida flew past them. She held the shotgun like a bat and swung it upward, connecting with Winslow's elbow. The knife flipped from his hand, and he spun away. He fell to his hands and knees beside the car.

Khalida wasted no time. She kicked him hard in the ribs, flipping him over onto his side. She pointed the shotgun at him.

"Give me one reason I shouldn't blow your head off," she said.

A spurt of blood popped from Khaldia's chest a split second before the sound of the rifle. She fell back, dropping the shotgun.

"Lida!" Derry yelled, trying to catch her as she fell.

Hyacinth made a move for the gun, getting a hand on it, but Winslow ripped it from her and squared up. He raised it, pointed at Khalida, and pulled the trigger.

There was a click. Winslow cocked the gun and tried again— another click.

That's when Paisley struck. She put one foot on the hood of the car and threw herself into the side of Winslow's head. She landed with her body on top of his wounded shoulder, wrapping her arm around his head and throwing the weight of her lower body down behind his back. It was a move she saw watching professional wrestling with her dad.

Winslow bent backward, his knees buckling, and he fell hard, screaming in both pain and frustration.

Paisley tried to get to her feet, but the man was no stranger to fighting, and he grabbed her by her recently healed leg and twisted her like a crocodile, spinning her and pulling her down. Hyacinth kicked at him, but his focus was on Paisley. He groped around in the grass and came up with the knife.

"I'm done with you, woman," he said, swinging the knife toward her neck.

Derry reached for Winslow's weapon-wielding hand, but the big man was too quick. Derry screamed as Winslow brought the blade down, but not on Paisley. He managed to divert the knife away from her. Instead Derry screamed as his pinkie finger fell to the ground.

Winslow pivoted on his knees, shoved Paisley aside, and pointed his rage at the boy. Once lined up with Derry, he lept off his feet and sprung up at him, driving him back and then down into the ground. A heavy breath escaped Derry's lips. Winslow knocked the wind out of him.

"Damn you, kid. You couldn't leave it alone, could you?" he yelled, driving the knife into Derry's side. Bone's cracked and blood sprayed out around Winslow's hand as he pushed the knife to its hilt. Derry tried to scream but the air he pulled in was lost through the hole in his side and bubbled out around the blade.

Paisley jumped on his back, and Hyacinth tried to grab his arm, but he threw them off with ease.

"Derry?" a voice rolled across the wind. It was soft. Confused. Hurt.

Patch stood looking down at his friend on the ground. The knife, still sticking from his side. There was a crack, and something tugged at Patch's shirt. Red bloomed high on his back and his chest.

"Derry?" he said again, not noticing the hole that went through him.

Winslow pulled the knife out, uncorking the blood that had been building up behind it and spilling it in the grass. He stood and wiped the blade on his pant leg.

"You really think you're ready to do this aga-"

Patch exploded forward, driving Winslow back like a tackling dummy. A stone statue of a woman with no arms cracked as the two behemoths slammed into it. Patch grabbed a loose block of the gray rock and pounded it into Winslow's head. Then again. And again.

The blade's flashing glint squashed any hope that Winslow was done. Patch released him and stumbled backward. He managed not to fall, but a curtain of blood draped over his side as a gash in his neck opened.

Winslow grabbed him by the shirt and pulled him face first into the statue, then let him fall into the grass beside it. He stood over the boy. His head bled from the back where Patch beat him with the rock, but it wasn't enough to stop the maniac. Winslow dug a hand into the boy's hair and pulled his head back, opening the wound in Patch's neck even wider, triggering a blast of blood that drenched the grass. He put the knife under his chin, perhaps to extend the cut across the rest of his neck, or, possibly, to take the boy's head clean off.

The knife pressed against the bloody flesh of Patch's neck, but the boy wasn't done either. He rolled, accepting the cut as it went, opening his jugular and giving up any opportunity he had to survive. With momentum from the turn, the boy swung the stone chunk of the statue he still held, connecting with the side of Winslow's face and taking most of it with it. His cheekbone and eye flew across the boy's chest, and his skull split backward, ballooning his brain out through the hole.

The man fell sideways and Patch climbed up to his knees. He brought the marble down hard on Winslow's head, splitting it completely in half and sending pieces of his skull and brain into the wind.

The boy stood and stumbled toward Paisley and Hyacinth, who raced toward him. He pushed past them to Derry, dropping to his knees next to his friend. He took his hand and fell to his side; using the very last bit of life he had to press his other hand into Derry's side, trying to stop the bleeding there.

96

Blue and red lights flashed in the distance, accompanied by the wails of sirens. Help was still a long way away, but coming. Paisley held a cloth from the first aid kit against Derry's side, staunching the bleeding. He was awake but not coherent. He just laid there looking over at Patch, who died looking at his friend. Paisley suspected he didn't want to look away since it would be the last time he looked into Patch's eyes. Though, if there was an afterlife, there was a good chance they would be there together soon.

"Stay down, and stay hidden. We don't know where that shooter is," Khalida said.

"Hy, are you okay?" Paisley asked. Hyacinth leaned against the car, not hiding, but staying low.

"I'm okay," she replied. "Just exhausted, that's all."

"Can you give me a hand over here?" Paisley said. She wanted to check in on Hyacinth, but there were bigger issues to tend. "Is there water?"

Hyacinth pulled herself together and turned to get water but stopped.

"Paisley," she said.

The sheriff emerged from the trees, carrying a rifle.

"Shit," Paisley said. "You think she knows we're out of bullets?"

"You think she cares?" Hyacinth retorted.

Sheriff Stacy strolled up to them as one might a neighboring campsite. She held the rifle, but did not point it at them.

"Howdy," she said, leaning the rifle against the side of the patrol car and resting her hands on her duty belt.

"Fuck off," Paisley said. The sirens grew nearer, but not

close enough that they could stop this woman from killing them all.

The sheriff looked over at Winslow and shook her head.

"I told Jackie not to marry that idiot," she said.

"Hy?" Paisley said.

Hyacinth looked down at her and nodded to the bandage she held against Derry's side.

"Yep," she said, switching places with Paisley to hold the bandage.

Paisley stepped toward the sheriff.

"You think there is a world where you go back to being sheriff of this shit hole town?" she asked.

"Way I see it, you and your friends here stormed my office. You killed the deputy there, attacked my idiot brother-in-law, and broke the boy out," the sheriff said, pointing at Patch. "Then you stole this patrol vehicle, which I tracked out here."

"I suspect you haven't been back to the station, have you? There's a lot there that won't be so easy to explain away," Paisley said.

"There's a lot of witnesses, too," Khalida added from where she leaned against the wheel of the car, nursing her gunshot.

"Doesn't matter. They'll believe what I tell 'em about that," the sheriff scoffed.

"And Stil? It's obvious we didn't shoot him," Paisley countered.

"No, I did. Because Stil was holding Winnie hostage. He was in on it with you. He's been in on it with you from the beginning. You came out here to cover it all up." The sheriff unsnapped the clip holding her sidearm and pulled it out.

"Cover up what?" Paisley asked. She thought about trying to grab the gun, but knew she wasn't close enough.

"The girl. The other one. The one Winnie had. I've been telling him for years that it wasn't no demon. He convinced my Jackie that they were doing something good, but it was all just sick."

"What girl?" Paisley asked.

Khalida stood next to Paisley.

"What girl?" she echoed.

"The one he found by the road," the sheriff answered. "He brought her home. There was some news story about a man and woman from Virginia with their adopted daughter who up and vanished one night, but no one knew where they were headed, so he never worried about anyone finding out what he'd done. Then little Heather, bless her heart, was taken, and they found her dead. Winnie thought it was his punishment for killing them. Convinced Jackie that the girl was a curse or something. He was always too dumb for her."

"I don't understand. Why would Winslow take a girl? Who was she? Why did he think she was a demon?" Paisley asked.

"Quit asking me all these questions. We ain't got time for all that," the sheriff said, turning the gun in her hand sideways and studying it as if it reminded her that they had unfinished business.

"He killed her? That girl?" Paisley asked.

"Yeah, he killed her alright," the sheriff agreed.

"And they had to take Lydia because someone saw him do it. They needed them to think it was Lydia he burned," Paisley said. It wasn't a question.

"Yeah, that's why he moved her. He worried someone would figure out it wasn't her," the sheriff said. "That fed lady had been out, talked to him, but steered clear of me. Guess he thought she was on to him."

"Why are you telling us this?" Paisley asked.

"To absolve myself," she answered.

"You think that by telling us it gets you off the hook?" Paisley asked.

"No," the sheriff said. Her hand tightened around the gun. "I just needed someone to hear it, though."

"Where did they move Lydia to?" Khalida demanded.

"I don't know. I didn't want to know. And, just so you know, he didn't kill those other girls," the sheriff said. She checked the gun in her hand and seemed satisfied with it.

"I saw him do it on tape," Paisley said.

"You don't know anything about that tape."

"I saw him torture the kidnapped girls. I saw him cut them up."

Sheriff Stacy shook her head.

"You don't know what you're talking about. Every one of the kidnapped girls was given some shot that paralyzed them completely, stopping their heart, that's it," she said. "And that wasn't Winnie. He wasn't smart enough to mastermind nothing like that."

"I saw it," Paisley said.

"So did I," Hyacinth called from her spot next to Derry. "It's sick."

"So did I," the sheriff said. "Remember, your friend sent them to me."

The sirens wailed as they turned into the cemetery entrance. The sheriff raised her gun and pointed it at Paisley. Khalida stepped in front of her.

"It don't matter who I shoot first," the sheriff said, cocking the hammer back.

Paisley stepped around Khalida.

"You're right, it doesn't. You're going to jail either way. What you haven't accounted for is why the police are coming here and not your office."

"Cause you called them. But that doesn't mean they'll believe you," the sheriff said, switching her aim from Khalida to Paisley.

"No, it's because I wear a camera that has been live-streaming this entire thing." She tapped the pin on her jacket, knowing that her bag was still at the station, and as soon as it was out of range, the feed would have stopped. But Paisley also knew that WhyItHurts had messaged Hyacinth after the feed dropped and she had told them where they were going so they could send help.

"What?" the sheriff asked. The gun dipped, but was still pointed at Paisley.

"Yeah," Paisley said, "and I had one on my bag as well, so everything that has happened, every admission, everything, has been broadcast live on the internet, and it's on tape. We've got it all. With all that research you all did on me, you didn't think I'd bust you the same way I busted the preacher?"

"You bitch," the sheriff whimpered.

"No matter what you do, you're spending the rest of your life in jail. You and your fucked up sister," Paisley said.

The first of the emergency response vehicles swung around the corner and through the cemetery gates.

"No," the sheriff said.

"You're fucked," Paisley said.

Sheriff Stacy raised the gun again, and Khalida, again, stepped in front of Paisley, but instead of shooting her, the sheriff put the gun under her own chin and pulled the trigger. The bullet exploded the crown of her head, spitting brain into the wind for the third time in just a few minutes.

"Jesus!" Paisley yelled. She stumbled back and fell. She beat her fists into the cold earth below.

Khalida came to her. "Go," she said.

"What?" Paisley shook her head, trying to recover from the trauma she just witnessed.

"Go. Get out of here. We'll take care of Derry. We'll deal with this. But you go, find her."

"Why don't you go? You seem much more *equipped* to deal with whatever you run into. I'm done. I can't."

"No, I've been looking for this girl for years and couldn't figure out what you did," Khalida said. "Find her before Vivian does. Whatever you do, do not let her get to her first."

The squad cars climbed the hill just a few seconds from the bloody scene.

"Paisley," Hyacinth said.

Paisley looked over at her. Her hair blew in the wind, and even though she was battered and bruised, her friend looked like a Hollywood actress playing a combat medic in some movie.

"Huh?" Paisley said. She really was done. She had nothing left. Help was at the bottom of the hill.

"I love you," Hyacinth said. "You have to do this. You're the only one who can."

"But Hy, I'm so tired."

"I know, girl. I know. And you shouldn't have to do this, but you take her hand and stand up. Then you find her."

Khalida stood above Paisley, extending a hand.

"Fuck," Paisley said.

"Go, Pais. You have to," Hyacinth said.

"Dicks," Paisley said, taking the woman's hand and coming to her feet.

"Go," Khalida said.

Paisley turned toward the building, looking into the woods where the sheriff had come from

"Paisley!" Hyacinth called after her.

Paisley stopped.

"Take this! You'll need your audience!" Hyacinth said, ready to launch her cell phone to Paisley.

"No!" Paisley yelled, running back to her friend and taking the cell phone from her. "I've only got one eye right now. There's no way in hell I would have caught that."

"There's only two percent left, so you'll need a charger."

"I need a lot more than that."

"Be careful, I love you."

"I love you."

And with that, she was gone. She wasn't sure where she was going but knew she was almost out of time.

97

Paisley stepped into the trees on the far side of the cemetery without being noticed by the arriving response vehicles. The sheriff's truck was just a few hundred feet from the clearing and stood out against the greenery, making it easy for Paisley to spot, even with just one eye.

She raised her hand and tugged the door handle. Her first sigh of relief came as the door opened. She climbed into the driver's seat and pressed the "Start" button. Another sigh of relief came when the truck roared to life. Of course, Sheriff Stacy was the type to leave her key fob in her truck.

She pulled out Hyacinth's phone.

HyBloom - *Hey, it's Paisley. Are you there?*

WhyItHurts - *Paisley! Thank god you are okay!!*

HyBloom - *Okay is a big stretch. But I'm alive. I'm short on time and I need some help.*

WhyItHurts - *What's up?*

HyBloom - *What was the last thing you saw?*

WhyItHurts - *The shootout at the sheriff's office. I saw what happened to the waitress. I'm so sorry. I know you liked her. I'm sure Derry and Patch are devastated. Tell me that the other departments caught Winslow?*

Competing feelings fought inside Paisley like caged dogs over a scrap of meat. There was anger that tore up through her, cursing Winslow. Sadness pulled at her heart. So much pain and death in such a short time. Then jealousy. WhyItHurts lived in a world in which Derry and Patch were still alive. A world that could turn the videos off and not have to see the girls tortured on camera.

HyBloom - *That's it! I get it! I know why they are looking for her!*
WhyItHurts - *Fill me in?*
HyBloom - *Shit! You don't even know about the spider!*
WhyItHurts - *There was a spider? Like, a big one?*

The screen on the phone went black. The power button was unresponsive.

Paisley looked in the console, the glove box, and the door pockets.

"Who doesn't keep a charger in their car?" she shouted.

She would have to go without it.

Pain needled Paisley's eye as she pulled the bandage off, exposing the swollen and stitched face that it covered. She blinked the dried blood and pus from it and gave it a few rolls to make sure it was still functional. She looked around the truck cabin and then out the windows. Her focus was okay up close, but that eye couldn't really latch onto things much further than the instrument cluster in the truck. But one and a half eyes would be better to drive with.

Paisley threw the truck into drive and hammered the throttle. It was easy to sneak out with all of the emergency vehicles crawling all over the place. Once she cleared the cemetery, she switched on the lights and siren, which she used the entire way to the salvage yard.

98

Metal screamed and tore from its rails as the hefty truck ripped through the salvage yard's entrance gate. Paisley barreled through the yard like she was running a slalom. An expanding hurricane of dust followed, accompanied with lightning strikes, when she clipped the junk cars sending sparks into the air.

She had no idea where she was going, but remembered walking to the back and along the drop. So she did exactly that. The headlights lit the way as the sun dipped behind the horizon, casting Paisley into the dark yard once again.

She turned when she saw a strip of caution tape that now hung in front of the drop. It led her directly to the car she was looking for, the one with the Virginia license plates. When she reached it, she aimed the headlights at it and jumped out. She had remembered something else that she needed to check. If wrong, she would be back to square one.

The door on the back passenger side was gone, and the sight of it hit Paisley as another reminder of Patch, who saved her that night, and how he had given his life for theirs that day. She looked through the opening into the back seat.

"Basil," she said, petting one of the cats. "And Ginger."

She scooped one under each arm and carried them back to the truck.

"I've got some work to do, and it may get a bit messy. I don't know what's going to happen to this car. So you'll be safer in here."

She put them in the cab of the truck and closed the door. Basil curled up in the driver seat, and Ginger jumped onto the dash where she would have a better view.

"Ah, the curious type. Be careful. That shit'll get you in trouble."

Paisley returned to the car with Virginia plates and climbed into the back seat. She lay on the floor where she had been when she died. It was a surreal feeling looking up at the roof of the car. She took a deep breath and rolled her head to the side as she had done that night, and there it was looking back at her from under the seat— a small green face with black buttons for eyes.

"Hey, you," she said, retrieving the small crochet turtle wedged under the seat.

A chill ran down her spine. The feeling of being watched.

"Hello?" she called. Something moved. Too big to be another cat, too small to be any of the people she was worried about running into out there. It moved again. It was just outside the car, shielded from the truck's headlights by the car next to her. The form inched closer. It was a girl.

Then she was gone, just as quickly as she had appeared. There was a noise. A moan? A dry scream? It was muffled and filled with pain.

Paisley tucked the turtle into her dad's jacket and zipped it up. She climbed over the seat into the front. The car was in ruins, and it was more apparent from there. The front passenger door appeared to be tied on. She tried to imagine the accident that caused this damage. The roof was crumpled, the side was smashed, the whole thing pummeled. She went to put her hands on the wheel, but the seat was so far back that she couldn't reach it. She grabbed the shift knob instead. It was in neutral, and she wiggled it back and forth a few times. Then she reached down and pulled the trunk handle. It made a creaking noise but didn't open. She prepared herself to force the driver-side door open, clearly mangled in the accident, but to her pleasant surprise, it opened easily.

Her heart beat like a subwoofer at a rock show as she hurried to the back of the car. The old metal whined as she wrenched the lid up. The noise sent fear through her body. She stopped to see if it had drawn attention but saw nothing.

A wave of relief and disappointment flowed over her. The

only thing in the trunk was an old tire iron and some stained rags.

"Shit," she said, sitting on the lip of the trunk. "Where are you? I thought for sure you would be here."

Paisley looked out over the drop. Another reminder of just how close she came to death. She couldn't see the bottom, which was for the best, as seeing the hummer in that condition would hurt. The thought made her uneasy, and she stepped back from the ledge. The fear of failure haunted her.

"No, not now," she said. "I can't."

She took in all the details, but without an audience to work them out with, she felt less sure of herself.

Her brain buzzed with information. Power lines jumped in her head.

"Come back, please? Let me talk to you," Paisley begged the darkness.

She stood there listening, hoping there would be someone to talk to so she could lay everything out. Her eyes shot open causing a whip crack of pain. She unzipped her dad's jacket, pulled out the turtle, and held it up to her face. She stared at it for a moment. Its soft face looked back at her, eager to help. It couldn't, but maybe something else could.

She ran to the truck and opened the door.

"So, listen," she said.

Basil's sweet eyes met hers. Ginger hopped down from the dash onto the center console to observe.

"They moved the body, and he wanted it to be somewhere he could keep an eye on it, right? It had to be somewhere he felt comfortable and secure. Then there's this." She held up the turtle. "I found it. It was in the car from Virginia, where Stil said you cats came from. The sheriff said the family Winslow killed in the accident was from Virginia, so I figured I'd better start here. I suspected he put her body back in the car where he found her in the first place, but it wasn't there. So where is it? I looked in the trunk, the backseat, the front."

It was unfolding now. "The seat. Someone pushed it all the

way back. It could have just been that way, but," she focused on the details that she couldn't see in that moment.

The cats watched as Paisley waved her hands about as if her mind was an investigation board full of red pins.

"The shifter, it wasn't dirty. There was a layer of dirt on everything, but not that, and not the wheel. Someone opened the door recently. But that's all just part of it. The important part, the part that I needed to see, was the dirt! Not the dirt in the car but the dirt *behind* it. There are grooves in front of the tires. I saw them when I was back there. This car has been moved since its arrival and then put back. It doesn't look like this happened when they found me, so I have to assume it was something else. And when I was here the other night, as you two likely recall, I spotted a mound of dirt that appeared out of place. I didn't get it then, but now I know. That's where they put the dirt, and they didn't get rid of what was left over."

The cats stared up at her with indifference and no opinion on the matter.

"I wish you could tell me if I'm right!"

Paisley dropped the turtle onto the seat next to the cats, slammed the door, and ran back to the Virginia car. She remembered Winslow having trouble pushing the Hummer backward, even in reverse, so she ran to the back. With the trunk closed, she was able to get a good stance. She lowered her shoulder and shoved. It rocked a little, but not enough to make her feel confident that she would move it on her own.

She went to the truck hoping that, as any good responder in rural Indiana should, the sheriff would have a recovery strap or chain to pull cars out of ditches during snow storms. The sheriff, for the first time in Paisley's brief experience, did not disappoint. Paisley grabbed the tow strap out of the emergency kit. Also in inventory was a small folding shovel and a flashlight, which Paisley assumed she would need.

Within a minute of finding the strap, she inched the truck back, pulling the car with ease. She wasn't in line with the car, so she worked at an angle, but it was good enough.

The dirt beneath the car told a story that Paisley felt like she understood. A section of the dirt dipped a few inches. Stil had told her about this. If it were in a cemetery, there would be a vault. She began to dig.

The earth moved easily. It hadn't been compacted when replaced, which explained the excess she had seen in the mound.

She dug furiously, ignoring the mental, physical, and emotional exhaustion that was trying to overtake her. She scooped dirt, tossing it mindlessly behind her. She had no plans to refill the hole, so it was of no concern.

After no more than half an hour, Paisley hit something.

"Of course, he only put her a foot deep. What an asshole."

Paisley's assumption was correct. He hadn't just moved the body but the casket as well. And without the protection of the vault, it had begun to collapse with the elements. Small sections had rotted and fallen in. Paisley stepped carefully, avoiding standing directly above the coffin, scraping dirt away rather than scooping it out.

Paisley busted a small hole in the bottom half of the casket. She bit her arm to hold back a scream. The earth wasn't wet at this depth, but it was damp enough to house a collection of worms.

Depending on the body's condition, she would grab her dad's jacket, which she had left next to the hole when she started digging, and pile the remains in there and tie it up using the sleeves. Then she'd take it back and use one of WhyItHurts connections to prove it wasn't Lydia.

The casket creaked under Paisley's feet. She shifted her weight, worried that she would fall through. There was something visible in the moonlight through one of the larger holes at the top of the casket. It was pale white. Was it bone? Was it the burial dress?

Paisley grabbed the flashlight. She steeled herself for the worst. The body had been burned. She saw the photos. As much as that should not bring a sense of ease, it did because the white had to be fabric. It would be the dress. She started to lean down and then had a thought.

"What if the bugs have eaten the burnt stuff, and now all that's left is bone?" Chills shot up her spine, but she had to know. She lowered the flashlight to the hole and peeked in.

It wasn't bone. It was too soft to be bone. But it wasn't fabric either. Paisley's mind raced to make sense of what she saw, but there was no question. It was skin. Pale skin. Nearly translucent. There were small crescent shapes that first looked like centipedes. She realized they were eyelashes. The skin stretched over the eye was thin and so white that the road map of blue veins was visible.

"Is that Lydia? How long does it take to decompose?" she asked herself.

She splintered a piece of the rotting wood away to get a better look at the child's face, but something tickled her brain, and she recoiled. She looked down at the eye, those blue veins. They pulsated. The eye opened. The body inside gasped.

Paisley screamed. She tried to flee the hole, but her foot broke through the wood. She clawed at the broken pieces that held her leg like a bear trap. She ripped wildly and lost her balance. She fell, putting her hands down, hoping not to be engulfed, but her right hand broke through and she could feel the body inside. It was cold, frail, dead. Yet, a hand shot out through the splintered coffin and latched onto Paisley's wrist.

The girl tried to scream but choked. It was as if she was suffocating. Once more she tried to expel her terror, but dirt and gravel spewed, clacking against her teeth as she voided herself of earth. She inhaled and let out a virulent scream that started slowly and slithered through Paisley like a plague. A scream that she would never forget if she lived to be a thousand. Paisley lurched back, but the girl did not release her grip. She screamed and scratched at the inside of the box. Her eyes, visible through the hole, didn't look angry but scared.

Paisley stopped struggling against the hand holding her wrist. She shifted her weight, propped the flashlight under her chin, and pried away the wood above the girl's face. The girl's other hand reached through the hole and grabbed Paisley's fingers. The girl strained as if trying to lift herself through the hole.

"Shhhhhh, it's going to be okay," she said. "It's okay, I promise."

Paisley stroked the cold, bony digits.

"It's okay. I've got you. I am not going to let anything bad happen to you. Shhhh."

The girl's screams faded. Paisley reached through the hole, brushed dirt off the girl's cheek, and then cupped her face.

"I've got you," she said.

The girl stopped screaming, looking up at Paisley. Color bloomed around her eyes. Her lips, which had been a pale blue, blushed.

The girl whimpered. Paisley recognized that cry from the videos.

"Oh my god," Paisley said. "It was you." Her breath caught, and her eyes burned. "Every time, it was you. God, it was you."

The girl blinked, her beautiful blue eyes blossomed like a columbine before her. Tears welled in them.

"I'm so, so sorry," Paisley said. The videos replayed in her head. The girls weren't just similar; they were the same one, every time. It was this girl. She was an Echo.

Neither of them could hold back the tears. Paisley held the girl's face, the skin under her hand warming.

"Let's get you out of there, okay?"

The girl tightened her grip on Paisley's hand.

"It's okay," she said. "I am not leaving without you."

The girl let go, and Paisley ripped chunks from the casket until there was room for the small girl to fit through.

"Can you stand?"

The girl sat up and gathered her feet under her. Paisley helped, and the two stepped out of the shallow grave.

"Okay, we're going to go to that truck, and then we're going to take you to a safe place to get help," Paisley said, wrapping her dad's jacket around the girl.

A shadow passed over them and into the truck's headlights. They were not alone.

99

It had been quiet in the basement, and Millicent hoped to stay asleep.

"Get up," the man demanded.

Millicent opened her eyes and saw the trap with Squeakers on it lying in front of her face. She didn't want to look at it, so she closed her eyes and sat up.

"I said stand up."

Millicent did. The man restrained her arms behind her back with tape. He had done this more times than she could count, and it always led to pain.

The man had a key. He bent, grabbed the chain around her waist, and unlocked it. He only ever did this when the woman told him to because they were going to hurt her very badly. The thought of running crossed her mind, but she hadn't been strong enough to run in a long time.

The man grabbed her, wrapping his hand around her arm and pulled her toward a red bag laying in the middle of the floor.

"Get in," he demanded.

Millicent didn't understand.

"Get in or I'll put you in."

Millicent knelt down into the bag, allowing him to bring it up around her. The zipper sounded, casting her into relative darkness. Then his foot crashed against the side of her head, popping her ear drum, which blew out right before she lost consciousness.

She woke when something smelly and wet soaked through the bag. She tried to push her feet out, but it was too tight in the bag to move. With her hands behind her, she did the only thing she could do and wiggled.

"Let's do this!" a voice in the distance yelled, followed by booming and quick footsteps. Then everything went bright, and within seconds, she was on fire. Her skin boiled, bubbling and popping, before sizzling into crisp black flakes.

The bag opened, and a young man screamed at the sight of her. He tried to pull her out, but the fire was too powerful, it bit his hands. She watched him until her eyes melted. She screamed until the air in her lungs ignited.

100

"You didn't think I was going to let you get away with her that easily, did you?" a woman's voice said.

Paisley raised her hand to shield her eyes from the headlights. It was Vivian, but she wasn't alone. She stood with Jackie. Vivian had a syringe to her neck. The side of Jackie's face was red and swollen, and blood dripped from her busted lips.

The girl saw Jackie and screamed.

"What is it?" Paisley asked, trying to calm her.

The girl hid behind Paisley, pointing at Jackie. Paisley hugged her, pulling her against her leg.

Paisley had an audience. Her mind kicked into gear.

"It was you," she said. "You did this. You sick bitch. It wasn't Winslow. You're the one who hurt her."

"I didn't do anything. She's a demon. You don't know what you're talking about," Jackie yelled. "Let me go!" She tried to free herself, but Vivian stuck the needle in her neck, but didn't push the plunger, and Jackie stopped struggling.

Paisley pointed at the car.

"The Virginia car. That's it, isn't it?" She looked at the girl. "Was that your car? Were you in an accident?"

The girl nodded but didn't take her eyes off Jackie.

"He thought she was dead. She was dead. But then she wasn't, right?" Paisley asked.

"Winslow tried to keep her, but that man, the boring one, was looking for her, so he couldn't. I told him he couldn't. Then our Heather was taken in exchange," Jackie cried.

"So why try to kill her?" Paisley asked.

"We had to sacrifice her," Jackie pleaded. "We knew we did. She's a demon. You see it. She's been in that hole for months, been in that box for more than a year, and she's alive. You saw the videos, you saw how many times we performed the ritual. You saw what we did to her, over and over. Then burned her up into nothing and she's still here. She's a demon and that man, the man who came, he's her devil."

"The man, it was him, wasn't it? The Neverborn, is that what it's called?" Paisley asked. "He was looking for her. Did he take Heather? Did he think Heather was the Echo?"

"He took a lot of girls to punish us for taking his girl, his demon," Jackie spat.

Paisley shook her head.

"No. That isn't right, is it? He would have known. Right?" Paisley looked at the woman holding the syringe. "Right, Vivian?"

"It's complicated," she said.

"Uncomplicate it," Paisley said.

"It was that man. He killed the girls," Jackie cried, trying her hardest not to move against the needle in her neck.

"No, he didn't. He would have known it wasn't her before he killed them. No, they were killed as a test, weren't they?" Paisley said. "A test to see if they'd come back."

"You don't know what you are talking about," Vivian replied.

"He wouldn't need to kill them to find out, but you would," Paisley said, pushing the girl farther behind her.

"I only took them to try to find her. We knew she was here somewhere. Those girls were collateral damage," Vivian said.

"And what about the cleaners at the Justice Center, were they collateral damage as well?"

Vivian's normally cool expression faltered and she sneered at Paisley.

"Oh, you didn't think I knew about that? When you came to the cell to ask for my help, because you weren't smart enough to figure it all out on your own, even with however many centuries you may be old, I noticed the coffee stain on the file. If they were copies, it wouldn't have been textured. You've been a step behind this whole time. And now I've beaten you to what you wanted, and I will be damned if I let you take her." Paisley stood up tall. She could feel the confidence welling inside her.

"She needs to be taken care of. She needs to be with her own kind. Not with a monster like this," Vivian said, shaking Jackie.

"How many girls did you kill in the process, Vivian? You call her a monster, but you killed innocent children."

"It was painless, I assure you. I used this," Vivian said, nodding at the syringe she held in Jackie's neck. "It paralyzes every single muscle in the body, including the heart and lungs. Sure, the brain is still active, but just long enough to register that everything else has shut down. Then they're just gone. Painless and easy."

Jackie stopped shaking.

"You killed my baby?" Jackie whispered.

"It wasn't personal," Vivian said.

Jackie turned, the needle still stuck in her neck bounced as she attacked.

Vivian was calm, easily dodging the weak swings of the beaten woman. She timed a swing perfectly and leaned back. Jackie's hand missed her face, and she stumbled forward.

The girl against Paisley's leg tried to pull back as the woman staggered toward them, trying to catch her balance. Paisley lifted a hand to stabilize the woman, but it was a pointless gesture. A crack ripped through the air, and something popped out of the center of Jackie Peck's chest. The bullet whizzed past Paisley. The woman fell forward into her, and Paisley caught her, helping her to the ground but not letting go of the girl on her leg.

Paisley knelt down next to the woman.

"I'm sorry about your daughter, but you tortured a child, you monster," Paisley said, allowing Jackie's body to slip into the shallow grave.

"Thank you for your help, Miss Mott. You were obviously the right choice." Vivian put away her gun and walked toward Paisley and the girl.

Paisley stood and backed up, keeping herself between Vivian and the girl.

"You're not touching her. Khalida doesn't want you near her," Paisley said. They had backed themselves to the edge of the drop.

"Khalida doesn't know what to do with her. She'll just take her off to live somewhere as a whiny child for a hundred years. Then she'll grow tired of her and leave her for the Neverborn. I can give her so much more."

"You're not taking her."

"You don't understand, child." Vivian reached out and brushed Paisley's sutured cheek. "I could just give you a little push right now, and you'd both go over. And since she's only been alive for a few minutes, he won't feel her when she goes, and he won't come. You, on the other hand, wouldn't be getting up."

"She's suffered enough."

"Do not speak to me of her suffering. You don't know the burden of immortality. Can you imagine being butchered over and over?"

Paisley recoiled at the thought and clutched the child tighter still.

"You can't take her," Paisley said.

"Imagine being buried alive when you just can't stay dead. Waking up every few hours as your body heals itself, just to suffocate on dirt and die again. You know what happens when you die? Your spirit detaches from your body. Now think about it: yoyoing back and forth because you can't stay alive and you can't stay dead. Imagine that and tell me you understand what this child has been through. You know nothing."

"I know that a woman I trust told me that you shouldn't have her. And that is enough for me," Paisley said.

"I don't think you understand. You can give her to me, or you will die together, and I will collect her while you wait for the vultures."

"No."

"You don't get to tell me no. I see why he hates you. I am a thousand-year-old God, and you are... what?"

"Paisley fucking Mott."

The answer surprised Vivian enough to buy Paisley the time she needed. She sidestepped, pulling the girl with one hand and swinging the other up into Vivian's neck. The syringe from Jackie's neck popped through the skin, and she pressed the plunger. Vivian tried to go for her gun but she froze. Her body locked.

"Normally, I wouldn't get involved in the affairs of Gods, but you don't fuck with kids."

Paisley gave Vivian a shove. Had the woman had any control of her body, she could have stopped herself. Instead, she fell over the side of the drop and disappeared into the dark.

Paisley didn't wait to listen for the impact. She just scooped the girl up and ran for the truck. She jumped in the driver's side, displacing the cats. They settled on the girl's lap once she was in the passenger seat. Paisley plucked the turtle from her seat and handed it to the girl.

"Here you go," she said.

The girl smiled, the most beautiful smile Paisley had ever seen. The first in a very long time. But not the last.

The truck started and kicked up dust as it spun around. It weaved past a few cars and then slowed.

Paisley rolled down the window. A man strolled through the dark. She stopped next to him. His perfectly combed hair, button-up shirt, and khaki pants looked as out of place as Paisley felt.

"That way. Over the edge. Can't miss her," she said.

The man leaned back to look around Paisley and see her passenger. Paisley leaned forward, blocking his view.

"That way," she said again, pointing out the window and back toward the drop.

The man looked off to where Paisley had just come from, then back at her.

"I'll see you again," he leaned farther to try and see around

Paisley again.

"You better hope not." Paisley winked and sped off, leaving the man in a cloud of dust as he unbuttoned his shirt.

101

The rising sun burned into Paisley's eyes driving her brain in a hundred directions. She shook her head to wake herself up as she took the steps of a small brick house that she had seen once in a crayon drawing. She looked back to check on the girl in the truck and gave her a thumbs up. The girl, cuddling two cats and a stuffed turtle, managed to return the gesture. Paisley checked the address before knocking on the metal screen door.

There was no answer, so Paisley knocked again. Nothing.

She went to the front window and looked through the metal bars but saw nothing but dated furniture.

She returned to the truck and opened the door.

"Hey, it's going to get loud, but I promise that everything is okay, alright?"

The girl nodded and Paisley closed the door.

She reached into the bed of the truck and grabbed a large metal cylinder with handles on either side and a pair of bolt cutters. Then looked back into the truck again and smiled.

"Be right back."

102

The hospital room was crowded when Paisley opened the door. Hyacinth sat in a chair on the far side of the room, allowing those who needed to be around the boy in the bed access. She struggled to stand when she saw Paisley. She looked ill but managed to get up to greet her. Paisley's dad was close behind. She allowed them to hug her.

"Oh my God, I was so worried," Hyacinth said.

"My baby," Paisley's dad said, pulling her in close for another hug.

Paisley's legs gave way and she began to fall, but her dad had her. It was probably imperceptible to the others in the room that he was holding her up, but she just couldn't stand.

"I got you, Dill, I got you," her dad whispered. Using the shortened version of her middle name, as only he ever did, solidified that she was safe.

Paisley sobbed into his chest, and everyone stood, waiting while she did.

"It's okay," her dad said. "You're okay."

Paisley planted her feet and stood on her own. She wiped her eyes and stood back. She looked at Khalida. "There is someone outside I think you need to meet."

Khalida's face morphed into a smile, and she nodded. She left the room, rubbing Paisley's shoulder as she passed.

"Hy, are you okay?" Paisley asked.

"Yeah, I'll be okay. I'm just glad you're okay," Hyacinth said.

"I know we've got a lot to cover, but can I have a minute with him?" Paisley asked Hyacinth and her dad, nodding to the man standing next to the hospital bed, holding his son.

"Of course," her dad said, as he helped Hyacinth to the

door.

Derry lay in the hospital bed, tubes coming from his mouth and bandages wrapped around his chest and hand.

"Mr. Knot, I'm Paisley Mott."

"Gerald. I know who you are," he said, not looking up from his son.

"How is he?"

"Bad. Real bad."

"May I?" Paisley asked, signaling that she would like to approach the bed and see Derry.

"Okay."

Paisley stepped up to the bed and took Derry's unbandaged hand, careful not to disturb any of the tubes or cords that were running along his arm.

"Oh, Derry." She blinked, trying to hold in her emotion, but knew it was a fight she would lose.

"They don't know if he is going to make it," Gerald said, fighting back tears of his own.

"I know it's been a hard day, and I'm really sorry you've been through so much, but there is something else." Paisley wiped her eyes, walked to the door, and opened it.

"Come on in," she said to someone outside.

Gerald's face woke slowly in confusion and then joy.

"Daddy?" a little girl's honeyed voice came from the doorway.

"Lydia!" he cried as he rushed over and scooped up the girl holding a teddy bear.

"I'm sorry about the hair," Paisley said, picking a small hair off the girl's sweater. "Her and her new friend were playing with cats in the truck on the way over."

Gerald dropped to his knees, holding his baby girl, and wept, covering her face in kisses while she laughed.

"How?" Hyacinth said, leaning against the doorway.

"The bear," Paisley said.

"The bear?"

"Yeah. Derry said she had it when he ID'd the body. But it

wasn't in the video or the crime scene photos. She didn't have it with her when she was taken on the Fourth of July."

"But how did you know where to find her?" Hyacinth asked.

"The picture in the sheriff's office. She said Heather, her niece did it, but the picture had her truck in it. She didn't get that truck until this year. Up until then she drove a Crown Vic and a Charger."

"And Heather's been gone a long time."

"Right. But in the truck photo there is a picture of a little girl holding that same bear. Same little green vest and hat."

"The brilliant Paisley Mott does it again," Hyacinth said, taking Paisley's hand. Paisley hooked her arm under Hyacinth's to steady her.

"Let's give them some time," Paisley said, looking down at the girl and her father. "I think I need more dad time, too."

In the lobby, her dad came up the hall from the vending machine with snacks and drinks for everyone.

Paisley's back popped as she stretched, adding a yawn that she couldn't have stopped if she wanted to.

Khalida sat with the girl who devoured a package of tiny donuts.

"It's going to take some time. She's been through a lot. Haven't you?" Paisley said.

The girl nodded. Then reached out with one chocolate covered hand and took Paisley's.

"Millicent," Paisley said. The girl looked up at her, brushed her hair from her face, and smiled cautiously. "Her name is Millicent."

Epilogue

Pale light beamed through the windows of Raven Bloom, waking Paisley. She had forgotten just how comfortable the beds were there. The down almost swallowed her whole. It had been three days since she'd been back. Everything moved quickly in Howling Ivy, and it was better for them to all regroup at Raven Bloom while they handled the fallout.

Thankfully, there weren't too many questions about why things went as they did. The official story was that the girls who had been kidnapped and killed by Vivian and her henchman were done so per some conspiracy theory. The proof of their involvement was easy enough with Prince's fingerprints at the sheriff's office. They ruled Deputy Morehouse's death an unusual killing, but with the appalling violence that Vivian and Prince committed against the cleaners, it wasn't much of a stretch to think they would rip someone in half.

Khalida had some friends in high places that helped with a lot of the connections that were harder to make. In the end, they made it look like the sheriff was covering for Vivian and Prince and Winslow and Jackie. The latter who was accused of faking someone's death to kidnap Lydia Knot, held captive at Sheriff Stacy's house, which wasn't completely untrue, though the authorities would never hear about Millicent. Winslow, Jackie, and the Sheriff would be posthumously identified in the kidnapping of Lydia Knot, the murder of Stilton Hawke, the murder of Steven "Patch" Simply and the attempted murder of Darius Knot. That would be elevated to murder if Derry didn't make it, but that was still up in the air.

Paisley had been mentally editing the story in her head, getting her story straight to make sure there was no mention of Millicent. Instead, painting Derry as the hero he was for faking the recording to get help in exposing his sister's kidnapping. She wasn't ready to start on it, but she was sure it was a story she wanted to tell.

There was a knock on the door, and Paisley toyed with the idea of just ignoring it. She knew who it was, though. She knew that knock. More than that, she knew the footprints that had preceded it. It was Hyacinth. She had been ill in Howling Ivy, so ill that they were afraid that she may have to be admitted to the hospital herself, but she refused. She said she just needed to get home. She claimed that she had forgotten to bring her medication with her, but Paisley suspected it was something else. She just wasn't sure what. As soon as they returned to Raven Bloom, she seemed better, but Paisley hadn't seen much of her, or anyone for that matter, as she had been hiding in her room since they returned. Hyacinth did bring her food a few times a day. She would normally knock once and leave the tray on a table in the hall. It had been a few days since she spoke to anyone.

The knock came again.

"Pais?" Hyacinth's soft voice came through the door.

She sounded healthy again, which made Paisley feel a little better. She worried that Hyacinth going out there had taken a bigger toll than she let on.

Paisley got up and crossed the large, beautifully decorated room to the door, stopping at the mirror on the bureau to try and press her wild hair down, but it was no use.

The door was locked. Hyacinth had a key, but Paisley assumed she would only ever use it if she had to for Paisley's safety. Paisley flipped the lock and opened the door. She felt ashamed for hiding for so long. She knew everyone was waiting for her. They had left Howling Ivy so quickly to get Hyacinth home that she didn't really address anything. Her dad had pressured her to come home to Oregon with him, but Raven Bloom felt more like home and she worried that Hyacinth needed her.

"Hey," Hyacinth said through the small crack in the door.

"Hey," Paisley returned. "You look like you're feeling better. I'm so glad. You pregnant, too?"

"No, just a little home sick. I'm fine now. You doing okay? Need anything?"

"I've got books, a warm bath, and some beautiful little fairy keeps leaving snacks at my door and running away. What else could I ask for?"

"I'm glad you are utilizing the bath. That way, if you wither and die in there, I don't have to worry about the stench."

"At least not for a few days."

There was silence for a beat.

"We miss you. You did something none of us could, and we want to support you in your healing," Hyacinth finally said.

"How are you feeling?" Paisley asked, ignoring the sentiment.

"I'm doing okay, now. I don't do well traveling. I always spring back as soon as I get home."

Paisley opened the door and leaned on the frame.

"I can't thank you enough for coming out there," she said.

"I owed you one, remember?"

"Does that mean we're even?" Paisley joked.

"Let's say, yes."

"Does that mean I can't crash in your guest room anymore?" Paisley's eyes got comically large, and she puffed out her cheeks.

"Raven Bloom will always be open to you," Hyacinth said.

"What a weird way to say that," Paisley laughed. "Get you back in your Gothic mansion, and suddenly you're Morticia Addams."

"You know what I mean," Hyacinth said, poking Paisley in her stomach through the heavy sweatshirt she wore.

"Thank you."

"Now, Grover is making breakfast and we are all hoping that you would join us, if you feel up for it."

Paisley paused.

"Rowan isn't home," Hyacinth offered. "He's been out at the cabin the last two days. He said if we needed him, to just call, and he would come running."

Paisley leaned her head back like a small child being told to clean up their toys.

"Fiiiiine. I'll be down in a minute. Let me brush my teeth and put on something I haven't slept in."

"Okay, I'll tell Grover to slow roll the bacon."

"That's redundant," Paisley joked.

Paisley watched her go. There was something about her, like she was more than a person. She didn't know that she'd ever felt that way about anyone else.

The smell of freshly cooked biscuits and gravy welcomed Paisley into the kitchen.

"Hey there," Grover said, offering her a plate as she headed for the table.

Hyacinth had a massive dining room, but if there were less than six people, they always ate at the table in the kitchen.

"Can I sit here?" Paisley asked, standing behind an open chair at the table.

"I don't know, *can* you?" Millicent laughed.

"Ohhh," Paisley said in mock offense. "I see how it is."

"She's got some spunk, this one," Khalida said, pouring orange juice into a cup for the girl.

"Reminds me of someone I know," Hyacinth said, setting a steaming coffee cup in front of Paisley and then taking a seat herself.

"Well then, *maaaay* I sit here?" Paisley asked.

"Sure can," Millicent laughed, looking at Khalida for approval, but she got it from the whole table as they shared in her laugh.

Grover joined them, sitting between Hyacinth and Khalida. The five of them ate and laughed and enjoyed the relative ease of not having anyone trying to hurt them at that moment.

When they finished, Grover cleared the table of all but the coffee cups.

"Well," Hyacinth started, "I think now that we are all here, we can start working through this thing, untangling some of the knots in all of it."

"Wait, you've all been here for three days and haven't talked about it?" Paisley asked.

"Didn't feel right to talk about it without you," Khalida said.

"Why not?" Paisley said. "Hasn't it been eating you alive?" Paisley looked at Hyacinth, then Grover. "Like, we have proof of some real paranormal shit here..." Paisley stopped herself and looked at Millicent. "Oh, sorry, some real paranormal stuff here."

"We do, but Pais, I think this is all a lot more shocking to you than it is to us," Hyacinth said.

"How is that possible? Immortals, giant spiders, homicidal maniacs," Paisley paused. "Okay, well, that last one I get."

"Grey Water Ridge has seen its share of odd things," Hyacinth said.

"We do have a Sasquatch," Grover said.

"Right, the Sasquatch," Paisley added.

Khalida nodded like this made total sense to her.

"Okay, well, if everyone else is already cool with all this, let's just jump right in, shall we?"

"We've already discussed it," Khalida said, eyeing Millicent. "So I think I am prepared to discuss it if you'd like."

"We're Heck-o's," Millicent said.

"Yeah you are," Hyacinth laughed.

"Echoes, dear. With an E," Khalida corrected.

"What is an Echo?" Paisley asked.

"You want the short answer, or the long one?" Khalida asked.

"Let's go with the short one, and see where that gets us."

"We're immortal," Khalida said.

"Okay, how about the long one?" Paisley asked.

"To understand, you have to accept that we are not alone," Khalida started.

"You mean like aliens?" Paisley interrupted.

"No, this is deeper than that. There are other dimensions that mirror the one we live in."

"Oh, like Marvel multiverse stuff, like Patch said?" Paisley asked.

"Yes, he said the same thing to me, so I watched all the movies, and they are close enough for the surface-level discussion," Khalida said. "Now, let's say that some of these nearly infinite number of dimensions have an alternate version of you."

"Weird," Paisley said.

"Oh my, I don't think we could handle another Paisley Mott," Hyacinth joked.

"Hey," Paisley said, kicking Hyacinth under the table.

"I'm kidding. A dimension wouldn't be complete without their very own Paisley F'n Mott."

"Right, so you all exist in other dimensions," Khalida continued. "But there are dimensions when your parents didn't meet, or dimensions where you died at birth, or a million, trillion other things that could have stopped you from being. Either way, you are possible in every other dimension. In every dimension, there is a soul, for lack of a better word, held for you. Does that make sense?"

"As much sense as any of this can, yes," Paisley said.

"Well, if you exist in even one dimension, there is a pool of souls for you that can be drawn from in every other dimension," Khalida explained. "So there is a possibility of your existence in every one of them. In the ones you don't exist in, your soul still does. Now, Echoes, like us, like Vivian, only exist in a single dimension. Just one."

"How is that possible if there are an infinite number of them?" Grover asked.

"Because we are an anomaly," Khalida said. "Every dimension will likely have one or two, but this dimension is boiling with them. Something happened somewhere on our timeline that caused things to get thrown out of whack, so we get a lot of people that shouldn't have existed. Which means more Echoes."

"What happened?" Hyacinth asked.

"We don't know," Khalida answered.

"And how many of you are there now?" Paisley asked.

"I don't know. We can feel the First Death of every Echo, but that doesn't help to know how many there still are."

"I'm sorry, the First Death?" Paisley followed.

"When an Echo is born they age and mature like anyone else. Then, when they die that first time, it is called their First Death. After that you are stuck at that age forever." Khalida looked at Millicent. "Which is why even though Millie here had her's nearly eight years ago, she is still the same age as she was then."

"I'm seven," Millicent added.

"And how old are you?" Paisley asked Khalida.

"By her logic? I'm twenty six, roughly. We really had a hard time keeping track back then."

"What, when did you have your first death? Like what year?" Paisley asked. It was starting to hit her that this woman could be very, very old and potentially lived through a lot of things.

"Best I can figure, the mid seventeen hundreds. Hard to say exactly when, though," she answered.

"Oh," Grover said. "That means..."

"Yeah. That's what that means," Khalida responded.

Paisley wanted to know more and hear it all, but knew it wasn't the right time. Khalida just revealed that she, a black woman, who couldn't die, lived through a few hundred years of slavery.

"I can't even imagine," Hyacinth said.

"You don't want to, I can promise you that," Khalida said.

"How often do you feel these First Deaths?" Paisley said. She didn't want to minimize the revelation but also didn't want to ask Khalida to talk about it if she didn't want to. She suspected there would be times when the child wasn't around when they could dig into the more difficult stuff.

"Not many. A few each decade or so. But sometimes, when there is one, there will be more. For instance, if an Echo is born, then every child they have has the potential to be an Echo. So we may have a few more when that happens."

"The potential?" Paisley asked.

"You don't just have an Echo. You have the potential for an Echo. There is a ceremony at birth. If the ceremony isn't held, the child will not become an Echo."

"That means her parents," Paisley nodded to Millicent, "performed the ceremony?"

"They would have had to, yes."

"My mommy and daddy died," Millicent said.

"In the car accident?" Hyacinth asked.

"No," Khalida responded. "Those were her adoptive parents. We don't know anything about her folks, and that particular information is surprisingly hard to find."

"I have so many questions," Paisley said.

"We will have time," Khalida said.

"How come we haven't heard of this? I'd think that someone who came back from the dead would be big news," Paisley said.

"There was one very famous one a few thousand years ago," Khalida said with a smirk.

"You mean..." Hyacinth said.

"That's what I heard," she responded.

"No way," Paisley said.

"Jesus Christ," Grover said, shaking his head.

"Exactly," Hyacinth added.

"Okay, so you can't die at all? You just like heal really fast?" Paisley asked, wanting to get as much info as possible before Khalida grew tired of answering, or Millicent got tired of playing with Hyacinth's tablet.

"Why don't we just put these on," Khalida said, grabbing a pair of headphones, plugging them into the tablet, and pressing them onto Millicent's head. The child didn't take notice at all. Khalida continued.

"No, we don't heal fast unless we die. Then our cells rebuild."

"But in the jail, you looked like you got crushed, and then

you were up moving in no time. Are you telling me you died?" Paisley asked.

"Yeah, I suffocated pretty quickly. So, it was a quick recovery. Just needed them to move, then everything started coming back. The ribs weren't really fully recovered, but we didn't have time to deal with that. See?" Khalida pulled the collar of her shirt out to show a bandage on her shoulder.

"This is so weird," Paisley said. "So you can die, you just always come back?"

"Pretty much. And before you ask, because everyone always asks, yes, even if my head gets chopped off," Khalida said.

Paisley looked over at the girl sitting with the tablet. She was thankful for the headphones. The image of the poor child being beheaded would never leave her.

"How long does it take?" Hyacinth asked.

"Depends on the damage done to the body. The injections Vivian gave those kids would have taken less than a minute. But other things could be days or weeks."

"Like burning a child alive," Paisley said, still looking at Millicent.

"Like burning a child alive," Khalida agreed.

"What about the spider?" Paisley asked, finally turning her attention back to Khalida.

"The Neverborn," Khalida said.

"That's a hell of a name," Paisley said.

"The Neverborn is sort of like an Echo, but instead of just being an anomaly, it is suspected that he was actually the source. He was born without a soul, a being that shouldn't have existed in any dimension. No pool of souls to draw on. Now he hunts Echoes."

"Hunts you?" Grover asked.

"We can only die one of two ways," Khalida started. "One is to be killed by the Neverborn. Also known as the Eater of Souls."

"I need a cooler nickname," Paisley said. "I want to be Paisley, Devourer of the Light, or some shit."

"I can get behind that," Hyacinth said.

"If he kills us or devours any part of our body while we are in the dead state, then we will die, and stay dead. No afterlife, no enjoyment of whatever it may be that everyone else gets to enjoy when you die, if there is anything. Just gone."

"And he knows when you die?" Paisley asked, remembering that he showed up after Khalida died and at the salvage yard after Vivian went over the drop.

"That's where the name comes from, Echo; when we die it sends out a reverberation, and he can feel it. The longer we are alive without dying, or the longer since the First Death, the more powerful the echo it sends out."

"But how does he get there so quickly?" Paisley asked.

"You don't get to be a renowned soul hunter who skips across dimensions without having a few tricks up your sleeve," Khalida said.

"Like being able to turn into a fucking spider demon?" Paisley said.

"I think that is probably more common than you'd think," Khalida said.

"Mutant spider people?" Paisley asked. "I don't think that's as common as you think."

"You'd be surprised," Hyacinth countered.

"I'm sorry, what?" Paisley said, turning dramatically to her.

"What? You've heard of werewolves, right?" Hyacinth asked.

"First off, yes, I have. Second, those are also fake. And they are dogs, not giant fucking spiders. That's way worse."

"I'm just saying, they aren't all wolves," Hyacinth said.

Paisley just stared at her. She trusted this woman who just told her the cryptid equivalent of the fact that the world was flat—something an intelligent person would never say.

"What was the second way?" Grover said, interrupting the awkward silence.

"We are not done with this conversation, young lady," Paisley said, flicking Hyacinth playfully on the shoulder before looking back at Khalida.

Millicent took notice of the dramatic move and removed her headphones.

"What's the matter?" the child asked.

"Oh, nothing. I'm sorry, sweetie. She's just being silly," Paisley said.

Millicent smiled and reached for her orange juice, returning her attention to the tablet.

"About that second way?" Paisley asked Khalida.

"You can give it away," she said. "Your echo. You can give it away. That's how most of us choose to go."

"What do you mean you can give it away?" Paisley asked.

"Just that. There is a ritual that grants it and a ritual that takes it away."

"So you could make me immortal?" Paisley asked.

"No, I couldn't make you immortal, but I could bring you back, once, but only right after your death."

"And then you what? Just die?" Hyacinth asked.

"No, we just go back to living," Khalida said. Her face pulled back in a forced smile as if she had spent a lot of time thinking about this.

"That sounds intense. Why would anyone do that?" Grover asked.

"I tried a few times," Khalida said. "The Reverend King, JFK, hell, I would have done it for Lincoln if I could have. Just never in a place where I could do a lot of good at the right time."

"With all due respect, in what dimension is Howling Ivy, Indiana the right place?" Paisley asked.

Khalida looked down at Millicent.

"We felt her, Vivian, and I. We knew where she was. And when an Echo goes off, we briefly get a picture of them. We knew roughly where she was and a basic idea of what she looked like."

Millicent smiled.

"She's special," Khalida finished.

"Of course she is," Paisley said. "But why is she special to the two of you?"

Khalida guided Millicent's headphones back onto her ears, and the child accepted it, returning to her games.

"There is a third ritual," Khalida said. "Only possible with young ones. And it doesn't allow them to live afterward."

"What do you mean?" Paisley asked. She could feel the anger rising in her. Just the idea of someone else hurting that poor girl brought her nearly to rage.

"The gift can be given, against the child's will, without their knowledge, through sacrifice. If this is done, the Echo continues."

"You mean that if they kill her, then someone else could become an Echo?" Paisley asked.

"Not like just coming back from the dead once, but immortal, like you?" Hyacinth asked.

"Yes," Khalida said. "But if you make an Echo out of someone whose soul already exists in other dimensions, they pull it from them."

"So they all die?" Grover asked.

"Yes," Khalida said, "it's happened a few times before."

"Then what?" Paisley asked.

"The Neverborn finds them pretty easily, so they never make it for long," Khalida said.

"Does that mean Vivian wanted her to make someone else an Echo," Paisley asked.

"I don't think so. I think she wanted her for herself," Khalida said.

"Why would she need her? She's already an Echo," Hyacinth pointed out.

"Yes, but the ritual, if performed and given to an existing Echo, could make them something more."

"More than immortal? Mormortal?" Paisley said.

"If it happens, the Neverborn is no longer a threat. It can no longer hurt them."

"That seems like a good thing," Paisley said. "But not at the cost of a child."

"It seems good, yes. They also have the ability to give their life, over and over," Khalida said.

"You mean they can just resurrect people at will?" Paisley asked.

"Yes. As one would imagine, this power would be amazing, in the right hands. And it was. But it is never the right hands that seem to seek it."

"Wait, so this has happened before?" Paisley asked.

"A few times," Khalida answered.

"Jesus Christ," Grover said again.

"Exactly," Hyacinth said.

"Well, I'm not letting that happen to her," Paisley said. "I'm going to tell you this right now. I like you a lot, Khalida. I owe you my life. But if I get any indication that you plan to do that to this little girl, I'll cut your throat while you sleep and feed you to that fucking spider."

Khalida smiled, not the smile of someone who just received a death threat, but of someone who just heard exactly what she wanted to hear.

"I don't want any of that, Paisley," Khalida said. "I've seen enough death in my very, very long life. I was looking for this girl so I could take care of her. What point is life if you don't use it to protect others?"

"Sounds like someone else I know," Hyacinth said, eyeing Paisley.

"I just wanted to make sure we are all on the same page. No offense," Paisley said.

"None taken," Khalida responded.

"You're all welcome here at Raven Bloom for as long as you'd like," Hyacinth said.

"Thank you," Khalida said. "I believe we will take you up on that, at least for a while."

"Great," Hyacinth said.

It was quiet for a long time after that until Paisley finally broke the silence.

"It's like we're the fucking X-Men over here."

Peace settled among them as they all sat, enjoying their drinks and the ability to rest in a blanket of safety.

"So," Khalida said, after a moment of silence. "Pregnant, huh?"

"Yeah," Paisley said, putting a hand on her stomach. It was joined by a smaller one as Millicent laughed.

"You've got two skeletons," she said.

Paisley Mott Will Return

About the Author

Do people read these? You're reading it. So I guess so! Kalvin Ellis is a writer. He wrote the book you presumably just read. He writes other books and stuff as well. If you want to know more about him you can check his website at KalvinEllis.com or follow him on one of his social media platforms.

Kalvin Ellis - photo by Dusty "Duck" LaPerriere

Content Warning

This story will have a scene or scenes with a little or a lot of each of these themes:

- Abusive relationship
- Amputation
- Animal abuse
- Animal death
- Anxiety
- Assault
- Attempted murder
- Blood
- Bones
- Bullying
- Car accident
- Child abuse
- Child death
- Death
- Decapitation
- Depression
- Emotional abuse
- Famine
- Fire

- Gore
- Gun violence
- Hallucinations
- Hospitalization
- Hostages
- Kidnapping
- Murder
- Needles
- Physical abuse
- Police brutality
- Pregnancy
- Profanity
- PTSD
- Slut shaming
- Spiders
- Starvation
- Suicide
- Torture
- Violence